SWIMMING

IN THE

STARRY

RIVER

SWIMMING

IN THE

STARRY

RIVER

A NOVEL BY

P. Carey Reid

HYPERION

N E W   Y O R K

The author wishes to thank the following readers of the manuscript: Ellen Dyer, Julie Morrow, Eleanor Reid, David Barnes, Julia Galosy, Diane Wald, and Neil Orleans.

COPYRIGHT © 1994 *P. Carey Reid*

FIC
8|07

LIBRARY OF CONGRESS CATALOGING-
IN-PUBLICATION DATA

Reid, P. C. (Paul Carey).
Swimming in the starry river / by P. Carey Reid
— 1st ed.
p.   cm.
ISBN 0-7868-6005-7
I. Title.
PS3568.E47658S92   1993
813'.54—dc20

92-41752
CIP

Designed by Holly McNeely

FIRST EDITION
10 9 8 7 6 5 4 3 2 1

For my parents,

Kathryn Lambrechts Reid and Paul C. Reid

SWIMMING

IN THE

STARRY

RIVER

O N E

I have one child, Stella, six years old. Our nightly walks take us down Pleasant Street, the main road of our nondescript subdivision. It is autumn now, and the feeble underwatered shrubs in the dirt circle at the end of Pleasant Street dim to gray as we look up at, first, Ursa Major, the big bear, then Ursa Minor, the little one, and on to other familiar and not so familiar configurations of glimmering points. At first, I hold Stella high in my arms, perhaps to allow her the sense of being closer to the distant stars. Neither of us is very strong, but I am blessed with enough upper-body strength to hold her for the duration of our sojourn. She is as light as a sack of sticks. She is little more than a sack of sticks.

As we stand amid the shrubs, Stella rolls her round head about and lifts one stunted mitt to the heavens. It is her job to orient us, and infallibly she has found the North Star.

"Polaris!" she cries.

Pride wells within me. "Yes," I say quietly. "That's right, honey."

"The tail of the doggy."

We laugh. "Right, Stella."

The small bear—or dog, as some cultures saw it—

3

has a bright tip around which all the heavens revolve in the sweep of its tail. That same star was a jeweled nail-head for the Norse, a golden peg for the Mongols, and for the East Indians, heaven's pivot.

"It's Polaris now," I say, "but the earth wobbles so much that Deneb and Vega might get their chance."

"When?" Her head comes down and regards my face only inches away.

"Oh, not for thousands of years, Stella. Not until long after we're gone."

She might be gone quicker than most. And for that reason my thoughts are forced often between the stars, pressed into the inked space at whose end the final answers are surely stored. For all of our slow journeying along the short stretches of these suburban lanes, Stella and I are in a great hurry.

"Dad, who's the boy who sits and waits?"

"You mean Dhruva," I answer, referring to a star story from ancient India.

"He sits and waits in the forest. He sure waits a long time, right, Dad?"

"He sure does, Stella." We begin to walk again. The houses of several neighbors, most of them strangers to us, have lit windows. The sight of these warm rectangles renders our solitude more precious. "The new queen was jealous, Stella, and sent the little prince and his grandmother away to live at the edge of the forest."

"But Dhruva wanted to know where his father was."

"Yes. He decided to go and find his father, the king, and demand justice. And he traveled from the forest throughout the land, wandering just as we are now. And, finally, he found his father, the king."

"But the king was scared!"

"Yes, unfortunately. He sent Dhruva away because he was afraid the queen would punish him. But he did help a little. Do you remember?"

"He told him to find . . . Who did he tell him to find?"

"Narada, the holy man, the lotus-eyed stranger. Do you remember the rest?" Her head is a round dark ball made rounder by the tight cotton caps that her mother makes her. Beneath a streetlight, I see the greasy dressing glistening at the corners of her mouth, where the skin continually cracks from so much smiling.

"Narada tells him, 'Stay here and pray to God till everything is better.' "

"That's right. So Dhruva sits in the forest, the steady praying center of the universe. He sits there still."

We both look up at Dhruva Lok, North Star, the "place where the young prince sits." Soon after, moving on, I think we might visit Dorie van Dusen, who lives on the far cusp of the cul-de-sac, but Stella's head is beginning to bob. And that's good, because these little walks are needed to calm her down after her long days of confusion, triumph, and disappointment. To speak calmly of the little prince praying patiently in the woods, or the Indians' starry hunt, or the two Chinese lovers who meet only once a year. . . . These stories smooth her frenzy, her rush to live as if, intuitively, and beyond her mother's and my control, she must live all of her life in the concentrated present.

We head back to our house, a redwood ranch at the top of a sloping drive, up which I trudge, dramatically huffing like a tired dwarf in a way that makes Stella laugh.

"Daddy, stop it!" Her giggling percolates through her words and her blunted hands wave in the air like puppets.

"But you're so heavy."

"I am not."

I'm stalling a little; at moments like these, with our private time about to end, I become selfish and hoard our moments together as greedily as any miser. It is convenient to allow others to continue in their beliefs that I am plying Stella with special hours replete with significance. It protects our time alone. Our visits with others, as we walk the streets together each night to view the stars, are few and brief. Stella is not an attractive child; in fact, to most she is hideous. Her better qualities are known by those, a very few, who have taken the time to know her, and I have become adept at intuiting the exact moment when another's eyes are about to veil with pity. Still, she cannot be long away from the house and that is just as well.

We turn at the top of the drive and look back at the neighborhood, the spattering of windows that spill patches of warm color onto the black lawns. Stella, a sack of bones so fragilely assembled, lays her head upon my shoulder. Soon, we will enter our home, a place predictably of strain and tears, but of moments of dazzling joy as well. But I have been tracing at some level, nearly subconscious, how the joyful moments are being winnowed.

I gaze at the lit windows, which normally spell warmth and comfort to the person on the cold street, but I know too well the heaviness that sits on certain homes. Stella, Marsha, and I, we are stuck. Yes, we are victims of more than congenital disease; we are victims too of the deadlier sorts of resignation. It is only lately that I have come to realize the existence of this problem, most recently signaled by a telephone call from Marsha into my stable workplace. In the call she told me that Stella's teacher had called home, that Stella had cried all morning at school. I had meant to talk to Stella about that.

Regarding her, light as a doll upon my shoulder, I think as I often have that my mission is to layer her world with richness—not *facts,* but other hearts, desires, stories, a world populated with angels and idiots, and papered with texts that she can enter and live more than one moment at a time. I have asked myself a hundred times, Will that not add up to a whole life?

But now, facing the night sky once more, I am wondering this evening, this particular evening which I want to force to become significant, I am wondering if all people die too soon. What is it about the world that presses us to leave it and, short of that, fall back to a posture of mere waiting?

T w o

We walk quietly through the house, past the front room and on to the kitchen where my wife, Marsha, has finished the dishes and the cast-iron frying pan dries upside down on one burner of the stove. Marsha is there, reading the paper at the table. Whenever she reads, her big reading glasses creep at an undetectable pace to the tip of her nose. Now we arrive, and she pushes them back as a typist might the typewriter carriage; then she continues reading for a time, stretching this single half-hour that has passed without interruption and is therefore so important to her. At last, she looks up, smiles, and acknowledges us, and lets the glasses fall to her chest, where they hang from their lanyard. As she rises and closes up the paper, the chair sighs to be relieved of her weight.

"Did you guys see any bears tonight?" she asks as she comes toward us.

"Two!" says Stella.

"Did you get any honey?"

"Not that kind, Mommy."

"Lots of talk, but never any honey."

Marsha lifts Stella from my arms and I follow my wife as she carries our only child to her bedroom. The two of them keep up a steady banter, which Marsha has perfected to distract Stella from the little pains and irritations of removing sterile dressings. Stella sits on the edge of her bed, and already Marsha has slipped off her cap and mittens and, grasping the tight pink stump of her right hand, begun to work down one jacket sleeve.

"Soon the bear will bleed onto the leaves," says Stella.

"Oh, my," says Marsha, and works the other sleeve loose. "That doesn't sound very nice."

Stella looks uncertainly at me. "The bear gets hurt, right, Dad?"

I am leaning in the doorway, watching the two of them. "That's right, Stella. Fall is on the way, and that's when the Indians in the sky hunt the Great Bear. When they shoot her, her blood turns the leaves red."

"That's very nice of her, I suppose," says Marsha. She has the jacket off, and as she speaks she is running her fingers over Stella's left hand, looking more closely than she lets on and running her own fingertips along its short, scar-encased length, into the shallow cavities filled with flaking skin that for one short year were the spaces that normally exist between human fingers.

"But she comes back, Mommy."

"Who, the bear?"

"Uh huh. She's dead for the whole winter, then she gets up again in the spring."

"Boy, I wish I could do that."

I smile, though Marsha's jokes sometimes have a little edge of irritation to them, which worries me because of the possible effect on Stella. Now she reaches down and lifts the edge of a strip of gauze that is wrapped around

Stella's right knee. She lifts her heel and carefully un-wraps the bandage, so quickly and gently that Stella doesn't seem to notice.

"Do what, Mommy?"

"Sleep through all the cold weather and wake up when it's warm again."

"Hey, yeah!"

"Lift up now."

With one of those gleeful smiles that always surprises me with a prick to the heart, Stella throws up her arms and stares at me with excitement as Marsha carefully peels her thick undershirt up and over her head. That done, she goes on with the examination of her daughter's small body. At times, she pats down the patchy wisps of the child's hair. I have thought that Stella would look better with no hair at all, rather than these scattered follicles, but the child finds comfort in them. They are the last strands that tie her to normalcy.

"Tea?" I ask Marsha.

"Yes. Dr. Roth called again today. I was out, but he left a message."

"Oh."

"He has time on Saturday."

"I see."

If he has time on Saturday, does that mean that I'm to take Stella to see him? I turn from the doorway, my shoulders suddenly heavy. By the time I've filled the kettle and set it upon the stove, my legs begin to ache. I think I'm coming down with the flu, but then I notice that I'm standing before the stove in a strange but fa-miliar position—hunched with both fists balled against my chest. Realizing that I've slipped into this posture is like coming out of a trance. The first thought I have is that I do not want to call Dr. Roth. It is not a matter of personal dislike; I have never spoken to the man nor do I know much about him other than that he will replace Stella's dermatologist, Dr. Lerman, who has moved to Florida to retire. There's more going on here than only my putting off calling Dr. Roth.

The water in the kettle begins to softly whine, as if it would rather not be heated. I turn to get the mugs from the pantry and fish two bags of peppermint tea from their colorful box. When I drop the bags into the empty mugs, I think, *You can reclaim your life. It's possible to reclaim a life.* I have no idea why these words have come into my head. It is silent in the pantry; the whirring of the refrigerator dampens Stella's and Marsha's banter. I wish the TV were on so that I could be distracted by its sibilant drone. It seems to be on nearly always, a convenient distraction. Instead, in the relative quiet, for one long moment I am pressed back into a world of whispers, of the thousand lies of two dark decades, when fear and confusion steadily overpowered the best impulses and desires of the members of my childhood home.

I have stood before with fists balled against my chest. When very young, I would stand this way among trees, or in the corners of the basement, hiding, and in the cloakrooms of special classrooms where no one walked straight and the most gifted among us could barely work a pair of scissors. In this waking dream, I am again in that room watching a tall woman with a long brown skirt of scratchy wool. I watch her from the cloakroom as she sits at one of the low tables, her legs crossed and her head leaning heavily on one hand as she watches a little girl painfully direct the tip of a crayon across the page of a coloring book.

"Well, look at that," she says. "Red will work as good as any, I guess."

There's a noise across the room where two children are standing by a toy box and one of them has just dropped a pail with a clatter.

"Darren again?" She shakes her head, looks to the newspaper spread before her. Then she mutters as if to be overheard, "Boy can't hold anything without dropping it."

Who is she talking to? Watching from the cloakroom, I can see no one else. There is someone invisible with whom she continually speaks.

A little girl with twisted knock-kneed legs comes trundling up to the woman, a paper waving about in her raised hands. "This," she says, with finality, and plunks the paper down on the woman's desk.

The tall woman peers down at the paper. "Now look at that," she says. "Can you imagine?"

Can *who* imagine?

That was the day I concluded that the tall woman in the wool skirt spoke directly to God.

The teakettle, which was purchased because of the happy lilting quarter notes printed on the outside of the box, has never whistled a single note in its long stay with us. It only wheezes in frustration when its contents are boiling. It has a speech defect. Stella whines too— often, repeatedly, and with anger laced through. She knows, more and more each day, what she can't do. Her whines are the first stirrings of fearful thoughts. Today, my wife called me at work and begged—there's no other word for it—begged me to leave work and go to Stella's school and pick her up.

"Her teacher says she won't stop crying, Jim. She's been crying all morning."

"Honey, I can't leave now. I'm right in the middle of something."

"Jim, I thought I would get a chance to do some shopping. She's just been back after her cold and now . . ."

My wife has never asked me to do such a thing before. *Crying all morning.* I must admit to myself, even if I cannot to others, that those words terrified me. To leave my job and to go to a place where my daughter is crying . . .

The two tea bags inflate in shock when I pour in the hot water. They gasp with pungent peppermint breath. I step back into Stella's room. Marsha has finished the child's sponge bath (frequent tub bathing is dangerous because it dries her skin) and is slipping her heavy flannel nightshirt down around her.

"Ah ha!" I exclaim when her head appears from the collar. "There you are!"

"Right here!" She smiles that big smile of delight, which invariably stresses the inelastic flesh at the corners of her mouth. To make her smile is to wound her.

"Where?"

"Here!" She throws out her arms to me and beckons by waggling their stump ends.

"Put her down, Jim," says Marsha. "I'm going to dig out some of the warmer socks for her tonight."

I come forward and kneel before Stella. Her arms drop

onto my shoulders and she lets me, as always, gaze into her face. A child will allow you to look long into its eyes, and can there be a deeper delight than that effective mirroring of souls? There are many colors in Stella's eyes, brown and a little green and blue. They are dark and bright as stars. "Stella-Capella," I whisper. Capella, the star of many fires.

She laughs and pulls me closer. Her thin arms hold on to my neck with surprising power. She begins to nuzzle my cheek with hers, then gradually with her whole face.

Crying all morning. She knows she is a freak. I whisper in her ear, *"Go ahead, you thing of wonder. Drink down every drop you need."*

THREE

Now I am at my desk at work, a wide desk of heavy metal that has been dipped in shiny black enamel and fitted with a new white-laminate writing surface because three years ago I noticed that our old serviceable postwar gray metal desks were gradually being replaced with cheap, tinny "office" furniture, and only because the new stuff seemed more attractive to employees and communicated a harder "executive edge" image. It was shiny black and had a phony wood-laminate top. But the handles popped off, and the laminate peeled, and I prevailed on Howard Long, the regional administrator, to consider refurbishing our old indestructible but effectively functioning desks. I made a study, provided comparative figures, then ran several refurbished desks past random personnel, and our old desks won out. Regionwide we saved over $300 thousand, up front, with a similar amount in long-term savings due to the old desks' great durability. I love these old desks. Their round corners do not have an executive edge, but nor do they clip your hips as you walk by. And their drawers slide in and out with conviction.

I could tell other stories, similar successes, which are not really impressive in themselves, but when you consider that I am only five feet three inches in height and around one hundred and twenty-five pounds in weight, and was once so much smaller and so dreadfully self-conscious as to be nearly autistic, then those successes mean more. My physical measurements were dictated by a bone-growth disorder, genetic in origin and still a pathological mystery. In my earliest years, my parents were told that I would be a dwarf, and in the climate of growing alarm that formed around me, I grew so quiet that everyone concluded I would be a moron as well. But nature, which loves balance, gave me certain gifts to compensate for my shrunken physique.

With these gifts, and lots of hard work, I've gradually cut a solid niche for myself where I work, and a good income. We need that income to provide the extensive care that Stella's affliction requires. I am the budget director of the Boston office of a branch of the federal bureaucracy that maintains government property. I review the budgets submitted by the many field offices that are scattered from Canada to the southern border of Connecticut and as far west as New York State—the New England area, or Region One as we feds call it. Not a dollar of the twenty million or so that we are allotted every year gets requested or allocated without my prior analysis. Over the years, fourteen by now, I've become somewhat close in a customized sort of way to the regional administrator, Howard Long. He has come to depend on me. I'm often in his office, conferring, and often find myself sent off to solve some financial problem or other. Sometimes I in turn send off one of my two staff people, Jennifer DiAngelis or Bobby Marco.

Today I am thinking how comfortable it is for me at

work. And I am haunted, at every moment when my consciousness drops heavily into the real present, by the knowledge that yesterday my daughter cried at school for an entire morning. Again and again, as I sit at my successfully refurbished desk, drafting memos and twisting about to check my computer monitor for specific figures, questions about my daughter slide into my thoughts. What happens in her life, really happens, when I am here and she is there? Running through these thoughts, ominous as a distant siren, is the pleading tone of Marsha's voice when she tried, unsuccessfully, to get me to leave work and pick up our sad daughter. Now I think of her, Stella, crying in a big schoolroom, a room I have never actually seen. All morning, the image superimposes itself over everything: She is standing alone, weeping evenly, the tears streaming down her face. She cries in complete silence—as if I'm watching from a distance, or through a closed window.

When I was a little boy, the world seemed to move by me like pictures painted on a long roll of canvas, or rise up around me like painted panels. I felt fixed in place, and if I moved it upset the perspective and then in those moments of confusion and panic I had to readjust to the rolling pictures and rising planes. It was better to stand still, if I were to have a chance of making sense of it all. At school, especially before there were such things as special programs, a typical day was a series of little dramas that exploded around me at a dizzying rate. Children to my right leapt to their feet and ran. I stared after them: *Where are they going?* A little girl behind me burst into tears: *Oh no, what happened to her?* All about me children dropped into stupors of concentration or burst into fits of hysteria. Some fell, cut themselves, bled. Some writhed while grasping a knee.

While all else reared, buckled, slumped, and wailed, it was the mysterious teacher who stood firmly in place, like a rock of calm, and if she ever moved it was only to execute slow quarter-turns. From my silent vantage, where I sat or stood, hunched and overwhelmed, I began to fasten a perverse degree of attention on these teachers. Miss Sullivan, with the pale blue eyes and skin so tender that the air seemed to bruise it, leaving pink patches on the rims of her ears or at the sides of her chin. Mrs. Laurenten, wide and dark, with large startling glasses that she turned full toward a child when she spoke. Mrs. Bell, bell-shaped and wrapped in pressed blouses, and smelling so strongly of rose oil that I grew drowsy during warmer afternoons. Different as they were, they all had one powerful thing in common: answers. From where I watched, children strolled, danced, or ran in long dreamy circles whose circumferences eventually passed through the still fixed point that was the teacher. At that moment of intersection, a question was always posed, born of curiosity or need, and an answer of some sort was always provided. "Yes, you may." Or: "No, you may not." Or: "That's because you're turning the lid the wrong way." But I can remember so few moments when those intersections occurred for me. I was one point, the teacher another, and the world moved in an elliptical orbit around these two loci, which did not meet.

In my silence was terror. I knew only this, that I knew nothing for certain. In my home, where my poor parents struggled against each other, I was adrift on an open sea with no instruments to fix on the stars. Nothing stood still, nothing was the same from one moment to the next. But there, in those classrooms, big solitary women stood in place and managed madness. Eventually, as they plied or pushed, caressed or yelled, the tossing tides around them would be quelled for a time, then swell again. My regard for them, the mute dependency of a lost child, swelled until I found myself in the company of the tall woman in the dark wool skirt who spoke to no one less than God. I watched them, wide-eyed, impressed to the point of fear.

It was during these observations of their powerfulness, which were so frightening and enheartening, that my love of the measurable was born. From my quiet place across the room from Mrs. Laurenten, I began to notice how, when the children were set loose in the room to pursue their natural play, their small bodies traveled around her. They swung toward her, then back, and then sometimes, if they did not stop to speak with her or show something to her, their momentum carried them around behind her. They wanted to be near her, all of them in turn, but then too their innate energy carried them back or beyond. The paths of their traveling stayed in my mind, like the afterimages of a sparkler twirled in darkness. Years later, when I saw illustrations of the planets' trajectories around the sun, or of electrons whirling about a nucleus, I understood instantly the interplay of momentum and attraction that they represented.

I am beginning to wonder if I ever had any real life at school, if instead I watched and thought to figure out how to live my real life, whatever that was and which certainly happened somewhere else. I do recall that by school afternoons I would begin thinking about being home again, and would just begin to allow myself to feel the first joyful stirrings, unbearable in full measure, of seeing my father that evening. Then, magically at home again, how I would busy myself until I heard my father's truck pull up in the driveway and I'd race into the kitchen and wait for him by the table. It was as far as my mother allowed me to go, because she worried that I would run out and under the wheels of his truck in my excitement. I can remember how acutely I listened as the truck door distantly slammed and how each step materialized and grew in volume. When my father appeared, his large body would be, for one instant, perfectly framed by the open back door. It was at that moment that my real living for the day would begin.

My father was a tall man, and from an early age that seemed significant to me. After years of never knowing why anything was happening, I began to see that up ahead, years ahead, lay the power to understand, to name, and perhaps to control. It all seemed to be based on numbers and measurements. Bodies, live or inert, traveled in paths directed by a balancing of forces, and the doors my father cut and the rooms he framed were templates of the human body. I wondered what the properties of teachers were that they would become the intractable loci of three dozen smaller bodies. Gradually, I believed I had my answer. One could become powerful, articulate, and assured, but first *you had to be tall*.

But with that knowledge also evolved a paralyzing counter-knowledge. And I still struggle with that fact of life today, that existence will slowly reveal what you need to know, and that what you need to know can sometimes block what you need to do. For what I gained from my penetrations to the "truth" of things was instantly neutralized by a whole new layer of terror, the growing realization that I would never *be* tall.

At my office desk, amidst the comforting piles of what I have assumed for so long is my real work, I wonder how my daughter is faring in school. The pins beneath my unshakable conviction that my work is meaningful have shifted a little, I find. I chose not to go to my daughter's school yesterday, where she was crying, crying all morning. The pages beneath my fingers, memos and sheaves of wide computer paper peppered with dot matrix, continually blanch as my eyes stare back and forth at possibilities rather than the realities which these purportedly represent. I look up: There are Bobby and Jennifer, both at their desks, busy with our common work. I must now face the fact that yesterday has altered things somehow. Why did I not leave work yesterday; why did I conclude that I could not?

FOUR

It is a clear, cool night, and Stella and I are on the prowl again. A tang of leaf mold enlivens the still air. Above, the first stars are pin-sharp on this moonless night. We have stopped to look up on our way to the cul-de-sac.

Stella leans closer and whispers, "Let's hide from the Dragon, Dad."

But we're in the open. The nearest bushes are those that Mr. Lester has erected around his shuttered home.

"I'm too tired to move very far, Stella."

"But he'll get us. Let's pretend like he's going to get us."

I keep moving straight.

"Dad-dy."

"But he won't get us while I'm around. Isn't that good enough?"

"No-o. We have got to hide."

With a sigh, I move us off our time-honored trajectory and head for Mr. Lester's enormous evergreens. I stand among them with my daughter, who is quivering with excitement. I am very tired and a little irritated to be rerouted. Around us, the trees are entirely silent.

Stella whispers, "Now he can't see us."

Together we peer up through a hole in the canopy of limbs and there, in the center of a ragged space, Draco glitters, long and twisting and trapped between the two bears. Some fathers read their children fairy tales, which project a rosy future, but Stella and I have gravitated toward the ageless and often sad stories that are tacked to the sky with stars.

The ancients put all of the heavens on the back of a huge, solid turtle that lumbered through eternity. They craved the solidity. When the sun began to fall in autumn, they seriously wondered if it would slip down one evening and never reappear. They fashioned stories of heroism and strength to stave off their own fears. At the point where Draco's tail makes its curve is Thuban, and thousands of years ago, the Egyptians built their huge pyramids to fix on Thuban because it was the polestar and would remain fixed. But the earth, like all bodies that we imagine fixed and dependable, shifted, and now the huge, immobile pyramids are obsolete. Draco reeks of failure. In the days when Zeus was fighting the giants to gain the throne of Olympus, Draco threw in on the wrong side. When the battle was fought, Zeus's own daughter, bright-eyed Athena, hurled the dragon into the heavens.

As Stella grows older, I can see that she grows moodier, more quiet and quicker to fear. Hiding in Mr. Lester's bushes, for example, is a new activity for us. What darkness does she feel emanating from the heavens? Which of the sad stories will she fasten on—the slain Medusa's, or that of Cassiopeia, the prideful queen who is hung forever upside down?

"The bears see the dragon," Stella whispers.

"Oh, good. Does that mean we can get out of these trees?"

"No, Daddy! Not yet. Shhhh. The bears are moving toward the dragon."

Up above, the two bears, larger and smaller, circle and close on the last third of the unwitting reptile. Poor Draco, it looks as if he's going to suffer another loss. Hopefully, it will be all over soon and we can start walking again.

"The big bear's got him. Oh, Daddy, he's got him!" Her hoarse whispering is snuffled up in the shaggy limbs that surround us.

"That's a relief." I start to head us out.

"Not yet, Daddy! The dragon is fighting!"

"Of course. I should have known the bears wouldn't have an easy time of it."

Why am I so restless? I remember that Howard Long stopped me in the hall and, pinching my coat sleeve, mumbled something in his overly significant way. I have to meet with him tomorrow. He mentioned a word I've never heard before. Defalcations. I had meant to look it up.

Meanwhile, the static battling goes on in the heavens. Tonight, the lumbering she-bear will be a hero. Her constellation has been many things to many cultures—a dipper, a plow, a coffin. Because she lives in all seasons, and never slides into the sea like the other stars fixed farther from the pole, she has a significance for all seasons. She is death and resurrection both. Tonight my daughter is adding warrior to her résumé, and as far as I know that is an original contribution.

"Oh no, the dragon is escaping."

"No, no, *I'm* escaping." I start creeping out of Mr. Lester's yard (what if he sees us?). "I'm sorry, Stella, but I'm just too tired tonight."

"Okay," she sighs. "The dragon's dead."

"Good girl. We needed a quick solution."

We amble on in silence, listening to each other's breathing. Then Stella says, "I think they won because Sinopa was riding the Big Bear."

"Huh!" I peer at the crook in the dipper's handle. Can Alcor be seen tonight? Yes, it's just there. "So what did Sinopa do?"

"She rode the bear and told her what to do. To, to . . ." She falters, her limited syntax failing to keep abreast of her imagination.

"Told her how to fight?"

"Exactly."

"Where did you learn that word, Stella?"

"Exactly?"

"Yes."

"It means yes, right, Dad?"

"Not exactly."

"What?"

"Exactly means . . . Let's see. Exactly does not exactly mean yes."

Stella laughs. "Daddy, what are you say-ing?"

"Exactly means exactly yes. Anyway, what about Sinopa? How does she figure in the fight with the dragon?"

Stella sighs as if impatient with my questions, whose answers she feels should be evident. "Sinopa rides the bear and tells her how to fight."

"Smart girl!"

"She's very smart, Sinopa."

But not in the original story, the Blackfeet's story of the starry hunt. It's not difficult to understand why Stella would come up with her more childlike version. The Blackfeet made a story for the whole family of stars that make up Ursa Major. An Indian maiden falls in love with a grizzly bear, then, when her seven brothers murder this unwanted suitor, she turns into a bear herself and plots to avenge him. She almost succeeds, but somebody shows up with magic arrows, which wound her and drive her away.

"The bear doesn't die, does she, Daddy?" Stella nearly whines. The stories of big and little bears and Indian maiden-turned-bear are confusing—to Stella the heavens must seem filled with bears—and a little gruesome. As the bear-maiden flees her heartbroken brothers, her blood stains the leaves of autumn.

"No, no," I whisper. "And now you've made sure that her little sister will protect her."

In the Blackfeet tale, the maiden's only sister, and the youngest in the family, hides among the protective brothers—and that is Sinopa, known to us by its Arabic name, Alcor, which peers out timidly from behind the larger Mizar.

Thump! Stella's head hits my shoulder like a melon.

"Honey, are you sleepy?"

She barely mutters a reply. The effort to develop a new role for Sinopa as a military tactician in the starry hunt has consumed her last energy.

"Sinopa's dead," she says.

There, *there*. That's the kind of thing that sends shivers up my spine. "Honey, don't say that."

"The dragon, it got her. Sinopa's dead."

"Stella, you are adding gray hairs to your poor father's head." (I have quite a few already, and keep my hair short to hide the fact.)

Then her head is up and her stumpy hands, cushioned in mittens that Marsha has fashioned from thick cotton socks, bump joyously about my ears. "But she'll be back in the spriiiiing!"

A laugh begins bubbling low in my stomach. An upsurge of relief feeds it, and then I am laughing out loud in the dark with the lit windows of Dorie van Dusen's house slipping by on our right. "Sinopa lives!" I cry.

"They keep each other warm all winter. It's lonely in the cave."

"Stella, you are a wonder. You are a jewel. I like your story very much."

She is very excited. I am very excited. I decide it is a good time to ask her something. "Honey, but why did you cry so much yesterday at school?"

She seems surprised. "I didn't!"

"Mommy says your teacher says you cried all morning."

"Oh, yeah. I don't know. I got shy I think."

"Shy? How did that make you cry?"

"Because . . ." She flails her hands, irritated with me, or at the words that won't come. "We were singing and I didn't want to sing and I got shy and I cried. When I cried the others couldn't sing and I felt shy."

More and more shy, I think, shy to an unbearable level. I press a bit more. "Why didn't you want to sing?"

"I don't know. It hurts, I guess."

The chronic blistering that slowly reduces my daughter to a living scar will—and this I have always considered the most unmerciful of all its hideous aspects—invade the tender mucosal membranes of her body: mouth, throat, anus, and vulva. To move her mouth may cause pain. When the bullae, or blisters, are especially tender, when they have erupted and are healing over, to smile is pain for Stella. Her singing comes out in an atonal wail. Once, I witnessed her attempt to sing around a Christmas tree with our few seldom-seen relatives. How courageously she attempted to manipulate the stiffened and painful parts of her throat to bring up a joyful sound. For a few moments, I had to leave the room.

I want to talk more, but at the top of our driveway, I'm surprised to find Stella's Uncle Jack, Marsha's brother, standing by the front door in the dark. He's over for the evening, as he often is, but here he is in the cold with just his suit coat on.

"Jim, Marsha sent me out to find you. There's a Dr. Roth on the phone."

"Oh, gosh."

When I hesitate, Stella reaches for Jack, and he takes her from me. She pushes her mitts into his coat and clasps his cranberry tie.

"No strangling tonight, Stella. You know I can't stand strangling." He looks to me. "If you don't want to speak with him I can easily tell him that you've moved out of range."

What is my problem? I can certainly take my daughter to a new doctor. I can handle that. I suppose my difficulty lies with a few quick words about Dr. Roth that

Dr. Lerman said. "You'll like him, Jim. He's young, a hotshot, full of new ideas." Why would I like that?

"No, thanks, Jack. I'll talk to him."

Jack is bouncing Stella a little. She observes, "Daddy, now I'm taller than you." She enjoys the higher vantage afforded by her uncle's height.

Jack says, "Stella, I hear you're going to get a brand-new doctor."

She nods, pursing her lips as if wisely resigned. "Dr. Lerman moved to Florida."

"Not a bad idea. They have wonderful golf courses down there. I'll be going down myself in a few months."

Stella protests. "No. I don't want you to go."

"Have to, dearest. I've got to work. Do you want me to starve?"

I regard them, smiling at each other. What is there about certain moments that make you feel an invisible hand touching you? Something from the heavens is reaching down and pressing me to my own front door, then guiding me across the rugs. Up ahead, on the little table in the hallway, I can see the phone, the receiver on its back like an upended turtle.

I speak with Dr. Roth. He sounds young, but he also sounds confident, eager, and concerned. I listen, he listens, we agree that he should meet Stella soon, and then we make an appointment to meet, for Saturday. It's that easy.

F I V E

How was I saved? How was I allotted a father such as the one I was given? It could have been much different, because my father was cut from very rough cloth and was never schooled in the arts of parenting, never read the books or listened raptly at seminars where members of my generation are given a shot at reclaiming the race's lost skills or learning completely new ones.

This fact remains, that this big man with hands so dried and callused that deep cracks appeared in the flesh, hands ravaged by driving nails, suffering cuts, working wood, absorbing splinters, shoving shingles about, or seared by caustic solvents brewed to dissolve sap and enamel and creosote, had only one son to dandle, a thin and shriveled one—and never once indicated the slightest regret at that lot. Those big broken hands held me with uncommon sensitivity, with gentleness, and—to this day I am astonished to realize it—with *pride*.

I was in another world entirely with my father. When he left the house in the morning, and until the moment when he reappeared filling the doorframe designed for a different standard of man, the day was drained of light and power. I suppose now that I only managed. I pushed myself through the endless, agonizing rituals of dealing with other human beings, suffering the inadequacies of language, treading in the viscous confusions that mired and impeded every effort, until my father returned to me and the light of his greeting illuminated the world and made everything so clear and simple.

"Jim! And what the hell did you do today?" He had a voice that came up from his heavy chest with just a trace of brogue.

We would sit at the table, he at the head and looking away from me toward its center as if the act of watching might reduce the acuity of his listening. Only when I heard his questions of me did the activities of my day stand before my mind as events of potential importance.

"We colored in our books all morning, Dad."

"Did you get that one you wanted?"

"I did, Dad. The one with horses. And you know what?"

"What?"

"I kept between the lines."

"With the crayons, you mean. That's good, Jim." He had a way with small words—*good, fine, bad*—that made them resonate with unsupposed significance. Thinking of crayons, he shook his head. "When I was your age I had a very bad time staying between those lines."

"Did you, Dad?"

He looked at me, nodding, his thick brows lowering beneath his crown of curling hair. "I did, and I'll admit it. And to this day I'm grateful for a square or a straight edge. I'd be all over a two-by-six without them, I can tell you."

Those were good times, evenings at the table. We could talk for much longer then; mornings, I would be poised over a bowl of cornflakes, and if he hadn't already left for a job site, there'd only be a few words and a fond pat as he passed through the kitchen and on out to the truck. My mother got a quick kiss as she handed off his lunch pail and enormous thermos of coffee. Then, he'd be out the door and I'd be left with only the dim and anxious prospects of my normal day. And often, at the other end, he'd be back so late that I'd be asleep already, though I'd been tucked in with the secret pledge to stay awake until he returned (but sleep would usually take me down quickly; my days were exhausting). Still, if we had even a few moments before my eight-o'clock bedtime, the whole day was reclaimed for me.

Summers were a mixed blessing. The longer days often kept him away, but sometimes, if the job was close enough, he would return for supper—and one summer he began to take me with him when he went back after eating. Gradually, those occasions began to include weekends too. Those were happy times for me.

The phone would ring around six o'clock, and from where I sat, usually alone in my room, or sometimes at the kitchen table where I colored and listened to the radio while my mother cooked, my ears would prick up like a cat's. My mother, thin, stiff with suppressed energy, would scurry toward the phone. There would be a brief conversation, and if the interchange was short and mostly monosyllabic, I knew it was my father. When she hung up, I would immediately hurry up to her.

"Was that Dad?" I'd ask eagerly.

Before she answered, she sometimes regarded me for a moment. She usually appeared to be hurt by the question, then her dark eyes would narrow and pin me with a scowl. In my excitement, I would absorb that scowl and seem to ignore it, but I can still feel the lash of those eyes. How bad she must have felt, she who could not quite secure the ineffable brand of love that I strove but failed to provide her, as she watched her stunted son moving eagerly toward her for news of someone other than herself. By then I had developed my characteristic tip to the left, the gnarled posture that eventually became permanent as my spine snaked uncertainly between my body's confused growth centers, and moved on bandy legs with a curious flipping of the feet. Who was this gnome who came scurrying toward her, and only when Dad was on the line?

"Yes, it was your father."

"Is he coming home for supper?"

I could see the tenseness settling high up on her back, at the base of her neck. My question must have seemed like a scream to her. Her taciturn child, who had moments before protested that he needed so desperately to paste and color and cut, so much so that he had no time to walk with her, to talk with her, now, with the prospect of a glimpse of his beloved father, had become a bubbling fountain of energy.

"Yes, Jimmy, he's coming home."

Jimmy, Jimmy. I cringed inwardly at the name, a version that I felt emphasized my smallness. I was Jim, *Jim.* As my father called me.

"Can I go to the job with him, Mom? Can I stay up a little later and go with him?"

By the phone still, her thin hand on the receiver yet. "That's up to him, Jimmy."

There is no heaven to compare with those seldom-materializing trips to the job sites with my father. I learned to tell time well, to gauge the lengths of days, simply to determine the chances of my being allowed to go to the job with my father. The three of us would eat together, my mother nervously hurrying to and from the table, and my father eating slowly, appreciatively.

"Doris, this is very fine."

"I'm glad you like it, Mike."

"I'm surprised a green-blooded Irishman like myself would go in so strong for a red sauce."

He'd grin at his own jokes, and give me a wink. Then he might point at my plate with his fork.

"Jim, you'll need to eat a bit more than you're doing. I'm going to need you at the site tonight."

How can I describe the transformation of feelings that words such as these would create within me? I'd been happy merely to be sitting there, happier by far than at any other moment during the long day, and now a layer of joy would be slathered atop my already high spirits. Soaring might be a good word. My feelings would soar, and with a yelp I would turn back to my plate and shovel down the remaining food. My father and mother would laugh.

In the truck I sat up very straight, loving the view from the high windows. It was all so loose and careless and manly in the truck cab. Stray nails underfoot, dust as thick as talc on the dashboard, a split in the bench seat where a spring showed, seat belts that tangled and whose ends had no counterparts to snap into. If we hit a pothole, the front end shook as if we'd dislodged the axle. My father worked the stickshift through the oversized gears with a reactive rasp from the metal works housed beneath us. On and on we drove.

At the sites we would usually encounter a home in some stage of construction. We parked on the bare ground, raising dust, and I hopped out and ran up to the house. My father would follow slowly, watching the house with concentration. A return to the site, I came to learn, meant that some problem had been left unsolved, one that he needed to get away from for a while and return to with fresh eyes. Meanwhile, I would reach the gray-pocked surface of the exposed foundation, or a pile of lumber stacked beside it, or rolls of tarpaper heaped like outsized licorice sticks, and stop, unsure why I was running or where exactly to. My father stood back, hands on hips, looking up at the house.

"It's the kitchen, Jim. That's where our problem lies."

Our, *our* problem.

We would negotiate what stairs there were, enter and ascend by way of incompletely placed boards or tacked-up two-by-fours affording footholds. The moist, rimy smell of curing cement hung in the house's interior. I slipped and slung up through the house like a monkey in the jungle, my knees and the seat of my shorts soon gray with dust. In the kitchen, my father found a spot in the center of the room where he could gaze across at a row of cabinets and countertops without their Formica as yet. Spaces gaped uncertainly at either end.

"They don't make the standard size the owner ordered anymore. We're stuck with some space to cover up, I'm afraid."

"What're you going to do, Dad?"

"I'm not just sure yet, Jim. I need to puzzle it out for a moment."

He stood with his arms folded, looking. If I could manage it, I would finally fall quiet and let him think. Then, with a sigh, he would set us into action.

"All right, Jim, we're going to need the saw, the one for fine work. And the square, not the one with the level in it, just the light one."

"With the wing nut in the center."

"That's the one. The hammer for sure, and you might as well bring me my nail apron as well. I think it's got a few of the finishing nails still in it."

And I would be off, down through the spacious latticework of studs, the cool curing air, across the thudding boards and on to the truck. "*We'll* need the saw. . . . *We*."

At the truck, I'd work the big pins free from the tailgate and let it crash down as I'd seen him allow it to do. With one foot to the bumper, I'd vault into the bed and kick the stiff toolbox catch free like a pirate hungry for gold. With the lid up, I'd pull out the square, the hammer, and the rolled-up nail apron. The saws, each in its original cardboard sleeve, were set vertically on their backs, side by side in a narrow space framed in wood at the front of the bed. As I began to struggle toward the house with tools sticking out from me in every direction, my father might appear in an upstairs window space.

"Two trips, Jim. We've got the light tonight."

And I would nod, and return the few steps I'd taken. Of course two trips. Did I think I would make it up the makeshift stairs this way?

Upstairs, my father would already be moving about with his tape measure out. In the dimming kitchen, he would measure wide and measure high, then finally step back and replace the tape. He wore that tape measure clipped to his belt like a pistol, so second nature to him that he often wore it about the house late into the evening.

"You got it, Dad?"

"I think so, Jim. I think what we'll do here is give the owner a nice surprise. We'll give the lady of the house a lovely little cabinet to slip her ironing board into. How would that be?"

"That sounds great, Dad. Where're we going to put it?"

"Oh, we'll just rough it in tonight. We'll need to eyeball it a little to see if it'll fit. Tomorrow, with the full light, I'll scribe it properly."

It would be a special treat if I got to see my father cut wood. From the first tiny mark of the pencil setting the measure, to the last sure stroke of the saw, it was to me an operation of great beauty. He used a hard-lead pencil so that he could push hard upon the point. ("You set the line deep, Jim. A deep line leads the saw.") I held the waste end of the plank while his saw stepped through the wood with long, sure bites. *Sssip!-a-sssip!-a-sssip!-a.* I learned to open the cut gradually to keep the blade from binding, and could hold back and just allow the cut end to come free without splintering.

"There she is. "Now, hold her up right along the wall there, Jim. I need to see it."

By now it might be nearly dark, but we two ghostly workmen were at it while others were thickening in front of their TV sets.

I held up the board, and my father regarded it. He might need to tack it up, and so would come forward pulling his hammer free. "Right there! Hold her steady now." *Pingk! pingk! pingk!* Three sharp strikes directly on the nail head, and the board would be tacked in place.

We would work a little while longer, and then my father would step back, study the situation a moment and say, "Well, I think we've made a go of it."

On the way home, we'd talk for a few moments about the details of the job, but as we approached the house he would invariably become more silent. He might even sigh, and I could gather over time that these were not sighs of contentment. Now his day was truly over, and he was going in to my mother—and eventually to their room, to their bed, to their tensions and silences.

On my tenth birthday, my father gave me a tape measure. It was not as large as his, but it was a fine piece with a flexible steel tape, a strong return action, and a stainless-steel casing with a belt clip. It was the ultimate tool for a boy with a love of numbers, and I never tired of measuring. I took to wearing it around on my belt, and to wearing belts so that I had something to clip the measure to.

In my room one night, my father and I selected a doorjamb and he showed me how to slip a pencil flat against the top of my head to make a mark, and then to turn and measure. Though I already knew the truth, something made me ask. "Will I ever be as big as you, Dad?"

He was sitting on the edge of my bed, his heavy forearms on his knees. He raised his brows, as if considering that the question had more than one answer. "It's not in the stars for you to be big, Jim. Not physically big. It's for you to be big in other ways."

With my new tape measure in my two hands, with the short mark on the doorjamb behind me, I felt so pitiful and inconsequential. I could not understand the feeling of shame within me, but worse, what to do about it. Couldn't he do something about it? He could do everything else, why not fix it so I would become big? With a sadness palpable and thick within me, I turned to him and quietly pleaded, "But Dad, I want to be big. I want to be big like you."

With a look of mild irritation, he reached out and took my shoulder and shook it. "Jim, you're ten and you work a goddamn slide rule. You already lay a better saw mark than a man of thirty. Don't you understand, boy? You already *are* big."

I've taken those words forward with me through my life. When your own father never, *ever* laughs at you, not even when your little twisted movements are unbearably cute, when there's never a little hidden snicker at the edge of his lips after you risk a question that exposes the very marrow of your soul, then perhaps certain spiritual muscles within you are given a chance to develop, and sometimes to a point where no one can overpower them.

About a year later my father died suddenly of a heart attack, keeled over on the job, scattering tools. That's the way one of his jobbers described it. A neighbor came to the school to fetch me in her car. She told me nothing, just drove in silence. All the way home I sat with my fists against my chest, waiting for my mother's awful news.

S I X

I will soon go down to Howard Long's office, and probably wait patiently for him to come in and explain to me what in the world he meant by "defalcation." I have looked the word up in the dictionary, so I know its meaning for the world at large, but it will be up to Howard to elucidate its significance in our smaller federal world. He is late, as usual, juggling the several commitments he tries to wedge into a given hour.

"It's a word that must bother him a lot," says Jennifer DiAngelis. She is sitting beside my desk and we are sipping our morning coffees together. Bobby Marco might have joined us, but he's busy tackling a problem that one of the field officers called in yesterday afternoon. We have no set coffee-break time in my office, nor do we often observe such a time, but we very often huddle together spontaneously to plan our strategies or to confer about a specific problem.

"You say that because of his indictment troubles."

Jennifer, her fine legs crossed so that her smooth knees have slipped below the hemline of her raspberry skirt, nods over her coffee cup. She holds the cup in two hands, taking its warmth into her long, pale fingers. Her beauty is, as always, unsettling. This morning, her straight dark hair, fine-stranded and dense, has been pulled back behind her ears and uncertainly pegged into place with a strip of leather impaled by what appears to be a piece of polished bone. Her hair continually frees itself. Now, before my eyes, already a few shining tufts threaten to work free. The prospect makes it hard for me to breathe.

She nods. "They never pinned anything on him, but doesn't he seem like the type?"

"To split contracts?"

"Sure. I mean, he was an effective politician, wasn't he?"

I think for a moment. To split contracts means to take a big maintenance or construction job and illegally chop it into a number of smaller jobs. That way, each is small enough so that it doesn't have to be reviewed by the watchdogs. By splitting up a big contract, an administrator can get jobs out faster and to more constituents—concrete people, bricklayers, carpenters, and maintenance companies—without having to be as accountable for the total amount of money being spent. Howard Long started out in politics, a mayor in one of the bigger Midwest towns, and politicians like to move fast and to please.

I say, "Yes, I can see him doing it. I can see him doing it with not entirely bad intentions."

"I heard that he left quite a string of them back there in Illinois."

Sometimes Jennifer betrays a little cynicism, and it always surprises me. First if all, where does she get her information—she's always coming up with some hefty chunk of gossip—and, second, why this nose for it? I have sensed, from a few partial disclosures in conversation and one or two tense overheard conversations on the phone, that she is not completely happy with her husband, a handsome, carefully groomed man who occasionally accompanies her to social functions, and she sometimes complains of nasty encounters with other men. I wonder if her clear blue-green eyes are at the bottom of her access to information and her nose for its darker variety; who can resist divulging what they ask or seem to ask?

Bobby Marco comes up. "How can I work when you guys are having all this fun?" He lowers his voice, standing before my desk with his too-eager hands temporarily sequestered in pockets. "Did I overhear that you've got the goods on Howard?"

"Just that he might indeed have done what they said he did in an earlier life," says Jennifer.

"That would be too bad."

I shrug. "Howie's a big boy. I sometimes wonder if anyone ever gets ahead in politics without breaking some rules. Our own field people pull their hair every time we send back a figure for revision. Why these limits? Why these signatures? Don't you want us to get the job done?"

"Because," says Jennifer, leaning forward as if to impart grownup news to me. "Defalcations."

"Unfortunately true," says Bobby with his small nervous laugh. When he smiles, his normally held expression softens for a moment and one notices then that his eyelashes are uncommonly long. Sometimes he lets his thick blondish hair grow out a little, to the point where its luxuriance becomes noticeable, but at that point he pays someone good money to hack it back. He has been looking at me, or at my blotter, or at my penholder. Now, with Jennifer pressed forward, he lets his eyes slide up to linger where they have wanted to—upon her pale cheek, the line of her fine nose.

I shrug. "Anyway, I think you're right, Jennifer. That silly defalcation word would make him nervous, if somebody above him is beginning to throw it around. I imagine he took some lumps because of the risks he took, but he'll be gun-shy now."

"You've got to tell us everything when you get back," she says. The tip of one brow rises slightly but eloquently. Now her eyes slide up briefly to include Bobby, whose gaze flits to my telephone.

While I'm waiting in Howard's office, I try to trace back my good mood to its source. I sit with an unread *Congressional Record* in my hands, breathing easily, feeling at peace with the world. I conclude that it is because my conversation with Stella about Dr. Roth went so well this morning at breakfast.

I said to her, "Your new doctor wants to see you, honey."

"The man on the phone last night?" Her mother watched me from behind her, smoothing a heavy sweater into place along Stella's pointed shoulders. Marsha's brown eyes were dark with significance. It must be Stella's decision, she telegraphed; we agreed to that.

"Yes, Stella, that's right. You remember?"

"You didn't want to talk to him, Dad."

I hesitated, not having foreseen that response. "I was a little nervous."

"Why?" She threw up her arms—How silly to be afraid!—which came back down as if dragged back by her enlarged hands. She usually sits with her shoulders slumped and her head thrown back, like a puppet on slack strings.

I took up bits of my oatmeal with just the tip of my spoon. "I guess I worry what it might mean for you. He wants to examine you, and you know what that means."

"Will he scrape me?"

I nod. "I think he might want to."

"Will he give me a shot?"

"I'm not sure. He wants to meet you, and if you feel comfortable with him, he would like to examine you."

Stella has been examined dozens of times by medical people. From the first moment that the troublesome scabs began to appear at her elbows, through the "cradle cap," which was not cradle cap after all, through the tiny red cracks at the edges of her eyes and lips that appeared and would not heal, and finally through the gradual taut scarring of her entire body, she has been scraped and pinched and jabbed. Bits of her have been sifted into test tubes or clamped between strips of glass.

"Will they help me, Dad?"

Marsha began to stroke the child, running her good hands along Stella's shoulders, down her hunched back. My wife uses touch to sweeten the bitterness of any medicine.

"Probably not, honey. He just wants to keep a close watch on you."

But Marsha added, "Doctors keep trying, though, and sometimes they come up with something new that works."

Stella considered her words. She nodded. Because she

has no eyebrows, and only a few short eyelashes, I have become attuned to less traditional indications of feeling. When Stella is thinking deeply, her eyes will slide to one side and her mouth will open. For an instant, she will forget where she is. This morning, she thought that way for longer than usual. Then her eyes came back to me, though her mouth forgot to close. She watched my face, watched me as I ate my hardening oatmeal.

"I might be shy," she said.

"Yes. I'm sure you will be, honey. You'll be shy for about twenty seconds, and then you'll charm the pants off him."

She started to laugh. "No pants," she said. "The doctor won't have his pants on."

"You'll charm the pants right *off* him," said Marsha. And then we were all laughing, laughing at the thought of poor Dr. Roth trying to be professional with his pants off.

I am remembering the laughter when Howard bursts in and catches me with a grin on my face. He waves at me to follow him into his inner office, where he falls into the chair behind his desk and sighs. He always sighs a lot. Without even looking at me, he says in the wheezing voice of a man who consistently neglects his health, "Do you think anyone in our region would steal?"

I'm usually flip as hell with Howard because he's so selfimportant—and because, to be honest, I'm more than a little afraid of him. He gets angry, he fires people, and I have a daughter with big medical bills. Normally, Howard appreciates the flippancy, possibly because he usually encounters only sycophancy from his subordinates. But I'm not flip now because I know he wants only a serious answer. In my mind, I'm quickly sorting through the wide range of personalities, from ornery to outrageous, represented by our field staff. I think of the ten men and one woman who compose the field-office managers, then the dozen or so equipment-maintenance and cleaning foremen, and finally the three dozen shift supervisors who guide the cleaning crews and elevator mechanics and groundskeepers. All of the men and women who keep the buildings running so that the government officials housed in them, and the citizens who visit them, remain comfortable and happy. Our field people are working-class people; they have worked long, hard years between widely spaced promotions, come up through the ranks with eighth-grade or occasionally high-school educations. They are prey to strange fears, persuasive rhetoric, and the vicissitudes of changing government administrations. They can be stubborn, sometimes mean-spirited, even racist, but more often they are smart, game, and helpful.

"I think it's unlikely, Howard."

He immediately shoots back, "Why?" I have seldom seen him so worked up.

I formulate a clear answer, one as tight as a clean budget. "I could cite their basic integrity, but I'll spare an old warhorse like you the sentimental stuff. The fact is that stealing's too easy for them. There's nothing they like more than to do things the hard way. Their self-esteem is based on persistently making chicken salad out of chicken shit."

Howard wags his jowls at me. "Just what I need this morning. A little shit like you spouting philosophy."

"Really, Howard. Who out there would steal?"

He's forward now, on his thick-padded forearms. His leonine head has nearly fallen onto them. "Jim, what we talk about from now on can't leave this room. Have you talked to anyone yet about this stuff?"

"No." I'll have to get to Jennifer and Bobby quick and put the hush-hush on them.

"Good. Because it's getting bigger by the second."

"Can you tell me what's happened?"

"There's been a call. To Riley's office up in Manchester." He is referring to the Republican Senator from New Hampshire. "It was anonymous, it could mean nothing, but it could mean that there's some stealing going on in Milo's office." Milo Pelletier is the field-office manager stationed in Manchester.

"Did they say what kind?"

"The caller mentioned collusion with contractors, but no names or details. Riley's a friend, so he called me."

So that the fire could be stamped out before it got to the papers? I think aloud, "So it could be Milo or any of a half-dozen of his foremen. Or it might be a disgruntled employee trying to nail his boss."

Howard wags his head. "Maybe. But it could be serious. I'm having Milo's contracts brought down from his office to your office and I want you to check them out. I don't want to bring in an auditing team if I don't have to."

I think of Milo Pelletier, short, white-haired, perennially in double-knit blazer and awful government-green pants. I like the man; he's kind, simple-hearted, and he runs an efficient field office. I begin to say something, then think better of it. Then I say it: "Milo's a friend, Howard."

He does not hear, or pretends not to. "You're the perfect choice. You know the operation, you've been part of plenty of audits, and you know how to analyze the shit out of figures."

Two years ago I would not have repeated what Howard did not hear. Since then I've learned what purposeful nonhearing can mean. I think of my wife's call to me, how evenly I had screened the fearful tone from her voice and dished back cool sense. My face heats up a little and I take a breath. "Have you discussed this stuff with Milo? Does he even know about the anonymous call?"

He does not answer either question, but I have my answers. I sense that our conversation is nearing its close. I am now being confronted with Howard's political dark side, his assumption that many, many people are on the take, a view of the world as cookie jar whose cookies steadily disappear while no one can remember taking any.

"Just start thinking about putting in a little extra time in the near future, Jim. I'll be back to you." He shoves his glasses onto his face, and I am miles away.

I have been dismissed, but I writhe and flinch in my chair, failing to get to my feet.

Howard looks up at me as if surprised to find me still there. "Jim . . ."

"I'm not going to become part of this, Howard—not until somebody gives Milo a decent chance to face the accusations."

Howard's face jerks and his glasses come up, flashing. "And what the hell would that do, besides allow him to dig in?"

"I wouldn't care if he *did* dig in. He's put in thirty years of hard labor for Uncle Sam, he jumps through all the hoops this office and Washington stick under his nose, and he never complains about any of it. Now some asshole drops a dime and suddenly Milo's guilty until proven innocent."

I can see Howard's big face softening behind his glasses. His head woggles. "Shit, I'm going crazy. I'll call him." He jerks his head toward the door. "Now blow."

In the hallway, Jennifer appears at my elbow as if she'd dropped from the ceiling. "Well?"

I'm still reeling that I got my way with Howard. I look at her. "He's really worked up. He's like a vet having flashbacks. We're going to be part of a secret little auditing team, and no one, absolutely no one, can know about it. Tell Bobby."

"He went to lunch."

"Already?"

"You know he can eat only when his stomach's calm. So, somebody's on the take, huh? Who is it?" A spot of pink appears above each temple on her porcelain brow. Higher still, her hair draws back in thousands of dark filaments.

"It's no one, Jennifer. We are only checking, and reputations ride on how we approach this."

"I'll say."

When Jennifer goes to lunch an hour later, Bobby returns and sets to work quietly in his corner. I have my desk and its quiet six square feet to myself. I have a sandwich in a bag, one of Marsha's extraordinary creations—cheddar and tomato in thinly sliced layers, fluffed with sprouts—but I'm not in the mood to eat. I like my work, but sometimes I don't like my work.

Then there's a security guard standing before my desk and he's holding out a memo. I take it and thank him and he's instantly gone. There is a short message from Bill Kelly, head of Federal Security for the region (his office is right down the hall, but we don't visit each other much in person). The message says that certain "materials" will be delivered to my office over the weekend, "apropos of recent directives by Administrator Long." What, they're going to raid Milo's office over the weekend? I grimace.

Again, I am confronted by the occasional malignancies of my job and must wonder what holds me so tightly to it. Something about numbers, I conclude. But what I am thinking is how the world conspires to hold me at this desk. Numbers and the lure of their potential power first placed me behind it, and there are many faces to this passion. I love the way numbers *look*. When I print them, they each stand distinctly, precise and beautiful, upon the page. I keep a dozen sharpened pencils in a juice can wrapped in a strip of construction paper colored by Stella. There is a moment when the thickness of a pencil point hovers between pin-sharp and spatulate when I can nearly pass out from pleasure; the point is then optimal for creating the slightly thickened tail of a two, the tapering top of a seven, or the twisted-ribbon quality of a perfectly executed eight. Then the point wears to merely dull, and I grab a fresh pencil to begin another short, happy episode of working from pinpoint to blade.

I marvel at the way numbers tumble and melt into

one another. How two 2's disappear and return as a 4. How 4 times 5 leaps into 20. To my mind, and its easily circumscribed territories, long division is miracle enough for any man. I will often perform it without a calculator so that I can witness firsthand the scores of identical numbers marching into a single larger one, and the final report of exactly how many such sums were accommodated. How a long column of numbers will collapse into a single total . . .

But beyond these joys, the look and action of numbers, is what they represent. That, I believe, is at the root of my real calling. Numbers are an invention of the human mind, and they represent aspects of that mind in ways that are continuously intriguing and often mysterious. I am not a cabbalist, or a wizard, but, as I said, I did as a child meditate deeply on the relation of power and control to the relative heights of teachers, parents, bullies, and saints. Later, when my earliest surmises were revealed as the rough gauges that they were, I broke into a new world of measurements—school grades, intelligence quotients, percentages, wages, income levels, census figures, congressional districts . . . and budgets. What is a calculation but a holding of one constellation of numbers in place while you impact it with another? Such little struggles occur infinitely as we attempt to pin down the elusive elements of existence. And where scores of these number battles are fought become the campaigns represented by mortgage rates and gross national product and immigration quotas.

When I review a budget, I see numbers, certainly, but as I look deeper and really *see,* the drama they represent gradually appears as a brightening stage set behind a theater scrim. Suddenly, a line item—$20,000 for supplies, for example—becomes a will to become, a desire to *do,* a hope or plan that requires fuel. Figures of salaries and wages, which make up the meatier parts of our government budgets, translate into large schemas of action: whole buildings kept clean for a year, with tons of dust sucked or wiped up, grime sluiced away, bale upon bale of paper waste gathered and transported to distant geographic points; entire inventories of equipment—heaters, boilers, fans, circulating pumps, elevators—serviced, repaired, or replaced; asphalt laid and pounded or ripped up, crushed, and trucked off; forms laid, concrete poured. I see men and women bustling about in offices, meeting, typing, filing, telephoning, inputting and outputting. A budget is a script for action. With certain numbers before me, I can envision an army of field personnel fanning out across the region, and as easily, one man on a scaffold patiently repointing a brick wall.

Because I can see these things, I can very often see into the hearts of the men and women who have created the documents that I review. It is not always a pleasant talent to possess. When Bill Kelly's office attempted to secure funds for a new line of sidearms, it was I who flagged the figure, many thousands of dollars, and ultimately initiated a series of adjustments. Budget figures, which implicitly reflect priorities, must be justified, and I saw that request for what it was—an attempt to feather a nest. Prior to that time, the Security Office, which is responsible for protecting federal space throughout the region, had been expanded in response to the threat of bombings by political activists. More officers were hired, more and better equipment was purchased, the salaries of supervisors were justifiably increased, and gradually a little empire was building around Kelly. But when the political activity simmered down on the domestic front, the budgeteers attempted to piggyback on the increase in international terrorism. Perhaps they thought no one would notice that only Washington and New York offices were the targets of such actions; at any rate, their attempt to represent and outfit themselves as an antiterrorist brigade struck me as an attempt to squeeze one more egg from the golden goose. I flagged it, and Kelly knows that; their subsequent justifications did not sway the administrative staff, and in fact, the increased scrutiny eventually led to a reduction-in-force.

So I am not considered a friend of the Security Office. But what can I do? Life is checks and balances, judgments like figures taken into account, added up, and assigned a value. I'm staring at Milo's last budget, long pages twenty deep, and I'm thinking about numbers, and the meeting tomorrow with Dr. Roth.

S E V E N

Marsha works on weekends, at the front desk of a psychiatric hospital, so that she can take care of Stella and me during the week. On this Saturday morning, Marsha is ready to go by eight-fifteen, early and excited and singsongy to be going to work. She goes into the living room and comforts Stella for a few moments about the pending visit to Dr. Roth. Marsha has her purse and coat, and she wants to be off. I can feel it. But I hear Stella say, in a thick, pouty voice, "I want *you* to take me to Dr. Roth's."

Then I hear Marsha say, "Honey, we talked about this already. You know that Daddy is taking you this morning."

"But I want you to take me. Why can't you take me? I hate Daddy."

"Stella, you do not. You're not cooperating."

I am eating oatmeal, as usual. It's a bit gummy this morning. I pour myself some more coffee and stare at the wall with its familiar wallpaper, colonial motifs of little butter churns and cranberry rakes tumbling down a green background turning yellow. My wife spends many, many hours each week with this wall in view.

The appointment is at nine-thirty. Stella starts to whimper. "But I want *you* to take me."

"Honey, you know I have to go to work. Now, give me a kiss."

Stella starts to cry.

"Honey . . ."

Stella starts to wail. "No, youuuu!"

I call out, "Just go, Marsha."

"Honey . . ."

I call out again, "Marsha, just go. We'll be all right."

Marsha appears, her face pinched with helplessness, but with a set cast to her brow that will get her out the door. Stella appears behind her, in her body-stocking pajamas with the sewn-on feet, running uncertainly with arms out. I rise and intercept her by reaching down to catch her at the belly.

She cries out, "No, no, no!"

"It's okay, Stella," I say, uselessly.

Marsha makes the mistake of hesitating, and Stella lurches in my arms.

"Go, Marsha."

Now I have Stella by the wrists, her cries sliding into my middle like knives. She is twisting about, tossing her head. I have to pin her arms and keep her from flailing because when this happens her skin might open at any of a score of points.

I hear the front door close, and Stella collapses into stricken sobs. "Mommm-meee!"

I pick her up and get her into her bedroom where she twists and convulses in my lap. Her screaming mouth is a raw red hole. She manages to slide from my lap, but when she gets to her feet I hold her in place before me by gripping her sides. She flails at my forearms with her pathetic mitts.

I start a litany of what I hope will be comforting information.

"Mommy will be back later, honey."

"Noooo."

"She wouldn't ever stay away."

"Noooo." Her cheeks are drenched, her nostrils bubbling with snot.

"It's just her workday, Stella."

I must try to remember that there are reasons for this behavior. That at certain junctures her cumulative disappointments, the frustrations of her crippling condition, the awareness of her appearance, which never sinks far below a conscious level, all of these will erupt in unmanageable sadness. But she is exhausting herself with these feelings. When she comes apart like this, I think her grief will kill her. She has so little energy in reserve that I can almost feel it burning away. Our appointment is in an hour; I have to get her dressed, a lengthy process, and it's a thirty-minute drive in. Marsha and I have read many books and articles, we've talked to dozens of social workers. So what have I learned? That I have to connect with the feelings that are twisting my daughter into a living knot.

"Are you angry, honey?"

Nothing. Just the tears, more cries.

"Stella? Are you angry?"

At the next breath, she wails, "Nooo."

"You're angry, aren't you?" I put calm into my voice, though I'm stinging from a dozen feelings of my own.

"I'm *not* angry," she says, angrily. But I notice that the crying is beginning to ebb.

"Are you scared, then? Is that it, honey?"

Before my eyes, her sobbing subsides. She stands still on her two thin legs and rubs one mitt into her right eye. "Yes."

"Of going to see Dr. Roth?"

After a moment of hesitation, she nods.

"Will you let me hug you, sweetheart? Maybe then you'll feel a little better about it."

She looks at me, as if to test my sincerity, then nods. I pull her toward me with her bony sides in my two hands. She comes into my arms easily, light as a doll, and I close my body around hers.

"I'm scared too," I say.

"No you're not."

"I want it to go easily for you. The examination."

She says nothing.

"But I think it will be all right, Stella-Morella."

Her head woggles in a nod.

"He sounds nice on the phone," I say.

"How old is he?"

"I don't know. I've never seen him. But I think he's about a hundred."

She snickers. "That's pretty old, Dad."

"He's a hundred, they tell me."

"What color is he?"

"Oh, I was hoping you weren't going to ask that. He's purple."

Her back starts to shake, and I move my hand to the shaking spot. I love her laughter, crave to feel it bubbling through her.

"Why is he purple, Dad? Does he eat a lot of grapes?"

"That's exactly right. He eats too many grapes. He eats grapes in bed."

"Is his bed purple?" She pulls back and hangs against my encircling arms. She is smiling now.

"Everything about him is purple. He wears purple clothes, and drives a purple car. . . ."

"And he's got a purple wife!"

I chuckle at that. "Yes, and three purple kids."

"And a purple baby!" Her laughter erupts, and she brings her head up to smile at me.

"Twins! Purple twins!"

Now she clambers deeper into my lap and up against me like a cat. When her thin arms sling around my neck, I hug her to me in the quiet bedroom and a familiar prayer flickers in my breast. *Oh, daughter of mine, if wishes were pennies . . .*

By the bed are tissues, lots of tissues, and sterile wipes. I dab away her tears, then clean her eyes carefully at their edges and wipe her nostrils clean, trying not to take away any of the raw skin that always pervades these delicate areas. I then strip her down, checking as I go for any splitting that her violent movements might have incurred. But we appear to be in luck; I need to adjust only a few of the dressings.

Soon after, I bundle her into her winter gear and then we are in the car together and heading toward the medical complex in the center of town where all of the specialty hospitals are clustered tightly like a battlement erected against disease. Stella sits quietly in her seat, her head back and swaying easily with the pitch and roll of the car. There is a history of trips to the hospital, trips to see specialists, and each trip has begun with hope and ended in disappointment. Finally, she settled into the maintenance care of old Dr. Lerman, but now he has gone away and turned over his practice to a younger man.

Filing with others through the revolving door of the hospital, I am struck again how coming here is like coming home in a way. Those people who come and go, bandaged and hobbling and sometimes carefully picking their ways, people leaning on steadier others, or standing before desks fishing identification cards from wallet and purse—they are like Stella and me. They are hurt and need healing. It's strange how the hurt ones must now ambulate to the well, rather than the reverse. The new equipment is heavy, immobile, and the tests are cumbersome and delicate.

Stella and I stand before the huge elevators, waiting. There are no escalators in hospitals or medical centers. Escalators challenge canes and walkers and unsteady feet. Stella stands beside me, one thick hand slung into mine, and I'm feeling easier about my decision to be the one to bring her here today. A year ago, she would have insisted that her mother go with her. As we stand together, she becomes more resilient by the moment, I can feel it. She's told herself something. Her curiosity has been aroused, and she wants to know what the next moments will bring. Her strength carries her through the next instance, when the doors open and the faces of the few exiters betray by tiny flinchings of lips and eyelids their awareness of Stella's damaged face.

Inside the elevator, in the company of several others, she blurts, "Hey, Dad, these buttons are big. Which one do we want?"

"Five, honey."

She turns to the button board and aims the end of her

blunted hand at the five. With two quick pounds, she gets it to come alight. Her face, suffused with triumph, whips around and up, and several people call out congratulations to her.

But as we approach Dr. Roth's office, a moment of deep fear, one all too familiar, seizes me. *An elevator button, an elevator button . . .* When she is ten, fourteen, sixteen, what will there be for her to do? I forget all about computers and thick-handled paint brushes and the extraordinary devices that the Swedes are producing—bottle openers, corkscrews, pliers, and even milk-carton openers, that people without fingers, hands, or even arms can use—and am instead haunted by a vision of my growing daughter's keen mind wrapped in a gnarled body that can manage only elevator buttons. I cannot tell when these moments will descend upon my heart, like a dark cloth swirling down, but most often they materialize late at night. I have seen her before the TV set, lost for hours in its facile distractions after her mother and I have exhausted ourselves in relating and caring and entertaining. I have wondered if her life will degenerate to a pandering for consoling and time-filling pleasures—ice cream, medication, soap operas, sleeping in. . . . I have come awake in the middle of the night and envisioned her older and alone in a small shabby apartment with heavy curtains drawn day and night. They say she will not live into her teens, but then some with her condition do. More than once I have come awake and have thought for a flickering instant to steal into Stella's room at her deepest moment of sleep and snuff out her life with a pillow.

Stella helps me locate the number of Dr. Roth's office,

and a very young woman in nurse's white slides back a glass panel and calls out, "Is that Stella Kaldy out there?"

Stella calls, "Yes!" and then looks at me, pleased with herself.

"Have a seat, Ms. Kaldy. Dr. Roth will be out to see you soon, okay?"

"Okay!"

Stella sits primly on the edge of a comfortable gray chair. She surveys the room, looking very brave, I think. There is another person in the room, an old man with a large strawberry smudge across one side of his face, but his eyes are closed and his head is hanging down.

"It smells like needles," Stella says quietly.

"Hospital smell."

"Look, Dad." Her hand indicates a Georgia O'Keeffe print of a flower on the opposite wall. "It's purple."

"I told you," I say.

The glass panel slides open again, and the young woman tries to hand out a clipboard to me without standing up. I rise and seize it. "Could you fill that out for me?" she asks.

"Don't you have her records?"

"It's just to get Dr. Roth and you into the same computer."

There's a pen on a string and a few forms clipped in place. I settle into logging in the usual information about Stella. Any allergies, unusual disorders, reactions to medications? She begins to flip her legs about, impatiently. Finally, she gets up and toddles to a pile of magazines on an end table across the room and works loose a *Glamour*. Marsha has ingeniously applied several flat rubbery buttons to the insides of Stella's mittens, and these provide the friction that Stella applies with surprising deftness to grip objects, turn doorknobs, and even flip magazine pages. She returns with the magazine and places it to one side of her chair. Then she works her little sharp behind up onto the chair again, leans to grip the magazine, and pulls it into her lap. I notice that the old man across the waiting room has lifted his head to witness Stella's little feat. He looks at me, a tiny smile of admiration on his lips, but I look away quickly. I have become good at sending signals to others—in this case that it's better not to publicly comment on Stella's actions. When a child is physically hideous, any reference to specific unusualness, no matter how positive, just underscores the physical unusualness. The social workers warned us, Don't turn your child into a freak show.

To my left, she riffles through the pages, whacking the glossy surfaces with her heavy hands and rolling them over and away. She never reads kids' magazines; instead, she invariably picks out these glossy paeans to idealized female beauty. Page after page of stick women with oversized breasts, their long bones hung with ornaments. Why does she look at this stuff, these images of forms she will never even remotely come to approximate?

I get back to the papers on the clipboard, but she whacks my leg. "Scratch this, Dad."

She indicates a scratch-and-sniff panel in a perfume ad, where men in tuxedos and half-naked women are assembled on a veranda that overlooks a perfect Mediterranean beach. The ad's subliminal intent—to shame and reduce the invariably less-than-perfect viewer to a state of anxious consumption—offends me in the extreme. Reluctantly, I lift a hand to scratch the panel, but I'm saved by the sudden appearance in the room of a man in a doctor's coat.

He takes another step and stands before the two of us. Then, before Stella and I can react in any way, he drops down to a squat before my daughter.

"Are you Stella?" he asks. He has placed his face on a line with hers, and now gazes at her through gold-rimmed glasses and dark curls. He has dark eyes and brows, but his skin is pale though flecked with small dark moles.

Stella says simply, "Yes." There's a hint of delight in her voice. It's fun to be identified, to be known without your knowledge.

"Well, I'm Dr. David Roth. I'm really glad you came today."

Stella says, "You're not purple," then giggles just a little.

"I used to be. But then I stopped eating all those grapes."

Stella's eyes go wide and her head snaps around to me. I shrug.

She looks back to Dr. Roth.

He says, "Hey, do you want to see my office?"

"We're in your office."

"No, the inside part."

A short tremor of indecision passes through her body. I place a hand on her two knees and squeeze gently. "Okay," she says.

"Can I carry you?"

The two of them smile at one another, mutually charmed, it seems. Stella's arms come up to his neck, a new body to experience and another person in the small company of those who care or might care about her, and Dr. Roth grips her thin middle and hoists her up. When he hugs her legs to his chest she is delighted to be held so high and looking down. At this height, she is carried off down the hall with a smile for me, following, over the doctor's head. The two of them slip through a doorway.

I discover Dr. Roth slipping off Stella's coat, which he hangs on the trunk of a flat plastic elephant's head screwed to the wall. Stella is perched on the edge of a standard examination table, padded, with a long blue strip of paper running down its length. There is lots of equipment in the room—blood-pressure machine and eye and ear probes and sterilization trays—but they've been softened by disguises, gay colors, and a crudely painted mural of Disney characters parading behind and among them. "Mickey," observes Stella simply. A friend.

"That's right. And Minnie, Daisy, and Donald. The whole gang's here. Now, your father can sit right there beside my table."

It's warm in the room. I slip off my coat and hang it on the giraffe's head next to Stella's elephant. Then I take a seat against the wall, facing the table and with Dr. Roth's back partially to me. Now Roth turns to me and takes up a manila folder, thick with papers—the legacy of Dr. Lerman, Stella's good friend.

"So, no adverse reactions to antibiotics, aspirin, Tylenol? That's very good."

"It's been fortunate," I say.

"Does she often run a temperature?"

"Yes. A slight one," I answer. He is asking because Stella's nearly chronic state of infection must be monitored carefully.

Roth nods at me, then rises and slips the folder into a plastic file holder on the back of the door. Then he rolls a high stool over to Stella and sits down before her. With a big sigh, he regards her for a moment, then says, "I want to take a really good look at you, Stella. Is that all right?"

Her eyes roll over to me. I raise my brows to communicate that it's her decision. Do you trust this guy?

She looks back at Roth and says, "I know this part."

He laughs. "I'll bet you do. Just like the other doctors, I want to take a really close look at your skin, Stella, and then I want to scrape just a little bit of you to take a really close look at. It won't hurt. It might tickle, though." He says this last part gravely.

Stella nods. "It's okay, huh, Dad? Mom said it was okay."

"Did she?" I say. "Didn't she say it was up to you?"

It's a tightrope we walk with Stella at moments like this. This little ravaged life is hers to live, and we ache to think that she might suffer humiliations to please us.

Stella is nodding quietly. "Yeah. Yeah, she did. But I don't mind, Dad. I really don't mind."

"That's fine then, honey."

But now a different sort of expression crosses her face, and then one hand comes up and lights against her cheek, pushing at the toughening flesh. She knows very well what will come next. He will look into her mouth to check the tissues inside her cheeks and along her throat, examining the esophageal strictures, the atrophic scarring that with some victims eventually results in the inability to swallow. Then he will slip the cool Bakelite cones into her ears for other signs of lesions, the clinically ascribed blebs or bullae—to the layperson, *blisters*. He will need to know how internalized the scarring has become. Then all of her clothes will be removed, and she will sit for a while on the edge of the table as Dr. Roth touches and stares at her feet, her knees, her hands, perhaps squeezing and rubbing each in turn. Certainly, he will pause at the extremities, rolling the mittenlike hands and feet to test the extent of flexion contracture in the joints. The fused digits are to be expected. He will pull the flesh a little, testing for elasticity. He might take her head in his hands, and roll it around to the points where her neck bones seize and ask if that hurts. He'll push the tips of his fingers under her arms and jaw, probing, then perhaps ask about past infections. Regarding infection, he will need at some point to draw blood to test for levels of hemoglobin and number of erythrocytes, normally depleted in victims such as Stella, whose repeatedly rupturing flesh must endlessly battle abcesses. One of the great ironies of the disease is that it cleverly outflanks attempts to defeat it; the anemia that sets in is usually refractory, resistant to the positive hematinics that can strengthen the blood to combat the septicemiae that will certainly poison it. After years of blood purifying, the kidneys often fail, but the victim's scarred epidermis provides no clean field for dialysis catheters. Direct oral nourishment is frustrated by the narrowing of the throat and the loss of appetite that accompanies prolonged physical suffering and emotional depression.

Stella waits and thinks, rubbing her cheeks. She knows that Dr. Roth will at some point lift her and place her face down on the cold paper—it's always cold—and run his fingertips down her spine to its base, then spread the small halves of her bottom to examine the chronic rawness revealed there. He may even elect to place her on her back and, while maintaining a slow stream of reassuring words, part her legs and peer into her vulva, where the scarring always threatens to invade the mucous membranes surrounding the urethra. At some point, perhaps while she lies upon her stomach, there will be the unseen clattering of steel instruments, the click of sterile glass plates, a few reassuring words, and then the sensation of cold, sharp metal brushing determinedly at the back of an elbow, behind a knee, at the edge of the jaw. She will lie still, as she always has, naked and tiny, her heart beating hard.

Stella looks away, at the wall, at Minnie Mouse. "Why do you want to see me?" she asks.

Dr. Roth, before her on the stool, seems not to have heard the question. While Stella rubs one mitt into her cheek, he sits fixed and quiet—rehearsing? Then he comes alive. "Well, Stella. I want to examine you because I want to be absolutely sure that we are doing everything we can to help you."

"How?" She looks directly into his face. At times, I am shocked to discover the face of a much older person in my daughter. This is one of those times.

Roth is silent again. I can sense him asking himself how much he should tell her. His shoulders drop; he has decided to answer her question completely. "I think I might have a way of allowing your body to grow more.

A way that it can stretch, at the points where it *needs* to stretch so that you can grow without . . . without your body hurting itself by growing. And to continue to move instead of growing stiffer."

I can't imagine that this explanation will comfort Stella, but she does seem to be considering it. But now her other hand has come up, and I believe we will soon see tears. She presses her other hand against her other cheek, a temporary control against feelings that are mounting fast. It's clear to me now: she does not want this, she wants no more of this. I'm holding on to the armrests of my chair as if preparing to spring forward and whisk her away at the signal from her.

Stella says, "How can you make me grow?"

Poor Dr. Roth. I assume he is struggling with the fact that honestly describing certain processes to Stella will scare her so much that she won't want to cooperate.

With a sigh, he says, "I think I might be able to put some extra skin on the places where your body . . . stresses it. On your elbows and wrists and ankles, Stella, so that when your bones and insides get bigger, there will be enough skin to allow those joints to keep moving." He waggles his own wrists and arms to illustrate.

He has said it all out loud, and I wonder with some regret if I should have stepped in. The burden that has suddenly been placed on Stella seems to have a nearly palpable weight; how could I have allowed such monstrous concepts to be pressed on her? Every day children undergo the grossest medical treatments, but within an insulating ignorance. But Marsha and I have made a pact: Stella must not be prevented from participating in decisions that affect her own life. It is our hope that these most often amount only to challenges of communication. I pray that this is the only challenge now.

Stella's hands have come away from her face. "I don't want to," she says, very quietly. With a look to me, she explains, "I'm scared," using the word we discovered together back in her bedroom.

"Honey . . ." I say, but I'm looking to Roth.

The doctor, meanwhile, merely sits and smiles at Stella. Then he takes her two mitts in his hands, squeezing them softly. "Will you think about it, Stella?"

"I want to see my mom now."

"She's at work," I say, inanely. Then I add quickly, "We could call her."

Dr. Roth sits back in his chair, hands in lap. "We don't have to do anything else today," he says. "Just think about it for a while, Stella. Maybe you could call me in a couple of weeks, so we can talk about it a little. Would you do that?"

Stella nods. "Okay."

I'm relieved. He's a pro after all. And he confirms this on the way out by handing Stella a lollipop in the only way she can handle one—with the cellophane partially removed and with the stick pinched between two fingers so that most of its length is free for her grasping.

Stella shucks the cellophane with her teeth and pushes it my way, then pops the top into her mouth. "Grape!" she cries.

But in the elevator, despite the presence of a small crowd, she looks up at me and says, "Sorry, Dad."

I protest. "You were great, Stella."

"I was too scared." She looks ahead at the buttons, no longer interested in pressing any of them.

"Sweetheart. You were brave to even come."

"I've come lots of times. But this is different."

The door opens, and, in deference to our discussion, kindly eavesdroppers make a path for us to the lobby. We pass on, speaking as we walk. But once we emerge into the bustling lobby, she throws up her arms, signaling to be carried. I hoist her up, and we head for the parking garage. Then, on an inspiration, I veer toward the street exit instead. "How about something to eat?" Neither of us had gotten much of our oatmeal down at breakfast.

Right across the street is a new pastry shop. French pastry has come to America! At the corner, the Walk light pops on for us as right as rain. "Here we go. Have you ever had a croissant?"

"With Mom. Ham and cheese. He was nice, Dad. I like Dr. Roth."

"I do too. At first I kind of wondered if he might be too much of a hotshot."

"What's that?"

"Somebody who's too busy with himself to listen. But I liked the way he listened to you."

In line, I put her down and we saunter forward hand in hand. Teenagers and smaller kids stare at my daughter, unable to conceal their curiosity. Feeling their gazes, Stella sidles closer to my leg.

Though we find a fairly secluded booth, she has little appetite. Her thoughts have taken her over, still wrestling with her feelings about the visit. "You know what, Dad? It's bigger this time."

"What, the croissant?" I'm pretty hungry. I'll eat her croissant if she doesn't finish it.

"No, Dr. Roth. I think I know something. The other times I just left. But this time it will be bigger."

"You mean that you'll have to come back again?"

She nods, now eying her croissant as if for the first time. "Lots of times."

"Oh," I say slowly. "You mean it will be different because he will really do something."

Stella grows excited that I understand. "That's right, Dad. Won't it be different? Won't we be coming here lots of times?"

Maybe, I think. I begin to see that Stella had correctly assessed the size of the decision. It wasn't just a decision whether to allow yet another doctor to prick and pinch her. It was a decision whether to commit to *many* such episodes. The magnitude requires time, thought, Mom.

"Stella-Morella, you're one smart kid," I tell her. "You take all the damn time you need."

She nods, munching steadily now. I think of the form I filled out on the clipboard back in Dr. Roth's office, of the name of the disease I wrote out on it, something that she is actually suffering from and is hard just to write. *Epidermolysis bullosa dystrophica.* I usually use this slightly shortened form; there is a fourth word I can never bring myself to write: *letalis,* Latin for lethal.

E I G H T

That evening there is no walk beneath the stars with Stella. Exhausted, she falls asleep right after supper, virtually in her mother's arms, and I take the nightly walk in the company of Uncle Jack instead.

"I should call up that fine woman," says Jack, nodding off toward Dorie van Dusen's illuminated ranch house. "I've been meaning to call her ever since I changed that tire for her."

I sigh. "Jack, I'm not going to say anything. Put up or shut up." He has been talking about calling Dorie, or some other eligible woman, off and on for years. He calls none of them. He meets wonderful women everywhere—at the country club, where he exploits his assistant pro status, or right here on my street. Something is always wrong with them.

"I almost called her yesterday. Marsha passed on her number." He looks off, strolling with his long-legged golfer's stride. "But I suppose I want to be certain that it will be good."

"But you don't want it to be *too* good."

He snorts. "I want quality. She hasn't been divorced that long. Perhaps she's still a little raw." He has a way of walking with his face a bit forward, as if he's always peering into the future. The face is pleasantly lined, tanned in and out of season.

I say, "If she's raw, then she's all the more likely to show a little anger toward foot-dragging bachelors with a commitment problem. Is that it?" I should talk; I've had more than one sinful thought about Jennifer DiAngelis.

Jack shakes his head, his tall club cap forming a funny silhouette against the night sky. "You are too brutal. I don't know why I put up with your abuse. I should get a lawyer, but concern for my sister prevents me."

We share a laugh, then walk on in silence for a while.

Jack came more fully into our lives four years ago when we confirmed that Marsha was suffering from nervous exhaustion. When Stella reached age one, the enormity of her affliction had become evident. For months, Marsha was visited with acute bouts of confusing feelings, a whole secret side of her coming out in a way that startled and upset both of us. It caught me by surprise; I thought her weeping would stop, that her long evenings awake in bed would end. She began to say inappropriate things in front of Stella. I carry always in my memory an image of her sitting on the edge of the bed, sighing, with Stella across her lap and freshly greased with Bacitracin. "There must be a reason for this," she said, referring to our child, and within her hearing. This from a woman of relentless good cheer.

I was damned thick-headed back then. My way of dealing with the whole matter was to imagine that it would go away. I thought it could only be that we hadn't seen the right doctor yet. There was medicine on some shelf somewhere that we hadn't yet tried. But Marsha's struggle was leagues deeper. She'd realized during our engagement that my growth disorder was unlikely to be hereditary, but we had never looked on her side of the family for signs of genetic weakness. She wondered aloud, in the midst of long late-night conversations that seemed to me to go nowhere, why her mother's chronic psoriasis had never loomed as a possible presage, a recessive nasty surprise. But what of that? I maintained. I showered logical words on her: Wouldn't we still have decided to have children even when fully informed of the risks? Husbands make poor psychiatrists. She remained subconsciously alert for signs of blame on my side, and eventually I supplied them. I blamed her for slacking off, giving in to what seemed to me an overly indulgent level of self-pity, failing to maintain a stiffer upper lip.

The failure was mine. I did not consider many important factors; most important, Marsha was at home *all day* with Stella. While I was getting my hand patted by fellow employees, she was watching spontaneous lesions form on the pale flesh of our only child. I gradually learned something else as well: parents begin as rank amateurs—and those whose children are less or more than normal are particularly at sea. Stella cried often, needed constant care, underwent long traumatic testing, was continually handled by strangers. We agonized over all of it, doing everything without ever deep-down really knowing what to do.

I got a call from Jack at work one day. I knew Jack, I liked him a lot, but I rarely saw him back then. He lived in an apartment out in Newton, near the golf courses, and just far enough away to prevent regular visiting.

"I've just been talking with our mutual girlfriend," he said. "You can tell her I called you, Jim. I promised her I wouldn't."

"Jack, what is this?"

He spoke in his casually elegant way, the tone of his voice even and reassuring despite the lousy news it imparted. "In a word, she's desperate. I think all the problems with Stella have undermined her mental stability. Family life was less than perfect for us, as I'm sure she's told you, and I think she felt she was going to set it all right with a good family of her own."

"I know she's tired. . . ."

"More than that, Jim." His tone becamse uncharacteristically firm. "She's coming apart."

We got serious professional help for Marsha and, by proxy, me. I went off to a group therapy session with her and four other couples with afflicted children. I assumed that I was just going to hold her hand, but it turned out quite differently from that. One by one, as the momentum mounted, the four women in the room began to reveal how alone they felt with their problems, how cut off from their husbands, how confused and guilty. Every man in the room grew pale and shaken in turn. In the face of our children's physical defects, we had on some level abandoned our wives. Our unconscious motives were based, it seemed, on a list of potent assumptions: that only women were responsible for making babies, that problems with babies were the fault and province of women, that whatever adjustments or sacrifices had to be made should be made only, or mostly, by women. It was torture for me, for I had conceived of my marriage to Marsha as an arrival of sorts. With the growth of our love, I had felt myself ushered into real life. But the therapy sessions upended all that, and it was revealed to me how much, truly, I had made my marriage into an escape—from pain, self-doubt, and responsibility. I married Marsha so that she would then take care of things, approve of me forever, and all the rest. Marsha, then, was raising two children, and it had become too much.

One day I called up the group therapist and blurted that I knew something was required of me but I didn't know what it was. This was very taboo; everything was supposed to happen within the group sessions themselves. But I think I sounded so desperate that, after prefacing her remarks, she did advise me that fairness was often the key. "A wife's needs and desires are equally as important as the husband's," she said, in that slightly patronizing way that always made me bristle. "It would probably help you both and your situation if you realize that as fully as possible." She quickly added, "And Marsha needs to realize that, too."

To ease the domestic burden, we hired a wonderful middle-aged homeworker named Velverleen Baker, who went about with Stella under her arm like a salami. Marsha and I started to talk a lot more; we made plans. It seemed best that she be home with Stella for the first few years, then I would come home and she would get a full-time job. Gradually, Marsha saw daylight, but Jack kept an eye on her the whole time. Because of his clout at the club, he could slip away and become Marsha's courier or chauffeur, ferrying her to appointments, alone or with Stella, and taking Velverleen to the subway station on late nights. When his lease in Newton was up, he moved into our modest house for several months until Marsha grew stronger.

"Blessed Jack," I mutter, remembering. He is off on his own thoughts, possibly a fantasy involving an unclad Dorie van Dusen. I look up at the stars. It is my nature to gravitate toward the few happy stories of the constellations. I feel wretched whenever I think of Hercules, performing all of those monstrous tasks then having to tear off his own flesh in death. I would much rather think of Perseus happening along with the head of Medusa under his arm just in time to prevent Cetus from devouring the lovely Andromeda, chained to the cliff. I am delighted when I find my happy-ending preferences borne out in real life, like the arrival of a Jack Willis on one's doorstep . . . or a David Roth?

Jack's continual reference to women always throws my marriage to Marsha into relief. Her breakdown realigned us in some good ways, but threw us off in others. After so many months without lovemaking, it was as if we had lost the habit. We are not as affectionate as we used to be. I had always managed to keep my sexual fantasizing at a minimum, but more than once recently I dreamed of Jennifer and woke to discover my pajamas drenched in my own semen. Poor Marsha. She is in my thoughts now because I know that she is back at the house, alone, wondering about herself and her child and how she ranks as a mother and wife. That truth is bothersome to me at the moment—beneath the stars I cannot long be dishonest—and as I'm trotting to keep up with long-legged Jack I'm remembering the therapy sessions and how much talk there was about self-realization, about how women should be something to themselves before they become something else to someone else. But then new treatments started for Stella and I got a new promotion and new responsibilities at work.

I had assumed I would never marry, had gone to college pretty much expressly to master certain career skills that would comfortably support my almost certain bachelorhood. I had never kissed a girl, never been on a date. I was not happy about these omissions, but I assumed that my small size, my slightly twisted trunk and bandied legs, and the curiously trundling quality that these distortions brought to my walk would relegate me to categories other than those in which women browsed for mates. At the same time, I had no desire to match up with the female misfits of society. I knew instinctively that inside my sorry body beat the heart of a true, robust spirit. I could see that other undesirables mismatched themselves in pathetic pacts, and I concluded that it would have to be very good or not at all. I suppose that at that time I assumed I would always live with my widowed mother.

I do not even remember when I saw Marsha for the first time, but I do recall the blurred presence of a dark-haired young woman always at the periphery of my sight from where I sat in the right rear seat of a statistics class. I sat there quietly, mostly following along in my text or glossing my prepared work as our instructor slung knowledge at us with an artificial lilt meant to stimulate us. I never raised my hand, but when called on I would supply the correct answer. Gradually, a certain reputation for accuracy accreted around me, and the instructor, after plying the class with a question about standard deviations or random samplings and encountering only silent faces around the room, would call on me with the certain knowledge of receiving the correct answer.

Marsha Willis was no slouch herself. Nor was she above raising her hand or simply stating an answer when she believed she had a correct one. When she was found to be correct, which was often, she sometimes looked around at me. I would look back innocently because I always assumed her look had little to do with me. But then I began to notice, as the semester progressed, that a certain twinkle of complicity informed her looks. It dawned on me one day that Marsha Willis assumed some sort of bond between us, and I recall that occasionally, late at night, while bent under the bright, expensive lamp I had purchased after solid consumer research to illuminate strongly the texts I had to master, I would be distracted by thoughts of Marsha's assumed complicity and puzzle at what the basis of it could be. I would sit with a pencil in the air, arrested. Finally, I toyed with the idea that she found me attractive, but while others, I noticed, dressed to be noticed and cut their hair and grew mustaches to affect an engaging image, I got up each morning and put on the cleanest pair of corduroys I had and a variety of sportscoat designed to stay marginally in style for the next four hundred years.

It struck me one day that Marsha might indeed be attracted by me because of my performance in class. I'd heard that women liked brains, but were brains enough to secure them? With this possibility in mind, I reverted to my habitual state of shyness and pointedly avoided looking in her direction. After a week of this avoidance, Marsha ambushed me outside the door of the classroom.

I rounded the doorjamb, my briefcase whirling outward, and nearly collided with the stationary Marsha. "Did I do something to offend you?" she asked immediately.

The question did not register. My socially autistic bent often led me to interpret such questions as dealing with someone else: Was she talking to *me*? I actually began to walk around her, but she nimbly turned and fell in step.

"I've noticed that you seem to look away from me. I'm just curious if my behavior has offended you."

I found words, but *what* words. "Me? No, offend you? Excuse me, who?"

She ignored this dialect of the wretched, and said, with a hint of pent-up excitement, "Have you noticed that we are the two top students in the class? We control the whole damned room. I love it!" She hugged her books to her large, soft chest. I remember thinking, When do women buy their briefcases?

I said, "Class . . . the instructor . . ."

"Yes," she said. "And you shouldn't keep yourself down so much, Jim. I'll bet you're anxious about your size, and I think that's a big mistake."

Had I heard correctly? I reddened to a degree that is hard to describe. It was a blush that filled the flesh of my face to breaking, that threatened to ooze in hot drops from my pores, that squeezed my eyeballs until they teared. Worse, all the while the blush felt precarious, as if it could precipitate into sudden cold paleness and even death at the sound of another word.

"You've got a brain the size of Texas, Jim. It's been seven weeks, and you haven't made a single error in class. Have you gotten *anything* wrong on *any* of the tests?"

Desperately my mind latched onto this question. It could save me because it required a quantitative answer. "None," I said. The word came through my nose, expelled by a pocket of air captured at the base of my restricted windpipe. Up ahead was the exit. I hurried for it.

For a plump person, Marsha moved well. Though she was wearing a long, snug skirt, she kept right up with me. My heavy corduroys scraped loudly as I struck for the door.

But once outside, she was still beside me. "I'm just going to go ahead and keep talking," she announced. "It might be a big mistake, but somehow I don't think so. So I'll be the big bad wolf who tells you the big bad truth. So what? It's a role I'm only too happy to play."

I had not the slightest idea what she was talking about. Outside it was cold. Thank God for that, because it cooled my skin to its usual pasty normalcy. I was heading, by pure instinct, to my usual solitary lunch, but as I looked ahead to the cafeteria door it occurred to me that Marsha Willis might think to join me. That would be a whole hour with her, with a woman to whom I had managed to say less than a dozen words and whose glowing presence, fortified by an astonishing level of self-confidence, would certainly blast me into simpering inanity.

I took a breath, even slowed down. "I feel sorry for our instructor," I said, amazing myself; I had conceived and uttered an entire independent clause. But what was I going to say next? "It's such a fascinating subject, but most students just assume it has to be boring."

"Exactly," said Marsha, as if she had been dying to hear these words. "They'll wake up in ten years and think, Hey, this is great."

"Long after our poor professor is dead."

Marsha laughed, startling me. I reached for the cafeteria door handle with my briefcase hand, clattering the case against the glass. I switched to my free hand, opened the door, watched Marsha pass through it, and, impossibly, followed her in.

In the cafeteria line we giggled at the gray, gummy food.

"Ah, my favorite! Dead cow with library paste gravy!"

"Have the instant potatoes, they're protein free!"

"Some industrial pigment for your coffee?"

When we found a table, the teasing solidified into genuine conversation. My God, how we talked. I can remember very few of the topics we discussed, nor can I adequately describe the heady elation of that introduction to unthrottled human communication. With Marsha's open, smiling face across a wide, polished table, my head opened like a split melon and words sluiced out in a torrent. The more I spoke, the more she listened, and then would blush with excitement and interrupt and shovel words back at me. I had not talked for years, had never, I could now see, really *talked* with someone else. I cannot even remember what we talked *about,* though it must have been the subject matter of our common classes, and then the personalities, foibles, physical appearances of our teachers, and then every member of the student body.

At one point during those first two hours, I ran out of words and found myself staring panic-stricken at Marsha. My face must have gone blank, and pale, as if I'd come awake in a dream and found my all-too-real life right there around me again. But Marsha peered back at me, then went goggle-eyed and shook her dark hair at me. "Jim? Have you *died* or something?"

She had acknowledged my fear. Just to laugh back would have been appropriate, but I thought to experiment with something: answering truthfully, as my father had suggested at several important points of my childhood. I looked at her and said, "I don't know what to say next."

Perhaps I expected that Marsha would gather her books and leave the company of such an unsophisticated companion; however, she did not leave, nor did she seem surprised or disappointed by my response. Instead, she made a slight scowl and nodded as if, yes, one of life's all too common trifling difficulties had come upon us. And then she, and then I, began to talk again.

Marsha Willis, I noticed, had pure, luminous skin, smooth cheeks, and when she smiled her bow-shaped lips revealed wonderful white teeth. But even more important, I could tell her the truth, and I think that moment set the mark for the rest of our relationship. We would, the two of us, always resort to the truth.

I laughed, she laughed. Over ice cream, we became very silly again, and laughed at anything. Then we remembered that we had classes to go to, and so rose and left the cafeteria, but talked some more outside the door.

We had a test coming up, why not study for it together? We parted on that.

The very next night we were in her dorm room, face-to-face on our stomachs on the rug. By ten we had mastered every facet of new information, and Marsha produced cold cans of beer, and we drank several of these, facing one another and again finding the sluice-gates for words.

"This is college to me," said Marsha at one point. She said that nearly reverentially, and I pricked for her next words. "All the new things, every damned moment something new. There's so much to learn, Jim. Sometimes I think I'm going to just pass out."

It was dim in her room (when had she turned off the overhead light?), and I could see past her head, past the rise of her large, soft bottom, to where her heels were gently bumping together as she spoke. Yes, there were things to explore, whole worlds of knowledge and experience that were opening before me.

I do not believe that I ever directly found Marsha attractive. Her size was threatening to me. She was actually an inch or so taller and she outweighed me, and from the way she hoisted piles of books against herself I suspected that she was stronger as well. But gradually these differences and dimensions came to matter very little, and because they mattered so little to Marsha. We must have looked like a comic couple, the dwarf and the fat girl, walking arm in arm across the campus in our wholly private space. I learned of the cruel nicknames that our classmates had labeled us, Little Jim and Big Marsha, but the source of this information was Marsha, her source was a close friend, and when Marsha revealed this information she did so with a laugh. And I saw in that laugh the relative sureness at the center of this young woman, a glimpse of the strength with which she was so lavishly equipped. She cared nothing for the casual cruelties of others, based as they probably were on jealousy and insecurity. She had, she believed, a seat at the table upon which life's banquet was heaped, and now, in me, she had someone to sit beside and share it with.

It was not always a smooth road; for example, we bumped into sex very ungracefully. Again, the matter posed no problem for Marsha, who slipped easily through steps that took us from friendly, grateful kissing, to oscular bonding, to lingering wet explorations. But once, during one of these long labial sessions, when she reached into my pants and drew out my penis, I froze. My body went stiff. I came awake, feeling as I sometimes did that I had been dreaming, fooled, and now needed to wake up. Wretchedly embarrassed, I could hardly answer her concerned questions. I literally fled her room.

I tried to avoid her eye during class the next day, but she knew my routes. She emerged from the bushes near the cafeteria, shouting, "Ah ha!" and nearly scaring me to death.

"Marsha," I whined. I could think of nothing more to say.

"My God, Jim, what is it? Do you think I'm a slut or something?"

Then I knew what it was that had so troubled me, but I was paralyzed to express it. It seemed too terrible. I credit myself with again having the guts to put things in plain words. "It's delicate," I said. "Last night, I remembered something. My a . . ." I took a breath. "Mom used to do that to me."

Her eyes widened and her voice fell to a whisper. "What? Jerk you off?"

I looked around at the students hurrying past us on all sides. "Marsha, that's not exactly the way I would put it."

"When did she do it? Recently?"

I cried out, "No! For God's sake, Marsha, it happened when I was a little kid. Don't joke." But I was already starting to laugh despite myself.

"Why, you lucky little stiff," she said with glowing eyes. "No pun intended."

"Marsha," I protested.

"My mom never did that for me." She pretended to be miffed.

She went on teasing me for days. Gradually, my shame at the strange ministrations of my mother became a secret comic topic between us, no cause for pain but instead delight. In fact, in time, *all* of my traditional shameful secrets were transformed into the common material of life. I think love, in its healthier forms, can do that.

My admission had a positive effect on our relationship, I now realize, because it was at this point that we moved beyond the unstated feeling within us both that this was our big, and *only,* chance for love. Despite our cavalier dismissal of any of our publicly perceived inadequacies, the effects of living in a culture that worshiped healthy, perfect bodies and concomitantly devalued any deviations from these standards could not be completely avoided. Our misgivings peeked out in our conversations, in our criticisms of other students' performances, or our keen memories of the occasional errors of professors, or observations about the "silly" ways that the so-called hip kids dressed. But now we had discovered a real bona fide perversion in one of us, one that was at least as monstrous as the supposed deficiencies of our peers. Now we could let up; we could let live. And with that another layer of living opened— as it has, periodically, throughout our life together.

Our conversations, late at night where we nested in a pile of books and papers on the rug, turned more and more to the personal struggles of the human heart. The travails of a fat girl before racks and racks of beautiful clothes cut for rail-thin anemics, a gnarled boy's survival on beaches where muscled youths ramped and tore like stallions. The terrifying, bottomless gestalt of sex, its mysteries and misgivings and terrific grip on the loins. Our most embarrassing moments; our greatest triumphs. The grade-school teachers who had changed our lives. Our fathers and mothers. What it was like to have a sibling (I hadn't met Jack yet). What it was like to be an only child.

Life is strange, for I could never have foreseen that my poor mother's gentle, desperate manipulations of my small, startled member, disappearing in a mitten of lather as I stood in the bath, would eventually open a new life for me. For as Marsha and I opened up deeper, hidden storerooms within us and revealed forbidden knowledge to each other, we were ineluctably joining the human race. The effect of these discussions was to reveal that all humans flailed and struggled, failed and succeeded. There was a whole population out there, just outside of Marsha's barricaded dorm-room door, that suffered terrible bouts of loneliness, as we did, terrible misgivings, as we did, deep worry about supposed inadequacies, as we did. We never, as I can recall, actually *stated* this great truth, but we began to act differently because of it.

We began to move out into the world together. Marsha, as always, led the way. We decided to go to a dance. I was terrified for every moment until the very last, when we entered the gymnasium and I could see, or rather feel, a common energy released by the slow song that the earnest provincial band was twanging out. Couples were moving together across the hardwood floor, their bare socks shushing, and in every worried glance, broad smile, tentative tug and pull, I could see enacted the great human struggle to reach out and connect. The mysterious terror of dancing fell away, and I took Marsha in my arms and we slipped into the dark pool of swirling couples. Later, when the music heated up, I became wilder than I wanted to, even tossing my coat into the bleachers and drenching my dress shirt in sweat. I laughed to think that in hard dancing *all* bodies appear twisted.

Marsha and I became a relatively popular couple. We became "the good students who can also have fun." I could make people laugh, I discovered. And when I couldn't, Marsha could. When we attended the first spring barbecue on the first greening grass of the college quad, we found ourselves in the center of a knot of what could only be described as *friends*. There was Jeff Moody, a tall basketball player who was also a brilliant engi-

neering major; Annie Bissell, a dorm mate of Marsha's
and the editor of the school paper, and her prematurely
tweedy boyfriend, Seth Blistein, a political-science
major who already worked full-time for a consulting
company; Tim Slight, a loud, seamy kid in a heavy
leather jacket who could never stop laughing, and his
date, Mary Beth Noyes, who stood slightly away from
him, as if frightened by his booming voice, but giggling
uncontrollably.

We all stood about with paper plates, stabbing at
chicken with fragile plastic forks, talking quietly and
laughing. Then Mary Beth, who had been gently staring
at Marsha and me, said, "How do you two do it?"
Everyone grew quiet. At the time, I thought that everyone might have been embarrassed by the question, but
now I am convinced that they wanted to hear the answer.

I said, "Usually with Marsha on top—believe it or
not—but if you don't know how to do it at this point
in your life, Mary Beth . . ."

Freud said that we most often laugh about the issues
that poke at our tender, vulnerable centers. Mary Beth
protested over her plate of chicken: "You know what I
mean. How do you just so effortlessly . . . stay
together?"

"Honesty," said Marsha. "Jim tells me everything.
And I'm smart enough not to do the same with him."

I faked surprise. Jeff Moody said innocently, "What
haven't you told him, Marsha?"

"Nice try, Jeff."

We continued to tease each other, but as the banter
went on, as we played out the fiction that Marsha and
I were privy to some sort of higher knowledge about

human love, the novel thought came to me that the two of us were not only quite normal, quite nice, but were even *envied*.

Out under the stars with Jack, I'm wondering why we don't laugh so much anymore, Marsha and I. It's a sudden sodden insight, the present measured against the vividly recalled past.

Jack says, "What was that story about the giants?"

I am puzzled by the question. "The sports team? I haven't heard anything."

"No, no." He's waving his hand in the dark. "You know. The giants' parts . . ."

"Oh! The Norse gods."

"That's it!"

"They used to throw parts of their conquered enemies into the heavens. So some stars are eyes, some stars are noses or swords."

"Giant trash," says Jack. "The Norse gods were the original litterbugs."

I snort. His teasing is like Marsha's, and she used to tease much more often. Gradually, a feeling of gloom settles into me as the road takes us back to the house.

"Jack," I think to say, but do not say aloud, "I'm remembering how Marsha and I used to talk all the time at college. We don't talk like that anymore."

He would say, "Quality versus quantity. I read somewhere that we say less as we get older, but it means more."

Is that true? I say aloud, "Jack, do you think all couples talk less as they get older?"

He thinks for a few steps. "No, I wouldn't say so. I go out on the course with couples all the time, and sometimes they chat away from the first tee to the last green."

"About golf?"

"That. And the kids, financial stuff. Anything."

When we go inside together, Jack heads for the TV and I search for Marsha. She is in our bedroom, sitting up in her bathrobe and reading a novel. She peers at me over her reading glasses.

"Did you two solve all of the world's problems?"

"No. We didn't even discuss them."

She looks at me, a touch more keenly than usual. But she says nothing. I am busying myself over by the dresser, but actually I am registering an essential difference in our past and our present. A few years ago, Marsha would have pursued the conversation—to the point of finding out what Jack and I *did* talk about, and if we didn't talk at all, why not, and if it was all right that we didn't, and if not, was there anything the matter. But she has stopped short of that. When I look over at her, briefly, I discover that her eyes have not returned to her book—which I think is significant. But neither are they fixed on me. Instead, she is looking at some point on the bedspread beside her. I am thinking, *We have always been truthful with one another. Doesn't that also require that we not withhold the truth?*

I do not know what truth I, or Marsha, may be withholding, but I can still approach her, still try with her. Later, when Jack's gone and I'm ready for bed, she's still reading. In my pajamas and robe I climb onto the bed and let my head fall onto her belly below the propped book. Her hand lights on my head and her fingertips slip through my hair, gently furrowing my scalp.

"How did things go with Stella?" I ask. The two of them must have talked during Stella's bath about the visit with Dr. Roth. I did not want to ask that, but the question pulls itself from me.

Marsha sighs. "It's bad, I think. I mean, more complex."

"What? Is she scared?"

"Worse. Embarrassed."

This is something new. "I don't understand."

Marsha closes the book, takes a breath. "I think she is becoming more aware of how she looks to others. She's much more self-conscious this time around. I gather that Roth is not so old, and maybe good-looking?"

"Yes, yes."

"Well, I think she feels ashamed to be seen by him."

A new problem, a whole new set of problems. I do not want to talk about Stella now.

With my eyes closed, I say, "Marsha, I want to go away somewhere. Maybe one of the islands."

"Nice idea, but it's too much trouble. She can't be in the sun, and the sand in her sores . . ."

"No, Marsha. I want to go away with *you*. With you *alone*."

My head rides her diaphragm as her breath goes in, holds, and then goes slowly out. Like the tide, like the receding waves on a distant, warm, sandy shore. But I suspect that our two visions are different; where I see the two of us walking hand in hand along that shore, Marsha sees herself there alone.

NINE

Milo Pelletier has already called by the time I get in on Monday. In the center of my desk are two pink message slips in Bobby Marco's precise high-school mechanical-drawing print. Bobby himself is at his desk and sitting before a pile of thick file folders.

I walk over to his desk, we chat a little about the weekend, and then I ask about Milo: "How did he sound?"

Bobby regards me quietly, clamping his lips. He fingers his sparse blond mustache, too small and too carefully clipped for his big, boyish face. He says, "Upset might be the right word. He asked a few questions I couldn't answer."

I'm embarrassed for Milo, a man in his fifties having to feel out a kid of twenty-five. "I see we got the package from Howard."

Bobby leans back from the pile of papers and files. "I thought I'd get them together for you. Sort 'em out. The whole bunch was sitting on your desk with this note on top."

He hands me a simple slip of paper, something neatly typed by Howard's secretary. "As per our discussion. I'll check with you around two." An approximation of

"Howard" is scrawled by a nib as thick as a freight marker's.

I shake my head. "Now what the hell can I possibly say to Milo?" I snap Howard's note, listening for inspiration.

Bobby, leans back in his chair and says, "You could lie. Say it's all being done for his protection."

"That's a good idea, and actually true. Except, I don't know what Howard has already said to him. I suppose I can stall calling him until I see Howard later."

"Sure."

But when I get back to my desk and take my chair, I am distracted by a picture of Stella that I keep on my desk. We have so few pictures of her. Her smile at the camera is broad, coaxed out by an effective school photographer, but I remember the curious way she looked at the proofs when we picked through them for ordering. "I'll be the only one with a hat on," she said. Long ago Marsha and I agonized whether to just let her baldness show. Fit her with a wig? Hair is an insulator, and without it Stella was catching every cold, so in the end the snug washable cotton caps were the answer; Marsha made them colorful, with flaps or fringes, which made Stella feel unique and perhaps envied for once.

But I recall how she looked at those first proofs, how confused to see herself more clearly as others did. With these thoughts of Stella, I become Milo Pelletier at his own desk up north in Manchester, New Hampshire. I can feel his concern. I feel the sharp blow to his pride, and the deep circling thoughts that are nesting and multiplying in his brain at this very moment. I pick up the phone and dial his number.

His assistant says he's out of the office, and I can hear the regret in her voice that he's not there to take my call. I can see her as I remember her, tall, white-haired, and straight, coming forward in her chair in the little office with its gray metal desks and file cabinets. Some of those file cabinets have lost their contents over the weekend.

"Will you be in all morning?"

"Absolutely. Right here in my office."

By now Jennifer has come in, and as always a certain light comes in with her. She is an excellent worker, very sharp and extremely competent, and I know I should be concentrating on those qualities, but I cannot help but marvel at how good she looks, or rather how good she *makes* herself look. The cut of her navy-blue skirt and jacket fits the cloth snugly to each curve of her body, and there's a bit of white in her low-heeled shoes to catch the bit of white in her scarf, which is gently knotted and lies like a lucky accident across one shoulder and around her long white throat. Dark blue earrings, square and shiny, peek out from under her gathered hair. There's a new fragrance in the room, floral but mildly sharp. She stands behind her desk, quite perfect, slowly working a plastic lid free from her coffee cup with smooth, pale hands, each nail precisely lacquered in maroon.

"Jennifer," I say, "do you have a job interview with a modeling agency or something?"

She chuckles without looking up. She gets the coffee lid free and raises the cup to her lips. I avert my eyes and notice that Bobby is averting his; the pursing of her pliant lips, the careful tactile kiss at the cup's edge, are too intimate to be observed without feeling voyeuristic. We hear the gentle sip, and then she says, "Ah, now I'm awake." Cup in hand, she walks over to Bobby's desk. "This the evidence?"

Bobby smiles. "I guess so."

She wheels on a heel and faces me. "So what's the plan, boss?"

I'm leaning back in my chair, thinking. I'm thinking to stall a little, because I've clearly chosen to assume Milo's innocence. I have piles of memos to write, a meeting later in the morning with Lease Management, which is about to run over budget, and twenty pages of a regional manual that have needed to be revised for at least a year now. I say, "Let's all meet after lunch and come up with a process."

She makes a mock frown. "That means I'll have to keep doing what I *was* doing—and *all* morning." She looks sadly down at her desk top, where three stacks of printouts are arranged beside each other, and each as thick as a New York City phone book.

"Wouldn't that be a pity."

She turns, advances. "I say we get on with it, Jim. Didn't Howard say to get right on it?"

"Jennifer . . ."

"I'll admit it, I'm excited."

"She smells blood," says Bobby behind her.

"I read every Nancy Drew mystery when I was a kid. Put me on the case, Jim!"

The phone rings; Bobby picks it up; he puts it on hold and looks to me. "It's Milo."

Jennifer says, "Ooh," and sits down on my side chair, gazing at me eagerly over her coffee cup as I pick up the receiver. I raise a warning brow her way and whisper, "No interference." She gives me the girl scout salute.

"Milo."

He blurts out immediately, "Jim, what in God's name is going on? I get a call from the maintenance foreman over the weekend that there's two guys from Security banging around in my office, and I come in and find my contract cabinets open and empty." He speaks in the slightly raspy voice of a lifelong smoker. I recall a quick image of him, one leg up on the bumper of his government car, squinting in the sun, tapping a long cigarette against the pack. At this moment, his tone is precise, angry, measured. "I wouldn't have known where the hell my records'd gone if I didn't get it out of Bill Kelly this morning."

"Your records are in my office, Milo. Howard hasn't spoken to you?"

"He said he needed to take a look at my contracts, not rob my goddamn office."

I take a breath; this isn't my job. "I can't speak for his motives here, Milo."

I feel rather than see Jennifer's eyes opening wide. She is an unwanted distraction now; I don't want to worry whether I'm showing off for her. On Milo's end there is only silence.

Then, "Well, I'll certainly be talking to him again, you can count on that. But Holy Jesus, Jim. What do you guys think is going on up here, anyway? This is Milo, Jim. Milo Fucking Pelletier."

I try a joke. "I'm glad you don't go by your middle name, Milo." I hear not the slightest chuckle from him, which I am straining to detect. I recall my reason for calling him earlier. "Listen, my friend" (and he *is* something of a friend), "I'm not exactly sure myself what's going on. I know only that Howard is concerned, and that he wants to be assured that nothing remiss is happening, and that he wants to keep everything internal."

"But what's he concerned *about?* That's what I want to know."

I get a sinking feeling. "He didn't tell you?"

"He said he needed to take a look at my contract records, that there've been some computer errors in the region and he had to check out some things. That's all. Oh, and not to go blabbing around the region, of course. He wouldn't want a scandal or anything, no sir, not that."

Now I am very confused. I have to think fast. "There's not much more I can say, Milo, because I've been told by Howard to keep my mouth shut and I feel I should trust him on that. I will tell you that I have been directed to conduct a preliminary audit of your office's contracting for the past several years."

"I knew it! Now *why?*" Already his tone has changed. Equipped with the truth, or as much of it as I feel I can impart, he whines less.

I say, "That's a question for Howard to answer, Milo, but let me finish." Jennifer's eyes are two wide pools. "Let's key in on something important here, something that I want to tell you by way of assurances. My office has been directed to do a preliminary analysis of your contract records, and the way I see it we should do the best job we can to prove conclusively that your office is performing according to the regulations. I plan to be exhaustive, Milo, and that way it will begin and end here."

"Do you think that's the way Howard is seeing it?"

I think for a moment. "I'm not sure. It's my feeling that I'm not being told the whole story" (Jennifer nods knowingly at this point), "but there may be a reason for that."

"Huh!"

"I'm meeting with Howard this afternoon, Milo." That's not true yet, but it will be. "I will insist that he speak to you openly and completely about this matter."

"Good, Jim. I'll go with that."

After I hang up, Jennifer says "Ugh," and rises from her desk. "I feel dirty."

"Me too."

As she walks slowly back to her desk, I keep my eyes off the taut parallel tendons behind her knees. My sadness for Milo has kicked up other sadnesses, recent and keen. Lately, I wake up in the middle of the night, and even with Marsha beside me I feel alone. Feeling alone means there's an error alive somewhere, I know that.

Bobby asks, "So what do we do?"

"Nothing," I say. "Put those goddamn records back in the box, Bobby, and go back to whatever you were working on before."

"Sounds fine with me."

Jennifer is looking down at her piles of fanfold printouts. "Should I go on fielding errors?" She has been steadily checking the accuracy of a new management information system that purportedly produces budget status reports. More than a few bugs have been discovered.

Someone has come into the office, and now the phone is beginning to ring. It's getting too public to announce that I plan to meet with Howard and that we'll plan what to do next after that.

Later, Howard proves elusive; his secretary takes messages from me, but Howard does not call back, and I know that he's been in and out several times. I see his bulk rounding corners in the company of others, and once just slipping into an elevator. When I get out of my afternoon meeting with Finance, he has not gotten back in touch. Now I'm certain that he's avoiding me. I stand beside my desk; it's four o'clock and I promised Milo a return call. I pace the hall, inwardly paralyzed. Howard will scream at me, tell me to butt out, remind me that these are his decisions to make. I continue to pace, and wish I'd opted for a private office when I'd had the chance. I have only the hallways to hide in.

As I pace I draw counsel from the air as some plants draw nutrients. I am my father's son, I remember. That helps. And I cull through my store of important bits of knowledge: modern philosophies about a man being the sum of his actions; the rectitude that Gerry Burke, the minister at our Unitarian Church, calls "the art of living"; a memory of Marsha smiling at me as I stand beside the forty feet of privet hedge that, on a dare, I'd planted in one day.

I go down the hall, and up one flight of stairs, to Howard's office.

He's not in, but I badger his secretary, Helen, until

she admits that he'll stop back before going home. I push harder and discover that he's only having coffee with someone, right down in the cafeteria, so I sit down with a *Congressional Record* and wait.

When he comes through the door, he sees me but says nothing. He starts to charge into his office, but I'm on his heels. "One minute, Howard, that's all I need."

"Of course," he says, as pleasantly as he's capable of. But his head has that grim set to it. In the inner office he heads toward his desk and pushes his large body into the generous leather chair. He gestures toward one of the empty chairs before his desk. "Sit down, Jim."

I sit. "I don't like the way it's going," I say.

He's taken his paternal posture, big arms out before him across the blotter and heavy head tipped and hung nearly between them. "Can you just help me out on this one, Jim? Do I have to always go through these heavy justification routines with you?"

"No, I can't," I answer quietly. "And yes, you do."

He closes his eyes. "You are an insolent little bastard, Jim, and sometimes I don't like you very much."

I begin playing the few cards in my hand that could back a bet. "Howard, I cannot be party to an audit in which the accused has not been informed of charges made against him."

He does not even bother to deny anything. "Audits are conducted all the time, Jim. It's part of the business."

"There's a difference, Howard. Those audits are conducted by schedule, they are not generated by accusations. And I should tell you everybody is feeling a little soiled by all this. Milo is very upset, he's personally hurt by your refusal to come clean with him, and my personnel feel like hangmen. And we haven't even *started* yet."

Howard shakes his head. He looks up at a corner in the ceiling as if an answer is floating there. "Okay," he says slowly. "Does the figure seven million dollars impress you?"

I do some quick figuring. That's at least ten times Milo's entire budget for one year. It's nearly twice the entire regional budget for all maintenance operations. "You're hinting at something much bigger than Milo's office."

"I'm not supposed to tell you this, but it will be in the papers in a few days anyway. Several field-office managers in Chicago were caught in a contract collusion ring. They've scammed seven million dollars over three years."

That's very impressive embezzling, but I suspect that Howard is revealing it in a manner meant to cow me. "And you're feeling pressure out here?"

He slaps a pair of glasses onto his face and flips open a leather folder—the one that holds his most sensitive documents. He reads, "In the very near future, a thorough agency-wide audit will be initiated of all contracting activities for the past five fiscal years." He slips the folder closed. "Now what do you think?"

"I . . ." Already I can see ahead to the next year, or two. The prying and prodding, the endless questions, the pointing . . . "It's Chicago. It's not us, Howard. I think we should ask, How would we proceed after that anonymous call if we didn't already know about Chicago?"

"But we *do* know about Chicago. We have to use all

the information at hand, don't we?" He thinks he has the upper hand now.

I must repeat, "It's Chicago, it's not here."

"But if it happened in Chicago, it could happen here. And now it might really be happening here. And I need to find that out, Jim. And that is why *I'm* directing *you* to check Milo's operation."

Despite all the diction, we are just arguing like little kids. I'm sitting forward, and probably more than a little red-faced. We're off the point, and every time I say "Chicago" he can easily say, "And maybe here." Then, I get an inspiration.

"When does the agency-wide audit start?"

"Soon. Why?"

"When it starts, will the field-office managers be informed of the reason for it?"

I've got him. My point sinks through his bulk like a stone. But it is not having the desired effect; he is becoming angry, he's running out of patience.

"Shall I deliver my instructions to you as a formal order? Will that convince you to begin, Jim?" The sarcasm is as caustic as acid. Now, I'm angry too.

"I don't care what you do, but consider this, Howard. Consider the numbers three and twenty-five. Which would you consider more impressive?"

"What's your point?"

"You've worked in this agency for three years. Milo Pelletier has worked here for twenty-five."

But our discussion has soured too much by this point; he will not be persuaded, so he has become insulted. I can see he will soon explode, but I hold his gaze and we both find a short instance of time in which to consider, minimally, that we are both human beings with limitations, good intentions, and burdens to bear.

"We're at an impasse, Jim. I'm going to send you a formal memorandum detailing your duties in this matter, and eliminate the debating. If you don't follow my directive, then it will be a simple matter of insubordination."

I rise, nod, leave.

There are a lot of people in my office when I return. Someone from Lease Management is talking with Bobby, and Jennifer is off in the corner with two field-office personnel who have come in to discuss some of the computer errors. The phone rings, but I let it go through to Howard's secretaries; he's got two, but my shop is too small to support a clerical position, so we share his staff. They'll take a message for me.

By four-thirty-five my staff begin to notice that something's not right with me. When he's free, Bobby comes over and says he's going to go down for coffee, asks if I want a last cup. I say yes and he asks how it went with Howard, but I wave him off. Jennifer is free by quitting time, but she hangs around her desk, eying me. Finally, she comes over. Bobby is there already, perched on the edge. "Tell us, Jim," she says.

I am very upset. I am determined to deliver on my promise to Milo, who has shown great trust already by simply not calling back. I know the poor bastard is in his office, waiting for my call.

Jennifer asks, "What did Howard say?"

I take a breath. "There's been some stealing going on in another region. Collusion with contractors. Millions of dollars."

Bobby says, "The party's over."

"None of us are supposed to know about this. Washington is about to launch an agency-wide audit, a big shakedown. Howard, as far as I can gather, doesn't want any surprises, so he's going fast after Milo."

"Because of a stupid phone tip?" says Jennifer. "There could be absolutely no connection."

"I never got that far. If I do not proceed with the preliminary audit, Howard will cite me for insubordination."

"That's nasty," says Bobby. "What do you think you'll do?"

I shrug. "I'm not sure. I get formal orders from Howard tomorrow. In the meantime, I've promised Milo a full disclosure today." I think for a moment, way back in my chair with my eyes closed. "I suppose I'll just have to demand to be relieved of this duty, or whatever the term is."

"Then he'll cite you," said Bobby.

"Which will be unpleasant, but not fatal. I'll have my job, but fewer promotions." I laugh.

"Don't demand to be relieved," says Jennifer, with much conviction.

I sit and rub my eyes. "I'm open to suggestions, gang."

"Follow the orders. Do the analysis." I open my eyes and discover that she looks very determined—but I'm confused. She would be the last to suggest that I go against principles. She goes on. "Look, tomorrow you're getting the formal directive, right? But today's today."

Bobby smiles slyly. "She's right, Jim. Whatever you do today is your business."

"You mean call Milo. Tell him everything."

Jennifer's eyes are wide. "Yes! Then he'll know the score, and he'll know that by tomorrow your hands will be tied."

"But they really won't be," adds Bobby, with a glance to Jennifer. She grins. "Right. Because *you'll* be running the analysis, Jim. If you go against Howard, he'll pull you and put someone less sympathetic on it. And what good will that do Milo?"

I feel a weight of considerable size toppling from my chest. "Excellent," I say, reaching for the phone. "You two are solid gold." I punch out Milo's number.

Bobby chuckles. "He might not even be there now."

"He'll be there."

Milo is there, all right.

T E N

Stella and I are huddled close this evening because it is getting colder, and the wind cuts.

"Winter is coming, Dad," she announces.

"Yes, Stella. It certainly is."

But we are fortunate that few clouds blot the stars this evening. With the coming of the winter sky, the constellation of the charioteer, Auriga, rises in prominence, and I take heart in seeing its pentagonal configuration. Why Auriga, a mythical shepherd, is pictured riding a chariot has never been clear. Like so many of the ancient stories, Auriga's has been lost. To add to the mystery, he carries a she-goat and her two kids on his shoulder; each of these little animals has its own star. The books that I have read during infrequent escapes to the library reveal some connection between Auriga and Vulcan, or Hephaestus, the lame dwarf blacksmith of the Greek gods who invented the chariot. But the idea of a gentle shepherd who also has the strength to control galloping steeds while simultaneously balancing additional animals on his shoulder has always appealed to me—riding that chariot, built by a lame dwarf. . . .

Stella says, "I'm cold," and hugs me with her head against my neck.

I pat her back, pressing her closer. "Should we go back, honey?"

"No. But I'm really going to like my bath, Dad."

"And I get to give it to you tonight, Stella." Her mother and Jack went off to a casino night together. It's just Stella and I tonight.

"Auriga's rising," I say.

"Oh, Capella!" she croons. She pulls away and comes erect in my arms, twisting around to view the sky. "There!" she cries, pointing at the brightest star in the constellation where it just comes above the horizon. Capella is the little she-goat that Auriga carries on his shoulder.

I am impressed. "Yes, that's it. And can you see its red and green flashes? Signs of inner strength, they used to believe."

"Who?"

"The ancient people. When they were afraid of the failing of the sun, Capella encouraged them. There is still fire in the sky, she said."

"Where's her babies?" She searches for the two faint stars that signify Capella's two baby goats. Auriga's shoulder is crowded.

"I think I see them there, Stella. Just above."

"I'm going to have two children too when I grow up. One boy and one girl. I'll name them after Capella's babies. What's their names, Dad?"

After a short silence, I answer, "I can't remember." We are passing Dorie van Dusen's house, lit as always. The woman lives alone, divorced now, owner of a home once shared by three, then two. I ask, "Do you want to visit Dorie tonight?"

"But what are Capella's babies' names?" She sounds irritated.

"I really can't remember, honey. They have to be 'hed' something because we named Heddie after them. Something Greek." It has always been hard to determine what to tell Stella about her future. We have discussed several times the nature of her congenital illness, and what "congenital" means. We have not discussed the relative length of the lives of persons afflicted with her illness. Most die young, but a few, a few do live on to reach normal lifetimes.

I am silent because I hope she'll drop the procreation topic, but she blurts out happily, "A boy and a girl, so they can play with each other."

"Ah."

We walk on in silence for a few more minutes and then Stella says, "Dad, I might get better now."

"Better" almost always refers to her skin. It's so cold out I'm nearly shivering. "How do you know, Stella?"

She answers in a singsong voice, "Be*cause* of *Doc*tor *Roth*. He's going to make me better."

"Is that what your mom said?" Dorie's house is passing behind us, and now the Lesters' dark trees are looming, their dark home peeking from between the obscuring limbs. They are a family of five, but after eight o'clock only the room with the TV is lit.

"No. But I know he will." I can feel her smiling. "You know, Dad. I'm going to marry Dr. Roth when I grow up."

She snuggles closer, shivering a little, and I hug her to me. I say, "Why not, Stella-Capella! But let's take a hot bath first!" And I hurry her the rest of the way back to our house.

Inside, as I peel the clothes from her, piece by piece, she is off in her own thoughts. The soft cotton layers that Marsha prepares so carefully, each rinsed clear of all detergent traces, go immediately into the hamper. As the layers come away, I run my hands, rinsed in alcohol, over the angriest of the blisters that ravage her tender dermis. There is some cracking, the increased peeling brought on by the drier winter air, and a little bleeding behind one ear and one knee. Low on her spine, I find some small splits with the telltale whitish edges indicating infection. It is loci like these—dozens in a week, a few undetectable, so the doctors tell us—where the blood must continually fight, depleting itself, and the kidneys must interminably cleanse, wearing themselves out.

"You really look good tonight, sweetheart."

"I'm *really* getting cold, Dad."

"Sorry." I should be hurrying through this; though we keep her room extra warm, if the human body is a furnace, her tiny corpus must be more than fully fueled to press it to a near-normal temperature. I should not keep her naked in the open air for long. I finish my examination quickly, then cry, "Go!"

She pops off the bed and heads for the bathroom, where the faucet is distantly gurgling. The sight of her attempts at running is always poignant to me. Without flexible toes, she has no forward spring to her run. Instead, her rising knees and legs churn nearly in place while her body moves forward only slowly. That she exercise is important, get the blood moving, but Marsha and I cannot help but wonder which tender blebs might break with these rapid movements.

When I arrive in the bathroom, she has one leg already hoisted over the porcelain side and dipped one clubby foot into the swirling water. "Not too hot?" I ask.

"Just right," she says, and slides over like a frog at pond's edge. Water is a good element for her. She is more mobile in it, but she is consigned only to bathtubs because her skin would dry terribly from the chlorine in swimming pools, and ponds are tricky with bacteria. At the moment, she is completely under the water on her belly, then she comes up with a spewing breath. I turn off the faucet.

"Done swimming?"

"No way." She paddles some more, frog kicking in the narrow tub.

"Maybe we'll put in a big hot tub someday," I muse aloud. "Like the Japanese have. They're as big as wading pools, but deeper."

"Hey, yeah. I can stay in for hours then."

"Maybe. If we put something in the water. Anyway, we'd better get going with the soaping."

We use a special cream soap on her, a custom mix of emollients laced with Betadine surgical scrub. It works well, rarely drying while working the skin flakes free. I squeeze some of the brownish cream into my palm, and one of Stella's legs comes up straight out of the water. Somewhere, an open sore is letting small pink puffs of blood into the water.

I enjoy the baths because of their inherent intimacy and because Stella enjoys them so much. But tub baths have dark associations for me; as the lather rises on Stella's flesh, I remember again the long, uncomfortable baths my mother used to give me. On the surface, they should have been joyous, because her careful, loving ministrations might have comforted my lonely heart. But while her thin fingers accurately furrowed my scalp, or slipped behind my ears, and pressed more deeply along my neck and collarbones, she spoke to me in a voice with an increasingly haunting timbre.

"Yes, yes, sweetie-pie. Yes, my little man. Doesn't that feel good?"

I would answer that yes it felt good, but hollowly, because I already knew what would follow.

"So what shall we share, Jimmy?" The fingers moved down my back, into the muscles beneath my shoulderblades. "What secret shall we keep?"

What could I answer then?

"I want us to be better friends, Jimmy. Aren't there some things we can do together? Some places we can go? Secret places where we can go together?"

She wanted something. She *wanted*. I could not answer, sitting up in the hot water with my eyes closed. The questions were not so mysterious in themselves, but I suspected that they were designed to accomplish something confusing and unpleasant. The secrets we were to share would be secrets from my father; the places where we would go together would be places where my father would not be.

As she cleansed and probed and rinsed, bringing handfuls of warm water up and over me, I would wonder where my father was. I knew instinctively that I could not speak of him then, because this was Mom's and my "special time." So while the poor woman plotted to somehow get closer to me, I burned with unanswered questions about *him:* Was he coming home soon? Had there been a fight or something?

"You need some new school clothes, Jimmy. Would you like to go out to Sears with me this weekend?"

Had there been a fight? Was he not coming home tonight?

"I saw in the paper that they've got these wonderful little corduroy suits. You'd look so cute in a suit like that. Want to go?"

"If you want to." *Was he never coming home again?*

"But tell me what *you* want, Jimmy." Then, with a sigh, "Stand up, now, little man. Time to wash your legs."

With her kneeling on the bath mat, we were eye to eye when I stood up. The bathroom steam softened her otherwise brittle hair, very light brown but with an early brindling of gray. Her eyes, hemmed with tight lines, fine as hairs, were dark brown with short stiff lashes. Her lips were generous, but normally pressed, her skin a pale white. It was the face of a stranger.

"So," the face would say, "let's get these feet pussycat clean."

I didn't want to be put into cute suits, to be associated with pussycats. I wanted to be big and dusty, like my father.

Her hands took each of my feet, her fingertips slipping between the toes, back along the heel. Then, soaping up, she brought her hands up my legs, around my knee-caps and gently behind the knees, her fingers pressing into the shallow cups there. Tenderly, her hands slipped up my thighs and she smiled as she brought one hand up behind my testicles, briefly massaging behind them, I suppose to familiarize my genitals with her touch. Then, while rolling the bar of Ivory around and around in her hands, she would say, "Now let's wash that little soldier of yours, huh?"

With one hand on my buttocks, she'd cup my penis and testicles in the other palm and begin to massage evenly, but precisely too. Her fingertips would gently roll each testicle, probing the scrotum, then, as my penis began to harden, draw down the short shaft so that the small swelling glans would slide back and forth in the slippery pocket of her palm. She might soap up again, then again. "Look at it," she'd say with delight. "It's standing out so straight, Jimmy. What a wonderful little soldier."

I suppose I assumed that all mothers washed their sons this way. The sensations were physically pleasant, as one might guess, but they only made the gloomy introversion of my feelings worse. I was too young to be brought to ejaculation, so we never faced that particular crisis. But, at the end of each bath, when she rinsed my tingling penis, she would often whisper with a small secret smile, "Now, don't tell your father about this. It's our secret."

So I was manipulated into a secret shared only with her, and from the one person from whom I wished to have no secrets. When I went about with my father, I found myself burdened at times with dark questions. Did she wash him that way? Why did we have to keep it a secret, she and I? Was there something wrong about what we did? Though I didn't know the words yet, I suspected I was experiencing something that was rightly his to experience, thus depriving the person I admired so much. It tainted things; all of my mother's strange, pressing efforts to wrest love from me tainted my living. Over the years, and only long after her death, did the startling news break in my brain that many are born who are not equipped to love. They are simply not outfitted for it, and what agony it must have been for her when she realized that she, who hoped so much for love and to love, was among that number.

The child in my own bathtub is now very clean and must be quickly and carefully dried. While sitting on the toilet lid, I blot her rail-thin body with a soft towel under the fierce, friendly glare of the infrared lamp. Then I wrap her in another towel and hoist her up and into the bedroom. Soon, she is laid belly-down across my lap. I grease my hands with Bacitracin and begin to rub it into her skin. I hum to myself.

"Dad, can I have a dog?"

Now what's going on in that brain of hers? This is a discussion that we have had a few times, and my answer has always had to be the same. "Honey, you know the answer to that."

"But I can keep him clean."

"Not clean enough, Stella." Even her stuffed toys must be washed often. We must remember that everything that comes in contact with her is essentially a bandage. "I know a dog would make you feel better, honey, but we can't risk it. Your little kidneys work hard all the time."

"But I don't *feel* them working, Dad."

"I know. But you'd feel it if they stopped. Believe me."

She's no dummy; she can conceptualize this even at her age. But my heart begins to ache a little because she will always, and naturally, invest in the possibility of a normal life—one with the things that other kids have: brothers and sisters, pets, summer camps, swimming pools, pajama parties. How Marsha and I have agonized. Our grim choice has been to put Stella in the company of other afflicted kids, thus reinforcing the stigma of the freak.

"But I want a dog, Dad. I can give him a bath every day, and that way I won't get any 'fections."

"That means getting yourself wet all over again, honey. And you know it's not good to get wet too often."

"I could wear rubber gloves. Like Mom does with dishes."

She's thought this out. She wants to love something, to care for something; she wants more out of her life. "I'll talk to Mom about it, Stella, but I'm not promising, remember."

"Okay, but I don't care about my kidneys," she slips in.

We are silent as we make up her bed, putting on fresh sheets. She has always insisted on helping with this chore, so we use flat sheets because she can't manage the taut elastic of the fitted kind. I lift first one end then the other of the foam pad while she pushes in the loose ends of the sheet. Then we tug on it from opposite sides, getting it smooth. Quite expertly, she runs the long sides under by sliding her two hands just under the edge of the light mattress. Then she is in, sitting up and half covered by her favorite pink blanket.

"Give me Heddie," she orders, reaching toward her stuffed bear at the foot of the bed.

"Hoedotus!" I cry. "Hoedotus One and Two, those are the names of Capella's babies."

"Oh, yeah." She thinks for a moment as she takes the bear from me, then her eyes go wide with excitement. "Dad! We can name the dog Heddie Two."

"No more talk about dogs. It's story time."

Kipling's *Just So Stories,* the book we're reading these days, sits on the floor beside the wide end table, whose top is too littered with tubes and gauze pads to accommodate it. I lie beside Stella and together we discover, again, how the elephant got his trunk. By nine, we've decided that she's too tired to wait up for Mom, and we hug a little, pat a little, tell each other that we love each other, and I back out of the room as she scrunches down to sleep.

I plan to read the paper and wait for Marsha's return. But first some tea. I put on the kettle to heat some tea water, and after it reaches its lisping boil and I have the cup before me, I think again of my mother's and my earlier years together, and especially the period after my mother's death, when Marsha and I talked a great deal about the guilt I felt—from my assumed failure as a son. Over and over I asked myself what it would have cost me to love my mother back. To fall in with her little plots and mysteries. If it was her only way to close the distance between us, what harm would it have done to play along? It made no difference that, as a child, I could not understand enough of the situation to help her. Later, when I was much older, and after an enforced separation that included college, business school, and a career start far from home, we found a better rhythm. I discovered I could visit her where she lived with my two aunts, both widows as well, and talk over coffee very pleasantly, just the two of us. She was eager to hear all my accomplishments, which she called "adventures" no matter what their true dimensions, and all my plans, which she called "projects" no matter how pedestrian their character. The strange pinched mask that had followed me through my childhood became the softer face of a friendly new acquaintance. Though I could not quite imagine that we had once lived in the same house together, that, in fact, I had sprung from this woman's womb, I discovered that I liked her. Her support was flattering and effective, her caring genuine and helpful.

We ended up going out together after all to pick through suits together. She had a great eye for a bargain, and with her face smoothed and reddened with makeup and a simple clasp purse pressed to her sternum, we moved through racks of clothing and I was sent back and forth to the dressing rooms as a pile of purchases accumulated. Very often, she paid for a number of these items, for my career was new and I still had lots of student loans to pay off.

This period covered the final few years of her life. I visited her, always alone, and then began to wish that Marsha and I lived closer to Boston and my mother. Marsha had always loved the city, and felt no special attachment to Ann Arbor, so in the year that my mother died we had been seriously considering moving East.

But my mother went down to quick incisive stages of cancer of the liver. Afterward, I experienced a surprisingly intense level of grief. For weeks I was virtually inconsolable, weeping without warning behind news-papers, or at the sink with a wet dish in my hand. I ranted to myself, angry at life for depriving her awkward loving of an adequate reward and angry at death for snatching her away just as she was beginning to experience one. I was visited with sharp visions of where our talks over tea, our lunches downtown, had been heading. I wailed at Marsha that we might have unraveled our damaged past and found footings to support a healthy loving.

"She knew," said Marsha. "Jim, she was a grown person. She knew, and I know she was grateful."

It's past ten when I hear the front door open. A loud whisper from Marsha: "We're home!" Footsteps, the rustling of shucked coats and scarves.

When she finds me in my robe in the kitchen, Marsha grins and whispers, "Everything go okay?"

"Like a dream. She is zonked out. Did you guys win anything?"

Marsha shrugs, her grin sinking. She looks at the floor and I think to myself, She is dissatisfied. That's it: *dissatisfied*. It's a word whose power I'd always underestimated, because its worst proportions amass over time. Could one die of dissatisfaction? What is wrong with my wife?

"How's her skin?" she asks.

"It looks good. The usual." I look to Jack, who steps up behind her. "And how did you do, Jack?"

"I lost forty dollars. But the room was full of striking women." For my benefit, he loads the word "striking," but I don't bite.

Marsha says, "He set up shop at the tiny cash bar."

"That's probably where he lost the forty dollars."

We stand around the stove, making more tea, chatting. The two of them recount all of their gambling adventures.

When Marsha asks what Stella and I talked about, I reply, "She mentioned a dog again. She was very persistent, said she'd keep it clean herself, all of that."

"That might have been my fault," says Jack. "She asked me a lot of questions about Arnold." Jack used to have a cocker spaniel, which he named after Arnold Palmer. The dog lived to a ripe old age, but died before Stella could know it.

Marsha says, "There's no fault. She wants things." She shrugs, staring at the kettle and looking very tired, I think. At dinner, while I chatted away with my news about work, I didn't hide how proud of myself I was for the way I had handled the situation, especially how "good" I had been to Milo. She listened with a spark of that old shared pride lighting her eyes. But she looked away at the end, and the spark went dim. Now, watching her watch the kettle, I think, *She wants things too.* The thought frightens me—because I might be asked to give them.

"Do you think we should see a social worker?"

Marsha grimaces as if I'd poked her. Jack finishes his tea, yawns, and heads for home, then Marsha goes into the bedroom to dress for bed. As they move off, I am surprised by a shortness of breath, a feeling that oxygen is leaking away from the air around me. A reflection of my face is spilled across the side of the kettle like a gleaming dollop of mercury. It is my face, lopsided and loathsome. I feel smaller by the second, quite ugly, the physical fact of my stunted spine muttering with the last angry sounds of the boiling water.

When my mother died, so much else came out. At a party one night, I blurted to Marsha in the host's bedroom, "You mother me." We were searching for our coats among those piled on the bed before us. "I looked around at the other couples tonight, and it scared me what we do sometimes. Do you think Sally Silverstein rocks Aaron's head in her lap and sings to him?"

"I don't care if she does or doesn't."

"Well, you should." My hands trembled as I tugged my scarf free.

"When his mother dies, I hope she does whatever needs to be done."

"Anyway, this all started before my mom died, that's for sure."

Outside in the cold car, I kept it up. I insisted on driving; that she usually drove seemed all too significant at the moment. "It's weird, Marsha. I wake up sometimes in the middle of the night and I'm curled up next to you like a fetus."

"Jim, I know that. And I *like* that."

"And what if our friends knew about that?"

"I couldn't care less. I like what I do to you and you like having it done. I also like what you do to me. For God's sake, let's not tamper with the *good* stuff."

I drove on silently for some time. "So, what do I do for *you?*"

"Plenty."

"Like what?"

"It would trivialize it to list it, though while we're

on the subject there are a few salient desires of mine that keep getting swept under the rug."

"Like what?"

"Like a child, for instance."

I groaned. "My genes are fucked up, Marsha."

"We don't know that. I've only asked that we check things out, and I'm sick of you dragging your feet and making us have this same discussion over and over again."

She was right. We checked out things on my side. It looked good. It looked just fine, so we went ahead. And we had Stella.

My tea is hot, infused with elixir-like potency. I take it down in sips, pacing the kitchen slowly and avoiding our bedroom. We bought a flat little ranch house so Stella wouldn't have stairs to contend with, but it's hard to hide with this floor plan. My wife's in there, and I'm out here. But my pacing about is working; I'm gathering strength with each step. I'm beginning to feel less ugly, then a little lucky, and then luckier. A fairly stable marriage, a loving child. Fortified, I step slowly into the bedroom. Marsha is in her slip, holding her dress by the neckline and glancing at its label. Her shoulders are hunched, deeply, in a way that recurs tellingly, tonight further pressed by the conviction that I expend less caring on her than I do on near strangers at work. With the sight of her sitting like that I realize again why I haven't broached, directly, the subject that now appears as such an evident dissatisfaction. I fear that what she wants is something big, something nearly unmanageable for me. With shame I recognize that I have been thinking, *What will I lose?*

"You're unhappy, Marsha."

These are magic words. After one slow nod, her face pinches. "I'm sorry, Jim. I've been trying not to be."

"What's wrong, Marshmallow?"

"I'm ashamed. I don't know if I can do it anymore." She sighs, painfully, then plunges on. "I look at her and think that every moment is another moment where I'm not getting my chance."

"What chance?"

She looks around at me, a little look of desperation flashing in her face. I brace myself inwardly. "At trying my hand at what I was trained to do. I was doing so well." She is talking about her job as the conference planner for a hotel in town. She left that job when she was five months pregnant with Stella. "Now I keep catching myself staring at Stella—with resentment. It's horrible."

She is twisting the dress in her hands now, over and over in a knot. I watch her, leaning in the doorway with my cup of tea.

"And that's the worst of it. I'm convinced now that I'm not being a good mother for Stella. I keep doing the mother thing, day in and day out, but she's not fooled. She can feel my unhappiness, it goes through her like a cold vibration or something. She's not happy, *you're* not happy."

"I'm not?"

She looks at me again, but there is no desperation this time. Instead, she looks angry. I brace myself even more. "You're going to make me mention it, aren't you?" she says. "You're going to make me the bad guy."

"Don't get nasty, Marsha." I hate it when she gets angry. It hurts me so quickly. "Mention what?"

"Our agreement."

Something goes thud inside of me, like a thick volume of old documents tumbling free—way back in a room in the house where I thought it would never be found. But I know just what to do; I play dumb. "What agreement?"

She knows. She looks right into me, and I am weakening by the minute. "For us to split the responsibility of caring for Stella," she says. "At home. We said until she started school that I would take care of her. Then we'd renegotiate."

I take a breath. "You're saying that you want me to come home."

An angry whisper bursts from her. "What a dirty trick! You're pretending like we never talked about this."

I put down my cup and come into the room. Whatever is going on, and a lot is going on, I need time. A short, stiff dose of it will do wonders. "Look," I say, putting a little tone into my voice, "you're not happy. That's the bottom line here. We'll just have to adjust so that you are."

"Now you're patronizing me."

I think, I can't win. "It's just that I don't know what to say. Not yet, anyway. Can I just think about this a little, Marsha?"

She rolls her wet eyes toward me, wary but, I'm glad to notice, a touch grateful as well. With my assurance hanging in the air, she makes no more demands for the moment, but later, in bed, while I lie as immobile as stone, she starts to talk, then continues, then talks a lot. About her ambitions, how much fun she had setting up conferences for all of these different groups, writing the memos and press releases and reports, how much money she might make if she went back to it, and how much we might do with the money. And she talks about her fear that she might come to dislike her own daughter. In the dark, lying beside each other, I listen until one-thirty. I cannot believe what I'm hearing. I remember this woman lying beside me, but only as a distant acquaintance. Marriage is tricky, even dangerous, with the way habit accretes like plaque around two hearts. At some point I fall asleep, and in the last sleepy instant I'm feeling dispirited at the silly thought that you can't stay on your toes all the time because your legs start to ache.

E L E V E N

Fear. There is no other word to describe the feeling with which I awake the next morning, and the feeling that grows within me like an extra-cranky organ, swelling and throbbing each time I think about giving up my job and, what? Spending whole days at home? I do not bring up the subject with Marsha again, though I sometimes pay a little lip service to "the new plan" whenever she mentions it—just enough to assure her that the issue is still alive and with the unstated agreement that I need more time.

A few days into it I call Jack at work and am lucky to find him in at the clubhouse. He takes Marsha's side. "She's a go-getter. Always was."

"But what would I do at home all day?"

"Whatever you want, I suppose. Freedom can be frightening though. I don't think I'd like a lot of it. Perhaps there are some things you've wanted to do all these years." As if he's sensing that I find this advice less than compelling, he adds, "You could take one of those tests. Skills and Interests, I believe they're called."

"Yes. Maybe." I sign off, unsatisfied, but later think that perhaps he's right. Maybe I'm just afraid to do what I really want to do—but then I remember that what I really want to do is stay right here at work with my colleagues and be doing something I'm very good at. Unfortunately, I've got a wife who wants the same things. I even experiment with saying goodbye to my job. I try to pretend while piecing through contracts and printouts with Bobby Marco one morning that I've come to the end of my creative rope with the division. But then somebody from Finance drops by with a problem, we put heads together, and I feel that old excitement. True or not, I seem important here. By the end of the day, I'm trying to figure out a way to get out of my promise to Marsha.

On Saturday morning, while I'm taking care of Stella, I descend on our good friends the Dorsets, Tammy and Bill D. Their daughter, Marissa, is one of the few kids who plays normally with Stella, who plays with Stella at all. While they're in the next room, I chase the two parents around the kitchen. Bill D. is trying to make coffee for us.

"Jim, you're like a caged animal," says Tammy. "Light somewhere."

"Can they hear us?" I ask with a nod toward the two kids in the next room.

"No, but don't worry if they do. You're not talking about strangling Marsha after all."

"Not so loud. I could be."

Bill D. says, "I'll make some covering noise," then runs the coffeepot under the tap. He turns and smiles stupidly. "Now talk!"

When the water quiets, I say, "Everyone's having such a good time with my problem. As if it were just a matter of my coming home and reading the paper all day."

"It will be a big change," says Tammy, patting the

kitchen chair beside her. "But it could be an adventure too, Jim." Her voice has some sparkle in it. "You can work on some projects, like painting or writing. Take piano lessons."

Bill D. says, "Didn't you use to work with wood a lot?"

As the kitchen begins to fill with the aroma of hot coffee, I tip back my head a bit, visited by a memory of my father, his big cracked hand wrapped around a coffee mug. Working with wood.

I come back. "I guess I'm afraid of getting bored, or of being no real use."

Bill D. brings filled coffee mugs to the table, then goes to the refrigerator and returns with a quart of milk. "We men identify with our jobs. You probably feel that you're going to lose your soul or something."

I nod.

"Give yourself time," says Tammy. "Let the ideas come. You don't have to have a detailed plan in place from the first moment." She leans over her coffee mug to blow on the liquid, her long bangs nearly dipping. "I think you're in for a surprise, though. Shopping and laundry and cooking take up an awful lot of time."

I groan at the thought of such chores. I still have a pile of light pink undershirts to remind me of the last time I took on the laundry.

From the other room there are angry words, and then the familiar sound of Stella crying. I'm about to rush off, but Tammy waves me down and heads off to see what's the matter. I look across the table at Bill D., who widens his blue eyes and says, "Days and days of Stella crying, is that what you're thinking?"

"Something like that. And what if Marsha doesn't make much money?"

He shrugs. "Bridges. You cross them one at a time."

After the visit, Stella and I drive to the grocery store. As we wheel around together, Stella in the wire seat, she looks idly about, always a little quieter in public, where a loud word from her will draw a look, and the look become a stare. Today, I appraise her as coldly as anyone else might. As I push, gathering cans and boxes into the cart, I envision whole weeks with her. She is afflicted; she grows tired and cranky; she becomes frustrated. On and on we roll, and with each step I'm more certain that it would not be a good thing, my coming home. Then at one point she looks at me, catches me watching her so coldly. She knows, as she always does, on some level. She finds the rejection in my eyes—what else is it?—and above her dark, clear eyes her paltry brows rise tremulously. Within me, I feel my love for her begin to seep back into my heart. She would like to smile, she tries to smile, but first she must ask: "Are you going to come home, Dad?"

She's heard bits and pieces; she misses little.

"Your Mom and I are talking about that." I run the back of my hand along her cheek as we cruise by a wall of cereal boxes. "What would you think about that?"

She thinks. "Mom would go to work, right?"

"Uh huh. I would pick you up after school. We'd do the shopping and cooking. . . ."

"Like right now?"

"That's right."

Then we look at each other for a moment. I know what she's thinking. How much fun could it be, if the air is thick and listless as it is right now? She deserves more honesty from me.

"I'm a little nervous about the idea, sweetheart."

She regards me with surprise. "How come?"

"I guess because everything will be so new for me. I'm used to my way of life now."

She thinks to herself as we roll on for the next few paces. Then her head turns toward me and, with a smile, she says, "Don't worry, Dad. I'll help you."

As the days wear on, Marsha becomes transformed. Smiling, laughing, singing around the house. I catch her poking in the want ads one morning at breakfast. So the decision has been made? What about the time I needed? I protest to her, and she replies, "I just want to see what's out there."

But what if she finds something she wants out there?

"What is Mommy talking about?" says Stella, milk dribbling from her chin. I think: Buckets, buckets of milk to wipe up from chin, tabletop, and floor. My life will be a continuous cycle of milk sopping.

I can see now that it was this year that really pushed Marsha to realize her need. Stella is home so many days; she gets every cold of the season, she gets ear infections, strep throat. Trying to piece together a part-time job while Stella was at school quickly became an impossibility, and I can now remember the exact moment that Marsha came to that conclusion, how defeated she looked late one night at the kitchen table. I remember saying nothing, thinking that it was her decision to make, but now she's called me on that policy of benign neglect.

She stayed busy, Marsha did. She painted every room in the house, she designed some wide, low shelves and waited for sales and then brought in a stack of precut boards for me to put up for Stella so that she could pull things down and put them away again. She got deeply into cooking and began making every meal a minor feast, even fine sandwiches and cold pasta salads for my money-saving brown-bag lunches. Now that will be my life. Whenever I suppose I can make a nice life for myself at home, I remember that Stella is so often there. School is a trial for her, as it is for any handicapped kid, or "physically challenged" as they call it now. How can I spend whole days in the company of a six-year-old child, even when she is mine? Cooking, washing, cleaning, trips to the doctor and the pharmacy and the super-market—these are now occasional duties of mine, and welcome distractions only because they are so occasional. But now they will be my core responsibilities.

Meanwhile, the added pressure grows that I will have little time to consider all these things, for it becomes more apparent every day that we have set the great machine of Marsha in motion. Now she cuts the want ads to shreds or types letters to old contacts. It seems to me that she has all but put out the word that Marsha Willis is available again, and the machine rolls forward.

But it is not accurate to say that Marsha has been transformed. As I come to realize, it is more accurate to say that she has been *restored*. The smiles, the laughs, the snippets of song, there is a bittersweet tang to their distant familiarity. Over the last two years, they have ebbed away, and a docile, nearly bovine resignation— pleasant, sweet, cheerful—set up store in my wife's heart. Now she is like my college sweetheart again, and I recall chunks of Marsha's past that I have conveniently forgotten: That she was involved in several on-campus organizations at Michigan, including the school newspaper, and continued to write articles for the alumni bulletins for years afterward. That she roused the neighbors to plant some decent shrubbery in the soil circle in our cul-de-sac (then slowly left off watering it). That it was she who asked the pertinent questions during the parents' tours of the schools where we had thought to send Stella, and which eventually resulted in our decision to send her to the Marion Healey School, which is not close by, but which has a good reputation for special-needs classes, and which Marsha managed through sheer force of will to get Stella into.

The day arrives when I realize that there is no way out; I made the promise years back, it was a fair one to make, and Marsha absolutely deserves the life she's asking for. But I still hope to hang on to a chunk of my old life too; so, late in the evening, after Stella's and my walk around the block and her sponge bath and the bundling of her into bed, I sit at the kitchen table with Marsha and say, "Why couldn't we hire someone to stay in the house during the day? Like Velverleen? A home-care person, who could do our cleaning, shopping, and cooking. You know, because we'll have two incomes."

Marsha thinks. "We could, I suppose, but Stella goes to school at eight and gets out at three. We'd get home no earlier than five-thirty, so we're talking about a life where she sees her parents only for dinner and then a little time before bed."

Of course. Feebly, I press the point. "But is that so bad?"

"What do you think? And with both of us working, we'd both be tired in the evenings. You're no ball of fire between six and eight yourself."

We talk on a little, and then she gets quieter. I smell a rat. "What are you thinking?"

"It's a bad time to ask you, but I've got an interview on Friday afternoon just when Stella gets out of school. Do you think you could get out of work early and scoop her up for me?"

"So now you're going to interviews?" I look at her and her face wears an expression so poignant, so poised on the edge of her deep personal struggle, that my feelings are blanched like a shadow flooded by light. I take her hand. "I guess we're on then."

She melts, I melt, we rub noses. Later, in bed, we ease into lovemaking. Her excitement about her new life can become public now, can expand; it has tapped deeper energies in her, and when her hand roots low in my pajamas I discover a very responsive energy as well. Things are breaking free inside of me too, opening up, and the energy is siphoning into my penis.

Later, in the dark, with Marsha's curly head wedged under my chin, I whisper, "It's just a little scary, all that time with her."

Marsha lies so still that I think she must have fallen asleep. But then she says, "Jim, remember when you told me that the absolutely happiest moments of your childhood were the times you went to building sites with your father?"

When I nod, my chin rustles in her curls. "I guess they were."

"Guess what Stella said to me tonight, while she was in her bath?"

"Tell me."

"She said: 'You know, Mom, the very best times are when Dad and me go walking under the stars. I *love* those times.' Those were her exact words."

"Really? You know, when we went shopping last weekend, I told her I was anxious about coming home, and you know what she told me?"

"What?"

"That she'd help me. Can you imagine?"

"She will!"

It's pitch dark in the room. My heart is rising in my chest. What can't I do when I have all these wonderful people to help me?

T W E L V E

I have no trouble at all arranging to get out early on
Friday; in fact, on the day itself I leave at noon, de-
ciding to take a long lunch near Stella's school, read the
paper slowly, and think about the new life that will
shortly fall upon what I envision as my poor, unpro-
tected head. But gradually the time after lunch begins
to weigh heavily and, noticing the mild fall weather, the
low sun and long, lovely shadows, I take a walk. I find
myself wandering closer to the school, then curious to
peek in and look down its halls. I've waited out front a
few times before, but never gone in during class hours.
I amble in, smiling at a custodian sitting behind a low
podium in the front hallway, then walk on. It's pretty
quiet in the building. I must have come right in the
middle of the last class period.

Something pulls me farther down the hallways, a
growing curiosity to feel again what a child's school
feels like. As I walk, I go back in time, testing old waters
that have lain still for decades, and with a feeling of
disappointment I sense those waters' darkening with
every step. The halls are dim, the walls so thick. Paint
peels in spots, but in most other places it has been layered
on so often that details in the old building's wood and

plaster have been slathered away. With every step I think, I could be in my own school but with all this paint and newer lockers. How much have these places really changed? Then two kids of about Stella's age, a boy and a girl, burst from a door and rush past me, though one of them limps.

"I'm supposed to get it!" one insists to the other. She has a leg brace, and her companion, a little boy, has very thick glasses and holds his head at an unnatural angle. I stop, glance at the partially opened door, the rear door of two to the room. I know something about that door, and I think that if I peer into it I will see children working together at tables, some looking off at Miss Sullivan or Mrs. Bell, standing at the front. But when I peer around this door, what I see instead is Stella, only Stella, sitting alone at a little table.

The table she sits at is in the rear corner across from the door. With her thin shoulders slumped down and her hands in her lap, she is looking toward the front of the room. Peering in an inch deeper, I can see that the rest of the children are standing around a bigger table near the front of the room. They are staring down at something, and the teacher sits among them, her head at the same level as the ring of their heads. Stella, yards away from them, sits before a fat crayon, which lies upon a piece of blank paper. Behind her, taped to the cloudy window, are pieces of construction paper crudely cut in the shapes of leaves. I see my daughter sitting beneath those rude leaves with a fat crayon unused before her, I see her looking off to the kids whom she has not joined, I hear their voices, which do not include her, and I grip the doorknob hard. I know every tremor that she is feeling behind that held-expressionless mask that she has made of her face.

When I enter the room, Stella's head turns to encounter me. She jerks as if poked, continuing to regard me but unsure that it is really me. She has been told that Daddy will pick her up, but she has probably rehearsed a scene in her mind that has me in front of the school and waiting for her. But now I'm there, right there in the classroom. Then her face falls in confusion and shame. Her father has discovered her sitting alone and far from her classmates.

"Come on, sweetheart," I tell her, quietly. "I'm taking you home."

Now the teacher has looked up; I thought I knew Stella's teacher, but this woman is a stranger. She is very young, a substitute? The room is so bare that when the kids quiet and turn to look the space around us becomes sensibly empty, bereft.

Then Stella comes alive, "My dad's here, my dad's here. I've got to go." She speaks over-loudly, wags her head, a faked gaiety.

"That's right," I say. "Where's your coat?"

She points to a hook with her name above it. "Those are mine too," she adds, pointing to a milk crate below her coat. Her satchel is there, and a few rolled-up drawings she's done. I remember the drawings I've seen before, so dutifully executed, and the scads of mimeographed doggies and pussycats with the crayon colors perfunctorily applied. By the second I become more desperate to get her out of there.

For the moment, I get her into the coat. She surrenders her limbs obediently for dressing.

"Ah, Daddy's here, Stella," says the teacher from across the room. I look up. The teacher leans forward on her elbows and calls, "That should make you happier, Stella."

The teacher rises and walks around to us, taking her time. She bends, placing her hands on her knees, and says to Stella, "Are we going to make up before you go?"

"Has there been a problem?" I ask.

When Stella continues to look away, absorbed with pulling her satchel from the milk crate, the teacher mouths knowingly to me: "She says she's stupid. Over and over again." But the young woman does not meet my eye. She's feeling bad herself, possibly at a loss, a professional caught without answers.

"Are you ready now?" I ask Stella.

"Same thing every day," the teacher insists on adding. Then she raises her voice. "Except when *I'm* stupid, right, Stella?"

"You're not stupid, Marie," Stella answers quietly.

"That's better. Goodbye now, Stella."

"Goodbye!" I call out, then lift Stella into my arms and step quickly from the room.

Now I have her alone.

"You are not stupid," I insist, pressing the words through my teeth. We fly down the hallway. "You are absolutely not stupid."

After we get down the large stairs, I let her down and we walk together toward the car. She seems very calm, but that bothers me all the more. I'm horrified that she might be accepting of a life that relegates her to empty corner tables, that my daughter might be making do with a minimum of joy.

"Are you all right?" I ask insistently and give her hand a shake.

She looks ahead. "Uh huh."

We pass the doorway to a bar, which from a glance looks pleasant and quiet. On an impulse I swing her toward the door and we go in and sit down in a booth. There's actually a waitress, just on, and she finds some drinkable orange juice for Stella. I have a beer, a full pint.

Stella says, "I've never seen you drink beer, Daddy."

"Honey, what happened today?"

For a few moments, she looks at me as if she doesn't understand the question. Then she says with a shrug, "We colored."

"Why weren't you with the others when I came in?"

"Oh. I had a book, but Michael took it away."

"But why were you sitting by yourself? And what's this 'stupid' stuff the teacher was talking about?"

Her two hands rest like stockinged clubs on either side of her orange-juice glass. Now she claps them to either side of the glass, at exactly the same moment, so that the glass is so precisely pinned that the orange juice barely ripples with the impact. Then, by moving one hand forward and the other back in sure, measured movements, she deftly twists it in place.

"I was telling you," she says. "Michael took the book away."

"And you called him stupid? Is that it?"

"No. He called *me* stupid."

"Why did he call you that?"

She's not looking at me but into her glass at eye level. She doesn't appear disturbed by the questioning, just curious about it all. She answers reluctantly, retreating into snottiness. "Because I couldn't get it back."

I can see it so clearly. She is working quietly with her coloring book, then a child runs up and takes away the book. She tries to get it back, without fingers. And the fresh tone: she thinks it's all somehow her fault. "Do they do that a lot, take your books away?"

"Yes." She answers firmly, as if I might not believe her.

They take away the book because it's fun to see her try to get it back, try to catch them on her toeless feet in the funny flat shoes and reach at them, crying perhaps, with hands that cannot truly grasp.

"Did you call the teacher stupid?"

"Yes," she answers again. She pulls the straw down and puts her mouth to it. The clear tube turns amber.

"Why?"

She stops sucking and the straw goes opaque. "Because she doesn't get things back for me. She sits in the front of the room and yells, but they don't listen to her."

There's not enough money in the schools, not enough training. Stella's hidden skills will go unnoticed. "So you called her stupid?"

"Yes," she says defiantly now, her eyes coming up to mine.

I find myself smiling. "Good for you."

Over dinner that night, our family first talks about Marsha's interview, which went well. She goes on and on about it over dinner. I listen as closely as my frustration with Stella's schooling will let me. But when Marsha asks how things went with the two of us, Stella and I say little about it. She knows though, Marsha does. She gives us the eye.

Later, I am still so upset that *I* need a walk. I want to be alone, to think, but Stella insists on coming with me. She stands at my very feet, clutching my leg like a puppy. I remember what she told my wife about our star walks being her favorite times. Why not? I should be talking to her about all this nonsense—but once outside I can't think of where to begin.

"It was terrible for both of us at school today," I say aloud. "I used to stay alone like that too when I was little."

"Daddy, were you being punished?"

"No. Well, in a sense, yes. When I stayed small, I was put into a special class, just like you, honey."

"I know."

"But let's not talk about that now. It depresses me."

We discover that Cassiopeia is high and bright, and that prompts Stella to ask for the stories. It's a complicated myth, and I'm soon lost in it, the vain queen punished by Athena for daring to rival her beauty, and Andromeda, her lovely daughter, chained to a cliff before the sea from which the whalelike monster, Cetus, slithers to devour her. Athena devises creative punishments. But there are so many characters in that story we keep stumbling over the names. There's Perseus to account for, the savior of Andromeda, but he does his saving on the way from an entirely different story. He's out slaying Medusa, and only later, coming back with her dangerous head, does he happen on poor Andromeda, chained to the cliff. But first Medusa's dripping blood drifts down into the sea, where Neptune, sad at Medusa's death, stirs up the waters and creates Pegasus, the winged horse, from the foaming waves.

"Perseus rides Pegasus?" Stella asks.

"Yes. He's just out for a ride and then he sees Andromeda chained to the cliff." It's cold and we're both shivering a little. I keep moving to generate some heat.

"Cassopee's not chained?"

"Cass-ee-o-pee-a. It's sort of like Ethiopia."

"Who's Ethiopia?"

"No one. It's a place. In Africa. But forget Ethiopia." I take a breath. "Cassiopeia is Andromeda's mother, the queen."

"Oh, yeah."

"Anyway, Perseus looks down from Pegasus and sees Andromeda chained to the cliff. And guess who's just about to gobble her up?"

"Medusa?"

"No, Cetus."

"Who's Cetus?"

"Cetus is the monster."

"Oh, yeah."

"So, just as Cetus is about to gobble her up, Perseus holds the head of Medusa in front of him and, whoosh! he turns into stone!"

"Persuss?" She's shocked.

"No, *Cetus!*"

"Oh."

We're nearing the house and I'm glad because it's *really* cold. With a flourish, I conclude. "So Perseus and Andromeda get married and everyone is very happy."

"What happens to the horse?"

"Pegasus. I think he just flies off somewhere."

"Where?"

"I don't remember."

"I know where he goes!" she cries, throwing up her arms.

I lean back and stare at her. "Where?"

"To Ethiopia!"

That slays me. We laugh all the way into the house. So much for calming her down for bed. But the whole house is in prickles, so much change and confusion. It takes all the tricks of both Marsha and me to nail Stella under the covers.

Later, Marsha heads to the basement to throw in a load of laundry, and on an impulse I follow her. "I want to see how to do this," I tell her.

"It's no big deal, Jim."

"I know. But all the germs have to be killed, right?"

She stares at me. "What's the matter with you? Did something happen when you picked up Stella today? Did you guys fight or something?"

I tell her the whole story. "It really got to me, Marsha, seeing her alone like that. I spent half my school years in the backs of rooms."

"I know. That's where I found you."

"Seriously. I'm very disgusted."

"I can see that." Her round brown eyes are upon me, her soft, smooth face impassive.

We stand together in the empty basement—which

does not necessarily have to be empty, I think at this moment: It could be a playroom, a place for kids to gather, friends of Stella's. It could be a science center, full of plants under grow lights, it could be . . .

"I just don't know," I say, shaking my head. "It did something to me."

"It was probably just a bad day," Marsha offers.

"Maybe." But the teacher had said *Same thing every day,* and there was that time that she cried all morning. . . .

Later that night, after sleeping very deeply for several hours, my eyes pop open. I lie thinking for a long while, then must turn and wake Marsha.

She regards me blearily. "What? What's the matter, Jim?"

"Sorry, but I've been thinking. Are you ready for this?"

"I hope so."

"I want to bring her home too. I mean, I want her home with me. I can teach her myself."

I feel my wife's stare, but she says nothing.

"A lot of people are doing that now," I say. "Home schooling."

I see her head nod slowly. Then she says, "You seem to be serious."

"Very."

She is quiet again. She takes my arm and says, "Go slow with this one, Jim."

"Maybe. I feel it's right though, Marshmallow."

We talk a bit longer, then sleep overtakes my wife again. I am too excited to sleep. An irony has gripped me. I have supposed so long that my freedom was configured by my life at work. How narrow! Such a small sphere. To prove this I leave my bed and walk to the front windows to consult the limitless heavens. The stars are sharp. Tonight, my guiding stars are the constellation Boötes, because he changes. As the Great Bear is modified across the civilizations, from plow to ox to bear itself, Boötes, following behind, changes from plowman to ox driver to hunter. I like his flexibility.

I am excited about the prospect of becoming a great father—not merely a procreant, or a breadwinner, but a true soulmate to Stella Kaldy. I recall how Michael Kaldy always listened to me, his son, to my every word—and those nights at the sites, how often was I truly needed there, or was I ever needed there at all? Perhaps I was needed in less of a practical and more of an emotional sense. My father had me on his turf out there on those sites, and it brought a surer element to our relating. Stella and I will just have to make sure that our home becomes a place for us, that we create a place to be together meaningfully. I'm not sure how that theory will play out, but it strikes me as a good guide.

I feel on the verge of a bold new adventure: being a larger father to my daughter, and a larger husband to my wife.

THIRTEEN

On Monday when I announce my plan to resign, Bobby and Jennifer are visibly shocked. In fact, for the longest time, Jennifer thinks I am joking. Then, when she sees I'm serious, she turns pale. "You should have warned us," she says. It's worse when I reveal that I will probably give the minimum notice—two weeks.

"Two weeks!" Bobby shouts.

We form three points around my desk, Jennifer straight and serious, Bobby leaning forward and looking down at his hands. I drop my eyes as well. "It was a very sudden decision," I offer.

"I'll say," says Bobby.

I have already decided to give them a full explanation, but I have to keep it brief because we might be interrupted by someone coming into the office. I conclude, "My whole family's adjusting to make things work better for us."

"And I guess *we'll* have to adjust too," says Jennifer.

They feel betrayed, which is natural. I have a pretty good finger on the pulse at work; it's my own family that continually surprises me. Perhaps the greatest comfort that men take in the workaday world is its predictability, seasoned by an occasional manageable unpredictability. When the unpredictability becomes truly unmanageable, then come the depressions and coronaries.

We natter on about when the resignation will be effective, what my future plans are, and a little bit about what will become of the office. Then they go off, to sort out their reactions. Later, I suggest meetings with them both. They agree, but only after a quick look to each other; it's just the two of them now, and already they're closing the circle.

For the moment, I have to get to Howard so that I can give the official word and thereby fulfill my obligation for a full two-week notice. But when I get back to the office, I learn that he will be out all day, and by day's end I simply leave the resignation letter with Helen Benoit. When I hand it to her, my face betrays me. She knows something is up and holds the envelope in her fingertips as if it's hot. "I'll give it to Howard as soon as he comes in," she promises. "You're looking pale, by the way."

When I arrive at work the next day, the office already seems a little different. I'm looking at it through different eyes, my psyche separating a bit from familiar tasks. I glance at the materials on my desk, the printouts, memos, circulating publications, Milo's contracts. . . . Some of those contract folders are three inches thick and I've barely been through a quarter of them. It will be the absolutely hardest part if I have to leave before getting to the bottom of this particular mess. I don't much care if I'm thought a quitter for my quick exiting, but it is hard to contemplate Milo's shock at the discovery that the person whom he possibly perceives

as his sole ally in the regional office will soon be leaving.
I think to work the ground a bit. I ring up Milo himself
and find him in. We share a few quick amenities, and I
find him calmer and more resigned than he was last
week.

When I give him the news about my decision to leave,
he's disappointed, as I expected, but less surprised than
I expected. Perhaps others are not as connected to their
jobs as I; perhaps the idea of leaving government service
looks good to him these days.

"Milo, I'll make sure that things are tight about this
contract business before I leave."

"That's a relief. It feels pretty much like business as
usual up here, except that half my files are down there."

"With luck, we'll have them back to you soon."

Then, soon after, Howard calls. He says only, "Would
you please step down to my office, Jim," but I can hear
an angry tremor in his voice. He's surely upset about
my resignation, but I'm upset too; I'm beginning to
realize just how deeply he has violated Milo and his
office. Meanwhile, Bobby has asked to have lunch with
me. It will be a day to remember.

In Howard's office, I sit in my usual chair and he in
his usual chair and we get directly into it. "This is a
blow, Jim." He rattles my resignation in his hand, peering through his comically small bifocals. "The timing
could not be worse."

"Is it ever good, Howard? I'm really sorry, but I made
a promise to my wife . . ." I drop my eyes, ashamed to
use Marsha as an excuse.

"I can read. But I can't help thinking that you're doing

this out of spite." He removes his glasses and I am surprised to discover a sadness in his expression whose genuineness unnerves me.

"Howard."

"I know we don't see eye to eye, and maybe I'm overreacting a bit with this Pelletier problem, but pulling out with a puny two-week notice . . . ?"

"I've enjoyed the not seeing eye to eye. I figure it has kept both of us honest."

He snickers. "Kept *me* honest, you mean. What the hell's going to happen with the investigation now? You know we're on the verge of some national-scale scum here, and you're leaving me alone with it."

I shake my head. "I have a plan," I announce; then, after taking a breath, I launch into it. When I suggest Jennifer as my successor, he raises his brows, but at least listens and lets me go on. "And I wouldn't immediately fill her position behind her. I think, instead, and you'll hate this, Howard, that you should leave some room in my office for a while."

"For what?"

"For regional auditors."

His face rolls into a hundred soft puffy wrinkles. "For *what?*"

"I think you should head off all this nonsense at the pass. Call for an audit, an official audit of our own people, starting with Milo, and let everybody know why and when it's happening, right out front."

His face softens. If I expected dumbfounded surprise, it would be because I have forgotten how smart he has had to be to get as far as he has. I can see he's with me. "Take the offensive," he says.

"That, and justify it by following policy. Periodic audits are supposed to be part of the process, but how often are they really scheduled? Just say the time is right, and you want to make certain that your own people are cleared before everybody gets swept up in a national witch hunt."

I'm about to hurry on, but he raises a hand. "I'm thinking, I'm thinking," he says, then his brow clouds. "But you want to sic DiAngelis on me?"

"She's the best. She's smart and tough and uncompromising."

"I'm sure you think that'll be good for me."

"She'll help you, Howard. I know it. She wants to grow, and she can't grow the way she needs to unless she's put in charge of something."

"But what about the audit you're suggesting? She doesn't have the experience to control those guys."

I've thought about that too, and, at the risk of appearing merely glib, I respond immediately. "Given her personality, that should work to everyone's advantage. She'll be the same with them as she's been with me; she'll ask questions, dozens of them, and that'll keep everybody thorough." I think to mention Bobby Marco too, how good he is with details, but then I remember the look on Bobby's face when he asked for the lunch meeting. He's spoiling for something.

"I'll think about this, Jim. I think I like it. I think I do." We talk on about the possible format of the audit, then on to other projects, lower priorities, which someone else will soon tend to. But it's almost time to meet Bobby for lunch. Howard and I have run out of topics anyway, and then we are left simply looking at each other. The look on Howard's face implies something that I'm grateful to suspect: that he will miss me.

In the hallway I find Jennifer at my elbow. "What's going on?" she demands. "I've been passing by this door, accidentally of course, every five minutes for the past twenty."

We stand together and I drop my voice. "I guess now's as good a time as any to tell you. I think you should go for my job, Jennifer. It's a year or so too early, and there'll be other contenders, but I'll back your application if you agree with the plan."

She has turned a little pale again, and her lower lip trembles slightly so that she has to press it more tightly. "Jim, I don't know. It's such a big job."

I laugh a little. "I think we flatter ourselves about how big our jobs are. You can certainly do it. If you don't want it, that's fine, but if you do we can sit down and go through every step of it. Just relax for now. I have to meet Bobby around the corner in about three minutes, so I have to run. And I'll be telling him what I've just told you."

"He'll be hurt. He was there before me."

"Maybe. But I don't even think he would really want the job. He might think he does for a while. I can't be sure."

When I start to go her hand comes out to take mine. She shakes it and says, "Thanks for the vote of confidence."

I smile, squeezing her smooth hand a little. "I'm just glad there's someone capable I can leave this mess to."

Bobby is in the corner booth at Maxwell's, elbows on the table astraddle a full cup of coffee. He is wringing his hands, slowly, just below his chin. I slide in across from him and, when a waiter promptly arrives, we both order a bowl of chili. The thick sandwich Marsha made me is still in its brown bag and sitting in the foot-square refrigerator in our office. I smile at him. "You look upset."

He scrunches up one corner of his mouth, making his sparse blond mustache bristle strangely. His shoulders are nearly into his ears. We talk a few moments about my plans. He says that he admires me for putting my kid first. I thank him, and then I help him get to the point. "Bobby, you're probably wondering what the future holds in store for you, as they say."

He smiles, clears his throat. "Are you going to recommend Jennifer for your job, Jim?"

I'm surprised. How much has shown, and for how long? "I think I should," I answer.

"I knew it." He falls back in the booth. "I knew you'd take her over me. And I was here six months before her."

I nod, think, ponder. His reaction confirms all my thinking. He's still a kid, really. Years younger than Jennifer, maturitywise. She had a boost—college-educated parents, the right schools, the fast track all the way. And the character to maximize those opportunities. Bobby is coming up the hard way. He's the first kid in his family to get a higher degree; now he's as shocked as they are to find himself holding down a solid position with good pay and benefits. His father still works in a factory in Waltham, worrying all the time about layoffs. Bobby has only one real problem: it will take him a long time to realize how good he really is.

"I've thought about you a lot recently, Bobby—you

and Jennifer. I guess I'd like to start with a kind of basic point, and that is that a job is worthless if you don't really like it."

"I'd like it."

"Really? Do you think you'd enjoy waltzing around with Howard every day? Would you get a kick out of interpreting packets of new regulations?"

"I do some of that now."

"You have lots of natural curiosity. But if I'm not wrong, you're intrigued because you're always trying to figure out how all this stuff hangs together, like how a line of figures impacts on an operation. Bobby, why not get out and see *firsthand* how it impacts? Push the buttons from the other end for a while."

He blinks at me, puzzled and suspicious, and I can see I've laid it on too fast and too thick. I have no choice now but to hurry on. "What I'm suggesting, Bobby, is that you should stay on here for a year or so, just to keep the shop moving smoothly while building up more experience, then get into field management."

"Leave the regional office? That's a demotion."

"It depends on how you look at it. I'm talking personalities here, and interests. Jennifer's good at the regional-level fights—she *likes* them, and that's what my position requires. Bobby, I see you as a man who likes to get his hands on things. I think this contract scrutiny with Milo is just the tip of the iceberg. Some of the older field-office managers are going to take retirement rather than stick around and put up with auditors crawling around their offices. The division will need good new managers."

He leans back again, leaving his hands flat on the table. The waiter brings our chili and Bobby picks up a spoon and I pick up a spoon and we both sit across from each other, stirring our chili. He sighs, "But it's what I came from. The guys in the field, the blue shirts."

"And my feeling is that you can talk to them, motivate them. Plus you've got the nerve and the education to master the new stuff coming down. Bobby, it's different now, it's all computers and zero-based budgeting and cost reconciliations. The old guard look at dot matrix and they get hives."

"But . . ." He grimaces, resistant.

"You think it isn't classy enough? I say don't buy into that attitude. You can make your office into what you want. You can run a field office like a locker room with mechanics sitting on your desk or you can run it like a boardroom."

"I keep thinking I'm not getting a shot because I don't wear a tie to work."

His reaction strikes me as absurd. I can't help it, I laugh out loud. But then I stop because there's some truth to what he's suggesting.

"Yes and no. Whether you are ready for, or whether you would even want, or whether you would be good at a certain job depends more on how you see yourself than what the job actually is. To be successful in a regional-office job, you have to be reasonably certain of yourself. There's not much room for experimentation. But in the field there's plenty of room for it. I see it as a place to try your hand, gain supervisory experience, deal with lots of different personalities and situations without the Boston administrators staring over your shoulder. There's a lot of freedom out there."

I've taken a more effective tack, but he's still shaking his head. "My parents will think I'm being kicked downstairs."

"That would be an erroneous perception," I explain. That his parents' opinion would carry so much weight confirms that I've been right about him. "It depends on how you present it. Entrusted with the operations of *whole buildings,* with the supervision of *dozens of people.* You could be in charge, depending on the office, of as many as forty persons. You will be cutting contracts for many thousands of dollars. It's enormous responsibility and it's also invaluable experience, the quickest way to learn firsthand how our blessed operation works—when it does."

I can see that I've got him listening at least. He's actually eating now, and sitting more erect. "So how come you don't think that Jennifer needs this precious experience?"

This is tricky; I've probably said too much and given him too many hooks on which to hang new arguments. At first I think to drop the whole damned thing, let him figure for himself, but then I feel I should at least be as clear as possible. "Your question assumes something that I cannot agree with. I'm not saying you *need* the experience, though who knows, it wouldn't hurt; I'm saying that you would make a *better* field-office manager than regional number cruncher. You would make a better field-office manager than Jennifer would." (A lie.) "You came in the back door—from a college coop program with good grades in your business courses. The

places that life takes us are not always the right ones."
The clouds of anxiety begin to lift from his brow. "Look
at me." I thump my narrow chest, and make a convincing sound. "I'm throwing all this over and going
home to spend whole days with my six-year-old daughter. Bobby, in the end so much of it is finding our own
places."

He nods, smiling shyly. "I'm not saying I'm not grateful, Jim. It just seemed like maybe you thought I couldn't
handle the job."

Maybe he could, but at some cost. It would chew him
up. But only because he would rarely see, or enjoy, the
point of the daily imbroglios. Bobby and I soon finish
our discussion, but I feel a strain of dissatisfaction coming from his side of the table. It's in his posture, the low
shoulders and heavy-seeming head. When we leave the
restaurant, he follows behind me, nearly shuffling. I feel
for the kid, I really do.

By the time I reach home, I'm exhausted from the day's
debates, but there's no rest for me here. Plans are piling
up for when "Daddy comes home to stay." It's all we
talk about at the dinner table these days. Visits to the
Children's Museum, the Zoo, the Museum of Science,
trips to Drumlin Farm, shopping at fruit stands, and
then, when the plans get wilder, a visit to Jack's country
club and maybe a round of golf with Stella strapped into
one of the electric carts. We talk about the schooling,
the math and science, the science projects, and, of
course, learning to read. We had concluded, Marsha and
I, that Stella's slowness in this area was natural, that she
simply wasn't "ready" yet.

While we're waiting for Stella to finish pee-pee on the way to church that Sunday, I whisper to Marsha, "You know, I think now she has been too damned sad to read. She hasn't thought to invest in herself, as if she weren't worth it. That will be key to the home schooling, the reading, because then she can teach herself whenever she wishes to learn something."

Marsha pulls on her gloves. "I've noticed a difference already."

"Have you?"

She nods. "She asks for help sounding out words. She's got quite a memorized list going: stop, no, exit, thank you, men, women . . ."

I am visited by a new fear, but more tantalizing, thrilling: Will we have enough time in a day to accomplish all we need to?

When Stella comes tottering down the hall toward us, snug in her church clothes and as pretty as we can make her, I say to her, "Stella-Morella, your Mom says you've already started."

On Monday, I have a long two-hour lunch meeting with Jennifer. She has decided that she wants to go for the job. We're back at Maxwell's again, but this time we're eating thinly sliced turkey on pale rye, and I didn't bring a sandwich from home to harden in the little office fridge. Jennifer has brought a long yellow legal pad. As we strategize, going over the status of each current project, she takes careful notes, back straight, head inclined, a small elegant calligraphy rippling from her pencil's tip. Most of the time, I am looking at a perfect part in her hair where two glossy plates separate and move away.

I can swear that some pure primal perfume wafts from that notch of pale skin.

"After all this, I'd better get the job," she says.

"There's no guarantee. Remember, it'll be an open recruitment, though your candidacy will be hard to beat. You'll be interviewed, and don't sashay in like you've got the job."

"Don't worry. What about Milo?"

I describe the auditing plan I laid on Howard. "I think he'll go for it. Be careful with Milo because the whole game will be changed with a formal audit. There won't be any more buddy-buddy calls, it'll all be strictly business. The best way to help him, and everybody else for that matter, is to keep the auditing people absolutely clear on what they're seeing."

Her eyes come up from her pad. "Like whether something is intentional wrongdoing or just a bit of mismanagement?"

"Exactly! They're trained to see dirt. Let's face it, Milo could be a red-handed crook. It's always possible. But it's more likely that he might have botched an input form or something. In that case, the record should point only to inaccurate practices."

"No allegations hanging around, no little innuendoes to haunt him."

"Yes, yes." It's encouraging how fast she gets things. "See, these investigations can be seen as supporting assumed innocence or failing to nail malefactors—depending on the twist given to it. It's an art to keep things clean, and you'll be the key. Howard's a damned cynic, always smelling a rat, and auditors have more fun when they get an indictment." I snort. "That is, until they really do get one, then they usually get so disgusted that they get out. But that's not the point."

"No, I get it." Her brainy head is poised above the straight, easy line of her shoulders. She taps her chin once, twice with her pencil. "I'm to be the one who knows the financial end better than anyone. I'm to be the engineer."

"And you cannot relinquish that role to anyone else, because then the amateurs have the day and everything will get nasty. I've seen it happen a dozen times: Something moves to what should be a constructive conclusion, but because of the way it was handled there's damage. Bruised egos, ruined reputations . . . resignations, lawsuits . . ."

She nods. She gets it.

"I feel good about everything but Milo," I say. "I've been thinking that the answer must lie between the cracks somewhere."

"Don't worry. I'll look into every one of them." Jennifer falls silent, and then smiles at me. "You'll make a good teacher for your daughter."

I smile, blushing a little. "Thanks. I hope so. She's tougher to please than most."

"Five years," she says.

"Six, actually."

"No, I was referring to our five years together."

"Oh."

With a rush I am sped back in memory, to my first interview with Jennifer and how impressed I'd been by her. She'd just gotten her MBA, full of plans that bubbled within the context of a new marriage. She wanted public service, she wanted to deal with people, and she asked lots of questions about those whom she'd be working with. I was disconcerted at how easily I began to open up to her, my answers verging on confidences. In the end, that had been the whole point. Her conviction that institutions were made up of people was unassailable. I was not wrong in my choice, and there were many good candidates—a few from inside the agency. Over the years, her talents positively bloomed; her self-assurance took even deeper root. But at this moment, with her a bit teary-eyed across the booth from me, I am ashamed at how far I've let my feelings for her develop. As I consider, perhaps clearly for the first time, that she will no longer be part of my daily life, I inventory a small sordid list of losses, each tainted by a kind of lecherous abuse of friendship. How many glances at her retreating legs, how many veiled peeks at the curve of her breasts? I can remember half-a-dozen times when, as she stood absorbed before a file cabinet, I allowed my eyes to rake slowly up and down her.

Jennifer, looking wistful, says, "We don't know what we'll miss until it's about to be taken from us."

I think to be firm, to make up for a few things. "I've enjoyed it, Jennifer. But it's also time for a change. This change will be better for both of us."

She nods, a new soberness inflecting her look, but as quickly blinks, puzzled. Neither of us speaks again, until the check arrives.

Just before four o'clock that afternoon, Howard calls me down for another meeting. To my surprise he offers me a ten-hour-per-week "consultancy," an offer I assume is motivated as much by his concern for my family's economic well-being as for his need for my help. I thank him and tell him I'll think about it overnight.

And I do, because Marsha and I don't know yet how much she will be making, but in the midst of the swelling pandemonium of our household, I can see that the consultancy idea will not work. There will be little extra time; already Marsha needs the extra overlapping weeks, subsidized by lump-sum payments for my unused vacation days, with me home so that she can get out for interviews. And I can see that even when I'm not directly working with Stella on some lesson or project or question, I'll be planning something for us, or doing a chore or two, or grabbing a little time for myself.

Home from an unsuccessful interview, Marsha shakes her head across from me at the kitchen table. "I'm frightened that we haven't been prudent, Jim. You shouldn't have given your notice so soon."

"We can last at least three months on my retirement money alone."

"But maybe we should have kept it as retirement, kept paying into it."

"It's better spent for this, now."

"But what if I don't get a job, or get one right away?"

"You will get a job."

"But what if I don't get a job I like?"

"You will get a job that you like, because that's the only kind of job you will take."

She looks across at me, with a touch of a smile.

"I guess you're the strong one today."

I smile back. "Remember, it's your turn again tomorrow."

The rest of my last week at work goes by in a dream. I have to spend lots of time filling out termination papers, checking on calculations for leave time owed me, clearing a few final car payments at the credit union. The guys from Security come down to check my equipment and relieve me of my office keys. Bill Kelly doesn't come himself, he sends subordinates down instead; still no love lost there. A woman comes from Computer Services and we sit together at the screen unstringing all my private access codes. Jennifer, on the other hand, comes at me with lists of questions on her yellow legal pad. She has already set up a working file on all the projects I will leave undone. All the while, Bobby stays quietly at his desk. I can only hope he is mulling constructively.

As my last week goes on, familiar objects look stranger. The careful arrangement of my desk appears arbitrary, even awkward. It seems that for five years I have been content to reach all the way across the desk for the stapler instead of placing it near at hand. All the undone and half-hidden projects and objects in the office begin to stick out. I notice rolls of paper behind one of the columns, a tall pile of unbound printouts that have needed to be sent to the archives for months. It saddens me to be reminded how raggedy-edged life really is, and I become as eager to slip from this tattered environment as a snake to slough its old skin.

On Friday afternoon, I walk into Howard's office in response to a call from him and straight into a surprise going-away party. I find myself facing nearly every angel and harpy that has collected around me for the past decade. It goes well; I drink some punch, put on two conical party hats at the same time, and crack some good jokes. All the while I'm thinking that in an hour I'll be out of there, but then the room grows quiet and Howard, immense and hang-dog, gives a surprisingly moving speech. He cites my "constructive irascibility," and I try to lighten the moment further by commenting on his "improved vocabulary." But I can see in the faces ringing the room that they wish to be serious. And I see too, now quite clearly, that my quick leaving is hurting and confusing some of them. I acknowledge the slow, oozy feeling in my middle.

Jennifer steps forward and takes a deep sigh. "The best bosses are the ones that trust you to try things yourself," she says, and goes on to totally embarrass me by listing several aggrandized qualities. Others follow her, quicker, more pointed. I nod at them, red-faced but deeply pleased. It would be good for me to realize that these have been useful and important years.

I'm given a gift, a wide box with a bow. Everyone's face is glowing and I dig in emotionally for an unexpected jolt. I open the box and inside are two heavy red sweatshirts, one large and one much smaller. Someone says, "We called Marsha to get the sizes right, yours and Stella's." When I lift the larger one out and spread it, it nearly covers me like a banner. Across the back in large white letters are the words DAD'S TEAM.

Howard's secretary, Helen, blurts out: "Don't lose touch, Jim. We want to know how it goes."

I could have kissed her. I have in the past, Lord knows, when she's pulled any one of us out of a scrape. With a deep breath, I slip out of my coat and, to everyone's applause, slip on the sweatshirt. I'm nearly lost in it.

"That's how they're wearing them these days!"

"It'll shrink!"

I speak. "I had a good father. He taught me to be honest." I look around, meeting eyes. "That sounds trite, but what I mean is that he taught me what it completely means to be honest. So I'm going to tell you all the truth. I owe you the truth, because otherwise you might think you're less important to me than you really are." And I go through the whole thing again, all the reasons I'm going to be home for good within an hour. As I speak, the room is so quiet it unnerves me for a moment. But I take a breath and go on; they want to know, I know it. "My daughter isn't learning. She remembers everything that my wife and I ever say to her, but nothing from school. She's frustrated. Her triumphs are not easy to spot, and in the big world out there they get lost. And so she doesn't get credit for her successes in life." I'm thinking as I go, but it's good for me to hear these things too. "So she's coming home with me because I want her to get credit for her successes." I smile and look around the room, one hand safely pocketed, the other gripping an empty plastic glass.

No one says a word. I've said too much, or it was more than they were prepared to hear.

Then everyone begins to clap and Jennifer exclaims, "So you *will* be a team!"

The room quiets and then fills with the sound of other voices. Then Howard is there beside me, his big, hammy hands on my shoulders. I feel the heat of his heavy face across the years. There's no escape. From this moment on, nothing will ever be the same.

FOURTEEN

The living room is for quiet work—for reading and writing; we confine our messier activities to the dining room, which Stella and I have completely taken over. Stella is there now, quietly playing her marimba. I am sitting at the table in the living room below the piano window. We don't have a piano, but the house came with the window, which throws down an even light that perfectly illuminates the page before me. I am writing out the final copy of a questionnaire that Stella and I will send to our relatives, using the return information to begin a project, the Book of Family and Friends.

I copy out, *"What is the date of your birth?"* Then: *"Where were you born?"* Then: *"Briefly describe where you have lived and for how long."*

I leave space between the questions for responses. Meanwhile, Stella plays on.

It's a mixed wonderfulness I'm hearing, the summation of a pattern that stretches over the past two months, moving under and through and upon the feelings that come up from her heart and move through the thickened ends of her hands to the clean, rounded tips of her marimba mallets. She will work, nearly every day, through the songs she is practicing, the sheets flat on the floor beside her. Then, when they are done, she will often regard the pile in silence, and after some time, return to the instrument and simply play whatever notes she feels like playing. At times, she plays in a lively style, wildly experimental, with real percussive punch, but this is one of her quiet days.

I write, *"Please describe your parents, grandparents, and other relatives as far back as you can go. Where did they come from? Tell us what you know about them."*

These are newer questions, prompted by our decision to push further back in time. We finished the questionnaire this morning after considering earlier versions over and over. We pinned each one up for a day or two and added to it as new questions occurred to us. We have learned to be more patient, moving beyond the start-and-stop frenzy that characterized our first few weeks together.

At first we were always returning things to the store because, once home, we found that they wouldn't work for Stella—or me. We learned, for example, that certain markers are permanent, and that made both of us anxious about accidental stains. Now we use only water-soluble materials. And I thought Stella would be able to work at a drafting table, because it tipped, but because we now secure most things to her hands with Velcro strips, such as paintbrushes or chalk holders, the angle proved wrong. It's also hard for her to place things so they won't roll. Now she works at a vertical easel for painting or drawing, her strapped brush or pencil straight out before her, and at a level table with very short legs for cutting or pasting while she sits or kneels.

"Were you ever married? If so, tell us about your spouse(s)."

"Do you have children? Tell us about them."

We're learning to plan; it saves a lot of time. I put up several painted four-by-eight Homosote panels for pushpinning things up, but then we decided to take up the rug and expose the linoleum (we were always having to vacuum the paper scraps or sponge off paint spills or paste dollops), which meant that all my handy-dandy four-by-eight pushpin panels had to come down so we could pull the rug loose. We are learning to go more slowly, to do three things well rather than ten not so well.

"Where was the best place you ever lived? Tell us why."

We have found that the best time for planning is first thing in the morning, at breakfast. We plan each day separately, Stella and I, sometimes consulting a list we make up right before she goes to sleep. Stella gets so excited some days, and the list helps to "put the day to bed," so she won't carry her frenzy into sleep time. And I want to calm her down a bit, because sometimes she goes at things with such fury that I fear she will burn herself out. (I love her quiet playing today; it bodes calm.) I made a whole stack of planning sheets, each with a space for the date and blocks of space for each hour, which we fill in together, and more and more often with Marsha now. Stella would fill the whole sheet with activity—day trips, project work, painting—and leave out rest periods, shopping, and math (her dislike of math is a disappointment for me), but Marsha and I wheel and deal with her.

"But I want to cut from the magazines today! Dad said I could last night!" With very developed legal instincts, she might even point to last night's planning list with some very canny revisions of her own.

"You know you agreed to do your numbers first."

Having Marsha in on the morning planning is good because she can arbitrate, or build in a consistent parental front—something I didn't have as a kid and which always left me confused. And the planning together is good for Marsha too because that makes her part of things. I liken our planning sheets to sheets of music, a sort of symphony for the day with everything orchestrated. I am teaching Stella to tell time by the big clock on the wall so that she can help us keep to the schedule.

The schedule also helps, a little, with the anger that Stella often feels. It's not always easy for us. Maybe I created too many expectations with my grand announcements about what we would do at home together. The reality is that the world is designed for grasping, and Stella has no fingers. Something so simple for other kids, like painting with watercolors, involves a fairly elaborate ritual for her. I can see why Marsha and I used to plunk her in front of the TV after school, or provide big, thick manipulables like dolls and blocks. Now she wants to paint and color and draw and cut. I've never seen how strongly the human need to express really is until I saw my daughter painfully working a red magic marker around a piece of pinned-down paper, or dipping just the corner of a moist sponge into a saucer of blue watercolor paint, or working a pair of marimba mallets as she's doing now, *plink . . . plink . . . plunk.* I am beginning to understand how critical each medium is: color, shape, sound, each is a form of the senses sending out in an interpreted form what was received through them. Stella works hard to express, and gradually the wide Homosote panels are filling with her colorful work.

"What was the happiest moment of your life so far? Tell us about it."

But there are also so many occasions for disappointment that they wear us both down. This morning has not been a good one, and I must admit that I'm glad to be in my own private space with this writing. Stella grudgingly did her numbers for the allotted half-hour, but after watercoloring she refused to clean up. It's something I insist on, to develop her independence, of course, but also because, earlier on, she began, with no real intention, to turn me into a servant—getting things for her, pulling things down—and I had to evaluate every situation: Could she get it or pull it down herself? I thought at first to use her as a guide in these instances, but she proved inconsistent; sometimes she is just lazy, or wants to be waited on for the extra attention. But then again, she is often simply tired. Her muscles are so thin and undeveloped. It becomes exhausting for me as well because nothing can be assumed. Once, when I tried to show her how she might use her eye as a guide to do a straight line with a watercolor brush, I imitated her straight-arm approach and was surprised to discover how quickly my shoulder muscle began to tire, then ache outright. So, when she throws a fit at the end of a session, when she is perfectly capable of filling two or three large pieces of newsprint with scads of blotches, swirls, and streaks in a variety of colors, I have to wonder how much is emotional lack of control and how much is physical exhaustion and pain.

"What is the greatest thing you've ever done? Why do you think so?"

On Thursdays, Jeanette comes by to teach Stella the marimba. She has loaned us a small two-octave instrument made of hardwood, which Stella plays on the floor, kneeling with her bony tush tucked against her heels. She is learning simple songs from sheets, numbered to correspond to the numeral decals on the bars. The sheets lie on the floor beside her. Someday we will make a small music stand—if she keeps up her interest in the instrument. I push the interest, because I can't stop getting hopeful that she'll latch onto something that will so consume her that she can forget, for long, long periods of time, how inherently difficult her life is. As it is, she will play, and well, then gradually small frustrations will amass around the act—an inaccurate strike because of a tiring, shaky forearm—and her heart will sink (I swear I can feel it sinking) and she will become angry, strike out at the instrument, begin to weep. At such times, I have to fight what I sometimes only later realize is my own personal expectation of the outcome; I have to fight my disappointment that she has not become, overnight and forever, a marimba prodigy . . . or a painting prodigy, or a montage prodigy.

Just yesterday I wrote in my journal, "Everything she does, everything she learns, brings out some new self-knowledge in both of us, and that forms the basis for what I feel is small but genuine progress." I must keep remembering that. Now, as I copy out the questionnaire, I notice again how deeply her music affects me. From the start, she never just whacked the thing, but tapped the wooden bars each time as if it were the first time she had struck them. Often she just touches them, curiously, with her mallet heads, coaxing out the sounds. She seems to have a respect for each note, as a separate sound and a separate event. She knows that her timing and pressure modulate those separate events, and the overall effect haunts me. I can write very efficiently—letters, this questionnaire, or the journal I've begun to keep—while the sounds of Stella's music soak into me.

There are certain sounds that she sends out into the room, and into the world, a joyous or boisterous or sly musical paragraph. And at other times I think she is sending me a message—affectionate or angry, it depends. But today, with my pencil held motionless above the pad, I feel more like an eavesdropper. Today there's a tad more significance to the tone.

What is different in her playing today is the length of space between notes. I hear a note, then nothing, and looking up I discover her sitting straight before the instrument with one mallet poised above it. At first, I think she is about to strike, and is merely waiting to do so; but then, listening as carefully as she seems to be, I notice that the last note is still faintly in the air, just barely there, traces of it, subsiding. She is waiting for the sound to end, for the instrument completely to cease vibrating before she decides whether to create another. I think she is speaking to herself, to her own troubled heart, and the plaintive sounds and spaces begin a sympathetic vibration in my heart.

I put aside the questionnaire and take up my journal and write, "I have buried too much. Stella's playing catches me unawares and brings up images of my own childhood terrors, the dread that dogged my days and blacked out whole weeks, months, of my early years. When I feel my own sadness, I can hear hers too. I am almost ashamed sometimes that I have not been ready for living because I have not admitted or accepted sadness, pain, loneliness, death as inescapable elements of living and have therefore been so often surprised, disappointed, even angry to encounter them. So why do I wish to prevent these darker elements from entering her life? It's confusing."

I put down the pen, grateful to listen idly, to stare into the room where she plays. On the big panels painted with white latex, many drawings are pinned up—bold charcoal swirls, stabs, and streaks; splash paintings; collages. So many were produced while she was completely consumed by the task, in a fury to do, sliding around and around her cutting table, pushing the paper weights to the corners of sheets before she hunched above them with the heavy craft knife pinned between her hands, or painstakingly pasting a picture in place, or standing before her easel and fairly slinging colors onto a fresh sheet of newsprint. . . . I scan the many watercolors with broad, intense purple swaths and pink curlicues, which she explains are wild animals, running, swimming, or flying, and sometimes, in the corner, a brown dog named Sally. There are maps pinned up too, and then the "tool table" that holds all the things—brushes, pens, paper punch, stapler, tape dispenser, paste pot, paper piles—and to which all must be returned. Next to the table is the easel, a kitchen chair beside it covered with newsprint, which Stella has refused to discard and must, by agreement, clean up right after marimba playing (a second chance). The easel sits beneath the bay windows, on whose ledge we have jars of water with rooting potatoes and onions toothpicked in place. On the other side of the room, next to the kitchen door, is a big closet, which we have converted into "the library." We put in shelves, which I sawed while Stella held the waste end of the board as I once did for my father. On those shelves are all her books—the purchased stories, texts, and an entire *World Book Encyclopedia*—but more important still, the budding collection of the books that she makes herself. There are only two so far, the Fable Book and the Book of Leaves. I feel satisfied seeing all this progress; proud, but wary, because the music is sad.

Stella stops playing. For a long time, she regards the small, dark instrument, whose sounds are dying to full silence. Then, with a sigh, she pulls the strips off with her teeth and, almost as if remembering where she is, turns toward me.

I wave. She waves.

"Did you finish the question-year, Dad?"

"Almost. We can make the photocopies when we go out shopping."

She gives me one of those smiles I love. A small, grateful smile. She gets up, then moves on stiff knees toward me. I shift about to open my lap, into which she immediately clambers, and we latch together into one of the long, long hugs that occasionally punctuate our days together. At these moments, I know that sadness as well as happiness was designed to draw human hearts together.

She stays a long time in my lap. "I'm sorry about the cleanup, Daddy."

"What happened there?"

"I got upset."

"With me?"

"No, with the colors. The red's almost black." She says this with a trace of disgust.

"You have to change the water more often, sweetheart."

"Uh huh."

Changing the water, a twenty-minute task for her. But I say no more about it because she is falling asleep before my eyes. Her head drops back against my shoulder, then, slowly, rolls and hangs. I sit in the completely quiet room, only the sound of the baseboard heaters occasionally gurgling. I say to myself, as I am saying more and more often, *Teach her to rest.* She was not made to push like this, it will kill her. I have to create some effective way of heading off her excitement, so contagious and, yes, *flattering to me,* which sometimes ends by cramming our days to an unmanageable, hectic, and irritating level.

"Relax," I whisper. "There's time. I swear to you, there will be time."

Later, when I shift a bit, she startles awake. "Are we going shopping?"

"After you clean up."

"Oh, yeah."

Everything takes time—rolling up a few papers and getting them into the waste can, even dressing for the outside. I am just learning to put in enough time for preparations to go and for the adjustments of returning.

We are always becoming more effective—our shopping
list is pinned where it should be on the small cork board
inside the door—but how many frustrating days we had,
for example, when we went out for specimens for the
Book of Leaves and had to return for the field guide or
wished we'd taken a plastic bag to hold the leaves. (I
must often carry Stella back; her toeless feet cannot negotiate rough ground, so I cannot assume to have hands
free; wadded plastic bags and a backpack are standard
equipment now.) How many times have we gotten off
late, and come back dissatisfied, anxiously behind
schedule.

Today it's better. At the Stop and Shop, I stroll
through the aisles, stitching in a reading lesson as we
go. I point to a can.

"Carrots!" she announces.

"Right. And this one?"

"Peas!"

"Big deal. You can see the pictures."

"But I did those at home, Dad. You're teasing."

"Then read from the list, smarty-pants."

She does, and not half badly. We do not follow exactly
the home teaching materials we ordered, preferring to
let Stella's (and my) interests guide us. But we lift ideas
from those books regularly, and one of them—so simple, really, like most good ideas—is to group new words
around concepts, like a place or an activity. On the wall
at home, a long list entitled "Food Shopping" has dozens
of words that Stella can now recognize. Where it makes
sense to do so, I have placed a small red dot between the
syllables (but•ter), so that she can sound out the syllables
and not be always simply memorizing. Though, Lord

knows, it seems her mind has an infinite capacity for stored information.

"Will Mom be back when we get home?" she asks.

I hold my watch up to her, but she's not interested in looking at the moment. "It's a little after four," I say. "And she gets home at . . ."

"Six. Will we be home at six?"

"Way before that, sweetheart. At least an hour before."

"So we can start cooking."

"Right."

We try to shop only once a week, but we usually need to make a second small shopping trip. We've run out of milk, and I want to buy some fresh herbs, which the store has recently begun to provide in small plastic pouches. I think Marsha would like fresh thyme on the steak tips we plan to broil. After shopping, we swing by the copy center to photocopy the questionnaire for the proposed Book of Family and Friends. Copying is a treat for Stella because the ready button on the self-service machine is wide enough for her to press.

Back in the car and heading home, Stella sighs. "I don't want to see Dr. Roth."

"Ah ha! Yesterday you did. Why the change?"

"He'll hurt me."

"He'll take blood, I'm sure. But it's time for that again anyway." Stella's blood must be checked every few months, for levels of erythrocytes, for potential anemia. "Then he'll want to discuss your results."

She whines a bit snottily, "Dr. Lerman never disgusted my results."

"I know, but he dis-*cussed* them with Mom and me.

I guess Dr. Roth thinks you're old enough to hear things about yourself directly."

"I don't like him."

I could ask why not, but that never gets us anywhere. Avowals of dislike, even hatred, are common, and usually don't mean what they seem. At least not directly. They mean instead that she is struggling with something associated with the person.

"Are you upset?"

"No."

I shrug. "Okay."

But when we're home again and getting dinner together, I at the stove and she setting the table, she says, "Dr. Roth doesn't like me. He wants me to die."

My back is to her. Slowly, long spatula in hand, I turn from the stove. "What did you say?"

"I said, I don't like him." She is pushing forks slowly into place beside the plates.

"What did you say about die?"

"What?"

"You said something about him, what, wanting you to die?"

I feel uncomfortable having to repeat the word. For her part, she seems surprised. "I didn't say that," she says. "I said . . . he makes me *cry*."

"Oh." I turn back to the stove.

I sear the steak tips, but I'm keeping an eye half-cocked in Stella's direction. One by one she pulls the plastic plates from their stack on a low shelf in the pantry. She carries each plate, cradled in her mitts, to the table and pushes it into place. She does the same with the utensils, new ones with bigger, more manageable handles, and all in all sets a pretty nice table. She turns quickly and finds me peeking.

"Dad, can I stir for a while?"

"Sure."

She trots to the corner and pulls an upside-down plastic milk crate from its place, sliding it to the stove, where I have stepped aside. I hold out the spatula handle and she clamps onto it. "Get your belly up against the door here, honey, to keep balance."

She stirs the tips around. "Each side. Right, Dad?"

"Yeah, so they're just a little gray."

"But it's okay if they're just a *little* burned, right?"

"Browned. Yes, that's okay."

I go to the refrigerator and take out a beer. I twist off the cap, toss it in the trash, sit down at the table, and watch Stella cooking. She has set the table especially nicely tonight. Each plate is centered, bracketed with utensils set fairly straight, and a blue plastic tumbler topping off each setting. At the stove, Stella works the spatula slowly in among the sizzling pieces of meat.

I take a pull on the beer. "You're a pretty neat kid, Stella."

She doesn't turn. "Thanks."

"I mean it. I really like having you around."

"I wasn't always around. Right, Dad?"

"No. First it was just your Mom and me. Then you too."

We are silent for a moment. Soon I'll transfer the tips to the broiler. "I think we should see Dr. Roth soon," I say.

"But I don't like him."

"I know. But I think I'm going to insist that you see him. I'm sorry, sweetheart, but I think it's important."

"Why?" She is stirring more slowly now.

"Because I like having you around. Know what I mean?"

She looks back over her shoulder at me. Sometimes her eyes are especially clear, brighter even than usual. Maybe the steam from the skillet has moistened them, but they are clear and deeply dark. Lovely eyes, really. Without brows and lashes, they can stare directly with great force, as they do now. She turns back to the stove. "I know what you mean. You don't want me to die. Right, Dad?"

Now I've done it. Marsha will not be happy to hear that this subject has been broached, though unwittingly, without discussing it with her first. "That's right, Stella. I want you to live as long as you can."

She nods. "Okay. I'll see Dr. Roth."

I rise and lift her down from the crate, hold her in the air a moment longer than necessary just to press my lips against her round head. "Good job. Into the broiler now."

"Not me!" She laughs.

"No, the meat!"

When Marsha arrives around six, we sit together at the table and wait for the rice to catch up with the rest of the meal. Stella asks, "How was work, Mom?"

Marsha replies with her brows pressed down. "I'm not sure." She has gotten a job as office manager of a small new software firm in Kendall Square in Cambridge. It was not her first choice, but the other was a bit too long a commute, and we both worried that she'd have less time with Stella. "I guess it would be easier if I knew who was in charge—or if anyone knew."

"That's too bad," I say. "Can't you push the issue?"

She thinks for a moment. "Actually, I'm thinking of just taking charge myself."

"They won't let you do that, Mom," says Stella.

Marsha laughs. "I'm just talking about their letting me take over more jobs in the office, without having to chase them down all the time to get their permission."

"Oh," says Stella, staring at her plate.

I say, "They'll probably end up appreciating it."

The rice pot is quiet. I get up and take it off the stove, then fork the rice into a bowl so that it makes a high, snowy heap. When will I bring up Stella's mentioning death? Later.

After dinner, Marsha and Stella read together for a while. Then Stella and I sit down and plan out the next day, pinning the neatly printed sheet in the center of its labeled rectangle on one of the Homosote walls. Then we go for our walk, and talk about stars and dogs—Stella continues to beg for one—and we do not talk about Dr. Roth or about death. Then we go in and Marsha gives Stella a sponge bath, pats her dry and greases her down, then clothes her and we all huddle around Stella's bed and talk about sleep and dreams and dogs.

Then, over tea, I tell Marsha about Stella's and my day: the drawings and lessons, the marimba playing, the shopping, the continual hints about wanting a real dog, her agreeing at last to be examined by Dr. Roth, and her mentioning death.

FIFTEEN

A week later, just a day before Stella and I will see Dr. Roth, the phone rings around ten o'clock, and I'm surprised to find Milo Pelletier on the line.

"I would never call," he hastens to explain, "but it's a last resort, Jim. I can't get any decent response from your old office so I'm turning to you."

There have been more than a few calls from my former workplace. Some matter or other that requires an answer from me alone, even as piddling as where I last placed something; each contact seems more strange and remote.

"What is it, Milo?"

"You may not know it but your office is falling apart."

It's not my office anymore. "What do you mean?"

"Marco has put in a grievance because Jenny Di-Angelis was put in over him as acting director, and meanwhile she's lost every friend she ever had with her ranting about the audit procedure."

I've heard stirrings of this, but at the moment it's too many things at once. I start to answer, but slow up. Across the room from me, Stella has fitted the lid of the paste pot into the toothed lid gripper, which I screwed to the underside of the tool table. She is trying to twist the lid open, but it is gummed shut because she cannot always clean things well.

"Bobby grieved, huh?"

"You didn't know?"

"And what's this about Jennifer's losing friends?"

"I get it all secondhand, but it seems that she's got the whole thing crawling at a snail's pace, always bitching about technicalities."

I wonder how much I can trust Milo's assessment of what an angry Jennifer might mean. "She's probably got a reason," I say. "I've seen a lot of botched audits in my time."

"I appreciate that, Jim, but I'm not getting much satisfaction is what I'm saying."

The paste pot twists free and falls to the floor. I wait for Stella to kick it across the room. Instead, she reaches down and gathers it up again, then places it carefully back between the jaws of the gripper.

"What would you like me to do, Milo?"

He sighs. "I'm in Boston now, for a meeting that never even happened. Can we meet somewhere, maybe for lunch?"

I think. I almost say yes, then I remember that there're two of us in my day. "Lunch wouldn't work, but hold on."

I put down the receiver, and go over to where Stella is beginning again to grip and twist the lid. I almost speak, but something makes me hold up. I stop in the middle of the room, like an animal sensing that it must not be seen. Stella is glaring at the paste pot, both eyes on it and her two hands pressed and quivering with pressure. As I watch, the bottle begins to turn while the lid stays fixed in the gripper. After a few more twists, she has it off. Now I nearly resent Milo. I could have missed this. I could have missed this small but extraordinary triumph.

"Looks like you got that old lid, honey."

She looks up at me, grinning. "I did!"

I crouch down beside her and give her a hug.

"I'm going to paste in the pictures," she says.

"That's great. Listen, sweetheart. A friend of mine needs to come by and speak to me about something important. Do you mind if he comes over while you're pasting? You might have to do it by yourself."

"Who?" she demands.

Though she swells with confidence at the moment, there is always the fear that accompanies the knowledge that someone new will see her for the first time. The way they look at her is rarely pleasant.

"He is a very nice man. His name is Mr. Pelletier. He just wants to come over for a little while."

"Okay."

"Thanks. He won't be here long."

I hurry back to the phone, but once there I hesitate, because Stella is right there and I can't warn Milo about what Stella looks like. I'll just have to catch him at the door and give him a whispered warning.

Milo agrees to come out and visit me at my home; I give him directions.

It's the early afternoon, and with the reduced traffic he will be here within half an hour. So be it. Stella and I sit cross-legged on the floor, and while she struggles with her fat craft knife, I cut out the photocopied pictures of Aunt Gladys and Uncle Ted and Grandfather Gus on Marsha's side, the pictures that we are gradually pasting into the new book. I want her to have a head start, because the pasting is easier for her and it will keep her occupied while Milo is here.

He arrives surprisingly quickly; he must know the area better than I'd assumed. At the sound of the bell, I rise and whisper to Stella, "I'll be right back."

I open the door to Milo, stamping and stiff in his long gray overcoat. "Freezing!" he yelps.

He steps in, huffing, his fair face pink and his hair's whiteness heightened by the vista of snow on our front lawn beyond him.

"Milo," I say quietly, "I just need to warn you . . ."

But then I hear Stella's shuffling steps in the living room and she is coming toward us. At such moments, I see her through hard eyes, as she physically is. The stumpy extremities, the rail-thin limbs and torso, the hard, stiff angry patches that ravage her skin. She comes right up to us.

"You're Milo," she says.

Milo has just gotten out of his coat, which I hold in the air between us. "And you," he announces, "are Stella!" Without a moment's hesitation, without a quiver in his broad smile, Milo reaches down, grips my daughter, and lifts her to his chest. She perches there, smiling into his smile.

"Do I get a kiss?" he asks. No one has ever asked my daughter for a kiss upon first meeting her. Her cracked lips are not attractive.

Stella, grinning, pops her face against Milo's cheek.

"Now, do I get to give you one?" he asks, with a

quick look to me. He is wondering if kissing could be harmful to her raw skin.

"What do you think, Stella?"

"Kisses are yecchy," she says, but there's a hint of approval in her tone.

"I can be quick," says Milo, and he plants a fast one on her cheek. "There!"

I put on coffee to warm Milo up. At first, Stella hangs around, showing off by grinding the coffee beans and insisting on tipping the grounds into the pot, but I prevail in shooing her away to continue with the pasting so that Milo and I can talk. We sit together at the kitchen table.

"Jim, it's still too early to tell, but it's beginning to look like my outfit is going to be the only one with a significant cost overrun."

"That's too bad, Milo."

"I wouldn't even care. I've got nothing to hide, but I've been over the budget sheets a hundred times, and the only thing I can see is overages in materials. We're right on target with everything else. We're one hundred thousand over on materials, no drop in the bucket, but those were all attached to approved leased space contracts."

"What sort of materials?"

"What you'd expect: paint, rugs, drywall . . ." He shrugs, gulping mightily from his coffee. He must hate being in Boston, so far from hearth and home and in a place where everybody seems mad at him but can't tell him why.

"How are your lease contracts? Those are the ones that usually go screwy."

He grimaces. "Those contracts are fine. Hell, there's been more emergency work this year than most but it's all legitimate, mostly in leased space where I can't anticipate a problem and then have to drive way out somewhere and force the lessor to take care of it. More work, more expense is the simple fact of the matter."

I watch Stella through the doorway where she slides around and around her cutting table. She has decided to finish cutting out the pictures and is working the big knife unsteadily along the weighted-down photocopies. Slowly she cuts loose the square images. "The anonymous call pointed at collusion," I say. "Are there any contractors or vendors you might not trust?"

He leans forward. "Jim, we're talking about Manchester, New Hampshire. It ain't New York City. I know every one of those people by name, I know their families and which school their kids go to. I order things from them, and I get the service and I get the materials. They wouldn't screw me, I know it."

It's hard for me to think because Milo's world now seems so far off to me. But then again I feel a sort of fresh perspective on it all. "Have the auditors been up to your shop yet?"

"Sure. Day and night for ten days! But now Jennifer's got them pulling out their hair in Boston. What I didn't tell you on the phone is that she's demanded a full reconciliation of figures even after they've already completed a full physical inspection of the contract work."

"So, now they know the work was done. But I guess Jennifer doesn't trust the figure base for the audit."

"She's not talking about the economic figures, Jim.

It's the physical ones she's bitching about. Actual square footages and the like."

I perk up. "The building profile reports? So she wants to double-check the building figures. She might be onto something. And that might give you extra time too, Milo."

"For what?"

"For you to check your space firsthand." I'm thinking as I go, but I'm also beginning to understand Jennifer's logic. "Here's what I think, Milo. I think you should check the building profile reports against actual space. Jennifer's probably working from the old records."

"Jim, I've got fifty-seven buildings, counting the leases. And the auditors have got all my records."

"You'll have to rely on your memory, and those of your foremen. And the agencies in the leased spaces, don't they keep a copy of their contracts?"

"There's probably a hundred projects, and fifteen different cities and towns."

I shrug. "Do it. Tank up the government car and go on the road for a week. I think you should take Jennifer's lead and see if the computer reports on space figures are really accurate. I don't think there's ever *been* an official reconciliation."

"And what am I supposed to find?"

"Inaccuracies, maybe. Contracts are costed out based on building dimensions—so many square feet of wall space means so many dollars for paint—and that translates into dollars paid to contractors. See if there's been any error creeping in over the years. I don't know, but I think Jennifer's not trusting the computers and I think she's got a point."

He thinks. Then he nods. "And we have our work-sheets too, the estimated manhours, the materials calculations. Come to think of it, there's a lot of hard figures around that aren't just in the contracts or the computers."

"There you go."

There's a clatter in the next room, and we both look through the open kitchen door into the activities room where Stella's craft knife has just twisted free. She looks up at us, smiling with a trace of embarrassment. She gathers it between her mitts, then presses on the blade-less end to bring it away from the linoleum for grasping.

"Get a good grip on that thing, Stella," Milo calls to her.

"Okay."

He sighs, beginning to rise. "I'll do what you say. I'll go on the road. Heck, it might be good to get out of the office for a week or so."

"And don't call it a fact-finding tour, Milo. Just pop in on your tenants and say you came by to see how things are going. A tour, an inspection, spot-checking contracted work to see how it's holding up."

He nods rapidly, "Okay, okay. That's good advice, Jim. Can I call you on the road?"

"By all means. More coffee?"

But he's already on his feet. "No, I'm fired up now. Want to get back. Thanks for the time, Jim."

He ambles away, into the room where Stella works. He hitches up his pants a bit and crouches down beside her. She keeps at it, cutting slowly between the weights she's arranged to hold the photo-copied pictures flat.

"What are you doing, Stella? Making something?"

"My Dad and I are making a book. These are pictures of family people."

"Oh, I see. Looks like you're doing a good job."

"Thanks."

For a few moments, he watches her in silence. Then he says, "You know what you might want to get sometime? To make things a little easier for you?"

"What?" She stops and sits up straight.

He cocks his head at her knowingly. "A paper cutter."

"What's that?"

He rubs his chin, choosing words. "It's a flat piece of wood where you put your piece of paper down. Like your papers here." He makes his hands into a flat board. "And on the side, there's a long, sharp blade, which you move up and down to cut the paper with."

"Oh," she says, uncertainly.

He takes her two hands in his. "You would just take the handle of the blade like this and raise it up." He raises her two held hands. "Then you let go and move your paper the way you want. Then, schuck!" He drops her hands quickly. "You cut right straight through and it's done!"

Stella thinks for a moment, envisioning. Then she pulls her hands free, leaps up, and comes running to me. "Dad, Milo says we should buy a paper cutter. Can we?"

I look past her to where Milo is still crouching, now peering quietly at the few cut pictures. I think to myself, *Howard, is this your thief?*

S I X T E E N

It is snowing this evening, and Stella and I stand by the front window and wonder whether to take a walk. Marsha comes in behind us. I see her reflection on the glass. "Looks pretty rough out there," she says.

It does. The flakes come down in a rush, then swirl aggressively against rising drifts. Mr. Lester's high pines are heavily shagged.

"Look," says Stella. "Those trees look like giants in fur coats."

"They do," says Marsha. She bends to my ear and whispers, "See. Take away the TV and they make up their own programs."

I chuckle. I'd thought to use the TV as a babysitter, a gap filler, and repriever for Dad—but it rarely goes on. There's no time. But Stella has overheard.

"Let's watch TV!" she cries. "We can make popcorn."

That's what we do. We watch reruns of *I Love Lucy* and *The Honeymooners* on an obscure channel. Stella stays up past her bedtime, and everyone silently seems to agree that this is all right—because tomorrow she goes to see Dr. Roth.

It's only when Stella's up to her neck in covers and Heddie tucked in beside her that she mentions the appointment.

"Tomorrow's Dr. Roth, right?" she asks quietly. Her dark eyes stare off, her lips remain parted after the question.

Marsha says, "That's right, honey. Do you want Mommy to come along too? It's still not too late."

"No, it's okay, Mom. I'll be okay with Dad."

Stella and I read a little of *Hansel and Gretel,* but we don't get much further than the children's first discovery of the house in the woods before Stella drops off to sleep. But I have a rough time falling asleep. First, Marsha and I go back and forth about whether she should come to the appointment—in case Stella becomes very frightened once she's there. We're torn between building up Stella's and my relationship and simply joining forces in this singular moment to support her. We decide that we should suggest strongly to Stella that Mom come too; we'll say that Mom wants to come, so Stella won't feel that we think she's not being brave.

"It'll be okay with work?" I ask.

"I've already told them it could happen."

"See. You're calling the shots there already."

She laughs, then quiets. "I'm nervous about the appointment."

"Me too."

And that's the last thing we say to each other. I lie awake, holding Marsha's hand, which gradually grows limp with sleep. I wonder if I should set the alarm ahead for more time to dig out the driveway, but I decide that if I get out there first thing I'll have time enough before the nine-thirty appointment.

When I fall asleep, I have a dream about my father. We are sitting together on the bank of a river and looking out over the water. It's barely light. The night is strange because there are many stars out, though the land is lit well enough for us to discern the blue-green of the high pine trees on the far bank. I can see then that the trees are bright on their own, and the big stones piled on the far bank are glowing from within. Clearly there is an animism—powerful, to be feared and heeded—informing the materials of our surroundings.

I have a bamboo fishing pole in my hand but without a line or hook; still, I move it idly over the waters as my father talks quietly. He is talking about my mother, something about how she couldn't make it that day. "She shouldn't come out here," he says. "She wouldn't like it."

I feel resentment rise within me at these words. "She would, Dad," I say. In my hands, the pole is heavy, oversized and cumbersome. Across the river, the pines heave although the air is windless. My father turns to me. He says nothing, but I feel in his look an assent. I do not look at him, careful of his reaction to my words, but he seems to be musing, carefully considering these words of a child.

Then he says, "Do you think that's true, Jim? What you said, I mean?"

I sigh, deeply, for effect. "She would love it out here, Dad. She's cooped up in the house all day. With me."

And then we both seem to be at a loss for words. Around us, the night has a life of its own, and we are uneasy guests of it. A wind comes up, chilling us and tossing dry leaves as if the season has suddenly changed. The leaves swirl about our feet. As if this new movement were a signal, my father and I rise and I leave behind the pole, an act that relieves me though it seems irresponsible. We link hands as we walk, then begin gripping each other's hands with uncommon pressure as we walk deeper into the woods back from the shore and the night darkens and chills further. We are missing my mother, both of us. Unstated regret hangs in the air, thickening the silence and weighting with sadness the black limbs around us. That she could be there, that she could be happy, that we could be the agents of that happiness . . . In our sorrow, implicitly shared, we step forward into the darkness. Both of us know that we are heading to our house, and that it is not pleasant there.

We reach the house, somehow my childhood home, but now a small shack pushed in among imposing trees. The house is built in an old style—wooden shingles on the roof, scroll-sawed lattices and window moldings. All is gray and peeling. Resigned, we both step through the small door.

Inside, a harsh light as if from exposed bulbs lights the center of the single room and leaves the corners dark. There are a wooden table and two chairs, all constructed of split unpainted planks. The floor is made of cement. In the center is the dark mouth of a rectangular pit slightly more than a yard in length. I am afraid to look at this pit. My father and I sit at the table, half-turned away from the pit and yet away from a corner where I sense more than see a small dark figure seated on a stool. It is a woman, her face inclined toward us, but silent and poised as if she assumes we do not see her. We both know this is my mother, though she is as small as a gnome and dressed in tatters.

My father says, "Well, Jim . . ." then falls silent again. More light drains from the room, as if the very last light of the day has slipped away. The limy air in the room chills. I realize that we will say nothing to the woman in the corner, though it is clear that both of us know who it is. We are powerless, as trapped in this small house as prisoners in a cell. Now my attention is drawn to the pit, which I have been careful to avoid considering since entering the house. I notice that my father is gazing toward it expectantly. I feel him growing thinner, and younger, and this frightens me. As long moments pass, I want desperately to speak or laugh or run about—to break the gaze fixed on the pit, as if something will happen soon that I do not wish to experience. Now I realize that my father's broken-off sentence was to be a statement that he had not the courage to complete.

Then, from the pit comes a soft, faraway sound. As if from a distant cavern, it is the sound of a child's crying. Soft, coughing cries, whimpers, muffled, they seem, but growing in intensity as we listen. The three of us in the single room become completely fixed on the sounds of helpless crying. Then my father motions toward the pit, as if impatient that I haven't acted yet. Am I supposed to approach it?

I look to it, the now unmistakable cries welling up from an awful depth. But what can I do? The child is too far away to reach. I'd have to go down into the pit, somehow, but the mouth of it is utterly dark and seems to exhale a cold breath. I remain paralyzed, unable to act. When I turn to my father to protest, I discover instead that I am sitting next to Dr. Roth. He is dressed in old farmer's clothes and seems embarrassed to be recognized. He grips my wrist, frightening me, and I cry out. I try to pull away.

I wake up with a gasp and discover that Marsha is shaking my arm.

"My God," I blurt out, "we're all so responsible for each other."

"Listen!" she commands in a whisper. "Is that Stella?"

"What?" I say. I'm not sure what she means.

We both go quiet, but I'm still blinking with stupefaction. The room is full of dream spirits. And there are the crying sounds again, quiet, lonely, as if muffled by a pillow. Marsha and I face each other in the dark, holding our breath and concentrating as if combining the powers of our hearing. At a particularly unmistakable sob, we realize that Stella is weeping in her room, and we both roll out of our separate sides of the bed and hurry together from the room. The little plug-in nightlight makes the hallway glow dimly. Then we are in Stella's room and heading to her side.

She is there, a nearly invisible shape beneath the quilt. At first I cannot discern her face, then I see that she has pulled her pink quilt up over her mouth. "We're here, we're here," Marsha croons, and gently turns the child toward her.

Gratefully, Stella snuggles into her mother's soft chest. She cries a bit more, then says, "I had a bad dream, about Dr. Roth."

"Me too!" I blurt.

Stella turns to stare at me. "You did, really?" she asks.

"Honest. He was a farmer."

With the tears still on her face, she coughs, then giggles. She has to snort because of her full nose.

"You're teasing, Daddy."

"I'm not, Stella-Morella. I honestly did one hundred percent have a bad dream about Dr. Roth." I'm standing behind Marsha, looking down into my daughter's face. "What was yours about?"

"He was chasing me. He kept laughing and laughing, but mean."

"Wow. In mine . . ." but I stop. I can't really tell mine, can I?

"What did you do?" Marsha asks her.

Stella pauses to think. "He chased me all the way home, and at the front door I turned around and hit him. Then he went away and I woke up."

"Well, that was damn brave," I say.

Stella giggles again. "You said a bad word, Dad."

"He sure did," said Marsha.

"Damn straight," I say, and all three of us laugh.

We bring Stella into our bedroom and snuggle her down between us. Heddie is there too. It's a crowded bed. When Stella's settled, she says, "I want you to come tomorrow too, Mommy."

"Good, because I want to come, honey."

"Good."

We all sigh at the same time, and then laugh at the same time because we sighed at the same time. Soon Stella is asleep, but I can't sleep that well. The windows glow from the snow light outside, evenly as if the storm has stopped. I want to talk about my dream to Marsha, but I can feel that she's already back to sleep. I'm still spooked, and thoughtful. My mind races with configurations of human conduct, strange familial pacts broken and unmended, the unstated pleas of my parents, and a deep, vague guilt at my childish inability to hear them. I am wondering and wondering, what could I have said or done to make my parents' life together happier? I can remember moments away with my father when I had felt a mild urge to say, "Let's bring Mom along," but the prospect would mean less fun. I was certain of that (why so certain?), so I said nothing.

It all becomes too much. I glance at the clock. It's later than I thought, nearly five. Quietly I slip out of bed and clutch about for my heavy clothes. Wife and daughter cuddle together, wheezing and snozzling in deep sleep. In the chilly kitchen, I shiver as I get into long underwear, wool socks, jeans, and a heavy flannel shirt. I fill the kettle from the tap and set it on very low heat. Then, at the front door, I pull on rubber boots with buckles, my parka, wool cap, and old work gloves. In the garage, I am so thickened that I have to squeeze around the cars to get to the snow shovel. The snow is banked so high against the wide garage door that I can't push it open; I have to backtrack through the house and out the front door.

Shovel in hand, I step into a transformed world. I could be in another land, things have been so altered. It has indeed stopped snowing, and the last clouds are moving away to expose a deep black sky with only the brightest stars. Auriga, the shepherd-charioteer, is prominent well above the horizon, Capella coldly brilliant on his shoulder. The lesser stars have been blotted out by the unearthly glow sent up by the smooth, rolling blanket that covers everything. It is quiet and nearly windless. Clumped tree limbs hang heavily, motioning slightly as if straining to move. As I watch, a feeble breeze passes like the last gasp from a distant wind, and a bit of snow smoke rises from the spine of Dorie van Dusen's roof.

In the silence, I set to work. With the first bite of the aluminum shovel, I grimace at the scraping it makes against the rough concrete driveway. But I have to make these sounds and so go at it methodically, gasping a bit after the first few shovelfuls. The snow is about a foot deep, on average, but fluffy in the icy air. The loose flakes spill from the shovel as I left them up and away. I'll have to sweep as well.

As I bend and scrape and lift, I am visited by a memory of my childhood, of a night also full of snow. I must have been very young when it happened to have escaped recalling it for so long. It must have been during a season when my father supplemented our income with snowplowing, before he became more successful in his home-building business. I remember the wide yellow blade fitted to the front bumper, and how the truck's dark blue paint shone without a mark. But the memory really begins with my waking in the night at sounds in the kitchen. It was not unusual to hear my parents doing something in the kitchen after I'd fallen asleep, but the sounds persisted, and they were distinct because the world around and outside the house was so very quiet. My room was lit as if by a full moon. Fully awakened, I stood on my bed and pushed the window curtains aside. Outside, the little street was covered with a new snowfall, and flakes were still drifting down. I hurried into the kitchen, where I discovered my father at the table sitting before a cup of coffee. He sat easily, heavy and confident-looking, smiling a little at the world and half-turned to my mother, who was busy at the stove.

"Well, young Jim Kaldy has arrived," my father said as I skittered into the kitchen.

"What are you doing?" I asked no one in particular.

"Your father's going out to plow the snow," said my mother.

"And your dear mother is fixing me up a big, thick sandwich and a thermos full of hot, black coffee to keep me warm. What do you think of that, Jim?"

"That's neat!" I agreed, though still not exactly sure what was happening. "You're going to use the new plow?"

"That's it."

I sat in my chair. I could see my mother taking down the can of Nestlé's Quik. She saw me notice from just the corner of her eye, and gave me the tiniest wink as she pried open the lid.

"Can I go with you, Dad?" I asked.

"Oh, now, it's two in the morning."

"Dad, I won't be any trouble."

"Let him go," said my mother. "He'll love it."

"Alice, he'll bounce around like a ball in the cab, rap his head . . ."

But I was aflame, and inspired. "Mom, you come too. We'll all go, and you can hold me so I don't bounce too much."

The two of them were silent for a moment, and then my father said, "Well, there's an idea."

But my mother said, "Oh, no, I'd be in the way."

"The hell. I'll strap you both in like a couple of rolled-up tarps."

"Yeah!" I yelped.

My mother shook her head. "You two go on. It'll be nicer that way."

"The hell," my father repeated. He gave me a narrow look. "We'll not take no for an answer, will we, Jimbo?"

"No!"

And so the three of us set out together on rough business. With my mother and me secured in the same belt, my father proudly took the wheel and fired up the wide Ford with its new heavy-tread snow tires. As we all grinned through the windshield at our own blanketed driveway, my father eased the truck into place at the head of it, then dropped the heavy blade with a thrilling clank. Leveraging the thick gears into first, he let up on the clutch and all at once we were pushing forward with the engine roaring, the blade scraping to heaven, and snow sluicing away in a white gush.

"Whee!" my mother and I yelled together, and my father grinned with the spray coming up and whitening away the world, then whisking clear instantly as the winds cut across the hood. Up and down we went, clearing the driveway to a thin pale skin of snow.

"Works like a charm," my father announced. He raised the blade and headed away from our home.

Down the magical empty streets we rolled, a world in arrest and lighted by bright lamps only for us. Nothing out but the three of us in our trusty truck. The snow beneath the wheels went down in squeaky protest; the very tamping of it gave a feeling of accomplishment. Then we came to a small, deserted shopping center, and my father took up his position at the head of its parking lot and began clearing.

When he fell into a rhythm, my mother and he fell into quiet conversation, a deep, lulling conversation that touches me even now, as I bend and lift, growing moist within my clothes. Am I imagining the unstated trust and caring in their words, the feeling that they were in something together?

"How do you figure where to put it all, Michael?"

"It's all been planned out, love. The developers own several feet beyond the tarmac. That's just for nights like this so's they can keep the whole parking area clear without having to pile the stuff on someone else's property."

And: "Careful there, Mike. I think there's a row of curbstones here just below the snow."

"You're right about that. I'm going to slip the blade right along them. Just . . . like . . . this."

And: "How's the Jimbo doing? Eyes still open?"

I felt my mother's head brush mine. "Still bright and open, Mike."

We parked at the edge of the cleared lot and ate our food together. My mother presided, unwrapping the thick corned-beef sandwiches and managing the two thermoses, one with coffee and the other with cocoa for me. My father let the engine run, the heater churning. We munched, lost pieces of sandwich in our laps, laughed at the messiness, slurped from our plastic thermos lids. Over my head, my parents passed their black coffee back and forth.

I must have been taken home between jobs, because I cannot recall the second clearing. When I woke up the next morning, in my bed, I felt for a long moment that it had all been a dream, and perhaps I have relegated it to that status over the years.

But it had not been a dream.

I straighten up, back in the present physically but saturated by the feelings of that distant memory. Across the way I see Dorie van Dusen's front door open and a neat figure step out onto the white lawn. It's Dorie; she's got a shovel in hand and she waves and waves at me. She raises the shovel and jumps up and down. She has to be forty at least, and there she is jumping like a kid. I wave back, laughing.

"You've inspired me," I can just hear her call.

"Do it!" I call back.

She raises the shovel again, then sets to it. Even at six A.M., out in the dark and shoveling snow, she has dressed smartly. As she moves by her front-yard light, a fixture set on a wooden pole, I can see the deep purple of her snugly fitting ski pants and parka. Her high boots, trimmed in white fur, hug her calves.

Though I am done with shoveling, I watch her for a little while longer, wishing to encourage her, but all the while I am very sad to see her out there alone, her husband gone to another woman and her son away at college. It is clear to me now that I was loved, loved very deeply as a child. Whatever damage was done by the confusion and pain that my parents eventually suffered, I was buoyed by loving as a body floats easily on warm ocean currents. And I love my family now, deeply love my wife and my child, and they love me. As I watch the lone figure of Dorie van Dusen, who has no one but a distant neighbor to relate to on this winter morning, I vow to remember that I am and have been extremely lucky.

We must be careful to remember that we have been happy, because otherwise our last bad time becomes our measure. And life will serve up enough bad times, the Lord knows, eventually to fool us.

Seventeen

We are waiting together in Dr. Roth's office, forming a family triptych in aligning chairs. Stella's in the center, sitting calmly. "What's he want to do again, Dad?"

I take a breath. It's hard to explain, and I wonder if Dr. Roth could do a better job of it anyway. "As you get older, honey, you suffer more and more from what they call flexion stricture."

"Your joints stiffen," says Marsha, "because your skin isn't flexible enough to let them bend."

"And he wants to make them loose?" says Stella, regarding her own wrists.

"That's right," I say, hoping she will ask no more questions.

"How's he going to make them loose?"

I'm grateful to see Dr. Roth coming down the short hallway between examining rooms. I can see in his eyes his quick appraisal of my strange family: the twisted little father with his hands kept still in his lap, the warm, wide mother with the hopeful smile, and the small blistered daughter between them. I preferred Dr. Lerman's more advanced age because it meant that he'd seen more configurations like ours. "Hi, Stella," Roth is calling.

She smiles at him, pushing the blunt tip of her right

hand into her cheek. He comes down to his knees before her and grins. "You came back!"

"Yeah," she said. "I had a bad dream about you."

His face falls, comically. "Oh no. That's not fair."

"Yes, it is," she says emphatically. "You were chasing me."

"That's because I *like* you so much," he protests.

Marsha laughs. "That's creative."

"Aren't you going to introduce me to your mother?"

"That's Mom," says Stella.

We all laugh nervously, good-naturedly, and Dr. Roth comes to his feet. "Let's go to the Mickey Mouse room."

"Okay," says Stella. She leaps out of her chair and takes Dr. Roth's offered hand. Marsha and I follow, our hands bumping, searching for the other's.

In the examining room, Stella has already pulled off her cap as if beginning to undress. This little gesture of bravery, as always, touches me and I warn myself to keep in control of my emotions. I feel within me that closeness between us that has grown so much over the weeks, living day in and day out together. She has become an extension of my own soul. I can feel the fear in her, and thrill at the courage with which she pushes through it. Marsha begins to slip off the child's other clothes, and gradually she becomes naked before us.

As she is revealed in the full horror of her disease, I am visited by an almost primordial sadness that might, before long, push me from the room. It is because we are here, under unsympathetic bright lights, and away from the insulation of our home, that I become dangerously close to cursing God and his cruel tricks. I can feel my own teeth gritting as I look at Stella, my little eraser nub, this skinny living scar, this small pure, ravaged thing. Soon she is laid upon her back on the white paper, thin and blotched like a strip of bad sausage. Marsha has hold of her hand, her arm outstretched. Before I sit down on the little desk chair, I step to the table and grab up one of Stella's toeless feet and press it to my lips. As I step back, making room for the doctor, Stella smiles back at me. Now Marsha must shift her chair back to allow room, and Stella is alone on the table.

Roth, his relative youth betrayed in some extra flutterings in the hand, bends over our daughter. "Now," he says, and nothing more. He begins to pass his hands over her feet. He rolls each in turn in his hands, bending them this way and that with a finger or two on her ankles.

"My hands warm enough?" he asked seriously.

"They're hot!" says Stella, and we all get to laugh again.

"Does it hurt when I bend your foot like this?"

"No."

"How about now?"

"Yes!"

Dr. Roth takes up a clipboard and makes a note. Then he puts it down and examines Stella's knees. More bending, more notes. Her hips, this way and that, then her elbows, her wrists. Then he has her sit up for a moment so that he can take her whole head in his hands and turn it first left, then right. He places Stella back down and makes more notes.

"What are you writing?" she asks.

He answers while continuing to write. "The big words are 'approximate flexion radius.' But that just means how far your joints will bend."

"Is it okay?" She has to push her chin down to get a good look at him.

He smiles at her. "Not bad, Stella. Better than expected. Now I need to look more closely at your skin."

Marsha says, "Her thighs seem the least affected."

"Yes, that seems to be the case."

He already has his hands on her legs, moving the fingertips along her thighs. He turns one in and runs his fingers up along the inside.

"That tickles," says Stella.

I reflect that this may be the closest she will experience of one of the traditional caresses of a lover. Roth, meanwhile, has swung a strong light over the table. Under its beam, Stella's scarring grows livid.

"I'm going to put on my funny eyes," says Roth. "Watch this." He places a white plastic magnifying headpiece over his forehead, and swings down the wide lens. "See?"

"Wow," says Stella. "That looks funny." But she seems more anxious than amused.

Roth swings his head to me so that I can see what Stella's seeing. His brown eyes are enormous behind the lens. "Wow," I say too.

"Okay, now for a closer look," he says, and bends to Stella's legs again. His fingers search carefully, keeping to the smoother, unaffected areas of her thighs. When he turns one thigh out, the child's vulva opens, shockingly pink and moist under the harsh light. The labia have been scarred, but the mucosal membranes within have never been attacked. Her sex, then, is a small area of physical dignity. She has not been so lucky with her throat, which occasionally develops painful sores, nor her anus, which remains raw and cracked from the normal strain of defecation. Since she has been home with me, I have become much more familiar with Stella's sufferings.

Later, Roth turns the child over on her tummy and then goes on with his examination. He looks closely at the backs of her legs, then the small of her back, another relatively unscathed area. He pauses at a flat, hard area just where her buttocks begin to separate. "Here's where you sit, right, Stella?"

"Sometimes," she says.

"Whenever her tush hurts, she scrunches back," I offer.

Marsha says, "Is that little hard place okay?"

"Oh, sure," says Roth, straightening up. "Every monkey has one, and ten million monkeys can't be wrong."

"I'm not a monkey," Stella insists.

"Are you sure? Let's put you on your back again, Stella. I have something I want to ask you."

She grunts as he turns her over. "What?"

Leaning up against the table, he looks over his shoulder at her. "I want a doctor friend of mine to take a look at you. She's very nice. Her name is Dr. Cejka."

"Checker?"

"No. Check-a."

"What does she want?" Stella's brow is calm, relaxed. Perhaps it was nice to be touched by those practiced hands. And now maybe the new doctor, a woman too, won't be so scary.

"I want her to see if those nice skin places of yours are as nice as I think they are."

For surgery, I think; for grafts. But please, Dr. Roth, don't say that aloud, I think next. I'm sitting across from Marsha, and we both exchange a look, checking in. Then Marsha turns back to Stella. "What do you think, honey? Are you up to it?"

"Uh huh."

"That's good," says Roth. "If you all would just wait here, I'll see if she can come down for a moment. I spoke to her earlier, and she seemed to think she'd be available." He leaves and we wait.

"Are you cold?" I asked Stella.

"No."

"Are you hungry?" asks Marsha. In her purse is a bag of Fig Newtons, fuel for the little furnace that consumes so quickly.

"No."

"You sure?" Marsha scrunches her chair closer, then reaches out to put her small, soft hand across Stella's middle. The child crosses her two mitts over the hand, then smiles as Marsha rolls her whole body side to side.

"Do you want to go out for lunch afterward?" I ask.

"Can I have a cheeseburger?"

"Yeah. We can go to McDonald's, and you can have a cheeseburger and a milkshake too."

Marsha says, "I'm going to have a Big Mac."

"What about you, Dad?"

"Me? I'm going to have a Blubber Burger."

"What's that! You're teasing, Dad."

"Nuh uh. Fried whale on a bun. I'm really hungry."

Dr. Roth comes into the room again. "She'll be right here," he announces.

We wait some more, bantering. Roth says, "I'm pleased with the examination. Stella's joints haven't stiffened that much. That was a concern of Dr. Lerman's. It's a good time." He taps the tip of Stella's foot.

It's good for us to hear Dr. Lerman's name. It makes me and probably all of us feel better, as if the old man is still nearby, watching. But I want things to hurry along, because Stella's been lying there naked for a long time and I'm wondering if she isn't feeling a little humiliated. Fortunately, Dr. Cejka soon arrives.

At the first step of this short, wide woman into the room, a change occurs in the emotional atmosphere. Roth steps back, hugging his clipboard, and a new pecking order prevails. Dr. Cejka already has her hand out to Marsha, then me, the two of us awkwardly trying to rise quickly enough as this dark-haired woman in a white coat comes at us. I have only a fleeting impression of her heavy black hair and eyebrows before she turns and approaches Stella.

"So this is the little munchkin," she says, with a strong trace of an Eastern European accent. Marsha pushes back her chair again, and Dr. Cejka sets right to work, nimbly grabbing up Stella's feet, then hands, then rolling her knees. "That tickle, sweetie?" she demands.

"No."

"No! Well, we'll see."

The room has gotten pretty crowded. Dr. Cejka's broad behind is practically in my face. Roth leans beside his colleague, pressing the clipboard her way. Now the new doctor awkwardly takes it from him, fumbling a little with bifocals. She lifts her head up to stare down at the board. "I see," she says, then turns back to Stella. With an irritated gesture, she bats the heavy light away.

"So, so, so," she says, running her two thumbs up one of Stella's thin thighs. "Not so bad, huh?"

Stella says, "*That* tickles."

"I told you so!" cries Dr. Cejka, then laughs so hard that she shakes. "We'll see, won't we?"

She continues to peer at Stella's skin, bending closer, her head bent back to get her bifocals at the right angle. Finally, she lifts them up to her hair and turns to all of us.

"Well," she says.

Roth cocks his head to her. But Marsha speaks first. "Can Stella get dressed now?"

Both doctors immediately assure her that that would be fine, then everyone shifts about, bumping and twisting, to give Marsha room to get Stella down to the floor, where Marsha and I get her into her clothes. As I grasp one of her arms I feel the muscles trembling. "Good girl," I whisper.

Dr. Cejka is saying, "I think we can talk further about this. Yes, we can." She rolls her head, looking at no one in particular.

Roth says quietly, "We should check Stella's blood to see how strong it is."

"Yes," agrees Dr. Cejka. She laughs pleasantly. Meanwhile, I fit Stella's cotton cap to her bald head. Now dressed, she climbs into her mother's lap and Marsha hugs her close. I pat her tush and Stella just lies there against her mother. She whispers, "Blood, Mommy."

"I know," Marsha whispers back. "Not much fun, huh?"

"I don't like that part."

And that will be the easy part, I think. I look to the doctors. "We'll take her out into the waiting room," I say. "We'll wait until you finish talking."

"Good idea," says Marsha, cocking a brow at me. The heavy talk is not going down well with Stella.

"Maybe you should stay," I mumble.

Marsha nods, then slips Stella to me. In the waiting room I walk about, bouncing Stella up and down in a protracted hug. No one else is in the room at the moment. She is fairly limp, at first, lying against me like a strip of heavy cloth. "Whoa, whoa, whoa," I chant, bouncing. "What a brave kid you are."

"Hey, Dad," she says, pulling back. "What does Dr. Checker want to do?"

"What does she want to do? Hey, did I tell you that I love you today?"

"Yes. You told me this morning."

"Oh. Well, I love you again."

"I love you too. But what did Dr. Checker say?" Strangely, her voice is not at all whiny.

We walk on, I bouncing a little less. "What we told you. She wants to add a little extra skin to your ankles and wrists. So that they'll keep bending as you get older."

"They bend." She demonstrates by waggling one of her mitts in the air.

"But less and less as you . . . get . . . older." I bounce out the words.

"Dad, you're giving me a 'set stomach."

"Oh, sorry." I stop the bouncing and fall back into a chair.

"Will it hurt?" she asks.

"Once in a while, but not too often. The important thing, Stella-Morella, is that you keep loose. So you can play the ma-rim-ba, and cut out your pic-tures, and all the rest. You see?"

She nods, but appears puzzled. "Do I have to do the blood?"

I nod, trying to strike an expression both blithe and sympathetic. "They need to keep checking as they go. Besides, you're past due for your regular check."

Now the examining-room door opens, and out come the other three adults. Dr. Roth leads the way, half-turned to Dr. Cejka. I rise and Marsha slips up close. "How are you holding up?" I ask quietly. I can see that she is preoccupied.

She shrugs. "The risks," she says simply. She gives Stella a pat. "Do you think you're up for giving blood?"

Stella wails. "Nooo. I don't want to."

Dr. Cejka protests. "But Mona's down there today. Mona's so good you don't even feel a thing."

"I *always* feel it."

"You will not feel it this time, I promise. Mona is the very best."

I'm not so sure I like this tactic. Stella will feel it, and then feel betrayed. At the moment, she is leaning back in my arms and eying Dr. Cejka carefully.

"Mona really is the best," Dr. Roth affirms.

Mona proves to be a small black woman with beautiful, delicate features and a very large but shy smile.

Her immaculate white uniform fits her like a glove, and she sports a clear plastic cap so assuredly that it seems like something from the latest fashions. She comes forward in her cubicle when Dr. Cejka hails her while standing at the entrance. "We have a little girl who wants to feel no pain today," the doctor explains. Marsha holds up Stella, who is smiling apprehensively.

Mona holds her two hands together at her chest, one hand holding two fingers of the other. She releases the fingers and waves them in the air as if gently scolding. "I do not allow it to hurt," she says in a voice strangely musical, laced with a delicate accent. "I am from another land where we do not allow it to hurt. Come, child," she commands, and opens her pale palms.

Dr. Cejka steps away, waving goodbye with a finger to her lips, and Marsha hands Stella to Mona. "You will sit where the big girls sit," Mona explains. "No longer in the finger, which is for little children, which you are not any longer."

Stella, intrigued, settles in the chair with the flat arm attached to it. Mona sits beside her in another chair and now stretches out Stella's right arm. "Now, the magic band goes on, round and round your little arm many times—one and two and three—ah, just right, and we pump up one, two, three." The pressure band is in place, covering the entire top of Stella's arm. Now Mona holds up a bottle. "This is the no-sting juice, very magic." She tips the bottle to a cotton swab and wipes the juncture of Stella's elbow in small slow circles.

"Magic," says Stella.

"Powerful. Now, you must get ready to sing the magic song with me."

"What song?" Stella looks deeply into Mona's face, her dark, bright eyes playing over the young woman's gleaming teeth and smooth, even features.

"The song goes like this." With her head wagging easily from side to side, Mona begins to sing, "I told my mother that I would not stay home—ta ta ta ta—I told her that I had to vi-sit the stone." She holds Stella's outstretched arm while she sings, tapping with one finger rhythmically. She pauses. "Can you sing that?"

Together they sing. "That's good," says Mona. "But for the magic to work, you must close your eyes and let your head go back."

Stella closes her eyes, smiling to herself, and lets her head drop back against the chair. "Good!" says Mona, reaching for a small syringe behind her. "Now, again, and I will add new words."

> I told my mother that I would not stay home
> —Ta ta ta ta—
> I told her that I had to vi-sit the stone.
> —New words now—
> The stone where the dog,
> Has hidden his bone.
> The stone where the frog,
> Has made his new home.

Stella sings, giggling. Somewhere in that song, the needle goes in and two vials of blood come out.

Mona's competence has given us confidence. At McDonald's, our collective mood soars.

"I didn't feel it, Mom," Stella insists over and over.

We all agree that Mona did a good job, and that Stella

was very brave the whole time. We are all very pleased with each other. I even tease the tiny Asian girl at the counter by asking for a Blubber Burger. With a smile she comes right back at me, tells me they are out of them. We sit around a table together, jostling our trays and laughing.

Stella is famished. She lights into the Happy Meal cheeseburger that I hold up for her and smears catsup all over her face. She talks on and on. "I like Dr. Checker," she announces. "She's very funny. Isn't she funny, Mom?"

Marsha says, "Yes, she sure is. So you think you might be okay with those doctors, honey? You think you might go ahead with them?"

"Sure. I want to see Mona again."

"You'll probably see a lot of her," I say, a little gravely.

"That's okay."

Marsha is staring at our daughter with one of her occasional misty looks. With a sigh she raises her eyes to mine. "Can you believe this little kid of ours?"

I rub my cheek against Stella's cap. "Wouldn't trade her for anything."

Stella seems embarrassed. "It's just me," she says, wagging her head. "Stella."

"I wonder," says Marsha.

E IGHTEEN

It is hard going on Pleasant Street this night. It seems that no one clears their walks anymore. I have to negotiate clumps of ice and slick patches with my light burden, Stella Kaldy, who talks and talks this evening. In the night sky, Perseus and Cetus move at an infinitesimal pace toward the chained Andromeda. Castor and Pollux, the two head stars of Gemini, are sharply visible. In the center of all this dynamic inaction is Auriga, directly above the ecliptic, the sun's invisible path, and his little she-goat, Capella, is ablaze with varicolored fires. But I've got to keep my eyes down, watch my step after the new snowfall on the uncleared walks. It's just as well, because of Stella's talkative mood. While I listen, or try to, something keeps nagging at me, something that the uncleared walks make even more irritating, but I can't quite remember what it is.

"Auriga is driving the chariot, Dad, but it's really a rough road."

"I see. Where's he going?" I step carefully off the sidewalk and onto the street.

"He's taking Capella and her babies to the pastures."

"The pastures. A new word." We looked in the encyclopedias that day, looked at Australia for a few moments, distracted by all the pictures of farms and sheepherding.

Stella continues. "Capella is up on his shoulder and she's looking over his shoulder behind the chariot and you know what she sees?"

"No, what?"

"A 'stralian sheepdog!"

We have had a pretty exciting time of it recently. Since her appointment with the two doctors, she has been lighting into our projects with a zeal that has me exhausted. We have completed the Book of Family and Friends (accelerated too by the purchase of a paper cutter), and are now busy with a new book, the Book of Stars. Stella is reading more and more, and has even developed a small taste for math—at least the shape of the numbers. With the Book of Stars, we are concentrating on the stories she likes best—Auriga, of course, and Andromeda saved by Perseus, the Starry Hunt of the Blackfeet Indians, and another Indian story about a spirit maiden who tries to come down and live in the world of people. I try to keep her on track with these stories, but she insists on adding new details and sometimes whole new plots of her own. At night she gets to expel more creative energy by rambling at will.

"Like the dog we saw in the 'cyclopedia, Dad," she explains.

I know only too well where we saw it. We tried to find Auriga in the *World Book Encyclopedia* but came up with Australia instead and Stella became very distracted by a picture of an Australian sheepdog standing on the back of a fleece-laden sheep.

"What's he doing?" she cried at the first sight of the picture.

The black dog, with pointy ears and snout, was standing splay-footed for balance in the deep fleece, its front legs forward but body pushed back and rump up high. Its tail was looped up, the tip nearly touching the back of its head, and a medium-length fringe of dark fur rippled along it.

"He's rounding up the sheep, I guess."

"But he's *riding* it, Dad."

"I know; he can do that. He also barks and jumps around and nips at them too. I guess when he jumps up on their backs they know he means business and go where he tells them to."

"Where do they go?"

"Back to the pens, I think. They go out on the pastures to eat grass, and then they have to be rounded up in the evening."

"Why can't they stay out?"

I had to read the text to answer that one, but there was no help there. We tried to find something about sheepherding in another volume, but that was the dead end I suspected it would be. Eventually, we ended up taking down the D volume and looking through the dog pictures. The Australian sheepdog was not featured, however, and so we vowed to go to the library and get some dog books.

But with this evening's walk, I can see that a real can of worms has been opened by all this dog talk.

Stella, waving her mitts freely in the winter air, is saying, "It's okay that the 'stralian sheepdog's out of the chariot, Dad, because he can run a lot. You know? And when he gets tired, he can just jump up inside. You know how they can jump."

"I sure do, Stella."

"Dad!" she cries, making *me* jump.

"What, honey? What is it?" I think she might have seen something, and I look around.

She has pulled back to look me in the face. "He can jump on the back of the *horse*," she whispers seriously. It's a secret sacred knowledge what this wonderful dog can do.

Later, passing the Lesters' dark pines, she says, "He can help me during the operation."

"Who can?"

"The dog. What's the name of that dog we saw, Dad?"

"It didn't give its name, Stella."

"But, Dad, he can help me when I'm home from the hospital."

She knows very well that she's earned high marks from Marsha and me for her bravery in the face of the impending operations (there will be at least two of them, one for her wrists and one for her ankles; elbows and knees later, if necessary or possible). She will try to parlay our approval into permission to get a dog. Now I must tell her again, for the hundredth time, what she least wants to hear in this world.

I stop and sigh and look up at the sky. There's Auriga up there, bright and shiny, and I'm down here dealing with sheepdogs and epidermolysis and something else I can't remember. So little is known today about the origins of Auriga, but it's a sure bet that a great deal of story was assigned to him at one time. Unlike the case with Hercules and Cassiopeia and others, his story has been lost, but at this moment I feel very much like an ancient man without answers, a simple creature who looks to the heavens for solutions. Now I remember what that other thing is: Marsha's bad news. She came home with the distressing report that her new job's health plan will not cover Stella's planned operations; they have determined that Stella's affliction constitutes a "pre-existing condition." You can walk around with a bad feeling and forget the reason for it.

I sigh again. So much rides on the stars. They are paths and they are the stories of people on paths and they are the paths of our dead and they influence the paths that we, the so-called living, tread here below. I walk on an icy walkway with a child whose soul might at any moment flee its inhospitable shell and streak into the sparkling canopy of lights that peek down like little thoughts, pieces of answers, glimmering hints. How shall I live? Tell me, stars.

I hear myself speaking. "You know you can't have a dog."

Stella hits me. She brings up both her mitts in the air, then down upon my shoulders. "Why!" she cries, whacking my shoulders again. She has been waiting for this answer, waiting like a coiled spring, angry that I would see through her manipulations. I can see from the streetlight how her face is wrinkling up. "I'll take care of it!"

"Stella, the risk of infection . . ."

"But I won't get 'fected. I won't!"

"Honey, no, I'm sorry but . . ."

She starts to cry. Her head rolls back and she positively

cries to the heavens. I pick up speed, pointing us toward home. Now she is wailing as if I've struck her with a stick. Her wails go out into the quiet neighborhood, echoing among the houses as among the stones in an empty valley. A light goes on in Dorie van Dusen's living room. Stella cries so that her lungs empty to the limits, and then she has to wrench them to get them to take in air again.

"My God, Stella, it can't be that bad." I'm getting pretty angry myself. I'm tired of this dog conversation, but I'm alarmed too at the depth of her frustration and anger. Her crying is genuine, and under the stars as we hurry forward, it strikes me as a primordial sort of anguish that I must take very seriously. Why should the many desperate stories attached to the stars be any more real than the anguish of a real suffering child? I can see Marsha coming out the front door. When we reach the top of the driveway, Stella rolls over into her arms.

"I heard her in the front room," says Marsha in surprise. "What's going on?"

"The dog," I say. It's enough.

For the rest of the evening, Stella whimpers, inconsolable. She goes to bed in tears, clutching Heddie after a defiant twist away from her noncooperative parents. Afterward, Marsha and I wander about, folding towels, patting the newspaper, waltzing among the dirty dinner plates in the kitchen without rhythm or purpose or synchronization. Finally, we find ourselves before the stove, staring at the lisping kettle. At the kitchen table with cups of tea, we begin to discuss the whole mess at last.

Marsha says, "I think she's made the decision to have a dog no matter what it means."

"She doesn't know what it means."

"She doesn't *care* what it means."

"It's no reason to let her have a dog just because she wants one. She'd love to dash into traffic too."

Marsha shakes her head. "She doesn't challenge us on that sort of thing, not seriously." She thinks quietly. "I think it's more important to her than we realize."

I protest. "We've always known how important it is. We've had three doctors tell us that her immune system is pushed hard." An exotic illness or simple skin infection, even flea bites, could push her too far.

Marsha nods with me, but she's heading into one of her powerful trains of thought that no human on earth can derail. "How about this: Isn't happiness, I mean real joy, an immunization in itself? Or a strengthening of it?"

"You're saying that her having the dog will make her emotionally stronger, and that will make her physically stronger." I say this, thinking to set up her premise to better knock it down, but having said it I'm confronted by its merits.

Marsha knows an opening when she sees one. "It's become a stronger and stronger desire of hers. It's beyond curiosity or cute or anything superficial. Having a dog is part of who she is, and what she wants to become." She peers at me, poker-faced, through the curls that have fallen forward on her brow.

I point out, "She's using the operation business to manipulate us."

"Which just goes to show how important it is to her."

"We *know* how important it is."

"But maybe not totally. I think it's tied up with how she perceives herself, how she's choosing to grow."

"She's learning to get her own way."

Marsha's eyes light up. I've played into her hands. But why am I fighting? I know: I want to be convinced. I want Marsha to be right, but really, really right. She says, "Getting her own way at this point is a form of growth—and the topic she turns to during such times is her desire to own and care for something else."

"Own? Is that a good thing?"

"Wrong word. *Be part of.*"

"Can't she be part of us?"

She shakes her head. "Only up to a point. A dog is her size, playful, cute."

"I'm playful, I'm cute."

We both laugh. We both know where this is heading. Somehow, some way, we are going to come up with a plan to get Stella her dog, and neither of us will sleep until we do. I move things in a more practical direction.

"What if we do get a dog? I mean, what about the cost and the feedings and all that?"

As it turns out, we have a fairly exhilarating conversation. If it's possible to train a dog so that it won't lick or jump up and would submit to frequent bathing, then perhaps Stella could have a dog after all, and that prospect excites us. We can envision very clearly in our separate brains how transporting an experience owning a little doggy might be for our daughter. But the training will cost money, and though we have no estimates on the costs of the operations, we know they can't be cheap. When the talk turns more and more to money, how much we have and how much we'll need, we grow quieter. The bad news about the insurance coverage hangs silently above us.

It's late. I'm tired. Stella's broadcast bawling and now this heady debate have absorbed my last few ounces of energy. I look across the table at Marsha, remembering that Howard Long left me with a standing offer to come back and work as a part-time consultant. That would be hard for me for many reasons. For one thing, I'm beginning to really like being home, and it would be damned embarrassing to show up at my old division again.

I take the plunge. "There's always Howard's offer."

Marsha peers at me. "Would they put you back on the health plan?" The health plan that covered everything.

"No. I wouldn't have permanent status. It would just give us the cash."

Her hand comes across the table. "That would be a lot to ask," she says quietly.

Though our hands entwine on the table, and though I get to feel noble for an instant, a sharp little prick of resentment starts up just below my sternum. Evidently she won't be suggesting coming home herself, or switching jobs to find the right health plan, or taking up a little part-time job on the side. It's going to have to be me that has to adjust—again.

"I would be grateful, Jim. Maybe there's some other way than that" (she can't even give my offer a name!), "but if Stella could be given her chance . . ."

Her chance, her chance. A second stream of feeling opens within me. It flows through me, a gentle energy, emanating from the consideration that if people are willing to take chances, then others should militate to support them. I had my chance—years of interesting work—and now my wife is getting her chance. The new feeling washes my resentment away. We're talking about Bigger Things now, and Bigger Things have a way of making me want badly to be part of them.

But I hold back a bit. "Let's sleep on this," I say, patting Marsha's hand. Howard, Milo, Marco the Discontented . . . are those elbows that I want to be rubbing again? And we need to ask Dr. Roth about this dog business.

I have a good night's sleep, dreamless and deep, and the next day, after lunch, with Stella down for an enforced rest (forced down, then invariably out), I sneak into the front room and dial Dr. Roth. He can't come to the phone but the receptionist says he'll call me back soon. I hang up, letting the phone rest in my lap while I look around the activity room. All the pinned-up pictures, the rubbings of leaves that did not find a place in the Book of Leaves, the seed pods taped to the window glass so that when the light is strong we can see the individual seeds snugly in place . . . I have a rich life now. At the moment, my annoyance at Stella's frequent moodiness is nearly forgotten. The thought of losing much of my time with her acts like the light on the seed pods . . . the good times are illuminated, separate and sharp. On an impulse, I dial Howard Long. I know the number that rings the direct line to his desk.

It rings four times. After one more ring, it will automatically bounce to Helen's line. Howard's voice comes on.

"It's me, Howard. Jim."

"Jim!" The same big voice, the same sometimes deep substrata of feeling. I miss him, whatever he is. He asks lots of questions about Stella and me, honestly curious. He laughs a lot when I describe her antics, and how poor Dad has to scramble to keep one step ahead.

"Sounds like working for me was a breeze in comparison."

It's as if he's cued me. "Well, that's why I called, Howard."

Because he's Howard he's not going to make it easy. His years of busting unions and swaggering through town fiefdoms were fueled by the thrill of power. He likes it that I'm on the phone with my hat in my hand. So, at first, it's "Well, things have changed a little around here," and "I'm not so sure . . ." But in the end, and also because he's Howard and will finally remember that genuine friendship is rare and therefore valuable, he makes a tentative promise. "I need to sort a few things out. What day is it? Thursday? I'll call you early next week."

I'm getting my first taste of crow and I don't like it. "I'm not sure if I'll need the work, Howard. I'm just calling to see if I still have an option open with the division."

"I understand, Jim. I'll call soon."

I pace about our room, rubbing my eyes. The thought of going back there artificially tires me. What could I say to all those puzzled faces? And something else that I'm only just beginning to admit to myself: Do I want to go back at a lower level of authority and responsibility? I feel little again.

The phone rings. It's Dr. Roth. I ask him how he is and he answers in his usual way: cheery but professionally opaque. It's the older ones, the Cejkas and Lermans, who've been at it enough to let their true personalities show through. "Stella wants a dog," I say.

He listens as I outline our plans to train and disinfect and all the rest. I speak quickly to outflank his opposition. At the end he sighs, "Yes, I understand all that. It's just that I have some of her test results before me . . ."

"Oh!"

". . . and while they're adequate and all, I'd have rather found some soaring erythrocyte levels. You know, a bigger margin of insurance."

I don't know what to say. "Are you saying, Dr. Roth, that Stella should not be operated on?"

"Oh, no no no. What I'm saying is that if we go forward we go forward at a higher level of risk than we might have hoped for."

I'm still puzzled. "What are you saying?"

He laughs grimly. "I know, it's not clear. What I'm saying, or rather, what I'm *doing,* is apprising you of the risks involved in the operation. To perform surgery is to ask the blood and kidneys to work hard. Stella does not have a lot of immunological reserves at the moment."

"Will she later, if we wait?"

"That's the tricky part. This could be as high as she gets—now or ever."

"So, if we don't go forward, she may never have the punch to survive in the future."

"Survive's a strong word. We'd lose what might be our best opportunity."

I take a breath. "What do you recommend, doctor?"

"I need to talk to Dr. Cejka. I haven't shown her the results yet."

"But what do you think she'll say?"

I'm asking the wrong question, because what I really want to know is what he will want Dr. Cejka to say. But he seems to recognize my inaccuracy. "I think, and I'm hoping, that she'll want to go forward. The point, Mr. Kaldy, is whether you would want to go forward considering the extent of risk that Stella will be facing."

"Oh, boy."

Stella appears at my elbow, rubbing her eyes. Panicky, I wheel about in the chair. Roth is waiting. I hold my mouth close to the phone. "I'll call you back. Stella's here now, and I need to get back to her." God, I'm already sounding like a bureaucrat again. I hang up and turn to my daughter.

"Dad, do we have to do math now?"

"Yep." Ceremoniously, I point to the schedule above the desk before me. I give her a detailed response to remind her of our planning. I sum up, "First a story, and then math." I tap a pencil against my knee. "You know all this, Stella."

She stands there in her red DAD'S TEAM sweatshirt. "But can we look at the 'cyclopedias instead?"

"Let's not, Stella. We have free time later."

"But I want to see the picture of that dog again."

Erythrocytes, dogs, Howard . . . I've had it. I shouted at her. "Look, Stella, I'm not going to take this dog business up again. We're sticking to the schedule and that's it.''

My eyes feel hot. Stella stands before me, a rickety little monster. In her shocked face, creased with sleep and blotched with blistering, I see her need. I hate her need.

N INETEEN

It's a windy Saturday morning. Marsha takes Stella to a puppet show so that I can get on the phone and secretly call up pet shops. I've already checked things out with Jack, who knows something about dogs, and he thinks I should poke around for one of the larger terriers. They are short-haired, nonshedding, and the larger ones may be more trainable, not so feisty.

I focus on the nearer shops. At first I'm not very lucky. The first two persons I reach are surprisingly unknowledgeable; it takes me little time to conclude that they are pushing the dogs that they have in stock. The next local owner I reach seems pressed and insists that I come in. "You have to *see* the dogs," he keeps saying. I reply more than once that I'm just looking for the names of certain varieties.

"I think *breed* is the word you're looking for," he says.

"And I think I've found a horse's ass," I think to myself. Into the phone, I keep it more pleasant: "My daughter is prone to skin infection" (maybe he'll be more sympathetic now) "so I have to be careful which *breed* we choose." He says again that I should come in. He wants me in, with Stella, so that she'll get hooked on something in stock and then he'll have a sale. I sign off, discouraged.

The next number is disconnected, with no forwarding number. An image of an abandoned pet shop slips into my brain. I fantasize about the causes: disease, too many returned dogs, unhappy penned potential pets that no one would buy. But with the very next call I sense an immediate difference. I reach a woman with a snagging dialect bred on the edge of West Virginia or the heart of the Midwest that invites you to talk.

"Yeah, yeah, yeah, I hear ya." I envision a big woman, one of those immense easy women who lean back with a phone and light into it, like they were born with one in their ear. "Don't know that I'd stick with the terriers, except perhaps the English fox terrier. They're well-behaved. But sounds like a Sharpei's more what you're lookin' for. They're real nice, gentle as can be, but they're expensive. We'd be talking around four hundred for a purebred."

I gasp.

"Say, who's this for? Your kid, you say?"

"Yes. She has a skin condition that requires sort of careful treatment. Can you bathe a Sharpei?"

"Oh, sure. They're real gen'l li'l beasts. But one thing is they got a mug on 'em that would stop a train. Some think it's cute, all pushed in—you seen 'em?—like they were chasin' a truck that stopped sudden? But not all the kids like that kinda face so much. But then some kids do. Their faces are real wrinkly."

"I've never heard of them."

"They look real sad, and it makes you feel sympathetic."

I wonder if that kind of breed would be the right one for Stella. I think Stella wants a buddy, something with some spunk, not something that looks funny or that she could feel sorry for.

"How about something that looks a little more normal. Pointy nose and ears. I think my daughter would like that better."

"Well, here's a stretch. How about the American Standard terrier. Short-haired, pointy snout, very friendly. They're strong-willed by nature, kinda got a bit of reputation for that, but they're trainable as hell."

"Now that sounds good."

"Own one myself—Jenny—and she stays here right in my shop."

"Can we come see you, and her, sometime?"

"Sure! Bring your daughter too, if you like. You say she's got a skin problem."

"A severe one."

"I got eczema myself. It can be nasty."

"May I know your name?"

"Helen!"

"I'm Jim. I think I'll be speaking to you again."

When Jack checks in later in the afternoon I blurt out the news. "I finally reached a very nice pet-shop person. It looks like we should go with the American Standard terrier."

There's silence on the other end.

"Jack, you still there?"

"Jim, that's a pit bull."

"What?"

"The American Standard terrier is better known as the pit bull."

"The ones that bite and never let go?"

"Yes. I guess it's an indication of their loyalty."

"Jack, that's not funny. I thought I had an answer and now . . ."

"But wait a moment. I've heard that their reputations can be very undeserved."

"Stella with a pit bull for a pet?"

"Why don't I come over. I'm bored stiff here, the wind's been too rough for even the diehards. I could swing by my apartment and pick up a couple of my books."

"I would be very grateful." I'm feeling so disappointed that the breed I've come up with is famous for chewing human beings. I shudder thinking of Stella's snappable little limbs.

I can't do anything for the hour that it takes Jack to wend his way to my door. He knocks on the front door instead of just coming in, so at first I'm not sure it's he. "Come in," I insist at the door.

He nods over his shoulder, eyelids lowered. "Let's take a walk. It'll do you good."

It's bright outside, though there is that biting wind that kept the golfers away. Jack stands there in his absurdly thin overcoat, a man used to the outdoors and someone who needs to walk a few miles each day. The golfer's curse. Soon I'm bundled up and huffing to keep pace with his par-five stride. It doesn't take long for me to realize that he intends to make a strong pitch for the pit bull. It tickles him to think of Stella with a dog like that.

"She's such a fighter herself," he says. "A survivor. I like her for that, immensely, and it seems so fitting somehow that she team up with a fighting dog."

"Jack, that's a great piece of philosophy, but I'm thinking about coming home and finding pieces of Stella all over the house."

He's off in his thoughts, very convinced. "We would need to look into it further, of course, but I do recall that incidents of viciousness could almost always be traced to provocation by the owners—who use them for gambling fights and the like."

"Almost always is not enough. What about a Sharpei?"

"Very lovable, but given to whimpering." He wrinkles up his face. "It would be hard to imagine Stella with a dog that whimpers all the time, don't you think?"

"This is very frustrating. Is there no dog *between* these two?"

"Certainly. We'll look at the books."

"You didn't bring them!"

"They're in my car, Jim."

I calm down. We head up one street, then down another, talking about Marsha's new job and Dr. Cejka's bohemian heartiness and Jack's plans to fly south in two weeks for all of February and half of March. At the corner of our street, we hear a car coming up slowly behind us. We turn to make room, and Dorie van Dusen comes up alongside and rolls down her window.

"Need a ride?" she says, laughing. We're a hundred yards from my house.

"Where're you heading?" I ask.

"Home with the groceries. Why do I shop on a Saturday? The stores were jammed."

"Jack and I are talking about dogs," I explain. "You remember Jack, don't you?"

Jack leans forward, touching a finger to his hat. "I remember you," he says.

She squints at Jack. "How are you? I've been thinking about getting a dog myself. I haven't been interested since my dog died a couple of years ago." Dorie has on a big fake fur hat, white but brindled with brown. When her round, soft face smiles broadly, as it does now, her eyes nearly close. The cold has pinked the tips of her wide nose and cheeks. In the bright sunlight, I can see the carefully dyed tips of her pale eyelashes.

"I lost mine a few years ago," Jack says. "His name was Ralph."

"Don't you miss him?" says Dorie with feeling.

"Immensely."

I lean on the door of her compact station wagon. "Dorie, we were just going to look at dog books before Stella gets home—she's not supposed to know that we're researching. Want to come over and help us out?"

"That sounds like fun! But is that okay with Jack?"

"It's fine with Jack," says Jack.

"I just need to get my groceries in," she says.

I tell her I'll put on the teakettle. When she drives off, I look to Jack. "How about that?" I say, proud of myself.

But he's peering at the retreating car. "She's put on a little weight, don't you think?"

"Will you stop that?"

Jack and I get the kitchen table ready. We clear the few remaining breakfast cups, wash them up, put the kettle on, set out the books. Dorie arrives within minutes, grinning in the doorway at me. When she passes in, I get a whiff of some potent new scent, sharp and spicy. I help her out of her outdoor things, and then she precedes me up the hallway, clasping her hands together and looking around. At the entrance to the dining room, now the activities room, she stops and peers in. "What's going on in here?"

I explain about my being home with Stella now, and Dorie listens closely and asks a lot of questions. "I've seen you and Stella out and about during the day, but I guess I never put two and two together." Meanwhile, Jack serves the tea and I set out cookies, the two of us circling Dorie. "Two handsome men serving my every need," she says, beaming.

"Within reason," Jack cautions, with a sidelong look to her.

"Don't worry," she calls out cheerily. "I can control myself." But she can't help laughing and tossing her head about. Her bright blond hair, surely a beauty-parlor creation, stays in place. "Are these the books?" she asks, unnecessarily. They have covers with glossy pictures of dogs all over them. "We should be very organized." She begins laying the books out.

"Jack thinks I should get my daughter a pit bull," I say, sliding into a chair.

"You're joking," says Dorie, eyes wide with alarm. But already she senses it's no joke and already she seems intrigued.

Jack has taken the seat at the head of the table, his long legs crossed and the tea mug cradled in his lap. "I don't know very much about them," he says. "But I do recall that their reputation is undeserved."

Dorie raises a hand. "I knew a couple who owned one. They swore by her. Gentle, smart, intelligent. It's an extremely intelligent breed, according to them."

"Is that so?" says Jack.

"Absolutely. This couple thought they might even raise them. But then they had to move and they ended up with a much smaller backyard."

"That's a shame," says Jack. "I still have the same place, out in Newton, and it's got a yard just big enough for one dog. Ralph loved it there."

"After my Sharon died, I couldn't even look into the backyard for a long time."

"I know the feeling. My entire backyard is a Ralph memorial."

Dorie laughs sadly. "Did you see that movie about pet cemeteries? I was close to Sharon, but I don't think I'd ever go that far with a pet."

I hear a noise. "Maybe Stella's back," I say. But neither of my companions seems to hear me. "I'd better hide the books." I scoop them up and rush them into the pantry.

Now Marsha and Stella can be heard coming in the front door. I go out to help Stella out of her things. She's already burbling about the puppet show. "There was a dragon, Dad. And real smoke came out of its mouth!"

"No."

"Yes. Right, Mom?"

"Right," says Marsha, taking a fatigued breath.

"Dorie and Jack are here," I tell her.

"Hey."

In the kitchen, the two guests look about at us with slightly forced smiles. I can see that they're not sure if they are supposed to be here anymore, and if my guess is right, they're disappointed at the prospect of the party's breaking up.

"Look who's here!" Marsha croons.

"Hi, Jack!" Stella calls out, and rushes up to her uncle. He just gets his cup up to the table before she reaches him. He hauls her into his lap.

Marsha says, "Dorie, Jack, can you stay for lunch? I'm going to make up some sandwiches. We're starving."

"Well . . ." Dorie says, looking to Jack.

"I haven't eaten in over an hour," says Jack. "I'll have Stella on light rye."

"Better not," says Stella. She turns and waves at Dorie. "You saw my dad shovel the driveway."

"He told you? Yes, it was very, very early in the morning."

In the pantry, I whisper to Marsha. "Got a line on a dog. Do you have the energy to go out to a shop with me?"

"What did you find out?"

"We can talk on the way. We can get Jack to watch Stella."

She nods, taking down cans of tunafish. "I could do it if you drive."

"And Dorie might stay."

After a lively lunch, we announce our plan and succeed in backing out the front door while Stella takes Dorie on a tour of the activities room, at Dorie's insistence, and Jack looks on in his patented state of amused detachment.

During the drive to the pet store, I slowly and carefully explain about the American Standard terrier. My caution is wasted because Marsha has never heard of the breed, but when I explain about its "undeserved reputation," she stares at me.

"Let's just see," I say. "The woman sounded nice."

"It's the *dog* I'm worried about."

It takes us some time to find the shop, which is one of many flat-roofed shops in a drab little mall. The sign is one of those all-of-a-piece suction-molded plastic items that always indicates a tight budget to me. I'm already anticipating that corners have been cut inside as well: cats with bald patches, wormy puppies dragging their little butts. We open the door to a shock of pet smells—sawdust, urine, the mealy smell of dry feed—but find it brightly lit and noisy with animal excitement. We have to push past stacks of plastic bowls and boxed cages before a heavy woman with a phone in her hand comes into view. There is no one else in the shop.

The woman seems to be standing on a raised platform behind a counter. "You Jim?" she asks, her round blue eyes popping.

"Yes!"

"I'm Helen. I'm on hold. Be with you soon. Take a look around if ya like."

I nod, staying quiet. I do so out of habit for people on the phone, but the air is full of parrot complaints and yipped greetings for Marsha and me. Marsha begins to cruise the rows of puppy and kitten pens. I stay in place and a full-grown white dog with big light-brown spots and clear brown eyes walks up to me and nuzzles my hand. When I pat its smooth face it carefully licks my fingers with just the very tip of its tongue. The tongue is pleasantly moist, not wet, and very warm. The color is the very pale pink of the interior of a conch shell.

"Well, it's about time!" Helen explodes into the phone, her party evidently back on the line. She talks for a short while about what seems to be a pet show in Providence, Rhode Island, and then, with a wink to me, gets off the phone.

"So, what do you think?" she says to me, coming from around the counter. I see that she has not been standing on a platform at all. She is just very tall.

"About what?" I say.

"About Jenny here." At the name, the brown-and-white dog comes up to her and sits before her, its hind-quarters quivering and front paws clicking up and down in place. "I see you two have met."

I still don't understand. Then I do. "*That's* a pit bull?"

"Gettin' to be the pop'lar term."

Marsha joins us and I introduce her. Before long, the two women are talking in great detail about the breed. Personality, level of care, training, who does it and how much it costs. When I start hearing hundreds of dollars mentioned I quietly slip away deeper into the shop. Across the whole back wall are tanks on top of tanks of tropical fish. I ease into the visual world of suspended colors and rippling forms. Goldfish the size of fists, with bulging eyes and dripping with diaphanous fins; darting black commas and iridescent purple smears maneuvering in a school; flat arrowheads dashed with orange and green, hung in the clear liquid. The gurgling and bubbling drown out the sounds of the women's voices and I'm wondering how Stella might like an aquarium, and how much it would cost to set one up and maintain it. At my eye level is a dead fish, bobbing on the water's surface and already fuzzed with fungus. Things die. I'd like Stella to have everything she needs, but I've learned from being home that in the getting you might miss the knowing. I'll go back to work, I'll make more money, and that will give Stella an operation and a dog? But how important *is* it that her wrists move another few millimeters? Things die, and life is short, and some lives are shorter than others. I wander from tank to tank, looking for answers.

When I come back up front, I hear the two women talking about Stella. Marsha is saying, "It is hard, Helen," as if agreeing with an earlier statement. "It's always weighing one risk against another."

"Uh huh." Helen is leaning against the counter. Her bare forearm lies there like a seal. I see that she is eying me. "You look sad," she says. There are flecks of dry eczema scales at the corners of her eyes.

I shrug, hating to admit to such a thing. "The expense," I say. Jenny is there beside us, looking on. I drop down lower and pat her head. "Are there any more Jennys around?"

"Sure. She's the product of love and care and she's grown to be a beautiful creature. I been talkin' to your wife here 'bout a gentleman I know out in Boxford. He trains these li'l numbers. He don't come cheap, though. I could call him."

I nod, coming erect. I'm too tired to speak, though. All the calling and thinking and calculating have me spent.

Marsha says, "Would you call us, Helen? We'd appreciate it." Marsha neatly slips one of her new business cards from her purse.

Helen says, "Sure, I'll call in a day or two. And bring your daughter by sometime. I'd love ta meet 'er."

"We will."

On the way back home we talk mindlessly about the whole gathering morass of our lives. "She could live to a ripe old age," says Marsha at one point. Her voice has no breath in it. "Then she'd need the physical flexibility." She's said this before; I've said it myself.

Later, I say, "The timing seems wrong. A pet at the same time as she's run down from the medical stuff." She's heard this before; she's said it herself.

When Marsha rolls the car up to the garage door and stops the engine, neither of us gets out. We sit in the car, side by side, staring at the dark front windows. Inside is what? Jack and Dorie and Stella. We don't want Jack and Dorie to be there right now. Maybe we don't want Stella to be there either. At the same time, Marsha and I sigh and our two heads roll over and bump to rest against each other.

TWENTY

Helen, the pet-shop person, does not call, but Howard does. He offers me a short-term spot in his own office, and I can see that he has given the matter some thought. I have feared that he'd come up with something awkward, like putting me back in my old office, which would have effectively imposed me upon Jennifer—which Howard might very well want to do. Worse, he could have come up with make-believe work just to help out an old friend. I've already had bad dreams about being in the middle of a workplace where no one listens to me but just looks through me. What Howard suggests is much different.

"I want you to be the liaison for my office regarding anything to do with the region-wide audit. It was your big idea anyway, so you should get stuck with it."

"I see. Do you mean handling correspondence?" I'm on the kitchen phone; Stella's coloring in the next room.

"All of it: meeting with the auditors, with DiAngelis, with the field, interpreting the reports and preparing responses. And organizing all the findings that come in."

"This is very interesting, Howard. Is any of that Jennifer's job?"

"It's *my* job, but I don't want it to be. I want to be

free from all of it. I've got better things to do, and to be perfectly honest I've a couple of irons in the fire, some serious promotional possibilities that I want to turn my attention to."

"You're leaving the agency?" I ask in surprise.

He chuckles. "At my level, you're always *leaving*— or getting pushed out by the newest administration. Not a word of this to anyone, Jim, but some of my old cronies down in D.C. are sitting on important committees these days, and one of them is pulling for me to get the top slot with Immigration in this region."

"More clout, more money," I muse.

"And a big office with a great view from the fourteenth floor of the JFK Building. And no building contracts to worry about."

I'm silent for a moment. Then I say, "I like the offer, Howard. You think I can do it all in ten hours a week?"

I hear him grunt. "It's hard to say. You wouldn't have to come in every day, that's sure, but I think it would be good if you were in three afternoons a week because you'll need to meet with people."

Of course. But Stella. "It's damned generous, Howard, but I don't know if that many days per week would work out with my family."

"I wondered if it would. It's the best I can offer, Jim."

"I understand, believe me. And I don't want you to think I'm not grateful. I can see that you've thought this out carefully, and I'm touched."

"It's good for me too. And I like the idea of having you around here again."

We sign off with my assurance that I'll talk over the offer with my family and get back to him soon.

After I hang up I am not alone with my thoughts, because Stella is here with me and it is not easy with her these days. Somehow the word got out about the dog. She's picked up some inaudible signal and she thinks that applying constant pressure will make it all happen. Her constant whining and complaining have pushed me to the limit; worse, they have set in motion some uncomfortable misgivings in Marsha and me. We now wonder if actually getting the dog will set up Stella for a sure and lasting disappointment. She has invested so much in the notion of a pet that the real thing will certainly fall short. The whole dynamic has gotten me very confused. As for Stella, I've found I have to send her to her bedroom at the very mention of a dog. At the moment, we are in the midst of a very uneasy truce.

This day has not been so bad, but I'm a disappointing companion. I'm simply too preoccupied. If I go in to work three afternoons a week, who will take care of Stella? Can Marsha rearrange her schedule, go in earlier and come home earlier, or do a split shift? It doesn't seem likely. Could we get a babysitter three afternoons a week? That would mean that a chunk of my new money coming in would be immediately going out.

"What are you thinking about, Dad?"

We're supposed to be doing math. At the sight of her numbers, I have been thinking that I haven't even talked to Howard about what he plans to pay me.

"Sorry, honey." I point to a number. "What place is the five in, Stella?"

"The ones. Were you thinking about a dog?"

I can't believe this. So blatant! But of course, she thinks she's being subtle.

"Stella, we talked about this. We are *not* going to talk about a dog."

But I haven't said that she cannot *have* a dog, and that looms as a potential yes to her. In fact, that difference— my no longer saying absolutely no—has probably tipped her off that the matter is under Mom's and Dad's consideration. Now my potential yes must be culled, pursued, coaxed along—and, in moments of pique or fatigue, demanded.

"Why not?" she asks.

"Stella, we are doing math. We are talking about place value, and that's all we are talking about. Do you understand?"

"But I want to talk about a dog."

"That does it." I get to my feet, take her by the shoulders, point her recalcitrant little body at her room, and move her along the floor so quickly that her slippers skid. Under my hands, her little shoulders are already shaking with anger, frustration, sadness, the works.

Before we even get to her room she has deteriorated into full tantrum, complete with screams and flailing. I get her on the other side of her door, which I shut tight. Normally, I could ignore her until she simmers down, but my nerves are shot. I haven't slept well, I'm worried, I'm fed up with the piles of unsolved stuff scattered throughout my psyche. Enraged, I throw open her door, stride across the room, yank her to her feet, whack her twice, hard, on the butt. I feel the shocks go through her body and up into her wrist, which twists in my hand like a short length of stiff rope. She shrieks to heaven. I drop her on her bed like a sack; she rolls on her stinging behind, mouth open and face knotted with pain and anger. I shout into her face, full force, "Stop that goddamn crying, Stella, and I mean it! If you don't calm down you will never have a dog, and I mean that."

Now she's hysterical, and I'm horrified at what I've done. When I lean to her, softening by the second, she backs away in fear, still shrieking. Without the slightest notion of what to do, I lunge from the room and slam the door.

I walk about the kitchen, then the activities room, then the front room, fidgeting, feeling miserable. The sound of her tortured little self is painful to me. I put my hands over my ears and remember that at times like this the good parent is supposed to offer children a choice, something about either calming down or having to stay in their rooms, but I'm too confused to formulate one. I'm upset because I can't make it all work and, on top of that, wretched to think that I might have ruptured any of her blisters. I look at my watch. It's only one o'clock! We have the whole afternoon ahead of us; we have to shop and cook too. The thought of pulling a screaming Stella through the supermarket . . . Marsha is miles away, and Jack will leave for Florida soon. I have been abandoned.

I decide to pray. Patience and reason have failed, so what other options do I have? I think about calling Gerry Burke at our church. I resolve to if things ever calm down, but for the moment I find myself actually getting down on my knees. It's surprisingly painful with my knees on the linoleum. I even pause for a moment to wonder how Stella can sit on this stuff for hours before I look up at the ceiling and whine, "Please, God."

The phone rings. God is calling. I struggle to my feet and lift the receiver, at the moment heavy as a small barbell. It's Jack.

"Did that woman from the pet shop call?"

"No." Stella's wailing has subsided to steady weeping.

"Too bad. But I've been talking to one of the members here. It just came up that he raises Airedales."

"What's that, a plane?"

"Are you all right?"

My voice must sound as if I'm speaking into a fifty-gallon drum.

"Bad day."

"How bad?"

Gratefully, I tell him all about my most recent troubles. I feel better already, pouring all this tripe into his willing ear. "And if I take the job, what the hell will I do with Stella three afternoons a week? Stella, who is now in the next room crying for Rin Tin Tin."

He laughs. "Why don't you and Stella give yourselves a break? Go to the movies. For God's sake, you both need it."

"There's shopping, dinner . . ."

"Buy a pizza! They make them just for days like these, you know."

"But we're trying to save money."

"You've got enough. It sounds as if you've just gotten a new job."

"But it may not work out, Jack." I'm playing the conversation out, buying more time with him.

"It will work out, Jim. It always does with you. It's just not going to work out *today*."

"Don't go to Florida, Jack," I conclude. "Stay here and take care of us."

"All right, so you're going to go to the movies. That's good. Now, about the Airedales. The gentleman with whom I spoke swears by these dogs and he's got a litter he's trying to move. I've told him about you and he would welcome a call. Would you like the number?"

After I hang up, I go to Stella's room and walk in. I squat down before her, a small quaking thing with a wet face. I say into her face, "It's so hard for you, isn't it?"

She nods, her small face pinched.

"If you could just lay off the dog stuff for a while, sweetie."

"But," she says, halting to snivel, "I can't help it."

Something breaks up inside of me. She can't help it. Of course. She's in the grip of something very big.

I open my arms. "Come here, gorgeous."

She falls into my arms, and we hug. We hug for a long time. Afterward, I hold my breath and slip down her pants to see if my swats have done any damage. Red and raw, but no wounds.

Stella and I go to the movies. We are two of five people in the theater. It's a silly movie for her, really inappropriate, but she watches gamely. Halfway through she grows tired, then sits in my lap, and we have fun with my reaching around in front of her face with handfuls of popcorn.

On the way home, with the pizza between us on the seat, Stella looks tentatively at me. "Did you like that movie, Dad?"

I have been thinking about something else (I can't

think of any way around the scheduling of the job Howard's offered; I'll have to ask for a hefty hourly rate to cover childcare for Stella), and I turn to her, puzzled. "When? What part are you talking about?"

But she does not answer. She only looks at me, her eyes searching my face in a way that seems new but actually strikes me as somewhat familiar. I feel as if she's looked at me this way before, and probably at moments when she sensed that I wasn't understanding something important. If I didn't know she was six years old, I would guess that she was applying the adult tactic of waiting for a better moment to bring something up.

Strangely, I'm shaken. I think first to press her with questions, but then I stay silent. I'm missing something. But even more, a heavy feeling of our essential separateness begins to press down upon my heart. She sits there, Stella Kaldy, across a pizza box from me, and she will not be, as I evidently keep assuming, a mere extension of myself. She is on a quest, a dog quest, and I am not Dad but the man who can get the dog but will not get the dog. And Stella Kaldy is a great, wise soul who knows what she wants and needs, but she's been pushed into a scarred little body and with only a six-year-old's tools to work with. My thoughts begin to swim, the trees going by rhythmically, the car engine humming a meditational chant. I think: The job of adults is to *ally* themselves with children, not control them.

I begin talking about dogs, praying that Marsha will forgive me for going ahead without her. I explain our fears about her owning a pet, how we've talked with Dr. Roth, how we've been to pet shops to find the breeds that can be trained, that won't shed . . .

Stella takes this all in calmly, punctuating my explanations with little comments, tapping the pizza box with one mitt. "I won't get sick," she insists in the end. I believe her. How strange; I'm completely convinced.

She asks, "Are we going to get a 'stralian sheepdog?"

I shake my head. "We can't get a dog that needs to run, honey. They hate to be in the house, always itching to get out. And there's no place for them to run near our house. It'd be in the street all the time, maybe get hit by a car. . . ."

She nods. "I want a big dog, Dad. 'Cause you know why? With a big dog I can hug him standing up."

I laugh. "I can see you've got this all figured out. I wonder if Airedales are big. Jack called and said he knows someone who has puppies."

"They are big."

We pull up to a stoplight and I look over at her. "How do you know they're big?"

She is sitting back calmly. Her head is leaning back on the seat and tilted toward me. "They're big in the picture."

"What picture?"

She rolls her eyes and whacks her mitts on the seat. "The picture in the 'cyclopedia, Dad! You *showed* it to me."

I blink. "You mean you know what Airedales look like?"

"They're the first ones in the book, Dad. They're big and brown and they have funny little beards."

"Stella, I'm very impressed that you would remember that."

She stares back at me. Evidently it's no big deal with her. The light turns green, and I head us down the last quarter-mile to home.

Marsha's home! She beat the worst traffic. We find her at the kitchen table, reading the paper with her glasses slipping down her nose. Within moments I have gratefully relinquished the whole matter, *all* matters, to her, and she has willingly assumed responsibility for them. I tell her nothing about the spanking, and hope that Stella too will say nothing. When I sheepishly admit to broaching the dog topic, Marsha nods instantly and waves a hand in the air. "It was time." Before long we've got the D volume of the encyclopedia on the table and are munching pizza slices as we huddle around the sole sacred picture of the Airedale. Then I remember Jack's books still hidden in the pantry and soon we have more pictures to look at.

Later, I can hardly wait to pour Stella into bed so I can get off alone and talk with my wife. We go into the living room, which we hardly ever do, and I fix myself a stiff drink, bourbon on the rocks, which I *never* do, and yammer at her from the couch.

"I can't describe this strong feeling I had in the car when we were coming home. It was like I was . . . in her way or something. Like I was holding her back."

Marsha nods. "She's ready. She knows the whole score, at some level."

"That's what I was thinking."

"And I was also thinking today that the whole dog issue is tied in with the operation." She shrugs. "It's going to be tough, she knows that, and so she's lining up more emotional support for herself."

I throw up my hands, my bourbon cubes rattling. "She's told us as much!"

"She's a sharp little cookie."

We smile at each other, wickedly taking credit.

We resolve to call the Airedale man and perhaps set something up for the weekend. When I tell Marsha about Howard's job offer, she's elated.

"Jim, that's great!"

"I know, but the three afternoons . . ."

"I'm so proud of you, Jim."

"Why?" I'm genuinely surprised.

"Because we needed extra money and, pow! you get something right away."

"But that was always in the works. Remember, he offered before I even left."

Marsha shakes her head. "Everybody says that stuff. But you, you're so indispensable to them that they actually meant it." She's absolutely beaming at me.

Let her think what she wants, I decide. I'm worried about how I can even take the damned job. But Marsha comes up with a promising idea. "We could call Velverleen. She was great with Stella."

I consider this possibility. "But what about the schooling?"

"Maybe Velverleen could do a little of it. I don't know how critical it is for a six-year-old, certainly less critical than her emotional well-being." She thinks some more.

"We could school her more on weekends. And how long will this job last, anyway?"

"That's true," I say, feeling a little alarmed. "It might only be a few months."

But overall I feel a lot better. I have a list of steps to take, and that is very consoling. It gets my eyes closed at bedtime and me unconscious.

TWENTY-ONE

I will call the Airedale man, and Marsha will call Velverleen. In the morning, Marsha goes off with a hopeful air—she has remembered the name of Velverleen's placement agency, so she's confident that she can get in contact with that old irrepressible woman—but comes back that evening with terrible news. I encounter her in the hallway, coming glumly forward, snowboots still on and leaving puddles on the linoleum.

"What's the matter?"

"Where's Stella?" she asks, her face as blank as putty.

"Over at Marissa's. The Dorsets wanted her for dinner."

"I have awful news about Velverleen. Brace yourself."

I do.

"She's dead," says Marsha. "Heart attack, just a year ago."

"My God."

This news takes the wind out of my sails. I myself have a mixed bag to present, but I only sit silently and think about cheerful, no-nonsense Velverleen, dead.

Marsha says nothing. This is a setback, and a tragic one to boot. Finally, I take a breath. "The Airedale man, Mr. Allbright, says that I called at a good time. The puppies are just now ready to be looked over, weaned and all. But he says that they won't come cheap."

"How much?"

"I didn't ask."

Marsha eyes me carefully. She's still wearing her coat, just sitting there at the kitchen table. Now she rubs her eyes. "That's not like you, Jim."

"How much can it be?"

"Not like you, Jim. You must be worried about how much it is."

"Let's trust in fate."

Marsha chuckles. "Maybe the spirit of Velverleen will intercede for us. Should we take Stella?"

I think about that for a moment. "She's been so patient since we agreed to the puppy. She deserves the trip. Besides, she should pick it out."

"Should she?"

I have assumed that she should, but then what would a kid know about the qualities of a potential pet? "Let's ask Jack to come with us."

Marsha shrugs. "We could. He's done at the club, but he flies to Florida on Sunday. He's a quick packer though."

I feel a bit silly going back to Jack again, but he seems to have an interest in the dog quest. And so that Saturday we have Jack over for breakfast and then the four of us get in Marsha's little car, Jack with his knees up under his chin in the front, and Stella and I bouncing around in the rear. And I do mean *bouncing:* Stella is very excited. As we drive she babbles plans.

"Mrs. Dorset says we'll need a box and a clock."

I look over at her. "A clock?"

"It misses its mother," she explains.

"The puppy? But why a clock?"

Stella, frustrated with me, throws up her hands. "Because . . ." but she has forgotten why a clock.

Jack looks over his shoulder. "They need sound. Moving from their hectic puppy family to a quiet basement is a shock."

"I'm glad we have a basement," says Marsha.

"Why do we need a basement?" I ask. "We need a clock and a basement?"

Jack says, "New puppies do pee-pee and poo-poo."

Stella giggles.

I say, "But this puppy will be trained."

No one says anything, but I feel puzzled. What's going on? I say out loud, "We're going to look at the puppies and possibly pick one out to be trained, right?"

Marsha says, "I thought we were going to pick one out and bring it home."

"No!"

"Yes!" cries Stella.

"Wait a minute. That won't work, folks. A puppy is a wild animal and we're not set up for it." I think of the puppy peeing everywhere, then hiding under the bed and not coming out, and chewing the legs of our only good chairs. But no one's speaking, except Stella. She's revving up for a mighty protest.

"But, Dad . . ." She is about to spout tears.

"Okay, stop the car!"

Marsha checks me in the rearview mirror. "Are you serious?"

"Stop the car. Please!"

Marsha checks the traffic and then rolls the car to the curb. I speak into the deep killjoy silence that is rapidly gathering around me.

"Here's the plan, my friends. We are going to *look* at these puppies. We are going to *consider* buying one of them. It will *not* come into the house until it's trained."

No one replies. Jack mutters, "Makes sense." Stella lies crumpled against the opposite car door beneath the raised cudgel of my finger. "Stella, if you raise a stink when we get there then we're just going to turn right around and come home. Do you understand?"

"Yes," she answers, but defiantly.

Marsha starts the car up again. "You're asking an awful lot, Jim," she says, a bit irritably.

"You're not going to be home to clean up after it."

"Big deal."

I don't like this divided-front approach to the problem. Stella will quickly sniff out the space between my and Marsha's thinking and slip right into the breach. "You forget I'll be starting a job soon. And who would we ask to watch a puppy then?"

"You're going to work, Dad?" asks Stella.

"Whomever we hire," says Marsha.

"We'll ask them to watch Stella and an untrained puppy? Be realistic."

Stella says, "Someone's going to watch me?"

Jack looks out the window as if he'd rather be anywhere out there than here in this car. And it's a long drive to puppyland. At least my letting out about the job possibility gives us something else to talk about than puppies. Stella demands again, "Are you going back to work, Dad?"

I can't find the appropriate words. Marsha says, "Only for a little time each week, sweetheart. We need to make some more money so we can pay for the operations." Wisely, she does not mention the puppy.

Jack says, "Is that so? They're not covered by your health plan?"

Now we have to explain the whole mess right out loud. "Preexisting condition," says Jack with distaste.

"What's that?" asks Stella. She comes closer to me, her voice has dropped, she's fed up with all the questions and their unsatisfactory answers.

"Sit with me, honey," I say quietly. She comes willingly into my lap and we look out the window together. We're heading out and away from the tightly packed neighborhoods to where the lots get large and the trees spread open as if sighing with all the room they have. In the gray sky, the tough winter birds are roaming for the next tiny course of their interminable meals, living to eat. I whisper into Stella's ear, "Did I tell you today that I'm so glad you were born? Did I tell you I'm glad you're a girl?"

"No," she says flatly. "Why are you going to go back to work?"

"It looks like I'll have to go back to my old office for three afternoons a week. We're going to look for someone to babysit you for those afternoons."

"You mean teach me," she quietly corrects.

I give her a squeeze, rub my chin against her knit cap. Inside her thick parka, I can feel her bones. "Yes. Teach. You're no baby."

"Babies can't have a dog," she declares.

"That's right."

We fall silent in the back, and Jack and Marsha chat on in the front about our family predicaments. Jack says we should push harder with the medical-plan people, but Marsha insists that she's tried everything. How much will it all cost? Thousands, of course. We plan to ask for an itemized reckoning from Dr. Roth; we don't want any nasty surprises after Stella comes home.

Outside, the sky is full of blackbirds. Some stand on the telephone wires like notes on a staff. I hum a familiar tune.

Stella stirs in my arms. "That's my song, Dad."

So it is, her marimba song. Three afternoons a week I will not be able to hear her music. Staring at the birds on the wire, at the huddled birds and the gray sky, I feel a chill. I'm so used to the things she gives. I could not do without them now.

Ten minutes later, Jack points to a narrow road with a mailbox at the entrance, and Marsha swings in, her hands shimmying along the wheel in her characteristic way. We putter up a long drive, trees leaning in on both sides. This place appears to be a genuine country estate.

"Somebody lives here?" Stella asks in disbelief, and we all laugh.

Then the trees draw back and we're in a clearing with a big white house and a series of rambling additions linking it to a shining red barn. A gray-haired man in high leather boots, a down vest, and a crushed felt hat motions to us from the yard.

"He wants us to pull up there," I observe, and Marsha obediently aims toward the man. She parks on the frozen ground near a split-rail fence. We all get out and the man ambles toward us. He is lean, unseasonably tanned,

and stoops just slightly. I always feel a little self-conscious at moments like this one, when my whole strange
family presents itself in a lump to a stranger. Coming
out of the compact car, we must appear like something
normally encountered at the circus.

"You must be the Kaldys," says the man. He waves
at Jack, then comes forward and takes his hand. "Jack."

"Dick," Jack replies. Then he gestures toward us and
crisply reels off our names. I hope he has warned this
man about Stella, but when she raises her face to him,
I see the nearly imperceptible flinch of shock on his face,
which she never fails to detect. Mr. Allbright executes
a forced smile, rallying quickly to a semblance of ease
and naturalness, but my daughter's face has already
dropped and she moves closer to my leg. Very quietly
she says, "I don't see any puppies, Dad."

The man hears. "The puppies?" he says, grateful it
seems to have a distracting topic. "They're out behind
the barn. Come this way."

Mr. Allbright drops back and walks beside us, staring
toward the barn with a small smile on his lips. He appears to go away in his thoughts for a moment as he
stares with what appears to be near-longing toward the
barn.

When Marsha says, "What a beautiful place," he nods
silently then drops his face. Then he raises it again,
walking on toward the barn. "Yes, isn't it? We were very
pleased to find it. It's nearly two hundred years old."

"No! It all looks so new."

The man smiles, mostly to himself. "We've completely restored it, of course."

There's a human-size door cut into one side of the huge carriage door. We go through it into a large swept space lit by shafts of light streaming down from high skylights. The slatted rays illuminate bridles and other bits of riding tack, a neat heap of straw, a medium-size tractor, green metal attachments, piled sacks of manure, potting soil, and sphagnum. Rakes, hoes, shovels leaning evenly against a wall, coiled hoses hung on pegs . . . We keep moving through to the far door, which Mr. Allbright indicates with a limp hand. We can hear the anticipatory yelping of excited puppies. Stella clamps my hand between her two mitts, pulling. We step up the pace.

Just outside the back door is a chicken-wire enclosure. As soon as we come out into the brighter light, there is a sudden swirl of activity in a wide pen. Puppies, puppies, puppies, leaping and yipping and trembling and darting. They trot quickly toward us in a wave, identical miniature brown creatures with short curly hair and boxy faces with the same black spot to one side of their noses. Stella reaches the chicken wire on one side as they surge up in a trembling, whining mass on the other.

She shakes at the wire. "Mom, can I go in? Dad?"

Marsha and I look at each other. I'm sure we are mirroring the same expression back at the other; how could we plan for every one of these unforeseeable decisions? Marsha shrugs, and I turn to Mr. Allbright.

But he is already coming forward, hands coming out from behind his back. He is gazing at the puppies in the same strangely remote manner that he was gazing at the barn. "Here," he says, and pulls a pin that allows the gate to open a crack. "Step in," he tells Stella.

Stella is spooked at first by the heavy flow of eager animals that jam against the gate, but she takes a breath and wades in. She keeps her hands high, giggling, then squealing, as the puppies leap about her, three or four at a time pinned up against her on their hind legs. "Look, look!" she cries to us. "They're all over me!"

"Stella, you're drowning in puppies," I call to her.

"I'm going to pet them," she tells us.

"Go ahead, Stella," Jack calls. I think he is pleased that his Airedale idea is going forward.

We're all at the fence, watching, grinning. When Stella dips a hand to one of the puppies, all the rest go for it, nipping, licking, yipping for a touch. Time and again, she pulls her hand up out of range with a startled laugh.

"Don't tease them!" Mr. Allbright shouts.

Stella looks around, puzzled. "She's just anxious," I explain quietly. "First dog."

Mr. Allbright grunts. "Makes them nervous. Mother doesn't like it."

All at once I find a huge dog standing between me and Jack, its muzzle up against the wire. It's just standing there, hip high, watching. I reach down to pat it, but before my hand touches its wiry fur it executes a series of sharp, angry barks. Stella jerks as if shot. I say, "Whoa, now," and look to Mr. Allbright.

"Better get her out of there," he says.

The big dog is now barking with feeling, its wide shoulders lurching toward the wire, and I wave to Stella. "Come over here, sweetie. It's the mother. She's worried about her puppies."

Stella understands, but she won't move toward me because the big mother dog is close to where I stand. Marsha heads off around to the other side, and Mr. Allbright grabs hold of the mother's collar. A few yards down the fence, Marsha reaches in and pulls Stella out. She turns in her mother's arms, looking back into the pen; her moment in puppy heaven is over.

Mr. Allbright then opens the gate and lets the mother into the pen. She trots in, proud and possessive, her tiny charges leaping in place all around her. Gradually, they settle into a large quivering pile on the gleaming straw.

I turn to Mr. Allbright, whom I have decided I do not like, and ask him, "How much do you charge for one of these puppies?"

He puts his hands on his hips, looking off into the pen. "Well, the pick went to the stud, of course. For the pick of the ten here it's eight hundred."

I stare at the man. Jack sidles up closer and says, "It's less, then, when there are fewer left to choose from?"

Mr. Allbright nods, looking at the sky, then the trees, and then the ground. Evidently I am a small black hole in his immediate universe. "The last one will go for six-fifty, I suppose. But it's nice to choose. Personality, disposition, those things count."

"Eight hundred," I say to Jack.

Stella calls, "Daddy, Daddy!" She's waving at me to come over.

I shake my head, walking off as Jack and Mr. Allbright take a step or two away. When I reach Stella and Marsha, Stella says in an excited whisper, "I know the one I want."

"Eight hundred," I say to Marsha.

Her eyes go round. "My God. What'll we do?"

"I'm not sure."

"There are other puppies in this world, Jim."

Stella says, "No, Mom! I know the one I want." She twists toward the pen, pointing. "See that one there, Dad? The one in the back?"

I'm very distracted, but I do manage to notice a particularly small puppy standing quietly, alone, just a foot or so from the quivering pile of dogs. The little thing stands quite solidly, its head perked up, and seems to regard the mass before it quizzically as if trying to discover a small space for itself within it.

I say to Marsha, "You said it yourself. We've been asking a lot of Stella here."

"Yes!" says Stella, without completely realizing what she is affirming.

Marsha looks off in that way I know, the way that tells me she's a little ashamed for having run out of answers. Stella's looking into the pen, her face puckering. At this point, I have nothing to lose; I might as well just speak my mind.

"We don't belong here," I say quietly. "This is a kind of place for perfect dogs with special papers—and money, and perfect things we don't even feel comfortable with." After a moment's silence, I get a nod from Marsha. Stella stares at me as if she's never seen me before. "I want you to have a dog, Stella, I want it so badly for you. But I don't think it's here."

Of course, she protests. She goes on and on, "But what about the one in the back there, the one standing there, Dad!"

Mr. Allbright has appeared in our midst. "That one?"

he says, hands deep in the pockets of his heavy canvas pants. "She's the runt."

"What of it?" I hear myself say. It comes out like a bark.

"Well, she's cheaper for one thing." He moves off down the fence.

Jack comes up. "I could work out a barter thing," he says under his breath. "Golf lessons for a break on the price tag."

"I think we should go," I say.

Mr. Allbright is in the pen. He has scooped up the runt, which now wriggles belly down in his palm, its four paws prancing excitedly in air. "Oh, look," Stella croons.

Marsha instinctively brings Stella to the edge of the pen, where Mr. Allbright, smiling fully for the first time, holds the puppy to her. He tweaks its tail, animating it like a toy. His even teeth are very white—false, I suspect. The puppy is nudging, licking, nipping at the tip of Stella's stunted hand. My daughter's face is suffused with barely suppressed glee.

And yet I say, "We have to go now."

These words go out as if spoken by someone in another dimension, parallel and uncommunicative. No one stirs. Except, perhaps, Mr. Allbright, who, if I'm not mistaken, lifts the puppy just slightly beyond Stella's reach. "We'll call if we're interested, Mr. Allbright. Let's go, everybody."

Jack leans toward me. "What in the world is wrong?"

I press out a few soft words between my teeth. "It's not right."

"I can deal with this guy. It's a done thing."

"Jack. Help me get us out of here."

His eyes, the dark round eyes of all the Willises, tip toward me, then toward the tight little circle around the puppy. He nods, he understands. With a sigh, he moves away from me and somehow we manage to get us all moving off and back toward the barn. Once out of sight of the puppy, with Stella yammering questions, we fill the air between us and Mr. Allbright with noncommittal pleasantries, promises to call, many thanks for the time, what lovely thises and thats. . . .

Stella cries in the car, her chest heaving with the pain of a broken heart. She cannot for the life of her understand how we managed to leave that place without a puppy. She does not want to be touched or consoled, but presses herself against the opposite door from me.

"I'm sorry, honey, I'm sorry," I keep saying. "I set you up."

Jack says, "*We* set her up."

Marsha, driving hands at exactly ten and two o'clock on the steering wheel, says, "I guess I don't see the problem."

"We're not going about it right," I say, a little desperately. I'm feeling as sad as Stella is. Why can't I function?

I'm getting no sympathy from the women in the car. They probably feel as if they've been bullied. Jack says, "Let's talk about it over lunch."

His suggestion goes into air so emotionally thick that it is immediately swallowed up in silence. Outside, nature continues in league against me by pressing glowering gray clouds down around the car. And we still have at least thirty miles more of this bliss! I will say nothing more; I look out into the flat lands that used to be farms but don't know anymore what they are and wonder what single people are doing these days.

When we round the curve into another nameless town a gleaming old-timey diner comes into view. I long to pull into its accessible drive, step through its all-weather door with the porthole window, smell the fresh coffee and the sizzling hash-brown potatoes. But I hesitate to risk disappointing my family further by imposing my will again. Then I feel the car slowing beneath me. In the front windshield, the diner grows, then looms, then is simply and beautifully there before us. The engine stills.

"Dear Marshmallow," I say like a breath.

I bundle the stunned Stella to me. As we cross the lot behind Jack and Marsha, I whisper into her ear, "Will you forgive me?"

She says nothing, just bumps against me. Little sack of sticks.

"You're not being fair with me, Stella. Just talk to me, okay?"

Her head has come to rest against my shoulder. I feel it move in a tiny nod.

It is empty inside, except for the man behind the counter, who turns toward us with a rag in hand. He is big, with rolled-up sleeves and thick hairy arms—the owner, the kind of man who gravitates to places like these. This man is about to tell us that they are closed. The clock on the wall between the felt-board menus says two o'clock. His mouth is open to say the words, and we stand there, the four of us, waiting for their sharp edges to cut us.

But the man takes it in, the round woman with her hands stuck in her coat pockets, the tall man with his shoulders pushed up to his ears, and the little man holding the crumpled child. He takes it all in and says, "We'll be closing soon, folks, but you're welcome to stay a little while."

"Thank you," Marsha says. The words come out on the breath she's been holding.

The moment turns, we begin to reclaim the day. We occupy a booth, sliding into it like refugees at a relief center. Gradually, Stanley, the owner and cook, produces several reheated hot dogs and a pile of french fries. The coffee has lost its fresh edge but I take in what qualities it has to give. Marsha pushes a hot dog, bite by bite, into Stella's willing mouth, and soon has her giggling. Jack sits across from us, spreading his elbows comfortably. I don't want to be the first person to mention the unpurchased puppy.

"I think Airedales are the wrong choice," Jack says.

Stella says, "They're cute!"

"But they get big. Did you see the mother?" he asks. "How mean she was?" Jack is smart.

Marsha adds quickly, "So big—and loud!"

"And angry," I venture.

Jack nods, wrinkling his eyes. "The dog for *you*, Stella, should be very gentle. A dog that can be your friend, and not jump and bark and push you around."

"But I want one . . ." says Stella, catsup all over her nose. She's listening, though.

Stanley comes over. "How's everything?" he demands.

I look up at him. Paper hat, pencil behind his ear, big gut wrapped in a greasy white apron. "Perfect," I say.

"And I'll bet you know about dogs too," says Marsha.

He looks to see if she's serious. "Some."

Marsha blinks, then turns on the winning Marsha smile, all soft cheeks and even, Chiclet teeth. "We've been trying to find a dog that's right for our daughter. We were looking at some Airedales, and they seem too high-strung."

Stanley nods in agreement. His eyes have been taking in Stella. "You like catsup?" he asks her.

Stella smiles, cradled deep in Marsha's arms. "Yep," she says, tiredly.

"Ever hear of an assistance dog?" He goes back on his heels with his arms across his expansive chest, hands just locking on the opposite elbows.

None of us has.

"Specially trained. I mean, trained to help out their owners."

"How?" I demand.

"They pick things up for you, or pull heavy things around. Lady in town here, sweet old thing, but she's, you know, in a wheelchair and all, and her dog, Skeeziks she calls him, can bring the phone to her when it rings, and it gets her shoes for her. . . ."

"You're not serious," says Marsha.

"They're wonderful dogs," says Stanley, warming to the topic. "Open a refrigerator or the front door. Just great."

"They must cost a lot, huh?"

"No, no. Free. There's an organization that trains 'em,

they pick 'em out at pounds and test 'em, and those that seem good they train and then just give 'em to people who need 'em."

He comes back later with a note with the name of an organization written on it. I clutch it all the way to the car. Stella is falling asleep in her mother's arms. "Mom, you kissed that guy," she says, dreamily.

"I'd do it again," says Marsha.

I hold the door to get them settled in the back. Jack gets in on the passenger side. Assistance dogs, there are such things? I reach for the driver's door, and just as I touch the handle the sun comes out and floods the earth with light.

T WEN T Y - T W O

I'm trying to tie my tie in the bathroom. I'm all thumbs, nervous as a kid before a prom. I sigh, fidget, reknot, because I can't remember exactly how it's done. Below my raised chin a mild rash is forming where I've shaved too closely. In the next room, in contrast with my little bathroom drama, all is peace. Stella plays the marimba—*bonk, plink-plink, bonk . . . pumb, pumb . . .* and next to her, at my last sighting, lies Sirius, a long grayish dog with a boxy snout and perfectly round eyes beneath shaggy brows. He is a kind, calm animal, very polite, with several interesting habits; for example, he usually listens to Stella's playing with his lower jaw flat against the floor—to pick up the vibrations through the floorboards, Marsha thinks.

I'm on my way to work, Day One of the new job, and I realize that I am not happy with this situation. My time with Stella will now be reduced, and in return for that I get the unsatisfactory prospect of a diminished role at my old place of work. I try to stay positive, but I'm feeling lonely and a little abused, and ashamed to feel so. In fifteen minutes, Dorie will arrive to take over Stella's care. The fact still rocks me, keeps my fingers from remembering the process for executing a four-in-hand. I can't believe our luck, but I'm nervous that it won't work out, that Stella will throw fits and Sirius will suddenly become rabid. There! The tying end *is* supposed to come around the front one more time. I slip the knot so snugly against my chin that soon the blood pounds in my temples. In the mirror, a very short man with a red face and short graying hair stares back at me. There's nothing to be done about any of that, so I turn to go.

In the front room Stella plays on while I talk to her. She's heard it all before. She knows what's in the fridge, and yes, she'll be good for Dorie.

"And the phone numbers are on the bulletin board next to the phone," I insist on adding.

Sirius raises his head and looks at me as if he disapproves of my intrusion. When he cocks his ears this way, the pointed tips just bending forward, he looks a little like Tramp in the Disney cartoon. In fact, his face often wears a slightly puzzled expression, as if he's trying to figure things out but doesn't have quite enough brain power. That must be a dog's lot: a great deal of stimulation and responsibility without quite the intelligence to sort it all out. Not so different from my present state.

"Okay, okay," I tell them both, then sit in the living room and wait for Dorie.

At some point, Stella looks in at me briefly, then looks down at her marimba again. *Plink-plink, pumb . . .* her thin torso, propped on tush and backs of thighs, is curved in a perfect C. "You look nice in your suit, Dad."

"Thanks, sweetheart."

"Siri thinks so too."

"Seriously?" I laugh, but the joke is already old. (My

nervousness has pulled it out one more time.) When we introduced the new dog to Dorie during one of his first walks, she said, "Serious? That's perfect. He *looks* serious." But then we had to explain that Sirius is the name of a star, and the brightest one in the heavens. Stella had thought of Capella at first, but we thought that because the name was so similar to hers the dog would be continually confused and, besides, Capella would be better for a girl dog. We went to Heddie next, because Hoedotus I and II are the names of Capella's baby goats—but Stella had already named her stuffed bear Heddie, and she thought that it would be disloyal to give the name away. Sirius is also in the Canis Major constellation, the dog constellation—and it *is* the brightest of all stars.

I hear Dorie's boots scraping eagerly on the mat outside the front door and hurry to let her in. Her pink-and-white face is there beneath the big fur hat. She has books in her arms, and records with heavy plastic library sleeves. "I found some great stuff," she announces before even getting in the door.

I am compelled to warn her right away. "Now, go slow, Dorie. It's just . . ."

"Oh, don't worry," she says, pushing me gently aside. (I have forgotten to step back to allow her to come in.) "We'll just take our time and go with the flow. Or we won't, and we'll make lots of fun mistakes and learn from them!"

I shake my head. "Where have you been all our lives?"

Stella appears, then Siri. Siri seems to recognize Dorie; at least his puzzled look has given way to a kind of surprised smile. He looks up at her; his long tail with its fringe of charcoal grey fur sweeps back and forth from his lean rump. Stella leans on his back like someone waiting for a drink at a bar, elbows pushing her shoulders up, head lolling comfortably, feet crossed. "Hi, Dorie," she says, casual as a sailor.

I get out the door, my fingers mentally crossed. The car starts; that's good. I back out of the driveway, throw the car into drive, head out. How long can this card castle hold? One week ago, Dorie and Jack came over for dinner (he'd even put off his trip a week just to see the dog episode through). All during that dinner, Dorie acted tense, laughing a little too quickly, even for her, and then going silent and gazing at Stella. I would have thought her staring insensitive if it hadn't been suffused with something akin to admiration. And she had questions for Stella too: "Do you like to read? Would you show me the star book?" And she was a willing audience for Stella's incessant demands of the newcomer, Siri. Showing off, she had Siri demonstrate his skills again and again, fetching her slippers from the closet, or continually slurping her fork, which she kept dropping on purpose, from the floor and returning it to her.

I didn't know then that Dorie was further testing waters that she had already tested in her mind. Finally, with Stella in bed and the adults drinking coffee, Jack cued her and it all came out. She said that Jack had mentioned the problem of getting someone to stay with Stella for three afternoons a week and Dorie wanted to apply for the job. At first, neither Marsha nor I could say anything, but that was just as well because Dorie had prepared a case and wanted to present it.

She lived alone, now, with her younger son, Bill, Jr.,

away at college on the West Coast, and her job at Raytheon was flexible enough so that she could move hours around and only lose a few a week—which we could make up in payment to her or not, it made no difference to her. Her mortgage payments were low, her divorce had left her on a sufficiently solid footing. And, surprise, she used to teach grade school before she got pregnant with her older son. She ended by saying that she liked and admired Stella a great deal and felt it would be a privilege to stay with her three afternoons a week. Then she sat back, picking at her napkin.

I sat speechless, Jack grinned, and Marsha started to cry. Stella came out of her bedroom, one mitt stuck in one eye, with Siri stepping dutifully behind. "You're talking about me," she accused.

I got to my feet and stood behind her, bending over her and patting her chest with the palm of one hand.

"We were only saying good things, Stella," said Jack.

"Why is Mommy crying?"

No one answered at first, so I offered, "Because she's very, very happy."

And then Stella went to the table and leaned against it in that way in which I suppose she has come to lean on things. Sort of solidly, comfortably, elbows as pinnings. I remember how she stood there, the four adults and one dog loosely surrounding her. I remember thinking, *It takes so many people to raise one child.*

But as I maneuver my Subaru wagon around the last corner to the big parking lot near the subway station, I find I'm thinking again about how Stella stood that evening, leaning against the table, and then again, leaning against Siri. I'm halfway into town on a nearly deserted train (who else goes to work at this hour?) when I remember that my father stood that way. Not often; in fact, perhaps only once or twice . . . And then I remember that it was a specific time, a time when I was sent in to get him at a bar.

My father was not a drinker, or not a heavy one. He came home nights, or usually did, but I now remember that there was a period very near the end of his life when he did not. My mother and I would be alone at supper, or my father would come in and then go, and this was in the gradually deepening period of their silence with one another. I have not thought very much about this period, but now it seems very important to remember that night. At the table with my mother, the food on the stove, the clock on the wall frozen in time . . . All at once my mother got to her feet and began getting us into our coats. I followed her orders as scarf and hat and coat were whipped onto me. Then we were in the car, and driving.

"Where are we going, Mom?" I ventured to ask.

"We're going to find your father."

"Where is he?"

"We're going to bring him home." She was about to say more, then hesitated, then spoke: "Where he belongs."

She rolled our wide family car right up to the door of a tavern with two bright-colored neon signs, one sputtering, in broad windows with curtains covering the lower halves.

"I'll wait here," she said. "Go in the door there and see if he's in there. If he is, tell him I need to see him."

I didn't think twice. I'd seen that look, or firm lack

of look, on her face before. She had stewed to a dangerous point, and could boil over now and blister the listening ear. When my mittens slipped on the door handle, her hand shot across me and yanked it up. The wide door fell back to reveal the bare sidewalk that moved in giant squares to the front door of the bar. I walked across each square to that door, and then waited as if I supposed it would open by itself. It did. Someone came out and I had to move back a step to let the door swing free. Two men stared down at me, surprised, then calmly stepped aside as I walked directly between them.

I went into the bar, into its smoke and noise, the sound of sports roaring from a TV hung from the ceiling. A knot of men with beer bottles and cigarettes balanced in their hands stood below the TV and looked up at the screen. As I watched, a few of them shouted at it. And there was a man leaning against the bar, just as Stella had, his elbows comfortably pinned to either side of a nearly empty pint of dark beer. He had not seen me yet. He had a leaning, easy manner, and a broad smile that stayed and stayed on his face as he listened to others and muttered and smiled broader still. Gradually I realized that this man was my father.

Then he saw me, and his face changed. The smile fell away. In detectable stages, a stiffness returned to his body, pulling his elbows up from the bar and forcing him to come erect. He stared at me and was again the quieter, more intense man I knew as my father. A new smile came onto his face, a terrible one to see because it was false and strained and it reduced him in a way that shamed me for him. I understand now that he felt how deeply trapped he was, and that there was no real escape for him. He was a man with an unhappy wife and a shriveled son (the proof publicly before him). He stood there, facing his lot, and I was a part of it.

I began to cry. I didn't know what I was doing there, didn't know what to say. As for my father, I could see him pulling deep within himself, pushing aside his great self-sadness and finding the place where he loved me. He huffed up.

"Well, Jim," he said. "Are you lost?"

"Is that yours, Mike?"

"He's mine! Come to fetch me, I see." He walked toward me, and I stood rooted and crying.

Would he let me hug him? I needed desperately to be affirmed, to be owned as his. He took me up in his arms and I tried to hide against his chest.

"Fine boy," said someone, kindly but without conviction.

"He is," said my father, almost a shout. Then, quietly, just to me. "Not a pleasant task, huh, Jimbo?"

He started to pay up, but someone waved him off. As we headed for the door, to return from his short-lived freedom, he called over his shoulder, "Duty calls, gentlemen!"

At the car, he placed me in the backseat and then got in himself. He said nothing as my mother dropped the car into gear and pulled out quickly from the curb.

"It worked, didn't it?" she said, as if he'd said something.

Silence. Then, my father: "So we'll ruin his life too, is that it? You should have seen him in there, half embarrassed to death."

"Better to have a father at home, wouldn't you say?"

"Depends on the home, wouldn't you say?"

Silence again. Perhaps they'd realized that their words were falling on a child's ears and concluded that quietly moiling resentment was preferable to honest shouting. My mother won that battle; my father was home more often, but in the end we all lost.

As my train nears Boston, I seethe at my dead mother for sending me into the bar like that. I'm certain there were many birds to be killed that night with her one stone: my father's absence, the powerlessness of her place, and the bond between him and me, which she envied so deeply. I am angry at this moment, angry at both of them for electing to walk about hurt and silent rather than having it all out, out in the open where we could deal with it—and angry that I was shut out of it, as if I could only be a little victim and not a full person with ideas and support and love to give. I could have helped.

I grow smaller and smaller in my mind as I reach the next to last station. I do not like to be angry at my father; it's a completely new feeling, a shock to be experiencing it. But I *am* angry—because I realize that he did not take care of himself, he did not see to his own happiness. We had it good, he and I, but didn't he see that we could have had it better still? If he thought he had a great son, well, I could have shown him what a truly great son he had—if he'd given me a chance. But he went into himself, and he hid a large portion of himself away from us. He was a good man, with very unusual qualities— the very ones that had drawn my mother to him in admiration. But when the impasses appeared, as they must—as they *must*—he did not recognize that kind of living as life anymore. In his decentness, he characterized his home life as duty; he directed great dignity and seriousness my way. I am grateful, but I am resentful that the broadly smiling man whom I glimpsed at the bar that night had lived in another part of the world from me. I see now that he came to me when he was ready, that he stayed on longer at the job on his darker days, stretching out his time away from us, and orchestrating our relating around moments he could control. It's so obvious to me now, perhaps because I'm ready to see it, that we shared few spontaneous moments. We stayed stuck in our home. We did not go to sports events or museums or on picnics, and I think the accumulating disappointment of our narrowed life grew to a great anger in my mother. On Sundays, she and I went to church together, without my father (he worked on our house on Sundays), and I remember how she sat with her head bowed and her hands clasped tightly as we sat together in the back pew.

Out on the familiar but strange streets of downtown Boston, I feel small, small, small. I am beginning to suspect that so much of my success is due to my own strength, and that pleases me. But I also know that I am not up to walking up the imposing stairs of the federal building and back into the confusing relationships I thought I'd neatly left behind. I vow to myself that I will not make my father's mistake: I will not be alone in this world. I need help, everybody does. I don't have a clue where I will get it on the steps of the federal building, but I do know that at the other end of this awful afternoon I have a wife with a brain as big as her heart and a kid with courage enough for an army.

I'm turning in circles in front of the building and petrified that inside I'll run into someone I know. A hale and hearty greeting would reduce me to a sack of dry leaves. I head across the street, loping with my head down as if someone's about to open fire. I find myself within a familiar coffee shop, which I recall has a phone booth in the corner.

I reach Helen, Howard's secretary. No, he's not in his office at the moment, but he'll be back soon for our meeting.

I take a breath. "Helen, I don't think I'm ready to come in yet."

At first she's silent. Then she says, "Oh, I see."

"It's stupid, Helen, I know, but I think I need another day or two to myself."

"Of course, Jim. There must be so much going on at your house these days."

I leap on this. "Yes! A new schedule for my daughter, and a neighbor taking care of her. And we got a dog, Helen, a new dog!"

"How nice. That certainly is a lot, Jim."

"Can I leave it to you to explain to Howard? I don't really want him to know I've got temporary cold feet. I mean, that's what we're talking about here, Helen."

"Leave it to me, Jim. I'll just tell him that it's the first day with the new sitter and you needed to break her in. Should I tell him that he can reach you at home if he needs to?"

I think for a moment. "No, I won't be home, Helen. I don't know what you should tell him."

She laughs. "I'll think of something, Jim. Maybe

you're out buying some special supplies to get the sitter started."

"That's good. I'll see you soon, Helen. You're great."

She laughs again. I know what she's thinking: *You men. Always so serious.*

I sneak out the back of this restaurant (it is frequented by people I have worked with), and head further uptown to the shops along the Boston Common. Across from the subway station with its green copper roof, I find a restaurant with a corner table, and there I sit and sit and drink coffee and feel mad about my father. There is a circle to be broken here. It is clear that I will not, as my father did, duck out of life by an early death. What little control I have over this I vow to exercise. But my daughter too must be saved from life-threatening aloneness; she may live beyond the point when most epidermolysis victims die; she may grow older and even decide to live alone—and may even *feel* alone, but must never allow herself to *be* alone. I am realizing more strongly than I ever have before the element that plain luck has played in my life. Back there in that statistics class, fifteen years ago, what if Marsha Willis had not come after me? What if she had taken no for an answer and left me to languish in the back of the class—as I languish now in the back of this restaurant? How many Marsha Willises can one expect to stroll into one's life? I could be sitting here without my family at this very moment—a man with only a job for his life.

This must not happen with my daughter. Her parents won't be around forever, and then . . . But then I think: *She got herself that dog.* Slowly, I begin to smile, then grin—thinking back on Stella's long quest for Siri. She wanted a dog, and she never stopped, just kept going and going until she got one. I think of her leaning on Siri's back like a sailor on leave, and all alone at my corner table I grin so hard it hurts my face.

T WEN T Y - T H R E E

We have had only five weeks before the day of the operation, and now it is upon us. It is half past five in the morning and still dark. Marsha keeps Stella's mind pleasantly occupied by checking over the little bags and bundles that are to accompany her to the hospital— there's a special new bag with brand-new pajamas in it—tricks by which Marsha manages to press little gusts of fun into the otherwise anxious atmosphere of our home. Meanwhile, I am nearly useless. I wander about from room to room, picking things up and putting them down again. Soon Stella will go into the hospital for her prep for the operation; then, at nine, she goes under the knife. These facts are big and weighty, and the adults can do only a little to lighten them. Our helplessness keeps conversation terse and tilts our smiles queerly. Only Siri seems effective. He hangs near Stella and receives her pats and poundings and lunging hugs with his usual grateful surprise. At breakfast, he lies on the floor near her chair. Once, in the midst of one of our more pregnant silences, he gets to his feet and barks sharply.

It's as if he's shouted, "Enough!"—and we all laugh. Released, we start getting ready to go. I take Siri outside and help him find a tree, and then a good spot to poop on under the privet hedge. All around us is the gray, wet chill of spring trying to happen. When we return to the house I find wife and daughter ready to go. Stella is warmly bundled, quiet and thoughtful—on the whole, acting in that "adult" way that children sometimes put on to deal with the unknown. Soon, Marsha is backing us all out of the driveway, Stella on my lap and Heddie on hers.

"Siri!" she calls sadly.

The dog has poked his head through the living-room curtains. He is barking soundlessly behind the glass, looking stunned and upset. Where are we all going? Where are we taking Stella at this hour? He is the most honest among us.

Then, all of Stella's questions, old and new, come pouring out during the drive to the hospital.

"Can I take Heddie into the operation with me?"

"I don't know," says Marsha. "We'll have to ask."

"Maybe she has too many germs, huh, Mom?"

"Maybe."

"Will I be able to play my marimba after?"

"Not right away, sweetie. Dr. Checkers says maybe only three weeks though."

Three weeks, I think. It will be terrible for Stella. An imprisonment. Marsha sighs. She must be thinking the same thing.

"I should have come back home," she says aloud.

"What?" It seems as if it's the first word I've uttered in ten minutes.

"You had a health plan. Now we'll all be off working . . ."

In my mind, I finish for her: ". . . while Stella's at home

with bandages on." But I say aloud, "Stella's used to bandages," and give my daughter's hands a squeeze. I've got my one hand around both of hers, where they are crossed over Heddie.

Marsha's mood, however, has settled deeply into her. Perhaps she's had to play the cheery role too often over the past few weeks and now her nerve is giving way. "We should have planned it better."

It's probably not a good idea to fill the air with regrets. It wouldn't take much of a dose of bleakness to frighten Stella. "We can't plan everything," I say, as blithely as possible. I give Stella's mitts a shake. "We're all together, and we love each other, and we'll help each other, and God will help us too."

"God'll be there, right, Dad?"

"Right there next to Dr. Checkers."

"Will Dr. Roth be in there?"

She knows that he will not be, but kids always wonder if there's been a change.

"No, honey. He's not an operating doctor."

At the hospital, it is eerily quiet. We traverse a wide waiting area spottily occupied by caved-in people. A few nurses are briskly traversing the floor as if pursued, or hurrying to scenes of pain and tragedy. The lights seem needlessly low, yellowish and lurid. We move toward the elevators, managing our baggage, plodding tentatively like refugees in the processing center of a strange new land. We have an entire enormous elevator to ourselves, but instinctively huddle in the square yard before one of the button panels.

"How're we doing?" I ask Stella.

She's staring at the closed door as the elevator moves

upward with hardly any sensation. "Good," she says, flatly.

We get off and a pleasant nurse hails us from behind a high reception desk. She's an older woman and wears one of those old-fashioned nurse's caps. The fact is comforting to me, as if she might usher us into an earlier, more hospitable world.

"I know your name," she calls out in a croon. "Stella Candy. Right?"

"Kaldy!" Stella shouts, coming forward.

The shout goes through me, because I can feel the rush of pent-up feeling that has been released in her. My heart starts up, hoping, hoping for the best.

The nurse whines, "But can't I call you Stella Candy?"

"Oh, okay."

"Stella Candy, Stella Candy," chants the nurse as she taps a keyboard and peers at a monitor through the lower half of her glasses.

"Is Dr. Cejka here?" Marsha asks.

"She'll be waiting for you in the operating room," says the nurse.

"What about Dr. Roth?" asks Stella.

The nurse says, "He'll be here just before you go down."

"Is that right?" I ask in surprise.

"He'll be here," says the nurse with utter surety. "He told me he wants to be here so he's coming in early."

This is news, and good news. Stella's insistent curiosity has been vindicated; the three of us look at each other, smiling.

"You all are in room 304," says the nurse. "And that's the best room I got." She picks up a phone and calls for another nurse. Moments later, a slim blond nurse walks down the hall to us.

"Hi," she calls out. "Are you Stella Candy?"

"Word gets around fast," I say.

The reception nurse says, "This is LeeAnne, and she's in charge of you, Miss Candy."

LeeAnne squats down in front of Stella and points to Heddie. "Which one of you two is having the operation?"

Stella laughs. "I am!"

"Okay, then you're the one that I'll have to get ready. Come on, let's go see your room."

We go into a room with three other beds, but no one else is in them. The room is partially lit by indirect lighting, bulbs and tubes behind panels and long metal sconces that pick at the early-morning grayness. "We'll be full up before long," LeeAnne explains. She lifts Stella onto one of the beds. "Okay, this is your home for two or three days." She steps back and takes up a flat package. In her hands, it unfolds into a hospital gown, blue, with a big Mickey Mouse face on the front. His big grin opens, an explosion of indomitable good cheer. "And off with *all* of these clothes."

She starts to take off Stella's clothes, but a certain order of process is violated and Stella looks to Marsha.

"Do you want your mom to do it?"

"Yeah."

Marsha slips off her coat and steps forward. She finds a place for Heddie on the side table, then mother and daughter reenact a ritual years in the running. The hat, the sock-gloves, the foot socks, the outer cotton jersey . . . There is no hiding the thin, blistered Stella

Kaldy from us now. The chronic rupturing along her throat and around her ears, the flat, stiff patches on her skull, and a line of new virulent blisters across her back, stress-induced, the disease pushing up through her, meanly sensing the weakness that comes from her lately diminished appetite. Her ribs, her tiny shoulder blades— under the scabby flesh, pointy little chicken bones. It seems almost a wonder that life goes on in such a paltry little body.

The gown goes so far around her skinny torso that Mickey's ears disappear behind her. Perched on the edge of the bed, Stella looks down at herself, then reaches back and gathers the gown forward to partially open Mickey's face again. She looks up with a grin at this accomplishment, kicks her stumpy feet back and forth in the air. We smile at her.

LeeAnne says, "Okay, Stella Candy, we're going to start your prep now."

As if this announcement were a signal, activity starts up around us. First, another whole family comes in the door, and now we have two, then three, nurses moving in and around us. Marsha and I have to stow Stella's things, map out and hold our turf in a gradually populating space.

LeeAnne rolls up a blood-pressure gauge and wraps the black cuff round and round Stella's arm. While the cuff is in place, the nurse takes her wrist and feels for the pulse. Then the air goes out of the cuff—*hisss*—and the nurse proclaims, "You have a strong heart. We're going to start your chart right now." She makes a note on a board that has two hooks at the top. Then she lays Stella on her back, and reaching into the sleeve hole of the gown, slips a digital thermometer under her arm, and then walks out of the room with a promise to be back in one minute. We wait, Marsha and I in stiff plastic chairs, teasing Stella about having to lie so still. Heddie watches from the side table.

LeeAnne returns with a few items, a plastic bottle full of clear liquid and some small cellophane-wrapped packages. I look more closely: enema, syringes, swabs . . . Perhaps they keep the rooms dim so that these items will not be so noticeable. LeeAnne takes up the thermometer and proclaims, "Not bad," then makes a note on Stella's chart and hangs it at the foot of her bed.

The nurse then leaves us again, and this time we have a long wait. We have no reply for Stella's questions, which she asks still lying on her back. Finally, I get up and lift her to a sitting position. "I'm getting cold," she says. Marsha rises and the two of us get her under the covers.

"Not so fast there," someone says, and we turn to discover a huge man in a hospital suit coming toward us. He's got on something like a shower cap and in his hand he carries a white metal tool tote, a much smaller version of the kind my father used to carry around his work sites. In the tote are two plastic squirt bottles, some cloths, and more cellophane packages. "Are you Stella?"

"Yes," says Stella uncertainly. She peers at the man from between Marsha and me.

"Well, Boodles, I'm here to give you a shave. And it looks like you need one."

"Boodles!" says Stella. She smiles tentatively, pushing

back some tight lines that have gathered at the corners of her mouth.

"I call all my customers that. It's simpler." He starts unpacking his tote at the foot of the bed. "Ready for your shave?"

Marsha laughs. "She can't have that much hair."

"Doctor's orders. Got to shave her legs." He looks at Stella with round brown eyes. "Have you started shaving your legs yet?"

"No!" She moves a hand toward Marsha, who takes it in her hand and steps back to make room for the newcomer.

"I'm Mort the Shaver. My job is to shave everybody before their operations so none of their hair gets inside them. Know what I mean?"

"But I don't have any hair on my legs," Stella insists.

"Oh, yeah? You do, you really do." The big man looks like he needs a shave himself. He has dark shadow lines along his jaws. "You have eensy-teensy hairs on your legs." He squinches up his big body comically and holds his large fingers close to his eyes as if staring at a microscopic hair. Stella starts giggling. "Now how about a little privacy," he says, and reaches around and pulls a curtain on wheels into place.

"That's better. Now! Let's get to the gams."

"Gams are legs," I say.

"Gams, hams, gams, hams," says the man as he slips down the covers. "Okay, okay, this is gonna tickle." We step back to give him room as he lifts Stella's legs and gently presses the loose gown up around her crotch like a diaper.

"His hands are really *warm,* Mom."

"Hot Hands, they call me. Solar Palms, too. Reason they gave me the job. Sometimes Mr. Tickle. Mort the Shaver you already know." He has arranged Stella's bare legs in a comfortable narrow V. "Which name do you want to call me?"

Stella thinks. "Mr. Tickle!"

"Mr. Tickle it is. Now, for the magic potion." He is shaking a bottle with brown liquid in it. He squirts some into a plastic bowl and swirls a brush around in it. "Mix, mix, mix. I'm gonna give you a tan, Stella. First kid on your block with a tan. Here goes."

He begins to paint the small unscarred areas of her thighs with the liquid, starting high inside and working out to the fronts of them, stopping where the blistering begins. "That's *not* warm," Stella reports.

I stand above her, watching her, touching her cheek. I take the thin edge of what remains of her right ear between thumb and forefinger. The older she gets, the more these important little extensions will be eradicated, gradually erased by the inelegant healing that follows the blistering. If successful, the operation will allow her greater motor flexibility, but it will not restore her ears or the tip of her nose, or lay out a fresh line of delicate brow hair. As if Stella has sensed my thoughts, her eyes roll up to encounter mine, and I press back the pity that has begun to well within me. She has never wanted pity, never asked for it. She wants just the acknowledgment of her pain and the additional understanding it might require. I smile down at her, and she smiles up.

"There!" Mort says, stepping back. Stella's legs are glistening with the heavy brown liquid. "Now, Mort the Master Shaver will perform his great task.

This," he says, raising an instrument, "is my own special razor."

"It's pink!" says Stella.

"And note. It has Donald Duck on the handle."

It looks to me as if he's glued a piece of a toy to the razor handle.

"Omigod," says Marsha with a nervous laugh. "It does. What next? Goofy enemas?"

I stare at her. Mort snickers, just beginning to slide the razor along one of Stella's legs. "Pluto," he mutters Marsha's way, his eyes forward and concentrating.

Helplessly, I fall in with this irreverent humor. "They'll make his snout into a point and then Pluto can snuggle right up into . . ."

"Stop," says Marsha, holding back a laugh.

I'm beginning to giggle. "Fetch, Pluto, fetch," I whisper. "Good boy."

Marsha quietly cracks up. "Stop!"

"What's he saying, Mom?" Stella asks.

"Everyone's being bad, honey."

"Mr. Tickles, I'm getting cold."

"Almost done, sweetheart," he says, in a new tone. Deeper, quieter, almost loving. After each pass, he wipes the razor on a damp white towel. "There. Now you're clean as a whistle." And he whistles to prove it. He wipes her legs until only a faint brown shadow remains—"I'm leaving ya the tan"—then pulls down Stella's gown and walks off, still whistling.

LeeAnne comes in and asks if Marsha and I would please go to the front desk and speak with the head nurse. "They need you to sign some papers."

"What kind?" I ask.

"The standard releases. Dr. Roth might have told you about them?"

He hasn't. She looks a tad flustered and I suspect there's been a minor mix-up. I look to Marsha. "Releases," she says. It's a little ominous to the two of us that something might have been overlooked. I can see that Marsha too is remembering that we're entirely in the hands of human beings, imperfect by nature. "Would you deal with them, Jim?" she begs. Then she shakes her head. "No, we should look at them together." I nod, relieved.

"We'll be right back, Stella," I tell my daughter. But as we get to the door I look back and see that she is watching us closely. The bed dwarfs her; her mouth is open, her pink stumps lie on the covers like sleeping newborn puppies, her eyes watch us leave.

At the front desk the nurse explains that we need to sign several medical release forms. "We have to do this these days," she explains in a whisper. "It's legal permission from you to perform the operation."

"And so we won't sue you later," I say.

"Well, that is about it, I'm afraid. We'll be administering some medications to Stella soon, and we'll need to set her up with intravenous feedings."

"And so the risks really start now."

"Well, that's about it again." She smiles at us, and we smile back.

Marsha's eyes come up to me. She looks tired.

"Let's take a little walk," I suggest.

She nods, and we walk off, to nowhere really—just down the hall a few paces. She takes my hand. "Just tell me we're doing the right thing."

I think to myself, "Roth's a puzzle sometimes. Why didn't he give us these forms himself, and a week ago? He's ambitious, but maybe ambitious people are the ones who push back the limits of the possible."

But what I say is "They always have the nurses do the dirty work."

"Yeah."

We walk a little farther.

Marsha says, "She looks so pathetic in there, swamped in that bed. I couldn't look back just now, see her and Heddie all alone in there. She's so little to be so alone."

"Now don't get worked up," I say to her, but I'm saying it for my own sake too. Her remarks are hitting home. "Are we doing the right thing here?—that's the question."

"Yes."

"Yes, we are doing the right thing?"

"No. Yes, that's the question."

We walk on in silence. We can't stay away from Stella too long. "It'll help her if it works," I say.

"If she has a long enough life to enjoy it."

"It's healthier all around if we assume she will. And remember, it has to be done now before her joints get stiff."

"Unless they come up with another new procedure down the line, when she's older."

We've been over all this, but we need to put these questions to rest again—as if at this point things would stop moving forward. "They might not, and she might be weaker then. I think now's the time."

"She looks so alone in there."

"It'll pass. It'll be awful for a while, and then it'll pass.

And she'll be able to walk more easily and use her hands more easily." But I just don't like it that Roth himself didn't give us those forms.

As if reading my thoughts, Marsha says, "It's great that Dr. Roth is going to be here this morning. I think that means he cares, don't you think? I mean, he had to rearrange his schedule with his other hospital and plan to come in so early. . . ."

"Yes. It meant a lot to me when I heard he was coming."

Marsha squeezes my hand. I hadn't noticed that we were walking hand in hand. "How are you holding up?" she asks. We pass by open rooms, some with children and parents, some empty. In the hallways are carts with supplies and towels and gadgets stacked on them.

"Oh, I'm fine. You?"

She nods. "Better. Shall we sign those forms now?"

"I think we should, Marshmallow. I think Stella would want it. She's not one to take the easy way and miss out on some living."

Her eyes come up, the fine brown eyes with—with what? Longer lashes than I remember? Sometimes I have a pretty wife, I see. In those eyes, what? Deep feelings, love for me, for us all. She's aging; I can see that there are new lines around those eyes. She is smiling. We have been together for many years now. We come to a halt, we face each other, we kiss very lightly once, then twice, brief brushing kisses, and then her head leans to rest on my shoulder.

"I could never do anything like this without you," she whispers against my ear.

"That's just what I was thinking about you," I whisper back.

After one more second, we come apart and walk back to the desk, where the nurse is now on the phone and the papers lie on the counter before her.

We hear Stella calling. "Mom!"

"You sign," says Marsha. "I'll go." And she hurries off to Stella.

I stand before the forms, reading, thinking, wondering. . . . Then I take up the pen and sign in several places to give permission to the doctors to cut strips of flesh from my daughter's legs and sew them onto her wrists. I put down the pen with an audible click.

Back in the room again, I find Stella on her tummy with her tush exposed. Her face is away from me and toward her mother when I enter, but she whips her head around on the pillow. "I'm getting an enema," she explains to me. "LeeAnne says it will be 'comfortable for a minute."

"I see," I say, a little angry that the release signing took us away from her for the time it did. I take up my post on the near side of the bed and pat one of her hands. "I don't think you've ever had one before, have you?"

"Uh uh. This is my first one."

Stella sounds almost excited, but LeeAnne looks concerned. She has a dollop of lubricant on the tip of one finger, which she holds in the air above Stella's bottom; I can see that she is noticing the dark red excrescences that blossom malevolently in the shallow cleft.

Marsha explains to her, "She's been a little nervous this week, a little diarrhea, and that makes her skin very raw back there."

302 | *P. Carey Reid*

"I think it's going to hurt," says Stella, as if she's talking about someone other than herself.

"Let me do it," says Marsha, reaching for the tube of lubricant. LeeAnne steps back without a word, and Marsha squirts a long nurdle of the clear lubricant onto her finger. "It's going to be a little cold, honey," she tells Stella. Then she gently separates Stella's buttocks with one hand and touches the lubricant to the scabbed pucker at their juncture. Slowly she circles with her fingertips, working the substance in.

"Cold," Stella confirms.

"Does that hurt? No?"

"No, Mom."

"Okay, sweetie, I'm going to slip in the tip of the bottle now. And then you're going to feel filled up a little bit."

"You just roll it up from the bottom," says LeeAnne quietly, handing over the little bottle. Kid's size. To Stella she says, "It'll feel like you have to go to the bathroom at first, but then that feeling will go away."

I grip Stella's mitt just a tad more tightly as Marsha positions the tip of the bottle and then, deftly, slides it in and immediately begins rolling up the bottle, crooning "There, there, not so bad."

But Stella has jerked a little in my hand. Her face grimaces. It has hurt. She's felt it now, the first pain. And now she knows: there can be pain here, and there can be more of it.

Marsha slowly removes the bottle and keeps one hand pinching Stella's buttocks together.

Stella immediately whines, "I have to go to the bathroom."

"Just hold on," I say.

LeeAnne says, "It feels that way at first. Just see if you can wait a few more seconds, Stella."

"I'm Stella Candy," she responds, defiantly, her free hand sliding about on the sheet. If she had fingers, she could comfort herself by clutching at the bedclothes. Another of the many things she's denied, gripping to get a grip.

"Stella Candy, hold on."

Slowly, Stella relaxes, but her cheeks are wet with her first few tears of the day. On her own, she tries to turn over on her back, and soon we have her propped up. "We'll just wait until you feel you have to go again," says LeeAnne, "and then we'll get you into the bathroom . . . *for a big poop,*" she concludes with wide eyes that make Stella laugh.

Someone rolls a TV into the room and one of the families begins watching together. The voices of the morning-talk-show people sound surprisingly awake, as if they've all been up for hours. Perhaps the case. Stella wants to watch too, at first, but she settles for talking with us. Both Marsha and I have found chairs by this point, and we sit on either side of Stella, talking about Siri, about how it will be when she gets back home in a few days, how we'll all manage. Then, Stella stops talking and announces that she has to poop, really poop, and Marsha lifts her up and takes her into the tiny bathroom, where it's a tight fit for the two of them, and there Marsha bends over Stella and gently enjoins her, in accordance with LeeAnne's instructions, to wait, to wait, to wait until she really *really* has to go. Stella waits, the tip of one blunted hand to her stomach, monitoring the moiling in her bowels. Then she really _really_ has to go and Marsha closes the door and then there's a rustling and squeaking followed by lots of convincing sputters.

When Marsha leads Stella out, the child walks on weak legs, as if she's already had the operation. She feels the eyes of others on her. A boy her age, his face lit by television light, stares out at her toeless feet, which the gown does not hide. "Mom," he says, about to point, but the woman with him shushes him up. In my mind I calculate again, for the tenth time, how the cost of a private room would have pressed our expenses to a prohibitive level. My talent with numbers can be a curse.

But Stella's no slouch, she's got resources. She moves more and more quickly toward the bed, where I catch her up and get her under the covers. She does not look at either of us, but her demeanor telegraphs, _Okay, what next?_

The intravenous needle is next, and we have our first real crisis of this medical undertaking. The nurse who wheels in the bottle is short and square, moving with authority but with a big smile for Stella, and Stella smiles back, guardedly, until she realizes what's about to happen. At her first sight of the needle, she says, "She's not Mona."

"Who's Mona?" I say.

"The lady, the one that sings."

"Who sings?"

"Oh," says Marsha. "She's talking about the nurse who took her blood that time. You remember, the first time we met Dr. Checkers."

Stella is beginning to panic. "I want Mona," she says again.

"She thought Mona would be here," I explain to the nurse with the IV bottle.

"Oh," she says.

"I want Mona, Mom," says Stella again, beginning to panic.

LeeAnne appears, moving in to take charge. She takes Stella's arm gently. As she talks, Stella starts to cry, resisting. But I notice that LeeAnne's grip on Stella's arm is tightening by degrees and the IV nurse is beginning to close in. Stella starts to wail. She's been shaved and jabbed and evacuated; she's had it.

"Dad," she wails at me. "Where's Mona?"

"I don't even know a Mona," says LeeAnne. Everybody seems fresh out of kindness. Marsha's been pushed off into the corner.

"Wait," I say. "Mona works on the third floor. I remember that."

"Yes, Hematology," says LeeAnne. "But it's only seven o'clock. Now, Stella Candy . . ."

"I think I know her," says the IV nurse. "But she works during the day only." I can see that she's trying a white lie.

Stella, whimpering and shuddering, looks to me. "Dad . . ."

"I'd like to just call down there, if you don't mind."

LeeAnne shrugs but stands in place. "It's better if . . ." she begins to say, but Marsha has interposed herself.

"We'll just make a call," says Marsha. "And if Mona's not there, then we'll just have to go ahead with Marie. Right, Stella?"

Marsha has come up with the other nurse's name by

reading her badge. Stella says, "Okay. But you'll call, right, Dad?"

"I'm going right now, honey," I say, and hurry off.

No one's at the front desk at the moment, so I can't use an interoffice phone. It's just as well because I'd feel more authentic coming back with a firsthand report. I find the stairwell, go down to the third floor, and come out into an area even darker than the floor Stella's on. I do find a few technicians working in one of the smaller labs, but I discover they do not know the "day crew," as they call Mona and her colleagues. Satisfied, I go back upstairs.

Stella looks disappointed when I come back alone. "Sorry, sweets. She doesn't come to work until much later."

Marsha runs a hand across Stella's brow. "Let's give Marie a chance," she says softly. "She looks very sweet."

Stella regards Marie, who, wisely, says nothing, but simply stands at the ready, hand on the bottle holder, and smiles. I can almost feel Marie's thoughts; she wants a chance to show her skill.

Reluctantly, Stella agrees, and within a few seconds her arm is down and dabbed, then jabbed. She grimaces. There is pain, and no magic Mona song to keep it away.

She lies there, deflating like a stuck balloon because she knew there would be pain and sometimes, as she's learning so quickly and much too early, we are alone with it. Despite Moms and Dads and all the others who might be hovering nearby, in the end we are alone with it.

TWENTY-FOUR

I'm on the road with Milo and Jennifer, tooling about the north country in a government car. It may come to nothing, visiting buildings and asking questions, but we have a solid suspicion that we want to test out. At the very least, we *feel* as if we're doing something. And I've got to be doing something these days because I'm no longer sure what I'm supposed to be doing, and mere movement must do for the moment. It's an idea I've gotten from hanging around with my postoperative daughter—who goes, goes, goes these days and will not stop. This is the first morning in a long time that I've beaten her out of bed, and only because I had to pick up Jennifer downtown by seven to be in Manchester, New Hampshire, by nine so that Milo could drive us out to Keene in time for a full day's work.

I sit in the backseat of the nondescript car, more than mildly distracted by the fine-stranded hair of Jennifer's dark head. When she slipped into the car as I stopped before her house earlier that morning, the whole dewy aura of her freshly showered self eased upon my consciousness like a cubic yard of iron. It's needing the artificial confirmation of a pretty woman's approval, I know that—and a dose of plain ordinary lust. I conclude that life is pushing me around like a bully in a schoolyard, and more and more lately. I wonder who I am at times. I feel that I am buried beneath cloying layers of responsibility. Perhaps because my life keeps changing so much I'm thrown off, psychically, and made to wonder what I am meant to do on this planet. I blush later in the backseat of Milo's government car when I catch myself in yet another ridiculous fantasy of Jennifer, naked, loving me, the two of us struggling in a motel room in a small northern New Hampshire township. . . . Too easily these images slide into my mind as I'm driven passively along, the fragrance of Jennifer's body spicing the spring air washing in through the windows.

I can push Jennifer from my mind, I tell myself. I have the will power. I distract my mind with a question: *What else would you do (besides make a pass at Jennifer DiAngelis) if you had a freer life?* I remember instantly that for years I have wanted a workshop set up in our single basement room. A big, heavy table with a vise attached, and a peg board with tools hanging within their painted outlines, and plenty of outlets, and a big twin-tube fluorescent hood throwing down a bright shadowless light. I always thought I would build things as I once did with my father, but now I wonder if the old skills would even return. Passing beyond the oily outskirts of Manchester, I think of the many things I would build: storage boxes that slide under beds on wooden wheels, cedar chests to hold the wool blankets in the summer, a long table in the basement for folding laundry. The growing list makes me cluck aloud.

Jennifer hears and her head comes up and around from a stack of documents in her lap. A bit of window light gleams on the bright iris of her left eye, but I avert my own eyes quickly. I do not want her to ask what I'm thinking about, and presently her head goes back to her work.

What I'm thinking about now seems embarrassing to me, as if I've been caught feeling sorry for myself. Though I did not choose to have an afflicted child, I chose to have a child. If I did not consider all the risks, they were not hidden from me; my own life could have served as a warning. Now I'm a father—a husband, the father of an afflicted child, and a part-time financial analyst. This ragged list strikes me as curiously full at one moment, and a patching of half-assed achievements in the next.

We pass the sad lawns facing the highway. Some residents have stuck exotic plastic animals in the dirt, as if a flamingo would come anywhere near this strip of dust and grease. Once, when I was little, my father came home with a homemade lawn ornament that he'd found discarded at a renovation site. It was a board cut in the shape of a chicken. It was a bit larger than a real chicken and painted on one side to look like one. "We'll make a puzzle of this, Jim," he announced. On the back porch, he set up the jigsaw, then drew looping lines across the front of the board. Snapping on the saw, he carefully fed the board through it, again and again, until he'd reduced it to a pile of pieces. When he'd sanded the edges of each one, he presented them all to me, and the new puzzle quickly became a special toy.

I was very young, perhaps only three or four, but I remember taking out the shoebox with the wooden pieces again and again and reexperiencing the wonder

of assembling it, gradually and with comforting predictability, into a whole chicken. In time, the matter
became too easy, so one morning, arbitrarily, I began
assembling the puzzle upside down. I was nearly done,
with only two pieces still in hand, when I noticed something surprising: the remaining hole, in the very center
of the puzzle, was in the shape of a smaller chicken,
though now right side up. I sat and stared, holding the
two remaining pieces; then I fitted them together to
make the littler chicken they were. I caught my breath
and ran to my father, outside on a ladder and poking in
the gutters.

"Dad, Dad!" I called and held up the two pieces.
"Look!"

He looked down, bits of leaf meal stuck to his cheek.
"So you've figured that out."

He knew already? I stood with the pieces in hand,
baffled, and he laughed to see my expression.

Is there always a plan? If I fit the puzzle pieces of my
existence together, do they amount to a complete life?
Or is it more the point that the pieces of our lives are
individual parts, each complete, that fit into the bigger
chicken composed of many other lives? If so, then we
are parts and wholes at the same time. The ultimate
solidity comes less from a private wholeness than the
integrity of each part we contribute.

It's job enough to be a good father. The truth is, it
gets harder and harder to be at work as Stella recuperates,
and now this whole day away from her. For one thing,
I worry about her. After the first few days, while she
lay stunned from the aftermath of drugs and trauma,
she got to her feet and, after a dozen or so uncertain

steps, lunged back into the world. At first Marsha and I just kept yelling at her, but the effects were only temporary; Dorie reports no better luck. The child forgets, begins to run, halts in pain, registers surprise, then runs again. Stella will not, cannot be slowed. We all worry about her depleting herself and getting an infection, of chafing the raw areas on her legs, or straining the stitches that tack down the grafts beneath her wrist bandages.

The instructions were clear enough. She is to rest, to be in bed early, to eat and sleep and let the tissues heal and her blood build up again; instead she wears herself down, and the rest of us with her, in headlong plunges into experience. What has happened? How can we stop her? She will not listen when we tell her to quiet down, to slow down, cringing as we witness her whacking her stitched wrists against this and that, or rolling on the floor with Siri, her bandaged legs flinging about. The poor dog has more sense than she; when she whispers hoarsely in his ear to go here or there or do this or that, he looks at her as if there must be some mistake. Only he, with his perplexed prancing in place, can slow her.

At bedtime she collapses. Through the day she gradually soars, higher and higher, then crumples under the covers. I wonder to myself if she is at war with her body; perhaps hope has been triggered in her at some elemental level, and she has answered to it, the results be damned. Her heavily bandaged hands are chrysalises, cocoons, like the scaly, pleated pouches she and I have found affixed to twigs: new potencies aching to be born. Or perhaps her cells have tasted death in the dark tinctures of the hospital rooms, in the acrid air and sopped-up blood, and now strain toward life.

But at what cost? I know only that I am helpless before my own daughter's energy. In the morning, the sound of her comic slippery trot precedes the ringing of my alarm clock. (Siri's clicking toenails gradually fall in step.) She, *she* must walk him in the morning, and as Marsha and I prepare breakfast, we take turns going to the window and shaking our heads as we watch our daughter stiffly pursuing her dog around the soggy back yard. Stella and I walk together every morning directly after our after-breakfast lessons, which she pushes to an early conclusion by wheedling and manipulating with an ineluctable childish canniness—"Oh, Dad, Dad! Look, Siri sees something outside." Now an excited whisper. "Let's go out and look. Want to?"

With those wide, hopeful eyes turned upon me, which of my many responsibilities—most now conflicting— should I exercise? Do I enforce the doctors' orders? Roth's nervous brow betrays him as he tells me, "I think it's all right. Those bandages are put on pretty tightly. . . ." The truth is, he doesn't know that much. None of them do. If they knew more, I'd have a beautiful daughter with skin rivaling Jennifer's. Those bandages come off tomorrow morning, in fact. Meanwhile, Marsha and I try to keep our trust in the doctors alive and hope that things will turn out all right. We watch Stella hurtling about, hold our breaths, and pray.

"It's wonderful," says Marsha, without conviction.

"Yes," I agree, without conviction.

What can we do, mere mortal parents?

A few nights ago, Marsha and I both came awake at the same time in the middle of the night and discovered

Siri standing with his front paws on the foot of the bed. Normally, he sleeps in Stella's room, and too often we find him up on the bed beside her. Now, here he is at the foot of our bed, smelling of the clinical shampoos that we periodically inflict upon him.

"I know what this is," said Marsha, laughing. "A family meeting."

Siri came over to me when called, grateful for the attention. I guessed that the poor guy didn't know what to do with Stella either—and he was not liking the tension in the air, the creased faces that apprised him when he and his charge engaged in what he had assumed was only play. I said, "He wants to know that we're all still friends." I patted his wiry head, let him lick me with my head on the pillow.

I went on to say, "I've been thinking. Maybe she knows what she's doing."

In the dark, I felt Marsha's shrug. "When you think about it, it's her damned life."

We started chuckling together, relieved. Marsha said, "Maybe we should just . . . get out of her way."

So I have become the holder of coats, the raiser of shades, the opener of doors. When I go to the front hallway to greet Dorie on her afternoons, Stella is there before me, excited at the prospect of a fresh adult to pummel with her demands. I greet Dorie and wave pathetically at my daughter. "Here she is. See what you can do with her."

Jennifer is watching me again. Pretty porcelain face, wide lips moist as berries. Beauty heals us, a gift that the beautiful must share; it's public property, spilling over into the lives of those who are denied it. Even Milo's white head looks beautiful, his pink scalp showing through.

"What *are* you thinking about back there?" Jennifer asks.

"What's the matter with him?" asks Milo, mock alarmed. "Is he gone off again?"

"Appears so." One of Jennifer's dark eyebrows raises its tapered end.

I grin at Milo's eyes perched in the rearview mirror. "It's hard to be away from my daughter these days."

"Why?" Jennifer asks, brightening. She turns half toward me, documents rustling in her lap.

I am about to talk about stitches and leukocytes, but I say instead, "Because she's so much fun to be with."

"I met her," says Milo. "She's a little terror. Into everything."

"It's worse now, Milo. She walks the dog four times a day and insists on visiting every bulb bed and budding branch in the neighborhood. She has cataloged all the snowdrops and crocuses in a mile-square area."

My companions laugh out loud in the front seat. "Get her a driver's license, Jim," Milo suggests.

"That's next, believe me."

"Are you, like, harnessing this?" Jennifer starts, uncertainly. I must admit that it is a kind of admiration that I see in her eyes at times like these. Childless, negotiating a shaky marriage, perhaps she regards me as successful in the deeper emotional ways that women value.

I try to play down my work with Stella, keep from boasting. "We're going to build a model of our neighborhood," I answer. Though I do not mention the scale of this undertaking—complete with papier-mâché trees, dyed Q-tips for flowers, real lichens for bushes, moss for lawns—Jennifer's eyes remain bright. I force myself to remember my workshop fantasy. With a workshop in the basement, I could build flower boxes, and planters, bring more of the world inside. I recall how it felt to put up those Homosote panels. The rasp of the saw thrilled in my wrist bone as I cut the one-by-two strips.

"What a project!" says Jennifer.

"A topographic model?" says Milo, incredulous.

We are a happy group, have been pulling together in fact for some time. At the office, I was wisely given a space up in Finance, off to one side as if it were always planned that way, and a whole floor away from Howard's and Jennifer's offices. People have been sensitive, they've given some thought to the potential awkwardness of my return and to the ways that I can best be effective. It turns out it was a good idea for someone to fill this role, for the role to be created, and perhaps for me to be the one to fill it. Gradually, everyone has looked to me to set the tone. I've called other regions to see how they're faring, and this is something that Jennifer did not have the authority to do, that would not have occurred to the auditors to try, and that Howard, with his penchant for discretion, would not have been willing to get involved in. What I've discovered from counterparts across the States is that our brand-new nationwide computer system is not so much bug-infested, as we've all been assuming, but mentally underequipped. Computer people are most often sales-people and are not motivated to point out weaknesses in their systems without provocation. I've not been studying our figures these days—everyone has done that to death—I've been studying the systems' programs, what they've been designed to do and what they leave undone. From what I have been able to determine, the largest single area of weakness lies in the programs' inability to distinguish between different kinds of space—office, storage, plant maintenance, and plain gross figures.

Maybe it's Stella's unbridled energy that's pushed me into these mysterious new sectors, even putting us adults on the road for this nutty hunt. Earlier this week, I got our own systems people together with Jennifer around my dark corner desk. I put it to them directly: "When reconciling a bill for payment, will the system apply specific types of space to the billing? For example, if a room's been painted, will it reconcile the square footage of the room's walls to the contract estimate?"

At first they said yes, they thought so, because in typical government fashion all contracts are based on measurable factors: even an estimate for painting could never exceed a certain cost-per-square-foot amount. But later, when pressed, they said that a bill *could* come in for thousands of square feet of painting and as long as the total did not exceed the total gross square footage of the building, regardless of what was actually painted and therefore to be paid for, the computer would generate a check.

"But the safety factor is the estimated amount of the contract," one of them hastened to point out. "That is, if anybody's watching."

Two days later, alone before a cup of coffee, the answer hit me like a silver bullet to the brain. I went down to Jennifer's office and said, "You know what I'm thinking? It's got to be sleaze."

"What are you saying?"

I lowered my voice. "When you consider everything, it *has* to be some kind of fraud. What does a computer do when you think it's working well?"

"It . . . computes."

I shook my head. "We *think* it computes, and therefore we think it's computing everything we need it to. But in this case, we've got programs that don't do that much."

Jennifer is not slow. "And if we think they're doing a lot, but someone else notices that they aren't . . . then you can slip them some bad figures?"

"Which we just haven't found yet."

Already, even then, it was mostly clear in my mind. It was just a matter of bouncing some scenarios off Jennifer's good brain. It would lead to this day, in this car, and by the end of the day it would, I knew, lead us to an answer. And the answer, unfortunately, would involve names of real people, people who needed more money—for a pleasure boat, a shotgun with a carved gunstock, or maybe an operation for a daughter.

Jennifer and I hashed out important details over coffee. "I wonder if there could be some breakdown at the beginning of the contract process," she wondered aloud. "The initial estimating."

I squinted at her over my cup. "No. We've looked over the contracts and they look good. I mean, the dollar amounts match the payment amounts very closely."

"But do the square-foot estimates match the buildings?" Bobby Marco would have been invaluable in such discussions, but he was up in a corner in Jennifer's office doing low-priority work, pending the outcome of his grievance. A loss.

"Most figures are checked by the buildings managers or their on-site foremen," I told her, beginning to push the point. "But in some cases they're only roughed in by our people, and then the contractors are left to fill in the blanks."

Jennifer nodded. "When the building is very far away from the field office."

"Right. Far away—from the buildings manager, the main foremen . . ."

"So we lose control. Now, let's build a model," she said. "Let's build crime as it *could* be committed given the gaps we know about in the system." Then her eyes went softer. "You're just trying to include me, aren't you? You've already got it figured out."

I shook my head. "I need your confirmation."

"It just clicks home: The system will accommodate bad figures, we've established that. But those bad figures must appear on a contract document. A contractor could pencil in those figures as long as the contract site is far enough away from the field office not to be checked directly."

"Right."

She shook her head, nearly sadly, it seemed. "You're a genius; it takes my breath way. We're talking about leased space in a small town far from Milo's office."

"I'm surprised we didn't think of this earlier. In leased space it's the landlord who's responsible for getting the work done, and that makes it even more unlikely that there'd be a government person watching nearby."

We had only to chart the largest concentrations of leased space in New Hampshire and then run a history of dollar amounts spent on those spaces. Marston, New Hampshire, jumped off the page. There were no federally owned buildings in the area, only a series of leased buildings spread across the town and its outskirts, and housing a surprising number of government agencies: Immigration, Bureau of Farm Administration, the Forestry Service, EPA. Our cost history showed dramatic increases over the last two years.

I'm brought back to the present by Milo's announcement that we have arrived at the outskirts of Marston. "I sure hope you guys are wrong about what we're going to find here."

"We're not," says Jennifer.

The drive has tired me, and my memories of heady meetings with Jennifer has left me with an erection. I try to deflate it by concentrating on the town. I see that it is small but scattered upon the generous north-country landscape. Soon a series of predictable downtown façades begins rolling by: hardware store, five-and-dime, interspersed with a number of shops named after their owners—Bob's Collectibles, Fran's Hair Salon. Milo knows the town and quickly gets us to the first lease, Health and Human Services. We breeze in and faces come up from among handsome work stations formed from low blue-gray partitions of sound-damping composition. Four people are busy—it's midmorning—but not pushing it as they might in Boston. A thin man in shirtsleeves and loosened tie, a short, graying woman in stretch polyester slacks and blouse, a gruff woodsy man, bearded and wearing jeans. A younger man who could be a student intern; it's a college town.

The director has been expecting us. He's a short, round man with suspenders and a bow tie, an attempt at nattiness that would work only for a thinner, taller man. He greets us quickly, then he sends his secretary, the graying woman in polyester, out to get coffee for us. Jennifer bristles slightly, but even in Boston a lot of the boys still don't get their own coffee. It's not a long meeting; we did not expect that it would be. We ask about all physical work done on site in the last three years, and the man's recall is good. Everything checks out: walls were painted, rugs were laid—not many, it happens, but those that were supposed to be laid were laid. He initiated the requests for the work, Milo's office got permission from the regional office, the lessor got the work done through contractors, and the work was inspected and approved for payment by Milo's nearest people—the maintenance foreman in Concord. At the end of our interview, we politely ask permission to do measuring.

I walk a measuring wheel across rugs, and Milo runs a metal tape up the walls. Jennifer insists on doing some of the measuring too. We discover that there is indeed fat in the contracts, ten percent more space here and there than there actually is. "Could be the contractor's usual insurance margin," says Milo. "Carpet waste, buying paint in full gallons." I nod, Jennifer nods.

Until a late lunch, we ply a series of visits on the quiet town. Every contract is fat, more square footage than actually worked on but never more than the gross square footage. By four we are still on schedule, and only Combined Recuiting is left.

"It's actually a pretty big office," says Milo, heading us downtown. "It's the biggest storefront space in the area, that's for sure. That's how they fill up the armed services these days, off-the-street recruiting in small towns."

"Huh," I say. I'm interested, but fatigued.

Inside are only a Navy and an Army recruiter, both clean and eager young men. "The Air Force guy took off!" Navy exclaims with a grin. They laugh like high school kids out early. "But we can answer for him."

I notice that they are taking in Jennifer very carefully. They don't know what to make of her—federal brass, but so pretty. "What's your job, ma'am?" Army asks politely after we're all seated around a conference table in a separate room.

Jennifer tells him, keeping her voice even, her face opaque. "Have you gentlemen been here long?"

"Gentlemen," says Navy. "That's us! And we're at your service."

Army leans toward her. "I've been here about a year, ma'am. And my assistant here for nearly three." He laughs at his own joke.

"Three years?" says Jennifer, eying Navy. "You look so young."

"Came in fresh outa college, ma'am," he explains, turning pink. He's flattered by the attention, but disappointed to be caught with so few years.

They're both pretty sharp. Navy remembers everything about the space renovations, which were actually fairly sizable. "When the all-volunteer army came into effect, recruiting had to become more aggressive," he explains. "Videos, glossy brochures, and expensive TV commercials . . . Our turn here eventually came up. Couldn't have a recruiting office looking like an old bus station."

"Anything unusual happen during the renovations?" Milo asks Navy.

Navy's hands clap on the Formica tabletop. He shrugs. "The owner came by with the contractor, they scratched their heads a lot, and then guys came in and rewired and replumbed and patched and painted and put down the rugs. It went like clockwork."

"Except for the rugs," says Army.

"What rugs?" I ask.

"Remember?" Army says to Navy. "The rugs in the basement you told me about?"

"Oh yeah!" says Navy, and scowls. "For the longest time there were three huge rolls of carpet in the base-ment. We finally called the owner about it, but on the day he came out we went down there and damned if they weren't gone."

We ask a few more questions, then set out to measure. Afterward, the three of us huddle in the waiting area. Jennifer punches the calculator and I make quick notes on a legal pad. Something looks wrong, so we recal-culate. "Nothing fits," she concludes.

"It's fat by at least twenty-five percent."

Milo blinks. "God, that's way off."

"This is where the bad guys killed the golden goose," I say.

The boys are hovering close, so we instinctively pack

up to go. Navy says to Jennifer, "We could use a recruiter like you, Miss DiAngelis."

"Guys would sign up in mobs," says Army.

They hurry their flirting as we get to the door.

"You're already in Navy blue, ma'am."

Out on the street we stand around the car, sighing and fidgeting at the measurement figures, Milo sneaking one of the cigarettes we won't allow him to smoke in the car. "It's frightening," says Jennifer for us all. "I can't believe that we actually found what we knew we'd find." But she's excited too.

"Why the rugs in the basement?" asks Milo. He looks a little pale.

I'm thinking, looking off into the strange townscape, familiar shapes and objects in an unfamiliar configuration, like an old puzzle turned on end. "Insurance," I say. "The contractor puts in an estimate based on inflated measurements then waits to see if anybody notices. If somebody discovers that he's put in costs for enough carpeting for every flat square foot in the building, including the kitchenette, the bathrooms, even the damned basement, then he needs the actual carpet there to confirm his 'honest' mistake. After the Treasury checks come in the mail, he just needs to sneak back one night and scoop up the extra paid-for carpet."

Milo groans. "I can't believe it."

"And use it somewhere else," says Jennifer. "A double payment for materials they never used."

"And the labor too," I put in. "That's also figured by the square foot."

Milo leans against the car. Abruptly, he flicks away his cigarette butt and yanks the door handle. "Let's get out of here. I know these contractors and it makes me sick."

We remain silent for many miles. Then Milo looks at me in the rearview mirror. "I guess Howard will have my head over this."

"Why?"

"It'll come down that somebody had to let this happen, and field-office managers are the local contract managers of the region."

I nod. "You might get your hand slapped, but it's more of a system problem. By the way, what kind of person is your Concord maintenance foreman?"

Milo sighs. "I know what you're thinking. He's got to be the anonymous caller."

"What are you two saying?" asks Jennifer.

"He's a damned good man, but addled. I guess he was getting puzzled over all these approved figures flying around . . ."

". . . which he suspected were phony," I add.

". . . and got worried enough to call his state rep."

"He probably thought he'd be helping you," says Jennifer.

"That's what I think," I say.

She looks over her shoulder and smiles at me. Her eyes, still so bright after this long, hard day, hold to mine for a fraction of a second longer than two colleagues would normally allow.

Back in Manchester, we part from Milo in the parking lot. "Remember," I tell him, "the guilty ones are the guys who stole." He smiles gratefully, but does not appear entirely comforted. He goes off with a few final words and a sad wave from his car window. Then Jennifer and I get into my car and start the ride home.

At first, we jabber about the success of the trip, plan how to break the findings to Howard, worry about Milo, then fall silent. We have talked ourselves to the edge of Boston, but now a kind of anxious silence holds the small atmosphere in the car's interior.

Jennifer sighs and says, "I'm too worked up to go home right away. You want to get a drink somewhere?"

I nearly say yes; in fact, my lips open to form the word. But what would this drink really be but a prolonging of the agony I'm putting myself through by indulging this silly crush I have on this pretty woman who happens to be much younger than I and married besides? What would we talk about while I and she, if I'm not completely mistaken, leave our most pressing feelings unexpressed? "Sorry, I can't," I say. "I want to get home before Stella goes to bed. Her bandages come off tomorrow and she'll be nervous."

Jennifer laughs a little, probably relieved to have her offer turned down. "Can I say something? I wish I'd had a father like you."

"You probably did. I'm pretty good at advertising my good side."

She looks over at me and laughs. Good, the tension is easing up. At some level, we understand each other. We're growing up more by the minute.

In a few miles we are at her house. "We did it," she says. "We caught the crooks."

We shake hands, and then, before I can react, she pulls herself closer to me and presses her lips onto mine. I experience a shocking warmth and softness, and then the lips are gone. "I had to do that," she says.

I stammer, "A celebration," stupidly labeling what cannot be expressed in words. Already she is out of the car, moving smoothly up the walkway. At the door she fits her key to the lock, then turns and waves me on.

I wave back, red-faced yet. One kiss has reduced me to a fool.

"Good, good," I say aloud as I gun away from the curb. I have been given a taste of the full foolishness I might have been in for. Happily, I head the car toward the house where I live. The roads gradually thicken with familiarity, structures and trees and road signs that pull me right, then left, then right again until the car finds the turn at Pleasant Street and, just before the circle of underwatered bushes, noses into my driveway and comes to a stop.

T WE N T Y - F I V E

"D ad," says Stella in a hushed whisper, "the stars are out. *All* of them."

She points to the window with a newly bandaged mitt, slimmer, whiter than a day before. The wrist is still thick, the swelling down but not down as much as Roth would have liked. But in Stella's eyes are mischief and hurry. The night is full of stars!

"Honey, you're supposed to be in bed."

"But, Dad, it's warm out, it won't hurt me. And I didn't get to see you *all day* yesterday."

Little weasel. Manipulator. But the flattery works on me. How can I resist tiny bright-eyed Stella?

"Just a short one," she says, standing there like a string bean in a denim jumpsuit.

On this evening, in response to the stars so long hidden by a week of uncertain March evenings, Stella must go out. So out we go. And above us, Boötes walks the plow through the airy spring soil of the heavens. We make a strange plowman of him, Stella and I, teasing about the glittering tiara, the Corona Borealis, that hangs from his back pocket.

"He's bringing it to someone," says Stella, laughing. "A present?"

"For me! For Halloween I'll be a princess."

"You're going to have to wait a few months first."

"And behind the C'rona is Herc'les, right, Dad?"

"Yes. A small constellation for a big man."

"Why did they give him such a small one, Dad?"

"It's a mystery. I guess the size of the constellation didn't have to match the importance of the person." We walk on, passing the Lesters' heavy trees, their mostly darkened house. Here it is, nearly spring, and the Lesters are still hibernating.

"Herc'les doesn't get many stars, Dad, and that's not fair. He did all those things." She raises her two cocoon hands, and then lets them drop heavily on my shoulders. In my mind I wince, imagining the incisions separating.

"Do your hands hurt, honey?"

"Sometimes. Not now."

"Do you want some aspirin?"

"Nuh uh. But Herc'les has the biggest *star,* right?"

"Now that's true. He has few stars, not much size, and most of his stars are very dim—*but* he does have the biggest known star in his constellation. Not the brightest, but the biggest."

"That's good. What's its name?"

"I can't remember."

She looks up, mildly disappointed. "How did Herc'les die again, Dad?"

"Oh, it's kind of grisly, sweetheart."

"I don't care."

Of course not. She's just been sliced up.

"He was tricked by the Centaur. Hercules shot the Centaur with an arrow because he had stolen his wife and was galloping off with her."

"He was married?"

"He didn't tell many people. Anyway, the Centaur got revenge. As he was dying, he told Hercules's wife to give Hercules a special coat that would make her stay in love with Hercules. You see, she was unsure that Hercules really loved her. Anyway, it's very sad; she gave him the coat, and when he put it on it stuck to his skin, and when he pulled it off, his skin . . ." I hesitate.

"Go on," Stella insists. Behind her I can see Dorie's lit windows.

"Want to visit Dorie?"

"Dad, I just *saw* her. What happened to Herc'les?"

I shrug. "His skin kind of stuck to the coat."

"It came off?"

"Yes."

"All of it?"

"Stella, I don't know if all of it came off. Enough to hurt him. Let's change the subject."

"Yech. And that killed him?"

"Not exactly. It hurt so much that he put himself on a big pile of wood and burned himself up."

"But that would hurt even more!"

"That's a good point. I think the burning purified him or something."

She starts laughing.

"Stella! What's so funny."

She's really giggling now. "He should have gone to Dr. Checkers, right, Dad?"

I laugh too, sort of. "I suppose he should have, Stella."

Stella thinks for a moment. "Where did Herc'les go after he burned up? Did he go to heaven?"

"Let's see, where *did* he go? I think he went to the Greek heaven. The Elysian fields."

"There's different kinds?"

"Yep. The Greeks believed that heaven was a beautiful field, like a spring meadow full of flowers and woods along the edge, where the best people walked about and enjoyed the sunshine and fruit and the long evenings and the stars." Soon, I think, summer will be here, and Stella and I will walk in our own earthbound meadows.

"What about the other people?"

"They went to a place called Hades."

"Where's that?"

"It's underground. A bunch of caves and dark rivers."

Stella shivers. "That's scary. I'd rather go to the fields."

"That's the place for you, all right."

"Up in the stars!"

"The fields in the stars!"

I think how smart the ancient people were. How much they *knew*. Even in the face of death's eventual taking down of the body, its inescapable triumph over the corpus, they fashioned an escape hatch for the soul. And so many of them created a seamless philosophy for the mortal's pact with death: How we treat death in living will affect the life of the soul beyond it.

I remember that Hercules is Gilgamesh in the Babylonian myths, and his life story is equally sad. He had a wonderful companion all his life, Ea Bani by name, a strange Pan-like creature, half-man, half-animal. When Gilgamesh spurned a goddess's advances, she struck Ea Bani dead in a jealous rage. For the rest of his days, Gilgamesh wandered in search of his dead friend's spirit.

This brought him to the gates of the afterlife, where he was granted a short visit with Ea Bani. But the story ends even more sadly; Ea Bani describes life after death as grim and dark for everyone, a continual wandering about and mourning the loss of life. For Gilgamesh it's then much the same: without his friend and in sadness for him, he wanders about mournfully in life. I think: What if it was only one cynical Babylonian who made up that story, and humanity got stuck with it forever? Why, it could have had a different ending. The thought makes me snicker to myself.

Stella asks, "What are you laughing at, Dad?"

"I was just wondering if we can be allowed to rewrite some of these sad star stories."

"Tell me the story of Young Tongue again."

"Tung Yung," I correct. Another story of parting and sorrow. "Aren't you tired?"

"A little, but not yet. Tell me, Dad."

Tonight the sky is so clear you can see the whole starry river. On one side is Tung Yung, the gallant farm boy whose star I cannot remember, and on the other is Chih-Nu, the heavenly princess who fell in love with him; her star is Vega, one of the brightest stars in the heavens. I take a breath and lower us to the curb, where I set Stella up high on my knees. "Tung Yung was a boy who sold himself into slavery to pay for the funeral of his father. He was a boy full of energy and promise, but he began to die as a slave. He became very sick, and in the heavens, Chih-Nu, the beautiful daughter of the great Chinese Father of All, looked down and felt pity for him."

"Did she live in a castle, Dad?"

"I'm not sure. I think they just floated around there."

"Okay, go on. She comes down, right?"

"Yes. She asked her father for permission to go down to visit Tung Yung, who lay in his dirty room, cold and sick." I lie back on the grass, which is just a little damp. Stella perches on my middle, a silhouette against the stars. "And so she stepped into a light boat and floated down, down, down the starry river to his side. She cured him with her magic, and fed him special food, and he grew stronger immediately. When she saw him well and whole, she could not help but fall in love with him."

"Did they get married?"

"Not officially. She stayed with him, and then they had a little baby boy together."

"But why did she have to go back?" Stella asks sadly.

"You're jumping ahead. She was not a human person, but a spiritual visitor and could not spend much time on earth."

"Why not?"

"I'm not sure. I guess it would upset the balance of things down here. Anyway, her father called her back, and one night, while her husband and child slept, she had to step back into the boat and float back up the starry river."

"I don't like that part," Stella complains, and throws her head back to look angrily up into the sky. "That's not fair."

"Chih-Nu accepted it, but she was very sad. Now she is Vega, right up there, sitting endlessly at a loom and thinking sadly of her husband and son."

"But every year they get to meet again. Right, Dad?"

I nod, then turn her around and pull her down so that

she's lying on her back on my chest. I rub my cheek against her head. "Her father could not stand her grief, and he could see how Tung Yung too was so sad. So one night every year, he lets them meet on either side of the starry river."

"Which night is that, Dad?"

"I'm not sure. We'll have to look it up."

"Which star is he?"

"I forget, Stella. We can look it up, though."

She nods, her head rolling up against my cheek. I fold my arms around her; she's so small and light, like a balloon that might float off if I open my arms.

"Can you swim in the starry river, Dad?"

I think for a moment. "Maybe if you're a spirit."

"Let's go swimming together, Dad. In the starry river."

"Okay. When?"

"Just as soon as it gets a little warmer. Promise?"

"Promise."

We struggle to our feet again and I lift her to my shoulder. She has taken on no weight, it seems, since the operation. As we walk on, I hold her more tightly to me, the two of us growing silent together.

I remember a favorite story of Stella's that we haven't spoken about in a long time. It's an Indian story about a starry maiden who looked down on earth and loved the people there, loved their ways and their lives. It was their senses she envied: smelling flowers, feeling rainwater, hearing the buzz of bees. . . . She visited and inhabited flowers, and trees, and birds, taking up each in turn as a possible new home. She reveled in life, but like all spirits she could only stay for a short time. On the day that she was called back to the heavens, in thankfulness she gave the earth the water lilies, which are like the reflections of stars in still water.

Stella shivers in my arms, shivers hard. "Okay. Let's go in now, Dad." Then she adds, "I'm really tired," and laughs, as if embarrassed.

TWENTY-SIX

We have a nice morning together, Stella and I. She's calmer than usual, so we get a lot of learning done. Near lunch, we have a great time with the Book of Stars. We have made several pages of our favorite constellations and Stella thinks the translations of the stars' names are fascinating and funny.

We read in Richard Hinckley Allen's *Star Names, Their Lore and Meaning,* that Castor and Pollux, the twin stars of Gemini, mean "the beaver" and "much sweet wine" respectively.

"I like that," I say. "Much sweet wine."

"But why did they say 'the beaver,' Dad?"

"I'm not sure. There must have been a shape that suggested it. There's no story given."

"What's the other one? The nose?"

"Menkar, from the constellation Cetus. It means the nose."

"The nose of Cetus."

"Yes. The nose of the monster that comes to gobble up Andromeda."

"But Theseus saves her, right, Dad?"

I start giggling. "Wouldn't it be funny if we used the English names instead of the old names? We'd say, 'Oh, look! The nose is out tonight.'"

Stella laughs. "Oh, look! The nose is so bright tonight!"

She didn't eat much at breakfast, and when she only picks at her lunch, I decide to call Roth. Later still, she surprises me by wanting to go to sleep, because she usually refuses to comply with commands to rest up. In her room, wrapped around Heddie, she falls asleep quickly.

Roth is in his office when I call. He wonders if she might be getting a little anemic and says he'd like to see her. He repeats what I already know, that the dosage of medications that Stella must take to suppress tissue rejection has to be monitored carefully. We make an appointment for the next day, Friday, which means that Marsha will bring her in because she's taking the morning off work so that I can spend a second, and hopefully last, full day up north with Milo and Jennifer.

At dinner, Stella eats more, and that's encouraging. Marsha and I debate whether to keep the appointment after all, but when Stella falls asleep before we can even get out for an evening walk, we think it best to keep it.

The next morning when my alarm goes off very early, I quickly reach out and grab to quiet it. It's to be another long day of meetings with lessors and contractors, potential felons actually. I do not look forward to this day and pray that it's the last of its kind. With a sigh, I roll toward Marsha and discover that she's not there. Her side of the bed is flat and cold.

The kitchen light's on, but she's not there, nor in the bathroom. I hear her voice in Stella's room. I find Marsha sitting beside Stella, her hand on the child's belly.

Siri stands quietly, watching in the dimly lit room. Marsha's eyes come up to me. She smiles good morning but there is worry there. The quiet is unnerving, I must break it.

"What's going on?"

Marsha looks down to Stella, who lies very still in the very center of her child-size bed. "We're not feeling so good."

I come over to the bedside.

"What's the matter, sweetheart?"

"I'm vibrating."

"Siri woke me," says Marsha.

"I told you he'd help me, Dad."

"What do you mean, 'vibrating'?"

Marsha says, "She keeps trembling. She seems very weak, Jim. I'm thinking we should take her in right away."

I sit down on the other side of the bed, and Siri slides in for a pat. I manage to rub his solid cranium while running a hand over Stella's forehead. Her flesh is cool but clammy, like clay. "Are you cold?" I ask.

Her small head shakes under my hand. She starts to speak, to explain, but stops. She just lies there, limp.

"I should call Roth," I say, but then add immediately, "but he won't be at the hospital yet."

"There'll be doctors there and they'll contact Roth or Cejka if they need to." She's speaking of the emergency room, of course.

"Will Mona be there?" Stella asks.

I laugh, clasping her shoulder. "You're irrepressible."

"What's that?"

"Nothing stops you. How about getting dressed and coming down to the hospital so they can see what you need?"

"Let's just bundle her," says Marsha.

I look over at my wife. Her eyes tell me we should not waste too much time—not to hurry, not to be fearful, but nonetheless to move.

"Should we eat?"

Marsha considers this. She asks Stella, "Would you eat a little something, honey?"

Stella shakes her head. "No thanks, Mom."

Should I be worried? Under my hand, a tremor passes through Stella's body. It's strangely unlike a shiver, more of a muscular clutching and releasing, but more elemental.

"All right, ladies, let's go."

As we get Stella to her feet, I can feel how weak she really is. Her limbs shake. Again I feel her forehead for fever. Nothing.

"I have to call Jennifer," I announce, and leave Stella to her mother.

I fish Jennifer's home phone number from the notes in my briefcase and ring her up. I hate to send a telephone call into her peaceful home, but she would be up and perhaps quick to grab the phone. As it happens, her husband answers.

"She's in the shower," he tells me.

"Gosh, I'm sorry. It's just that it looks like I won't be traveling with her today and I wanted . . ."

"Wait, the water just stopped. Hold on."

A few moments pass and then Jennifer comes on the line. "Jim? What's up?"

Of all things, with my daughter getting bundled up for the emergency room, I am distracted by the thought of wet Jennifer wrapped in a bath towel. "My daughter's sick. I'm afraid you'll have to go it alone today."

Marsha appears at my elbow. "I could take her in, Jim. You go ahead."

Though this suggestion is meant to help, it only irritates me. "Hold on," I blurt to Jennifer. I have to leave her dripping on the other side of town. "No, I think I should go with you," I say to Marsha. "We might have to make some kind of decision."

She nods. I have worried her further, I can see. Should I be so worried? Jennifer's voice is squeaking against my palm.

"Go on ahead, Jim," she is saying. "I can handle it."

"You're sure?"

"Let's just spend a couple of minutes talking now."

"But you must be freezing."

"No, I've got a big bathrobe on. I'm fine."

"Oh, okay."

I wave Marsha on, and then think of what to tell Jennifer. Finally, I take a breath. "Here's the way I see it. It could be that certain lessors kept going back to the same contractors, adding a little extra fat each time they didn't get caught."

I can sense Jennifer nodding. "I could draw up a graph or table, showing the overages chronologically. Add in everything that we found and what Milo and I find today."

"That's a good idea. And start getting names of contractors and lessors. If we can show that certain people fudged more and more over time, then I think we've got a case."

"I'll call you from the road at some point. Just to check in."

"Okay. This thing with Stella could be nothing."

"I sure hope it is, Jim. Good luck."

Wife and daughter are ready. Stella has on her robe and slippers and a little bag of toys and books. On an impulse, I fetch Peter Lum's *The Stars in Our Heaven* from the activities room in case we're stuck in some waiting room for a long time.

I drive. Marsha bundles Stella against her. Stella submits to the bundling, watching out the front window as if lost in thought.

"What are you thinking about, sweetheart?"

"Siri. I don't like to leave him."

"You'll see him again soon," I say.

No one says anything in reply. I drive on, and through a surprising amount of traffic. "Lord, how many people start work at seven A.M.?"

Again, no response. I resign myself to the job of simply getting Stella to the hospital with reasonable speed.

At the emergency room, I expect to have to make a lot of explanations, to justify our appearance there, but the nurse who comes out to see us takes one look at Stella and ushers us to an area partitioned off with curtains. She takes the child from Marsha like a package and sets her on a padded gurney. "What are these bandages?" she demands.

"Skin grafts," says Marsha, efficiently. I'd opened my mouth to launch into a medical history. Marsha adds,

"When I called ahead I mentioned that so you could get her records."

Really? When had she called ahead?

"Oh, yes," says the nurse. "They're on the way. Now let's see here." She peers into Stella's eyes and feels under her throat. She goes "Hmmm" and I wonder what she's finding. I peer harder at Stella, who perches as if about to tumble from the edge of the gurney. She slouches there, taking things in, expressionless. She watches the nurse take her blood pressure, feel her pulse, then, before our eyes, her whole body shudders. That same muscular grabbing, but stronger and deeper.

To my right, Marsha makes a little sound and her hand comes up in the air. Someone comes up with records, and the nurse starts to walk off. "I'll get Dr. Silber," she says.

I feign surprise and whisper to Stella, "Dr. Silly?"

She smiles wanly at my cheer-up tricks. "No, Dad. Not Dr. Silly."

Marsha goes off in pursuit of the nurse and I see her catch up to and literally grab the woman. They confer out of hearing. I see the nurse shrug, then move away, then Marsha close the distance again. More conferring, then the two of them separate and Marsha returns.

"What?" I ask.

"She doesn't know for sure. She's wondering if it might be a graft rejection."

"This late?"

"Remember, Roth said it could happen anytime."

I become self-conscious because Stella is listening. "Do your wrists feel different, honey?"

She shakes her head. "I don't think so."

A young doctor comes over with the same nurse. He introduces himself as Dr. Silber, and when he says his name, Stella looks at me and grins weakly, which is encouraging to me. He examines Stella superficially, then consults the records again.

"So she had autografts on her wrists?" He seems puzzled by what he is reading.

"Yes," says Marsha.

"Not allografts? I mean, it was her own skin that was used for the graft, correct?"

"Yes."

"That's good. Do you know if they were full-thickness or split-skin grafts?"

Marsha and I look at each other.

The doctor says, "Were there stitches at the donor site—on Stella's legs, I mean?"

"No," I nearly shout, grateful to be able to supply a firm answer. "Why? Is that significant?"

"Well, a full-thickness graft brings up fat cells too, which is often done with grafts at the joints. It's a more serious graft, obviously, and chancier."

I think for a moment. "Dr. Roth said that her problem was one of superficial inelasticity and . . ."

"Ah. So it was to relieve surface stricture that might eventually lead to joint contracture?"

"Yes. That's exactly what it was."

"What does all this mean for Stella now?" Marsha demands.

"I'm not sure yet. We might need to contact Dr. Roth, but it's good to know that if there is a rejection going on it's unlikely to be virulent. We'll need to take blood . . ."

Stella's eyes open a little and she looks at us. Her head begins to shake. "No," she says. "I don't want that. No blood."

"I'm sorry, honey . . ." says Marsha.

"No, no." She begins to weep. It's not childish crying, but something akin to the quiet grieving an adult might do. "I can't," she says.

But there's nothing to be done. The doctor has to have blood tests to see what's going on in Stella's system. Stella is laid down and weeps on her back while a nurse comes up to do the job. Marsha holds her other arm, but it appears to be small comfort. I don't know what else to do but ask Dr. Silber a lot of questions.

"I'm not a dermatologist," he says, "but I'm sure we'll be looking at her antigen levels. There could be what's called a cell-mediated attack going on, and if that's happening it could explain the anemic-like lethargy she's experiencing."

"Why would there be a rejection at this point?" I demand. "After all, it's her own skin."

The doctor nods. "True, but your daughter suffers from a genetic skin disease. Chromosomally speaking, the grafted area might eventually decide not to recognize a patch of skin from another part of the body. But let's wait for Dr. Roth on that one."

He's drawn off to another case, behind another curtain, and from that point on we see only glimpses of him. The blood has been taken (how many drops can she spare?) and Stella, limp and sad, lies in her mother's arms. Marsha sits rocking her and I stare off across the room of curtains and cubicles. We wait for Dr. Roth.

After an eternity, he comes. No white coat, just his street suit and tie. Stella appears to be asleep. "Let's get her up to my office," he says, looking around with distaste.

"With Mickey," says Stella, surprising us.

"Right. With Mickey."

Marsha lifts her and we all take the elevator to Dr. Roth's office. It's so early that he has to unlock his own office, laughing to himself as he tries to find the unfamiliar key. "Dr. Cejka will be in later," he says. "If we need her."

Back in the familiar examination room, Stella is laid out on the table like a length of rumpled cloth. Roth feels her all over, running his hands over her limbs with her pajamas still on. He backs away as we watch, then spins out of the room and out to the receptionist's area. We hear him on the phone, and then he returns.

"They don't have the blood results yet. I'm wondering if we should take a look under those bandages." He smiles at us.

"What would you be looking for?" I ask.

"In the blood or in the tissues?"

"Both." Marsha and I are still in our coats, each perched on the edge of a chair. Stella is directly in line with our eyes.

"In the blood, evidence of what are called HLA antigens, or group A leukocytes. They are the initiators of a rejection response. In the tissues, discoloration, atrophy . . . Let's take a look."

I don't want to see this. I find that I have no stomach

for it. Perhaps if this were a slide presentation and not my own daughter. . . . Roth, meanwhile, has taken up one of her bandaged hands and is beginning to snip through the cloth. When I reach toward Marsha for comfort, my hand bumps against hers coming toward mine. But when the bandage is nearly cut through, I have to rise up and look.

I wish I hadn't. The flesh there is purplish and puffy, the stitch marks risen in angry little puckers.

Roth sighs. "Well."

I can't bring myself to speak. Marsha reaches up and pulls me back. "Give him space, Jim," she says.

"But . . ."

"I know."

Roth looks closer, puts on his funny magnifying headgear and waggles his face at Stella, who smiles gamely back. "So you don't like the new skin, huh?"

"Maybe it doesn't like me."

She rolls her head toward us, pleased at her joke. I force a laugh; it breaks out of me like a bubble coming up through thick soup.

"Wait here," he says to Stella. "I want Dr. Checkers to take a look. Okay?"

When he leaves us we say nothing for a long time. I think to mention a nice breakfast somewhere, but then I don't know if we will be leaving the hospital anytime soon. Should we call Dorie, let her know that she might not be needed this afternoon? Should we call her just to tell her what's happening with Stella? I want to call someone.

Marsha says, "Guess what? Tomorrow Uncle Jack comes back from Florida. Won't that be nice, Stella?"

Stella smiles and nods. I smile too. Jack.

While we're waiting for Dr. Cejka to appear, Marsha and I stir ourselves enough to get out of our coats. When I go down to hang them up in the waiting area, I hear a radio quietly playing pop rock. The receptionist is just in, her cubicle brightly lit and animated by her youthful presence. I glimpse her through the sliding glass panels, but then I am compelled for a moment to stare. I keenly note her clear skin, her piled hair tied with a sparkly band. How old is she? Eighteen, nineteen? Twisting about in her chair, snapping gum, alive . . .

No one's in the waiting room, but the magazines have been neatly restacked and the door to the hallway is ajar. Life is going on. When I come back to the examination room, Stella is sitting up with Marsha.

"Well," I say.

"I'm thirsty, Dad."

"I wonder if we can go down to the cafeteria or something."

"We'll see," says Marsha, giving Stella a sideways hug.

Now comes Dr. Cejka, Roth in tow. We make room for them both, and Dr. Cejka greets Stella heartily and taps her cheek gently with one knuckle.

"It's this," says Roth quietly, lifting the wrist with the opened bandage.

"Yes, yes," says Dr. Cejka, peering closely. "And it was taking so nicely."

Marsha and I have pressed ourselves back against the walls. The elephant's plastic trunk stabs me between the shoulder blades. Dr. Cejka turns and faces us. "Can one of you take a little walk with me?" she asks.

Marsha looks at me. "You go, Jim."

Cejka and Roth and I huddle closely in the hallway between all the examination rooms. Dr. Cejka says, "There is definitely a rejection taking place, my friends."

"What can be done?" I ask.

"This is not uncommon, Mr. Kaldy. What we usually do is increase the dosage of azathioprine, perhaps double it—two pills instead of the one that Stella now takes."

"Yes," says Roth.

". . . and that usually suppresses the immune-system reactions."

"More drugs," I say.

Dr. Cejka nods, picking up on my cue. "There are risks. As always." She removes her glasses and rubs the bridge of her nose. "We will need to watch our little friend here to see that her blood contains plenty of white-cell platelets."

"It might be good if she stays here with us for a few days," Roth puts in.

"Yes, I agree," says Dr. Cejka.

"What could go wrong with her blood?" I ask, but I already know. I've asked these questions before, back when Marsha and I demanded a full accounting of the risks from Roth. Azathioprine suppresses the activities of the immune system, heading off the body's attempts to reject grafts or transplants, but in so doing it increases the potential for infection; in higher dosages, it can even damage the tissues of the bone marrow that produce blood cells.

"What about new blood, my blood?"

They both shake their heads. "Transfusions are just another form of transplant," says Dr. Cejka. "Her system will be doing the same checking and possible rejecting as it's doing now."

"So . . ." I begin, but I've run out of questions.

Roth says, "We should keep her here, Jim. Increase the dosage, and just watch closely to see that she's got the punch to keep off infections. It should be all right."

But I hear that tone in his voice, that calming tone that doctors put on because, after all, they are still part witch, part shaman. Their cutting and chemicals can only do so much, and the rest is a bolstering of the mind and spirit to support what healing the body can manage on its own. They don't want a pair of hysterical parents lurching about. I nod at them, accepting the tone, the gotten-up hope.

"Should we get her something to eat?" I ask.

She pats my arm. "Yes, go downstairs for breakfast. Then come back."

"I'll set it up with the hospital, Jim."

Marsha becomes very worried when I start to tell her what the doctors have told me. It unnerves me all over again to see her eyes jump and to field her quick questions. I should have told her away from Stella, but there's no room anywhere in this place, nowhere else to go. But Stella just regards us calmly.

"Are we going to eat soon, Mom?"

"I guess so."

"I might go home and get some things," I say.

"Bring Heddie, Dad. We forgot Heddie."

So we did, in our rush.

"Let's eat together first."

"Okay. Yes, let's be together."

Stella is actually able to laugh in the cafeteria, though

she refuses to eat much and only sips from a glass of orange juice. Marsha and I don't have much of an appetite either, but we press upon ourselves a bland array of wrapped and chilled and semiheated dishes. We notice that other kids are there too in pajamas, and we point this out to Stella. "It's a pajama party," she says.

"I arranged it for you," I say.

"You're teasing, Dad. Right?"

"Yes, I admit it."

We make plans, Marsha and I. She will go home to get things for Stella's stay; her knowledge of what's needed and where things are remains superior to mine. For her own peace of mind, as she explains, she leaves us soon after we finish eating. When she's gone, it leaves a bigger hole in our mood.

I decide to take Stella for a little walk. I lift her up and she rests her head against my shoulder. I think that she is sad now, and if not exactly frightened, then resigned in a way that is frightening to me. I do not know exactly what she is thinking, and I am afraid to ask. I do not want to disturb thought processes that may be important in ways that I do not understand. But at the same time, I want her to fight this nonsense and to survive it. I think to myself that I deserve to have her in my life. I recall my father and his strange inability to get what he needed and wanted, and my mother, who knew what she wanted but lacked the skill to secure it. I want to be clear now about what I want, and I want Stella.

"You've got a fight ahead of you, Stella-Capella."

"I know, Dad," she says quietly.

"Are you up to it, honey?"

"Uh huh."

"It'll be hard. They'll need to take blood, sweetheart, and they'll be giving you more drugs."

"It's okay, Dad."

I'm amazed to hear her comforting me; how adult to try to put me at my ease. I leave off the prompting, though. It's not her job to comfort me, and what battle she fights within her body and soul is actually, in the end, none of my business. Stella tells me, every day and every moment now, that living is risk. To hold on to is to lose, to let go of is maybe to get. Every day, the sun mounts higher on its ecliptic. We are not, after all, ancient people afraid of the sun's refusal to return; we know now that it will return. Auriga in his chariot, Boötes at the plow, Pegasus in sea and air, all ride the hills and waves and gusts that roll back and forth between life and death. Life's strange pact with death is that to avoid death, to hide from it, is to die.

But while my mind struggles to convince myself, my heart's not so sure. It is pumping blood hurriedly, sending it banging against my temples. We are walking down the long hallways, Stella and I, as we have walked together so many times before, but in different places and for far different reasons. Lurking at the edges of my thoughts is the ugly possibility of an end to these walks. I find that I'm holding her closer, tighter with each step.

"Little weasel," I whisper. "Thing of wonder."

Our heads are so close together. I wish that I could hear her thoughts. I wish that she were inside my skin.

"You're hurting me, Dad."

"Sorry." I let the pressure ebb from my arms. "Sorry."

Dr. Roth finds us wandering about. "I've got a room for you, Stella," he announces. We follow him. In the elevator he says to me, "It's a private room, Jim. Much more expensive, I'm afraid. I might be able to rig the bill a bit, but I think we need to keep a close private eye on her."

"Sure."

The room is a nice one, not large, but it has a window with an actual view. There are ailanthus trees outside the window, normally not my favorites, but they do bud early and that provides us with some spring growth to see. I get Stella under the covers and then the two of us wait for a while, for Marsha, just talking. She has so few questions; she asks only about Siri. After a while, she drops off to sleep.

I can't take my eyes off her as she sleeps. Several times I start to stare out the window, but then my eyes come back to her. I can see every raw patch on her face, the several small hairs that make up her tattered brows, the three or four lashes that her own cruel skin has allowed to grow out. And yet she's so beautiful to me. How can this be? I suppose because I know her so well. I can see now that I have not made the single most devastating mistake that a parent can make, the failure to know his child. Stella, the single thing, the one and only. Stella herself, who never sleeps like this in the day, who is never long between laughter and tears, who must therefore be very sick right now.

I hear Marsha's step in the hallway and walk out to discover her clunking about with a full shopping bag and peering at the room numbers.

"She's sleeping," I whisper.

"Is that good?"

"God, I don't know."

"I brought her own blanket and pillow, but I guess she didn't need it to fall asleep."

"Where's Heddie?"

We stare down into the bag together. Marsha says, "No, did I leave her by the front door? I can't believe it. She was the first thing I grabbed."

"Not like you, Marshmallow. Better calm down."

"I'm a mess."

"I'll go back and get Heddie. You stay with Stella."

She sighs. "All right. Maybe you'd better."

While she's telling me where the car is parked, a tall, thin woman in an immaculate nurse's uniform walks up to us. "I'm Rhea," she says. "I'll be taking care of Stella." She smiles at us kindly, crinkling her pale blue eyes.

"She's sleeping," Marsha and I both say.

"Let me know when she wakes up so I can start her chart."

Start her chart *again,* I think as I go off. Instead of heading for the garage, I go to find Dr. Roth. His receptionist tells me that he's in with a patient, but meanwhile Stella's blood results have come in. I decide to wait. I pick up a magazine after a few minutes. It's a *Glamour,* and it hurts to remember that the first time Stella and I came here together it was with such hope. She trusted me, all the big adults, and we let her down. My eyes blur and I toss aside the magazine.

Roth comes out much later and we go back to that same awful examination room to talk. "I wish I had better news," he says. "The platelet counts are way down and she's anemic to boot. I wouldn't even chance trying to suppress the rejection at this point."

My face feels very cool. I think to wait for a moment, to see if he'll speak again and say different words. But when that does not happen, I respond. "What does that mean? What else, what other options are open?"

"It basically means we'll have to remove the new skin and reattach the old skin the way it was before."

"Another operation!" My own voice surprises me.

Roth nods, all business now. "And soon."

"I'm confused."

He sighs. "We can remove the rejected skin and return Stella's wrists to just about the way they were before. That's no problem."

"But," I think, "they'll be even stiffer than they were before. What a mess."

"The bad news is that we need to get her strength up before we can operate. I don't want to tax her system in its present condition." He thinks to himself, leaning back against the examination table. "The stress, the risk of infection . . . Dr. Cejka would be the one to answer."

I shake my head. "It seems to me that the risk of infection might be greater with her skin going bad."

"No, no. We'll pack them. Keep them cool while she rests and gets stronger."

"Should we take her home, doctor? I mean, aren't hospitals full of germs?"

He smiles. "So they say, but she needs special care and she needs to be watched, and that can't be done at home."

I nod. "Of course."

When I get home I find a huge note from Dorie taped

to the door. I guess that Marsha must have called her when she went home for Heddie. I'm reading the note on the doorstep—"If there's *anything* I can do . . . " *anything* underlined twice—with Siri scratching on the other side, when I hear Dorie charging up the lawn behind me. I turn, trying to put on a happy face, but her own concerned look penetrates me in an instant. We hug briefly.

"It's bad," I say, admitting the fact to myself for the first time. "We're caught in some kind of vicious circle. The new skin's gotta come off, but they can't operate until she's stronger, and while she's rejecting the new skin, she stays weak." I shake my head, fumbling for my front-door key. "We shouldn't have let her play so much."

But when I look up at Dorie I can see that she's about to contradict me. We are having the same thought.

"Can you imagine telling Stella not to play so much?" she says.

I grimace. "Ridiculous."

"You'd have better luck telling the sun not to rise."

"Right. Come on in." I open the door.

Siri wags his tail, but he's irritable and whiny. His puzzled visage asks, "Is Stella with you? What have you done with her?" Heddie is right there, on the bookshelf where Marsha left her. Even the stuffed animal looks worried.

"I should take Siri home with me," says Dorie. "For the time being. I came over earlier and fed him."

"Thanks. I'm just going to come and go now."

"Go ahead. I'll pack some food for Siri. Do you think I could come and see Stella?"

"I don't know yet, Dorie. Why don't you call later?" I remember the room number and give it to her.

The phone rings and I answer it because I think it might be Marsha. It's Jennifer, calling from New Hampshire.

"We were dead on, Jim. We've pretty much tracked two contractors who were adding roughly five percent fat to each successive job. The whole mess keeps growing. Is Stella all right?"

"No. And I can't talk now, Jennifer. I'm on my way back to the hospital."

"Oh, Jim, I'm sorry! I thought I should . . ."

"No, no, Jennifer. It's all right. I'm glad you called. I'll be back in touch soon."

When I hang up, I accidentally put the receiver upside down on the cradle. It feels like an alien device.

At the door I follow Dorie out. "Dorie, Jack's coming back today. He must be on the plane now. If you see him, tell him what's going on, would you please?"

"Of course."

I drive back to the hospital with Heddie on the front seat beside me. It's eerie. I want Stella there, not a fake creature. I get spooked with the silly, complacent object sitting there beside me, feel its dead teddy bear stare pointed toward the windshield. The feeling grows so strong that I reach over and toss it onto the back seat. Then I feel unlucky, as if I'd enacted a curse by tossing about Stella's favorite toy. So I reach back and grab it and replace it on the seat. "I'm sorry," I tell it aloud.

At the hospital, Stella is still asleep. I look at my watch and can't believe it's nearly 6:30 in the evening.

"Has she slept the whole time?" I ask Marsha.

"Yes. Dr. Roth came by and took a look at her, but he said sleep is good. Jim, take off your coat."

"Okay."

Stella is hooked up to an IV. They're feeding her with liquids. "We're giving her a high-powered mix," says Rhea cheerily. "She'll come awake a dynamo."

Later, when I lift my jacket to the wall hook, I feel a weakness in my arms. I'm exhausted. In a corner chair, I keep dropping off. I think to nap a little, but the chair cuts into my back.

Rhea eyes me during her next visit. "There's a bed open down the hall. You could lie down for a while, if you like."

I look over at Marsha. "We're staying, right?"

She nods at me. She has brought a book from home, and reads with her glasses slipping down her nose. "Go on. Maybe I'll lie down later."

"Shifts," I say.

I follow Rhea down the hall and she points to a bed with no sheets on it in an empty room. I lie down with my shoes hanging off the end and feel my breaths coming deeper and faster and then I'm asleep.

TWENTY-SEVEN

My father and I stand, side by side, on the banks of the river. It's dusk, and the first few stars are out in a sky suffused with a tincture of deepest blue. "I think you can just walk it from here, Jim," my father says, but I'm not sure what he means. I stare down the short bank to the water. On the slow-moving surface are water lilies, pure and full, drifting and turning on the water.

"Aren't you coming too, Dad?"

He looks at me with surprise. He is thinner, more frail. He is an old man, I can see. "Well, I guess I could," he says, taking a tentative step down the bank.

I reach out to steady him, and the two of us step fully clothed into the water. It's warm, which is a relief. We both begin to titter, feeling foolish but committed to the gradual plunge. The water is not so deep as we thought, and with growing confidence we raise our arms and step forward more assuredly, the slow current rising to our chests. Across the way I see my mother standing among a few low bushes. She is nearly a silhouette, but I can feel her laughter from the way she shakes her head. I know what she's thinking: *Men!*

"Now how did she get over so quick?" asks my father.

She begins to motion to us to hurry as we get closer. The water lilies float by, behind and in front of me, like small, bright boats. I think to lift one in my cupped palms, but I sense that their journeys are not to be disturbed. Now my mother is starting to hurry off. She makes a last gesture to us and calls back, "Hurry, she's getting so far ahead!"

When my father and I get to the other side, we hurry up and find ourselves on the crest of a small hill that overlooks a magnificent descending slope. The sight takes my breath away. The whole rolling slope is covered with a deep, tawny grass, heaving like fur, swaying rhythmically in the dusk. The few trees, low and full, bend in the wind. In the distance, a dense forest composes the horizon, above which I am startled to see the stars rising like slow, vivid rockets in the purplish dusk.

My mother comes back to us, to hurry us, but she is not my mother now. She is Marsha, and her face expresses a different kind of hurry. She looks back over her shoulder and says, "Jim, Jim! She's getting so far ahead."

Then I am awake and Marsha is beside me, shaking me. I sense immediately that it is very late. Marsha's face is grave.

"She's got a fever, Jim. She's burning up."

Then she's gone and I have to find my way erect. My feet feel stuffed into my shoes. In the hallway, I brush my hand under the water fountain splashing my cheeks, then rub it dry with my handkerchief.

Stella's room is surprisingly bright. Rhea is pressing something down on the bed, down onto the pillow. But where's Stella? Then, I see that Stella is there, her head on that pillow. I cannot remember her this small. I approach the bed, my hand clutching my own chin. The pillow takes in her whole head. She is smaller, so much smaller, her face thinning to nothing before my eyes.

Marsha takes my arm. "Roth's on his way."

"What time is it?"

"I don't know."

How can she be so calm?

Rhea says, "We've packed her wrists. Just in case. That will cool her further."

I drop down beside the bed. The lids of my daughter's eyes are wrinkled like wet tissue. They adhere to the balls of her unmoving eyes.

"Stella?" I say.

"You'd better let her rest," says Rhea.

"Stella?"

Her eyes ease open and she looks up at the ceiling. I am visited with the terrible feeling that I've called her back from somewhere. Her eyes roll over to encounter mine.

"How do you feel, honey?"

Her flushed brow clouds. She feels awful. It's obvious. I don't know what to say, so why am I doing this? I've brought her back to her pain.

"Listen, you little shit. You better not leave me."

Slowly she smiles. "You said a bad word, Dad."

I laugh quietly, a bit relieved. "I mean it, Stella-Morella. I've got a lot more star stories to tell you."

She appears to be considering this. "What was Herc'les's wife's name, Dad? Remember?"

"No, I haven't looked it up yet," I say. I feel awful that I haven't done this yet. "But I will. I brought the book! I'll look it up and I'll tell you, okay?"

She smiles a little. Then grimaces and swallows slowly. "My chest hurts."

Roth appears on the other side of the bed. He has her chart, and Rhea hovers nearby. He turns to her and they confer. Then he turns back to the bed and bends to Stella.

"Let's check her blood again," he says to Rhea, more like an order.

Then nothing happens, though I feel that something should. I can feel that Marsha expects the same. We are waiting. Roth goes and does not come back, though I thought he would. Rhea comes back in and takes blood from the catheter in Stella's arm. Then another nurse, whom I do not know, replaces the IV bottle. A man comes in and puts tiny tubes in Stella's nose and tucks a metal bottle beside her pillow. The whole while, she only lies there, her chest barely moving. Once in a while, her dry lips move as if she's about to speak, but she makes no sound.

Later, I find Roth in the hallway with two other doctors. They form a phalanx of white coats, which I have trouble penetrating. "Dr. Roth . . ." I insist.

"Just a minute, Mr. Kaldy."

I drop back and they keep their voices low. I look into the room, and Marsha's wide, pale face is turned to me. The windows are bright behind the heavy curtains that keep the room dim. I can see the light seeping at the edges, feel the ailanthus stretching out and budding in another world. I realize that Marsha has not slept all night. She appears calm, but defeated and helpless too. I resolve to be strong for her, if only because I've gotten some sleep.

Roth and his crew are in tight, bending toward each

other. They keep their body language noncommittal, but I do not miss the telltale shrugs, the little tremulous shakes of the head. They don't know, they don't know what to do.

Eventually, Roth breaks free. We start to walk off together and I look back briefly to see Marsha's face watching us. My good friend Marsha. When our eyes meet, I wink. I get a grim, tiny smile back and then her face slides away behind the doorjamb. I cannot bear to look past her to the bed.

"It looks like pneumonia, Jim. But it's septicemia by any other name."

It is the way the disease eventually claims all of its victims.

"Advanced?" I ask.

"It's always advanced, by its very nature. There's a blood infection and she's already into the first stages of kidney failure."

The worst. The absolute worst. Every defense in the child's tiny ravaged system has been shut down. "There's no hope, then."

"There's always hope. It's just that, well, she could beat the infection, but then what? Kidney transplant? More rejection risks?"

I nod. "It's better if she dies now."

He grips my arm. "I'll be back soon," he says.

I go to get Marsha, feeling my chest caving in with every step, but she comes to the door to meet me. She sees my face and starts falling apart. I had thought to weep myself or cry out or fall to the hard, cold floor, but all these burning forces are driven back into me by the sight of my wife's face.

"No," she says.

"I guess she's gotten all the life she can out of that little body."

She keeps trying to speak, but sobs burst painfully from her. She lurches farther from the doorway, explaining in jerky phrases that she doesn't want Stella to hear, though I feel that Stella is already far beyond hearing. Then, outside of a little room full of vending machines, Marsha gives in to her grief. The hallway has become populated, but we hadn't noticed. She falls against me, weeping in a fearfully shuddering way, and people draw away in deference. Her bulk will not be contained by my arms. My heavy wife's legs are giving way, and I must dance about and dig in with my heels to keep her erect.

"So unfair," she wails. "I curse God for this."

"No meaning to it." I'm blinking hard now, throat tight as a straw.

Marsha suddenly finds her legs. "Got to be with her every second now."

"Yes, yes!"

We hurry back to the room and are shocked to find it empty. No bed, no bottles or tubes. Only Heddie sitting silent on a chair. Turning in the doorway, we collide with Rhea.

"We've taken her up to intensive care," she says.

"Where is it?" Marsha demands.

But Rhea is already leading us toward the elevator. "Just a couple of floors up."

We get an empty elevator, but no one says a word at first. I can smell Marsha, a strong, unwashed odor of suffering. Her eyes are black with smeared mascara. "You're a mess," I say, nudging her.

"So are you. All your fault. You and your little soldier."

"Wouldn't have had it any other way. Right?" It's no joke. I need to know.

She nods. "A privilege. A goddamn privilege."

Rhea watches the floor lights. "Almost there," she says.

They've got her in a fancy room, all right. Her bony chest is exposed and wired between the small pink nipples that will never bud into breasts. I look away. I have no strength left, it is too terrible and I do not care who knows it.

"She should have Heddie here," says Marsha.

"Yes!" I exclaim, gratefully, and rush to the stairs. My plan is to weep in the stairwell, but staff people are coming up, two by two, with plastic trays of food. Is it lunchtime? Time is rushing forward, running through our fingers like water.

I will weep in Stella's old room. I cross the hall and walk in and Jack is standing there. He is wearing a jacket and holding a rolled-up tube of paper. We stand a few feet apart, staring at one another.

"I came directly from the airport, Jim. Where is she?"

I have never noticed before how strongly Stella resembles her uncle. The same bones, the nice oval shape of the head. She would have been tall.

"Jack," I squeak, "Stella's dying."

I blurt something else and then there's spit on my lips and my face opens like an angry boil. I fall against Jack and have to be held a long time, pain lurching in my chest too fast to get out in sobs. I hunch forever against him, fists balled against my chest to hold back the grief whose volume frightens me. But it spasms out from between my hands.

It seems to take forever to subside. Afterward, breathing more and more evenly, I can hardly remember who I am.

"Easy, there," says Jack.

"I'm better now," I say, finding my legs. After I blow my nose and blot my eyes, I look at him. His face is ashen.

He slowly holds up the roll of paper. "Look," he says. His hands are shaking as he takes off a rubber band and unrolls it. I see that it's a certificate of some kind. "I had a star named after Stella. I was planning to surprise her. Did you know you could do that?"

Helplessly, I look at the sheet. It means nothing, but it is comforting to look fixedly at something. "No, Jack. I didn't." My voice is a nasal wheeze. I stare at the document. It has a seal on it, and a pattern of blue star shapes printed across the lettering. And in a space it says in fancy calligraphy that Star BD + 59°1915A has hereby been christened Stella Kaldy.

"It's right on line with a visible star, Jim. One in the Canis Major constellation. Was that a good choice? I'm no star expert."

We should go back up, but I know he needs two more seconds to comprehend the horror that is befalling his niece. "Jack, it was the perfect choice. Sirius is in Canis Major. Stella's will be beside it. Let's go up and tell her."

I turn and bump into the wall. We find the hallway,

ascend the stairs (the elevator is so deathly quiet and
slow), and then I'm nearly running into the intensive
care room. I find that it has become very populated now.
Marsha comes out into the hallway and she and Jack
walk off. I can hear her weeping again, just see the back
of Jack's head shaking.

I go in and take up a position by Stella's bedside. Now
she's covered up to her chin in a spotless white sheet.
Her little cap is off. I wish it were back on because then
she has a bit more dignity. I am embarrassed for her,
the baldness of her. But no one seems to look upon her
with anything but respect as they come and go.

Rhea touches my arm during one of her visits. "We
were planning to set up an oxygen tent, Mr. Kaldy, but
Dr. Roth thought you might not want that."

I realize that she is saying that when death is nearly
certain the survivors might not want hanging sheets of
plastic in the way. "I prefer not," I say. "I think my wife
would prefer it that way too."

An hour passes, Stella worsening by the minute.
Dorie arrives. We take up positions around the bed, in
its center the small guttering cynosure of our affections.
Stella, looking more and more like a flat white sack.

More hours pass. We walk in and out. Once I eat
something and it has no flavor that I can detect. Sometimes we stretch and walk a little, say things like "She's
all worn out" and "She'll have peace now" and "So
much living in a little life" and then we nod and pass
before and behind each other.

Around 4 P.M., a small rasp starts within Stella. We
each find our spot around the bed. We are compelled,
each in turn, to bend and press our lips hard to her hot

cheeks. Then I get down close and take her arm, thin as a twig. "The absolute best daughter a father could ever have," I whisper.

"Jack named a star after you, sweetheart," says Marsha.

"The best, the best . . ."

Her eyes remain closed and the breathing shallows further. Roth is there now, on the far side of the bed. Pale, with red-rimmed eyes, he gazes down, just staring.

Already the flesh is puddling around her bones. Within me a wave of new grief is rising. I press my face close to her chest. I can no longer hear the tiny clicking of her heart in her ribs. I feel rather than see a final breath pass through her, like a breeze beneath a sheet.

Then my mind goes away. Something implanted in the deepest recesses of my cells activates itself and lifts away my brain and coats the backs of my eyes with blackness. I know only that I am making a terrible sound. Arms have me, and it is I who am dead and feeling the great good sense of dying.

TWENTY-EIGHT

Today I have decided to finish the Book of Stars. It has been buried a long time in the basement room, in a box among a stack of others that have remained carefully sealed. There was nothing particularly different about the start of this day, but all through it, in little imperceptible steps, it became all right, for the first time, that Stella is gone. I'm not sure exactly when I became consciously aware of this fact, but I know that it began with something that Dorie said over bridge.

I do know that at no moment before that moment was it all right. I had been down to the boxes only once before, to move them a little because a plumber was coming later and he would need to get to a certain pipe. I moved one box, just one, and something rattled and made a sound. The sound was so hideously telling, a muffled thump that ended quickly. It was Stella's marimba. I instantly thought of Stella herself, muffled and boxed away, and a pain went through my chest like a knife going in and twisting. I was no good for a week.

It was Dorie's idea to start the bridge games, and eventually it proved to be a good one. Morose blobs staring at each other for months, Jack and Dorie and Marsha and I. Sitting around a table, bidding diamonds and eating peanuts and drinking beer was better than that. Better than the long watching of TV, immersions in the newspaper, the staring into space, the general taking of us away. Perhaps all that was necessary. The worst was directly after: all the phone calls, the poor stricken Dorsets, the flowers from relatives who had only a few moments for Stella when she was alive. Even the Lesters briefly crawled from their lair—I imagined, uncharitably, at the smell of death. The bridge games were all of the world I wanted to see.

But what I wanted and what I was required to have were quite different. At my new job with the state, I imagine my coworkers see me as a quiet, competent man who minds his own business—those, that is, who are not privy to my controversial dismissal from my position with the federal government. After Stella's death, I found I had to keep working, for the distraction, for the distance from our sunlit rooms at home where Stella and Marsha and I had worked and played so intensely together. I stayed on to see the mess through at my old division, sat in on meetings and prepared reports, and then gradually, in a long stretch of time that I remember more as a tone or texture, dark and bristling, I found myself leading a schism that broke ranks with Howard Long and his determined response to the contract fraud in New Hampshire. Jennifer and I and a few stalwarts from both Finance and Lease Management had pressed to investigate other cost overruns in the region, and before long discovered more instances of possible fraud. At first we were frightened, then disgusted, but over time a kind of dour elation set in. We knew we had discovered a gap in the contract-management system that was virtually invisible to the honest insider but more than a little apparent to wily contractors.

We did not know it at first, but Howard did not share our elation at discovering a system weakness which, once fortified, we were certain would keep potentially dishonest people honest. After initial disbelief, and then suspicions that grew to certainties, we realized that he wished to contain the all-region audit. For what reason? Each member of our splinter group had his or her opinion, but we all agreed that it must have something to do with potential damage to his career. We had a fight on our hands; Howard had sympathetic advisers, a few of the auditors in his pocket. More important, he was in a position to block inquiries, drag out responses to our reports (when he did not completely ignore them), and divert work time in other directions. Those among us with the moral conviction to be outraged turned to me to raise their standard. I nearly did not.

In my private meetings with Howard, I was peculiarly attuned to his deep sadness. I was attuned to any sadness. I was willing to perceive, as he did, how very unfair it would be if he were left, in some minds, holding this nasty bag so late in a mostly accomplished career. I was almost willing to conclude, as he did by way of intimation, that leaving a smaller man, such as Milo Pelletier, with a smaller bag might be more fair. I very nearly believed all that.

But I kept having this nagging ugly feeling. Then I remembered something that my father said to me during one of our summer evening trips to a job site. We were going back to work on something that had bothered him all through dinner. When he thought he had the solution, he clucked and turned to me beside him in the truck. "You know, the truth's a funny thing, Jim. Sometimes you *feel* it before you *know* it."

Thinking of Howard and fraud and a half-dozen other matters, I held on to a feeling through one evening, and held on later as I stared up at the bedroom ceiling where I lay next to a sleeping Marsha. Then I imagined Stella alive, and older, imagined her at eighteen or so, and wondered if I could justify myself in her company. I might discover, over sandwiches in some restaurant, or side by side on the way to a movie theater, that I could not spontaneously boast of my behavior during this awful episode. . . . Well, the very prospect was unbearable to me. And when I imagined the opposite scenario, how she would cheer and laugh at my recounting of the good battle fought to the end, how she would beam at me, the matter became pretty simple. I could not deny either of us that kind of victory.

To make a long story short, I raised the standard of our little group and we forced Howard's hand. In some thick way, I feel he was eventually grateful, but at the time his anger, fueled by my perceived betrayal, was swift. In the end, I was the only vulnerable target, a part-time consultant whose contract was imminently cancelable.

I had assumed I would be poison in the local job market. Marsha and I had some weeks of worry to endure. I hated being around the house, and Stella's medical bills loomed large. But in the end a good job came looking for me. It seems that there are employers out there on the lookout for workers who will not roll over and die. Stella taught me that we always have deeper reserves of strength than we realize; the trick is to find and release them. I was chatty and confident at the interview. Now, each day in my airy office high above Cambridge Avenue, I step among tall, soothing columns of numbers.

It took a longer time for things to get better at home. At first, in the evenings after work, Marsha and I would go out for long walks together with Siri. He has been so good for us. His animal ability to live in the moment, to run about and sniff and piss and seek for the source of every noise, showed us what might lie ahead in our distant future. But for the moment, Marsha and I, walking slowly hand in hand, would watch him and say nothing. We just talked, and watched Siri. We'd go in just before it got dark. Daylight savings had come just in time for me, blotting out the stars.

But tonight we were playing bridge, just as always except that it felt a little different. I guess I knew that someone would mention Stella, but I wasn't sure who would do it. Then, after I'd gotten up for the fourth time to fetch beers, I said very innocently, "We need servants." We chuckled, then there was a moment of quiet, all of us facing center with our cards fanned out before us. Then Dorie said, "That reminds me of something Stella said once."

At first we made no response, and then Marsha said, "Really? What did she say?"

Dorie's eyes went around the table. She was smiling slightly. "I was reading her *The Enchanter's Daughter,* the one about the girl who is raised all alone with her sorcerer father in a palace? Anyway, there's a part where the book says something like 'The Enchanter had no need of servants; whenever he wished for something he would just wave his hand.' " Dorie started to giggle. "And Stella said, in this very serious voice, 'And as we know, servants are *sooo slooow*.' "

How we laughed at that. We all agreed that that certainly was Stella, and that it was a relief to laugh. We started coming up with other things, nearly competing for the most telling memory of what she'd said or done. We exhausted ourselves with the topic, glutted ourselves as if we'd been famished for months. We parted somewhat happily, agreeing out loud that it had been good to talk about her.

After Marsha and I cleaned up, we took a walk, and there was a difference there, too. We talked together of Stella, and not just hand in hand but with Marsha clutching my arm and rubbing her head against mine. We cried a little, but we kept smiling too, full of Stella and happy to be full of her. Siri noticed the difference; he barked several times, his contribution to the conversation. Once, briefly, I even let myself look up at the stars. It was deep autumn, and the stars were coming out earlier and earlier. I let my eyes slide up to the heavens, and there was Capella, one bright point of a triangle formed with Polaris and Dubhe. The little goat that rides Auriga's shoulder . . . It was hard to look, too much to remember and feel at once. Canis Major, where the star named for Stella rides near Sirius, will not be visible until the winter, and perhaps that's just as well.

With a deep sigh I said to Marsha, "I have to make a place for her in my mind. A place where she must be."

"Me too, Jim."